Praise for A Land So Wide

'With all the wit of a classic fable and the dreaminess of a modern romance, *A Land So Wide* is like the woods themselves: lovely, dark, and deep. I was beguiled by every word'
AVA REID

'No one does it like Erin Craig. *A Land So Wide* is a dark, atmospheric love story that takes you by the hand and leads you straight into a snowy folktale'
HANNAH WHITTEN

'Wonderous and haunting. A mystery told by firelight and shadow with all of the heart, danger, and destiny of our most timeless folktales. Erin A. Craig strikes gold again'
MARISHA PESSL

'The Canadian wilderness has never felt so wild and untamed. Erin Craig has masterfully woven the stark beauty of nature with the eerie pulse of the unnatural, where the land itself seems to come alive. *A Land So Wide* is a breathtaking exploration into humanity's unyielding drive to conquer, and the cost of ignoring what lies beyond the boundaries of the known world. This book is an undeniable triumph. Beautiful and dark and unforgettable'
SHEA ERNSHAW

'*A Land So Wide* is a spellbinding journey through a landscape as beautiful as it is treacherous. With lush, enchanting storytelling, Craig crafts a world so vivid you can taste the air and hear the whisper of the trees. I was utterly enthralled from the first page to the last'
ELIZABETH HELEN

'All hail the queen of gothic fantasy!'
MARA RUTHERFORD

'With a setting both lushly expansive and desperately claustrophobic, Craig invents a new mythology of terror and determination. I couldn't get enough of this romantic, tense, and thrilling tale'
KIERSTEN WHITE

'An achingly gorgeous tale of love lost and love found, of magic and of longings unforeseen. *A Land So Wide* is a dazzling, sumptuous story that lingers in the imagination well after the last page'
CHRISTINA HENRY

By Erin A. Craig

STANDALONES

Small Favors
The Thirteenth Child
A Land So Wide

SISTERS OF THE SALT

House of Salt and Sorrows
House of Roots and Ruin

A LAND SO WIDE

ERIN A. CRAIG

Copyright © Erin A. Craig 2025

The right of Erin A. Craig to be identified as the Author of
the Work has been asserted by her in accordance with the
Copyright, Designs and Patents Act 1988.

Published by arrangement with Pantheon Books,
a division of Penguin Random House LLC

First published in the UK in this hardback edition in 2025
by Headline Publishing Group Limited

1

Apart from any use permitted under UK copyright law, this publication may
only be reproduced, stored, or transmitted, in any form, or by any means,
with prior permission in writing of the publishers or, in the case of
reprographic production, in accordance with the terms of licences
issued by the Copyright Licensing Agency.

All characters in this publication – other than the obvious historical characters – are
fictitious and any resemblance to real persons, living or dead, is purely coincidental.

Cataloguing in Publication Data is available from the British Library

Hardback ISBN 978 1 0354 1107 8
Trade Paperback ISBN 978 1 0354 1108 5

Maps by Rhys Davies

Offset in 12/14.75pt Bembo Book MT Pro by Six Red Marbles UK, Thetford, Norfolk

Printed and bound in Great Britain by Clays Ltd, Elcograf S.p.A.

Headline's policy is to use papers that are natural, renewable and recyclable
products and made from wood grown in well-managed forests and other
controlled sources. The logging and manufacturing processes are expected
to conform to the environmental regulations of the country of origin.

Headline Publishing Group Limited
An Hachette UK Company
Carmelite House
50 Victoria Embankment
London EC4Y 0DZ

The authorised representative in the EEA is Hachette Ireland,
8 Castlecourt Centre, Dublin 15, D15 XTP3, Ireland (email: info@hbgi.ie)

www.headline.co.uk
www.hachette.co.uk

*For my dad,
teller of stories and keeper of the very best animal facts,
and who has taught so many people to always
speak for the trees. I love you so.*

Geographers . . . crowd into the edges of their maps parts of the world which they do not know about, adding . . . "Beyond this there is nothing but prodigies and fictions . . . there is no credit, or certainty any farther."

—PLUTARCH, *Plutarch's Lives*

A Land So Wide

Prologue

THE VOYAGE BEGAN with a whispered secret and a most peculiar piece of wood.

Upon first impression, it was nothing extraordinary. Just a simple cut of log, brought back from an explorer's journey to the new world. The whole continent was nothing but vast forests, untamed, unclaimed. Lumber was hardly a surprising resource.

But this cut, this tree, was different.

It was not oak or pine.

It was not walnut or cherry or maple or birch.

It wasn't like anything the man had ever seen.

Impressively strong. Surprisingly flexible. Impossibly light.

Lumber from this tree could be fashioned into the finest fleet of ships ever known. It could create bridges that would span for miles. Houses and buildings and palaces. All would spring up like weeds and last for centuries.

This was a tree that could build an empire.

The man paid the explorer three times.

Once, for the cut itself.

A second time, for the explorer to show the man the exact place he'd found the trees. Together they crossed the sea, then a bay, then a cove. The explorer canoed them deep into the new wilderness, tracing the routes he'd marked on his maps, charting where he'd gone, where the trees grew.

The man had stared with wonder at the vast forest, thousands of trees strong, thousands of gold coins in the making, and a strange hunger kindled within him.

So he paid the explorer again. This time, for his silence.

The explorer, gladdened by his heavy pockets, set sail once more, now heading south. He wanted to be somewhere warm enough to burn away the memories of those trees, of the dark and wild world in which they grew. Even as he basked half a world away, sun-kissed and surrounded by swaying palms, those trees made him shiver.

Back at his home in the north, the man drew up a plan, put together a ship and supplies, gathered a crew and equipment. He thought through everything. He left nothing to chance. Day after day he toiled, driven more by that strange hunger, that gnawing ambition and greed. He wanted to be the first to conquer this new world, to bring it under his heel, one fallen tree at a time.

The man was clever. Very, very clever.

He knew that the most important piece in this endeavor was not the machinery or the blades, not the rations or the transport. The thing, the one thing that would make his schemes work, was the morale of his men.

So, when he told them of this new expedition, he instructed them to pack it all. Pack their homes, bring their wives and children, their maiden aunts, their elderly parents, their sweethearts and livestock. They were meant to bring anything holding them to the old world. They would not be returning. They were on a noble mission, a greater destiny. They were bound for glories unimaginable.

He spun the men stories and, starry-eyed, they followed after.

Their voyage was long and hard, crossing the cold northern sea, one punishing wave at a time. Sickness claimed some of the older ones. Tears flooded the nights, the children certain they'd never see land again. Doubts crept in, stalking through the crew, taking hold of the men and their women. These doubts clouded their thoughts, corroded their hope.

The man would not listen to doubts. He pressed ahead, pointing the ship west, his gaze fixed on the watery horizon. He reminded them of the wealth that awaited. He restored their dreams.

For a time.

When they did finally reach land, finally spotted the thick black slabs of rock rising high from the water like slumbering leviathans, any cheer the company felt withered away.

They stood in an awestruck line along the ship's starboard side, watching the ancient cliffs draw nearer, silent and grim. There was a strangeness to this land, an uncanny watchfulness that set their neck hairs at attention. This was not a land to be conquered, as the man had promised. This was a land to be feared.

But the man did not heed those who wanted to turn back, who wanted to flee for the comforts of home. Instead, he pointed them up the coast, following the lines of the explorer's maps until they reached the mouth of a vast waterway, bordered by primeval forests.

They gave one last look to the sea behind them, then entered a vast bay.

Rocky cliffs grew steeper, forming forbidding granite mountains. Blackflies and mosquitoes festered, swarming and hungry for flesh to feast upon. Bloodcurdling cries were carried upon fierce and howling winds. At night, the sky burst into shimmering flames that danced silently across the dark void.

Women clutched their children close.

Men cried and whimpered for their own mothers.

In his cabin, the man studied his maps.

He just needed to keep going, to lift everyone's spirits long enough for them to see he'd done right. Once they saw the trees, they would understand. He was certain of it.

The morning's sun rose red and bloody, bringing with it the promise of storms. Angers flourished and tempers flared. Wives bickered and children wailed. Roiling clouds of thunder piled high. The air crackled with doom.

They begged the man to stop, to turn around.

Grown men knelt on their hands and knees. They grabbed at his clothing. They rent their own.

Still, the man would not be dissuaded.

The first mate was the first to whisper it, that sly, sneaking, treacherous word.

Mutiny.

It lit through the crew like a line of gunpowder, racing from man to man until the entire ship was clamoring for action.

But then an excited cry rang out from the crow's nest. The man's oldest son, high aloft with a brass spyglass, had spotted them.

The trees.

They grew in a clustered grove along the far edge of the shore. Tall. Wide. Packed together in numbers so dense the man's heart raced as he imagined the staggering prices he could charge.

They only needed to sail their way through a narrow channel flanked by a series of rocky peaks, and the trees would be his. The man's spirits buoyed and he laughed aloud.

His ebullience was carried away on a sharp draft.

The sky turned black. The wind pitched sharper, and waves climbed over the bow of the ship, heralding the storm's approach.

The mutiny would have to wait.

There was no time to turn, no time to alter course. To remain on open water would lead to a most certain death. The tree-lined cove beckoned, offering the promise of protection.

Without option, the first mate gritted his teeth and pointed for the narrows.

They nearly made it.

Just as they cleared the channel, the hull scraped against an underwater crag. The ship shuddered. Planks split apart. Brackish saltwater flooded into the lower decks. Cargo toppled over. Goats bleated in terror. Oxen and horses trampled their stall doors, fighting for their lives. Lightning flashed, and the echoing thunder boomed so loudly one man's heart burst inside his chest.

The world was noise and darkness, blinding light and fear.

As the ship grew heavy with filling water, it cracked into pieces, throwing men, women, and children into the bay. Some swam. Some sank. All rued the moment they'd chosen to follow the man.

The storm eventually blew east, leaving behind a sky so brilliant it looked obscene.

Those still alive sputtered and pulled themselves to shore, surveying the wreckage. They took stock of their surroundings. They counted their dead.

They found the man underneath one of his trees.

At first he appeared to be sleeping.

Then they noticed the branch jutting from his abdomen, mixing its strange red sap with his innards.

His first mate touched his shoulder with caution, jarring the man awake for a moment.

"This was a mistake," he whispered, flecking his lips with blood. "Coming here was a mistake. A mistake and . . ."

"Mistake and . . ." the first mate repeated, but the man did not answer.

With dead eyes fixed upon his grove of trees, Resolution Beaufort's ill-fated voyage had come to an end.

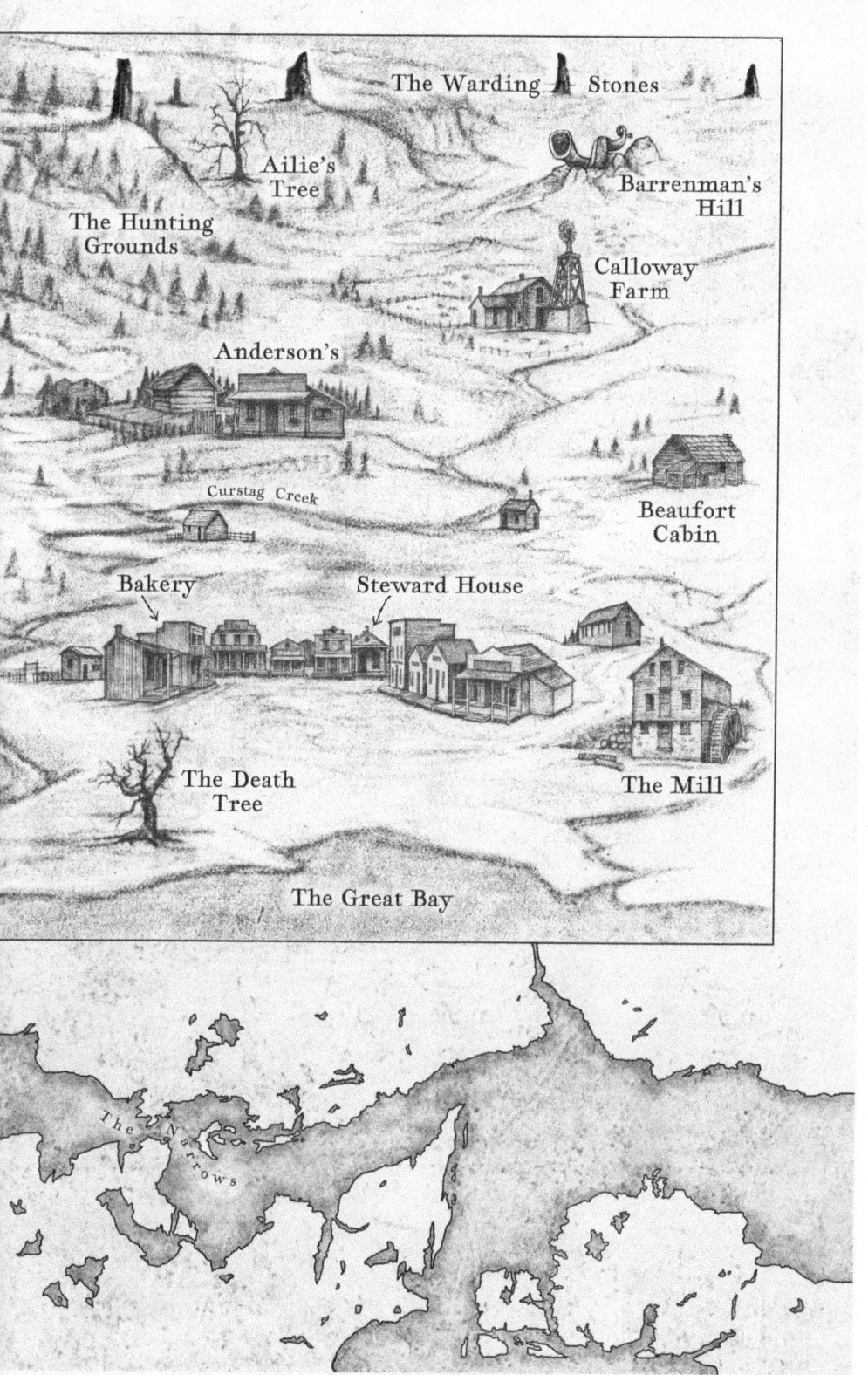

PART I

Mistaken

If they just went straight they might go far;
They are strong and brave and true;
But they're always tired of the things that are,
And they want the strange and new.

—ROBERT W. SERVICE, "The Men That Don't Fit In,"
The Spell of the Yukon, and Other Verses

1

*S*critch, scritch, scratch.

Even with her face buried in a sketchbook and her back turned away from the bloody business, Greer Mackenzie could still hear every bit of Louise Beaufort slicing into the hare's pelt, splitting a bright seam down its stomach.

The flick of the knife.

The wet squelch as fur peeled away from red meat and glistening sinews.

Those cords of muscle stretching taunt, then snapping asunder.

"Last one," Louise announced as an eagle screeched overhead, circling them in lazy, hopeful patterns. It beat its wings against currents of air, once, twice, before drifting off for a more promising meal.

The tip of Greer's pencil dug divots into the soft paper as she doubled her concentration upon the map, forcing the noises away as she made sure her lines were tidy and accurate.

"Take your time," she said, glancing back, regrettably, to see Louise twist the rabbit's heart free, her fingers stained with rust-colored offal. "It's probably our last trip out before Reaping."

"A good one, too," Louise commented, sounding distracted. "So many hares, and I'm sure your father will be pleased as well. Never seen this many Redcaps."

Greer's gaze fell on the copse of scarlet trees, standing out starkly against the forest's green pines and yellow tamaracks.

Named after the murderous goblins found in whispered childhood tales, Redcaps were wide and squat. Their limbs spread farther out than up, as if they were monstrous spiders moving in for their prey. The red bark was thick and riddled with bulbous whorls. When it broke off, shedding jagged bits and pieces across the forest floor, a pungent scarlet sap flowed forth, raining down like blood. Gray moss clung to the creaking branches, like tufts of straggled hair.

They were not attractive trees, not by half, but the wood was surprisingly strong and flexible. Perfect for lumber, for boats and buildings.

It was what first drew Resolution Beaufort and his workers to this land: the whispers of bounty, the lure of untold, easy wealth.

Her butchering done, Louise sat back on her feet and stretched, tipping her face to the sky. Rich amber sunlight sparkled down, turning the forest around them to flame. "That's all I want to carry back today."

"I'll put up the flags, then," Greer said, pulling out the strips of cotton from her pack. They'd been taken from other trees nearly a mile back. It gave Greer a thrill to move the flags on each of their excursions, claiming more of the surrounding unknown, yard by yard, bite by bite. She loved knowing that, even though she might be stuck behind Mistaken's border each night, there were small pieces of her remaining out in the wild, tiny scraps of defiance that would not budge, that were not subject to the Warding Stones' pull.

The markers were made of blue-and-white ticking, their stripes bold and unmissable—perfect for warning any travelers from Mistaken that they were about to venture too deep into the forest, that they wouldn't be able to return before sunset. Anyone who went blithely by those bright strips of fabric needed to know they weren't coming back.

Alive, at least.

Greer tied them along these new Redcaps, careful to keep her fingers from the sap. When brushed against skin, it caused painful rashes, burning as bright as the trees themselves. She jotted the flags' new positions along her map, adding the marks to the others running along the ridge's curve.

She glanced at the sun's position before turning to her friend. "All packed? Only a couple hours till First Bellows."

Autumn had toppled heavily over the land, the night nibbling in earlier each day, swallowing up more seconds of sunshine, and leaving Mistaken in a shroud of hazy twilight by mid-afternoon. Soon the sun wouldn't even bother to rise, leaving them in the clutched fist of unending night, trapped inside the town's Warding Stones, hunkered down against winter's fury.

Greer didn't mind the cold, didn't mind the dark, but the weight of the cove's limits pressed down in those long stationary months, flattening any potential joys or cheer. She could already feel the serpentine squeeze of claustrophobic dread tightening around her, as binding as shackles.

She rubbed her hands over her forearms with brisk efficiency, stirring her blood as she tried to think on better things. "Are you going to the barn warming tonight?"

Louise shrugged without commitment. She tied the hare to her rucksack, letting it join two others, already cleaned. The pelt went inside the bag, but as she reached for the organs, Greer stopped her.

"Wait. Aren't you leaving those?"

Louise's hazel eyes darted past the flags; her face was cloudy with hesitation. "I wasn't planning on it." Her voice was careful, the words delicately formed. "It's not yet Reaping."

It wasn't, but lacy patterns of hoarfrost stretched fingers over the little pond behind the Mackenzies' cabin, and Greer's breath lingered in frosty puffs even throughout the afternoon's warmth. Great flocks of black-and-white geese had long since flown for warmer climes, and golden stalks of wheat rustled and whispered against one another, nearly driving Greer mad with their secrets. The farmers' silencing scythes couldn't come soon enough. The Benevolence would soon descend from their colony high up in the Severing Mountains.

Some might already be here.

Greer reached out to stop Louise, her fingers covering the bloody bits. "Just these, then. Please?"

Irritation flushed over Louise's face, nearly drowning out her stain of freckles.

"Louise," Greer persisted. She could feel the discontent building between them, like a wall grown taller with every stone her friend dropped in place.

Louise pressed her lips together, and Greer could tell she was struggling to hold back a mouthful of sharp words.

"You're right, it's not Reaping," Greer tried again, gently, quick to avoid confrontation if she could. "But . . . we shouldn't give only when it's expected. All this"—she gestured to the trees, to the rabbit—"it's a gift. Their gift to us. We should be grateful for it."

Louise snorted. "You sound just like Martha."

A blossom of pride swelled in Greer's chest—she adored the older woman who'd lived with their family since she was a small babe—even as she realized Louise hadn't meant it as a compliment. Still, she held her gaze with firm resolution, refusing to be the first to back down.

After their silence grew thorny, Louise turned, facing the forest beyond the flags, and offered out a deep and disingenuous curtsy. "Thank you for the rabbits I had to catch and kill and clean myself. It was very good of you to let me work so hard. I'm wildly grateful," she called out, her voice mincing.

"Stop it!" Greer hissed, disappointed. "What if they hear you?"

Louise choked on laughter. "It's only you and me. No Benevolence. No Bright-Eyes. There are no people in this valley for miles all around us."

"Maybe not here, right here," Greer sputtered, swallowing back the urge to remind her that the Bright-Eyes were not people at all. "But there"—her hand rose toward the Redcaps, toward the flags—"they're out there. All of them," she added.

"They're not real!" Louise said, laying out each word with heavy care. "They're nothing but stupid stories to scare children at bedtime."

Greer glanced into the deeper forest, her eyes darting as she tried to catch a telltale glimpse of eye-shine, certain Louise had just brought perdition down upon them. "You don't mean that."

Louise was always poking at things she shouldn't, eager to argue, quick to show that she wouldn't fall into line just because the rules dictated she should. She loved saying startling things to see how people would respond, only ever redacting them when given a sharp look from her older brother.

But Ellis Beaufort wasn't with them now.

Louise licked her lips. "What if I do?"

"You're just acting like . . ." Greer sighed, tossing the last of her words away, ready for the conversation to be over. For the first time in her life, she wished she could snap her fingers and instantly return to Mistaken. It was bound to be a miserable hike home with Louise in such a contrary and foul mood.

"What? What am I acting like?"

"A fool!" The words fell free before Greer could stop them. She reached out, intending to console her friend, hoping to smooth the abrasion over, but Louise looked anything but wounded.

She stared at Greer with a mix of disdain and pity and let out a bark of laughter. "That's a fine accusation coming from a grown woman worrying about the monsters under her bed, leaving out trinkets and treasures, trying to buy approval. Do you ever stop to consider how foolish *you* act?"

"The gratitudes aren't foolish."

Louise shook her head, bristling. "They're a waste! So much food and resources left to rot out in the woods. Do you know how even a fraction of that could benefit families in the village? Could benefit *my* family?"

"They're not left to rot. The offerings are always taken. There's never a single one left," Greer snapped, though she knew she was skirting around the uncomfortable truth.

There *were* families in Mistaken whose gratitudes were a hardship, families who missed the extra bushel of apples, the side of venison, the bags of flour in the dark months of winter. The Beauforts certainly. But the gifts returned to the town well outweighed such a minor cost.

They had the Warding Stones.

They had the Benevolence's favor.

No other outpost up or down the coast could claim such fortune.

Louise sighed. "There are a thousand things in these woods ready to snatch up whatever is left on the altars. Ospreys and kites, martens and lynx. Black bears. Foxes. Wolves. I . . ." She trailed off with a strangled noise of frustration. "The Benevolence is not what takes them. In all the years since our supposed truce, no one has ever seen a hint of them. Because they're not there," she spelled out.

"Then who is protecting us from the Bright-Eyes?"

Louise rolled her eyes. "Those aren't real, either."

Horror unfurled in Greer's stomach, making her queasy and sick. "But they . . . ! Of course they are! Martha has seen them. They killed her entire family."

Louise had the decency to look uncomfortable. "We don't know what killed them. We never saw it."

"What about the survivors from the other towns? They all say the same thing. You know their stories as well as I do," Greer said, imagining the bloody chaos, the cries for help, the sky shattering into violence.

"Stories told by the men in charge. Men who have a vested interest in keeping everyone on edge so that they'll be better listened to, so they'll be better obeyed. Men like Hessel Mackenzie."

"What does my father have to do with any of this?"

Louise pinched the bridge of her nose, smearing rabbit blood across her face. It made her look wild and feral. "How do you not see it?"

"See what?" Greer could feel anxiety thrumming within her, could hear the racing cadence of both her heart and Louise's. The air between them felt charged and heavy, like in the moment just before a thunderstorm crested the mountaintops, ready to unleash its torrents. Greer was bewildered by how quickly her insistence on today's gratitudes had turned into such a tangled, barbed mess.

"Our differences! The way you came trampling through the woods today in a dress nicer than my Sunday finest. The way you can carelessly leave an entire dinner behind on a tree stump. The way I've been foraging and hunting and trying to store up my family's winter rations while you spend the whole day messing about in that damned book of yours, doodling pictures and notes and maps that will never matter!"

Greer's mouth dropped, stung by the harsh words, stung that they'd come from her best friend. She turned, unable to take the weight of

Louise's fervent glare, and crossed her arms, holding back the tears that wanted to come.

Only then did Louise soften. "Greer, I didn't mean that."

Her spine stiffened with resolve. "You said we were sharing today's hunt."

"I say that every trip," Louise began uneasily. "You never take me up on it."

"I am today. I'll leave my share as a token."

Louise huffed with disbelief. "Are you . . . are you in earnest?"

Though it pained her, Greer kept still.

After a long, taut moment, Louise cast the organs to the ground, letting them land near Greer's feet. With a snarl of disgust, she grabbed her bag and stalked off.

Greer glanced back in time to see the flayed rabbits swinging from Louise's rucksack like broken marionettes.

"Louise," she started, but her friend had already disappeared into a thicket.

To Greer, each footfall was as loud as cannon fire, reverberating down her sternum and making her heart ache. She wished Louise would come back. She wished Louise would come and apologize. They'd lay out the tokens and go home, their friendship cleanly restored.

Though they'd certainly fought before—they'd been best friends since they were schoolgirls—the fights had always been small and incidental. Squabbles over dolls, hurt feelings on summer afternoons when the weather was hot enough to spark anyone's temper. The week of silence after Louise learned Ellis had kissed Greer on the little footbridge spanning Curstag Creek. Greer hadn't told Louise, because she knew it would upset her, and because, after over a decade of sharing every single thought with her friend, it felt delicious to keep one small thing for herself.

But this fight felt different.

They weren't little girls anymore, fighting over hair ribbons or secrets.

They were grown—Greer twenty-seven and Louise twenty-two—and these stakes were higher, these words were crueler.

Still, Greer waited, certain her wishes would come true.

But as seconds turned to minutes, Greer's hope began to wither.

Giving up, she glanced to the line of flags shifting in the listless breeze.

"She didn't mean that," Greer called loudly, ready to catch the attention of whoever, whatever might be listening. She sighed. "I'm sure she didn't mean any of that."

As if in response, the forest fell silent, the quietest it had been all afternoon.

Greer scooped up the scattered organs before ducking under the branches of the Redcaps and stepping past the flags to search for the right altar. She could tell the exact moment she'd crossed over, slipping into an untouched world, alien and new and unmarked on any of her maps.

She was the first person of Mistaken to stand upon this ground, so far from home, so far from the Stones' hold. She took in a deep breath, basking in the sensation. But even as the wonder coursed through her, as heady as a shot of Fenneck O'Connell's best whiskey, she noticed footprints pressed deep into the spongy moss all about her.

Greer blinked, certain the impressions were a trick of the heavy afternoon sun.

They remained.

She stooped down, inspecting them with her artist's eye.

They'd been made by feet bare and too big.

Too irregularly shaped.

Her mouth dried as she counted just two toes per print.

Greer knew the woods around Mistaken as well as her own cabin. Her mother, Ailie Mackenzie, had taught her every kind of tree that grew there and every type of animal who roamed its depths. But she could not think of a single one that boasted only two toes.

This was it.

This was a sign.

Louise was wrong. The Benevolence was real, as were the dreadful Bright-Eyeds they protected Mistaken from.

Unable to show her friend this irrefutable proof, Greer wanted to howl in frustration.

From somewhere deep in the woods, a branch cracked, and her heart seized as she suddenly realized she was alone in the woods with whatever had made such enormous two-toed tracks.

"The tokens," she whispered in a rush. "Find an altar, set the tokens, and go home. The Benevolence will be grateful. The Benevolence will bless your endeavor." The words fell from her in rote succession, instinctive turns of phrase Martha had spent years drilling into her.

Greer stopped at the first fallen tree she came across, a long length of birch, its papery bark curling back to reveal spiky clusters of combtooth mushrooms. Their white branches were as jagged as vertebrae.

She knelt and placed her fingers along the tree, pausing for a moment of genuflection before beginning her task.

Though Martha had given her the words and ways that would be most pleasing to the Benevolence, it was Ailie who had taught Greer to offer reverence for the land and all the marvels it held. Much of Greer's childhood had been spent exploring the wilds with Ailie. During each journey, they would find somewhere to pause for a moment of reflection. They'd kneel down, skirts pooling together, and the wind would carry away their whispers, tangling them so tightly they sounded as if they'd come from the same person.

Martha's practices inclined more toward pageantry: laying out the viscera just so, making sure her entreaties held the appropriate note of awestruck fervor, keeping everything rigid and orderly, familiar and routine.

But Ailie had been infused with a profound sense of wonder, urged to see more, learn more, experience *more*. She'd believed the only way to show true appreciation was to take what was given, to wander as far as the Warding Stones would allow, basking in the world's messy glory, reveling within it, and allowing the wild pounding of her blood to be its own sort of prayer.

Greer's faith was a blend of both women's teachings. She could almost feel their hands on hers now, telling her to stop and feel the textured warmth of the tree bark, guiding her as she arranged a tableau of offerings, ghoulish and macabre.

A string of intestines.

A liver.

Kidneys.

The heart.

They were covered in dirt after having been cast aside by Louise, and Greer wiped them clean as best she could. When she was pleased with the arrangement, she sat back, scanning the darker depths of pines.

She cleared her throat, feeling her voice waver even before she spoke. "With gratitude and thanks, I leave these tokens as an offering for thee." Every hair on the back of Greer's neck stood at attention, attuned and ready. "May they be of good use and bring you great pleasure."

She held her breath, wondering if today she'd finally hear the Benevolence's answer. She waited, watching for any sense of movement, any stirring however small.

But it wouldn't be small, would it?

She glanced to the right.

The tracks were big, so, so big . . .

Then to the left.

Two toes, what has two toes?

The spruces' trunks remained in place, unfaltering and still.

The tamaracks' glow dimmed, and the surrounding woods grew darker.

Closer.

Was the dying light due to an approaching storm, a bank of clouds rolling down from the mountains high above? The falling night?

Was it the Benevolence?

Or, worse yet . . . the monsters they held back?

The woods waited, stubbornly refusing to offer up its secrets.

Greer kept her eyes fixed on the garish lumps staining the tree bark before her. She could be stubborn, too.

But as she knelt, waiting in a moment drawn too long, Greer felt it, the falling of the sun, the pull of Mistaken. The Stones tugged on her bones like a fisherman testing a catch on his line. Gentle for now, but persistent.

Greer had counted her footsteps today, as she always did when she slipped past the town's boundary. Ten thousand paces, give or take.

Nearly five miles. It would take her more than two hours to return. At least.

She had enough time before First Bellows.

Just barely.

She could wait a moment more.

Another minute. Surely, she could last another minute.

When the strain grew again, tugging at her with unchecked doggedness, Greer gave up and stood, certain that the moment she turned, the trees would come to life, stooping forward to snatch up her gifts.

Greer blew strands of dark hair from her eyes and rubbed her fingers together. They were smudged sticky from the offering. She'd wash them at the first creek she came across. Martha would never let her hear the end of it if she returned home looking like the butcher's apprentice.

Now that Greer's feet were pointed back toward Mistaken, her lungs released a breath of air, momentarily free of the incessant pressure drawing at her body. She gathered her supplies, but paused before she could roll up the map.

She'd been so proud of it before Louise's hateful words had bitten in, poisoning its joy.

She studied the clean lines, the accurate scale, the series of checks marking each copse of Redcaps they'd come across.

It was good work, Greer knew that.

With resolve, she rolled the map into a tight scroll and tucked it into the satchel carefully. She wouldn't let Louise taint it. She'd stop at the mill and show it to Ayaan Adair, her father's second in command. He was certain to be pleased.

As she eased the satchel's strap over her head, something from the periphery of her vision shifted, a pale slip of movement sliding through the trees.

Stealthily.

Soundlessly.

Greer strained her ears, baffled by the silence.

For as long as she could remember, Greer Mackenzie had heard things. Big things, small things. Things improbable. Things most impossible. The beating of wings far overhead, conversations from the wrong side of the room, flakes of snow landing upon branches deep behind her home. Sometimes she feared she could make out the heartbeats of every person within Mistaken, tiny, relentless pulses of life demanding to be acknowledged.

She didn't know why or how, only that it was a truth she could not escape.

So why were the woods so still now?

A sudden terror staked into her middle. She could feel it pressing close, as suffocating as a damp blanket: the eerie weight of the uncanny.

Strands of her hair danced by her ear, swaying as if someone had softly exhaled just behind her, but she was too scared to turn. Too scared to see.

Something had crept up behind her, and she'd heard *nothing*.

The impossibility was too dreadful to bear.

Greer scrunched her eyes closed, unwittingly conjuring up images wild and fantastic. Demons and monsters too horrifying to believe. Trees that could move soundlessly through the forest like a wisp of mist. Trees with shining eyes. Trees with two toes. Trees with long, knobby fingers reaching out to scrape her bare neck . . .

"Hello, little Starling."

Her eyes flashed open.

She'd heard *that*.

Hadn't she?

A voice, low and beguiling. Just behind her shoulder. A voice, as real as her own.

Greer licked her lips. She wasn't going to look. She couldn't bear to look. Except . . .

When her resolve slipped and she whipped around, the forest was still, and her offerings were gone.

2

Black clouds rolled in off the mountain range to the northwest, setting the world dim long before Greer stumbled out of the tree line. They hung low, seemingly close enough to pluck down, as angry as a fresh bruise.

Great drops of cold rain soon began to fall, soaking the earth and Greer's skirts in equal measure. She could already hear the tongue-lashing Martha would give her for tracking mud through the parlor.

She passed by one of the monolithic Warding Stones—the widest of their lot, with a chunk chipped away from the top that reminded Greer of a missing tooth—and traced her fingertips over its wet surface. Red iridescence flickered across it, as if welcoming her back. She felt an instant lightening as she crossed over the town line, like the setting down of a heavy satchel after a long journey. Her muscles loosened; it felt easier to breathe.

The Warding Stones were towering shards of black basalt that appeared wholly unremarkable until sunlight hit at just the right angle. Then they shone with a red-hued luminescence. Hundreds of them dotted the perimeter of Mistaken, a gift from the Benevolence, part of their decades-long truce.

The Stones were their protectors, holding back the Bright-Eyeds from ever crossing into town. The Stones were their jailers, keeping the people of Mistaken forever bound to the land.

Giving the forests behind her one final longing glance, Greer turned her focus toward the town. Whether she liked it or not, she was home for another night.

She paused at the crest of Barrenman's Hill, and glanced across the cove at the rocky cliffs of the Narrows and into the Great Bay. It stretched out as vast as an ocean and was just as salty. Sleek whales, dark with banded fins, were regularly seen spouting close to shore, hungry for plankton and krill. In the spring, the harbor was loud with the barks of young seal pups. Louise had even claimed to have once spied a shark in deeper waters.

There'd been a schooner docked outside the Narrows for the last two days. Its crew had ferried in much-needed supplies while the captain negotiated lumber prices with Hessel and Ayaan.

Mistaken boasted the only mill up or down the coast that cut Redcaps and turned the bedraggled trees into handsome planks of wood. Demand for these trees was so high that merchants sailed thousands of miles across the sea, facing untold perils, just to reach their remote and isolated community. As mill owner, Hessel had been waiting for this schooner's arrival all summer, rubbing his hands with impatient glee as he pre-emptively tallied the profits.

But the Narrows were now open, and the tall masts and full sails gone.

A burr of worry dug into Greer's middle as she surveyed the empty bay.

Just that morning, Hessel had said they were still haggling over a final price. Could they have already come to an agreement and transported the lumber across the cove?

The rain began to pound heavier. The sound was so deafening that Greer nearly altered course, leaving the village for the sanctuary of her bedroom. She could hide away on her straw mattress, covering her ears until the worst of the storm's fury had passed and everything returned to its usual decibels.

On the other hand, if the schooner *had* left without buying the wood, her father would undoubtedly be home, banging about in the foulest of moods, darker than even the sky overhead. Greer winced as she imagined the sounds of that rage permeating the house.

As she stood motionless with indecision—the house or the mill? the mill or the house?—her ears pricked with a new sound.

A group of young boys was ambling down the road, careless of the rain or the puddles they stomped through. Greer took in the hems of their trousers, inches deep with splattered mud, and pitied their mothers. They carried their writing slates over their shoulders, holding on to the leather straps with a lax air, and were snickering over something from their day at school.

The snickerings stopped when they spotted Greer.

"Isn't that Old Man Mackenzie's daughter?" one asked, his voice hushed.

Greer heard it through the chaos of raindrops as clearly as if he were standing right beside her.

"Don't look!" another warned. "My ma said she can see everything you're thinking, just by staring into your eyes."

"My sister said her mother could hold your hand and tell you exactly how you were going to die," a third boy hissed.

This elicited little noises of astonishment from the group, and Greer's stomach began to sour.

It was no secret that the people of Mistaken thought the Mackenzie women peculiar on even the best days. On others, their rumored talents for the impossible verged into absurdity. Even before Ailie's death, Greer had heard her mother accused of drinking blood from a neighbor's horse, bursting into a flock of birds, and foretelling the future. In her absence, the stories had only gotten worse.

There were never any outright accusations. Hessel's rank on the council of Stewards and status as mill owner granted them certain levels of protection: no one wanted to anger the man who employed most of Mistaken. But the whispers still found their way to her ears.

Usually, Greer ignored them. But Louise's hurtful words still echoed in her mind, and she couldn't bear to push aside the boys' mean-spirited chatter.

"Is that Benjamin Donalson I see?" she called out, raising her voice to carry through the rain, squinting at them.

The boys froze.

"I'd be cautious going home today if I were you."

Benjamin glanced from one of his friends to another with wild-eyed wondering. "Wh-why's that?"

"Your father knows who pinched the coppers from his purse last week. He's bound to be on a warpath."

The boy's face paled, but he shook his head and stormed away, yelling at the others to follow.

It had only been a guess.

But, evidently, a good one.

Just yesterday, Jeb Donalson had been purchasing a tin of nails at the general store. On the other side of the aisle, Greer had heard him mutter under his breath, counting his coins and coming up short.

Greer smiled, watching them go.

"What little shits."

She turned to the row of shops behind her and caught a bright flash of russet.

Ellis.

He stood under the cover of Tywynn Flanagan's bakery awning, wearing an apron once blue but now thoroughly mottled with flour. He watched the cluster of boys scurry into the storm, with his arms folded over his broad chest.

Her smile turned to a grin.

Ellis Beaufort's voice was Greer's favorite sound in all the world. It was a warm, rich baritone that felt like that magic hour between Bellows, when the falling sun painted the world in shades of gold.

A Beaufort through and through, with hazel eyes and a shock of chestnut hair that burned as blazing as autumn leaves, Ellis had a loud, easy laugh and was always smiling, but never quite as widely as when he spotted Greer.

She approached the bakery, tipping her chin to stare up at him.

"Get out of that mess." Ellis reached down and hoisted her to the raised wooden promenade that ran the length of the town's storefronts. It kept the customers out of the worst of the snowbanks in winter and from the thick sluice of mud that plagued Mistaken during every other season.

"Afternoon," he greeted, pressing a quick kiss to the top of her head. He smelled *warm,* of rising dough and yeast and the oven's flames.

"It's a good one now." She tightened her grip on his hand, wishing she could grab him by the collar and pull his mouth to hers.

It had been days since she'd last seen him. They'd been caught in an endless town meeting, stuck and separated by the wide aisle running down Steward House. Greer had watched him watch her from the corner of her eye, and after the meeting was over, they'd sneaked into the shadows behind an outbuilding to steal as many kisses as they could before Ellis's younger brothers began to shout for him.

He grinned widely, dimples winking. "How was the hunting?"

Greer hesitated, remembering the way Louise had snarled before leaving the forest. "Fine. Louise shot three rabbits. Didn't lose a single arrow."

One eyebrow, as thick as a freshly drawn line on one of Greer's maps, rose. "Her aim is improving. Stew tomorrow," he said, clearly pleased, then tilted his head. "What aren't you telling me?"

She blinked, feigning innocence.

"I know your face better than my own, Greer Mackenzie," Ellis said. "And right now you look as though you're about to burst into tears. What's wrong?"

Greer was certain her forced smiled looked as pained as it felt. "It's nothing. It's fine."

His gaze was unwavering.

She sighed. "Only . . ." She stepped past him, avoiding the weight of his stare. "Louise didn't . . . She didn't want to leave any tokens behind."

He made a sound of understanding. "And you did."

"Obviously." She tucked a curl of hair behind her ear, uncomfortable.

Ellis rubbed at his jaw, unsurprised. He'd stopped shaving as the cooler weather had set in, and the auburn stubble had grown into a thick beard. "And Louise said something hasty and stupid."

Greer paused. She didn't like putting Ellis in the middle of their messes. It wasn't his responsibility to work through them, and it seemed unfair to make him choose a side. Reluctantly, she nodded.

"The pantry *has* been stretched a bit thin lately," Ellis confided, dropping his voice even though the promenade was empty. "The boys are worse than a plague of locusts. Growing pains," he added.

Rhys and Riley, the Beaufort twins, had turned twelve over the summer, entering that awkward phase of childhood when limbs stretched too long and out of proportion. To Greer they looked like nothing so much as a pair of downy goslings, tripping over their own feet as they struggled to understand the strange shapes their bodies now formed.

Guilt pooled in Greer's belly, making her feel off-kilter and uneasy. Some of what Louise had said was true. The mill brought in fistfuls of money each summer. Greer had never gone without, had never been hungry or worn clothes patched or too small. An only child, she'd never even scrapped with siblings for her portion of dinner. It was a far cry from the Beauforts' household.

"And . . ." Ellis trailed off, his eyes glancing to the sheets of water rolling off the promenade's tin roof. "She's been in a mood since the Stewards told her their ruling."

"About letting her sit out this Hunt?" Greer frowned. They'd been together all day, yet Louise hadn't mentioned it once. "I didn't even know she'd presented her case. She hasn't said anything. Neither has Father."

With Ellis and Louise's father's death, grief had settled over Mary Beaufort like a thick, sticky cobweb, impossible to break free of. Her mind had always been prone to flights of whimsy, but now it wandered further away, drawn to confusion and paranoia. Strange tics riddled her gestures, and she'd often fall short in a conversation, sometimes mid-sentence—there one moment, then gone the next.

When it became clear that Mary could no longer run the Beaufort household, Louise had left school and taken the reins, to look after her younger siblings, tend to the cabin and livestock, and watch the accounts with a sharp eye. She'd turned twenty-two during the last snowmelt and, though this should be her year to run in the Hunt, Louise had confided that she planned to ask the Stewards to let her stay home, reasoning that her family needed her more than Mistaken needed another bride.

"What did the Stewards say?"

Ellis looked uneasy. "I feel like she should be the one to tell you."

Greer recalled the look on Louise's face before she stalked back to Mistaken. "I don't think she wants to tell me much of anything right now." She let out a humorless laugh. "Or, whatever she might, I'm not sure I want to hear."

Ellis licked his lips. "They're making her run in the Hunt."

"But . . . that can't be right."

Ellis shrugged helplessly.

"Oh, Louise . . ." She studied Ellis, unsure how to read his expression. "We don't know she'll be found," she began tentatively, trying to think of something hopeful to say. "She always was the best at hide-and-seek."

A corner of Ellis's mouth lifted, but it was a far cry from his usual smile.

"But if she is caught . . . we'll be together," Greer assured him. "You and me. We'll take care of Mary. The twins, little Norah, everyone. We won't be far away."

For the past year, Ellis had been preparing a cabin for the two of them, building it on the back half of the Beaufort land. With the Hunt only a few weeks away, it was nearly complete, but Ellis insisted it remain a secret till after the Hunt and Joining Ceremony. He wanted the first time Greer saw it to be when she was carried over the threshold as his bride.

He nodded now, looking appeased. "Don't let her bad mood trouble you. I'm sure she didn't mean whatever she said, and one offering won't make a difference anyway."

"Martha and I picked a bumper crop of blackberries yesterday," Greer began thoughtfully. "Perhaps I could bring some over before the barn warming . . ."

"Not tonight," he warned. "Give her time to stew. But tomorrow, that would be a kindness I know she'd appreciate—as would I. Nothing beats Martha Kingston's jam," he added cheerfully. The matter was—in his mind—laid to rest.

He was so unlike her.

Whereas Greer was prone to fits of worry, endlessly fretting over mistakes real or perceived, Ellis was fast to forgive, and just as quick to forget. He reminded her of the black-and-white eider ducks on the Great Bay. They paddled up and down its breadth no matter how perilous the weather, content to ride out whatever waves might come.

Ellis poked his head out from under the awning to peer at the sky. "Storm's likely to last awhile. There's sourdough in the oven. Should be done soon. Come on in."

Ellis had begun working at the bakery once his schooling ended, seven harvests ago. He'd started out as nothing more than an errand boy, wrapping orders and counting payment, making sure the barters were fair. Now Tywynn allowed him to work in the back, pounding out the dough, and even entrusting Ellis with his best recipes. Though unstated, it was common understanding that once the old baker—long widowed, with no children of his own—was ready, he'd pass the business on to Ellis.

"It's tempting," Greer said.

"Is it?" His voice lowered still, warm and husky with longing.

He laced his fingers through hers, tangling them into an affectionate knot. A spark of hungry warmth caught in her middle, and as he traced little circles over her knuckles, Greer suddenly forgot all about Louise.

"Is anyone else around?"

"Haven't had a customer since noon."

"What a shame. I suppose I should come in and buy something."

"For Tywynn," he reasoned, brushing his thumb across the delicate skin of her inner wrist.

Greer's breath hitched, lodging in the hollow of her throat. "For Tywynn." The words almost didn't come out.

As she stepped inside, Greer was struck by a wall of delicious heat. She could hear the flames in the ovens crackling, the hiss of baking bread. The front shop was clean and tidy and gloriously empty.

Even so, Ellis tugged her to the far corner of the room, away from the large storefront window. Eyes were everywhere, and with only days until the Hunt, nothing would please the town gossips more than catching a pair of lovers in a moment of indiscretion.

Ellis traced the curve of her ear, murmuring how much he'd missed her. Then, after he gave a quick glance back out the window, his mouth was on hers.

She nearly laughed with relief as they fell against each other. Pressed between the wall and Ellis's long, looming frame, for one blessed, heady moment, Greer heard nothing but the whisper of his breath, the deep hum of his appreciation, and the racing patter of his heart and hers. In that moment, the rest of the world washed away, leaving only the two of them behind.

"I've missed you, Ellis Beaufort," she murmured as he left a trail of kisses down the column of her throat. His hands roamed along her sides, squeezing the curve of her hips, bundling folds of her skirt as if he wished to tear them away. She drew lines up over his back, tugging at his suspenders, across his scalp, her fingers curling into his hair. She wanted to hold him in place, wanted to keep this moment going.

Just a little longer.

Just a little . . .

Ellis chuckled as he broke away, giving her an admonishing tap on her nose.

"You're going to bring Old Lady Cowen running in, making noises like that," he teased.

Greer cupped his cheek, pleased with how his beard prickled, and snorted as she pictured the widowed seamstress bursting in, brandishing a pair of scissors, ready to snip the inflamed couple apart. "Do you ever feel like the entire town still thinks us children?"

He pressed a kiss to the center of her palm and shrugged. "I suppose, till after the Hunt, we are."

"If we had just run in the last one"—her hand fell as a wave of bitter melancholy washed over her—"we'd be married. We'd have children of our own already. But instead. . . ." She waggled a crooked, admonishing finger at him, approximating the widowed Cowen. She bit the inside of her cheek. "It's my fault—"

Before she could finish her sentence, Ellis kissed her, silencing her worries.

"None of that," he said. "You were in no shape to be thinking of anything but Ailie."

"But you were," she countered, sinking into a pool of guilt so deep she wanted to cry. "You were ready. You could have run and found some other, a girl who doesn't hear things she shouldn't, a girl who isn't strange—"

"Greer." Her name on his lips was enough to stop the anxious spiral. He tilted her face to his so that their eyes met. "Why would I ever settle for some girl when I have you? I would wait a thousand years if I had to. Happily. Joyfully. It was never a hardship. Never," he emphasized, squeezing her hands.

She could only stare, caught in a strong current of too many emotions. Shame and gratitude, guilt and wonder, and so many shades of love. Each demanded to be acknowledged and felt in equal measure, all fighting to come to the forefront of her inner storm.

Ground yourself.

The memory of Ailie's voice cut through the turmoil.

When things are overwhelming, ground yourself in truths.

Greer took a deep, centering breath. With Ellis, there was only ever one truth that mattered.

"I love you." She stood on her tiptoes, feeling strangely shy as she pressed a quick kiss to the cheek of the man she'd loved for more than a decade. "Always."

"Always," he agreed and a light flickered in his eyes. "I forgot to tell you: something special came in today."

He crossed behind the counter, and Greer followed, watching him take a loaf of bread from the case and set it on a length of brown paper.

"Is that cinnamon chip?" Greer asked with surprise. It had been an age since the bakery had had the spice in stock.

"Tywynn was able to talk that merchant captain out of an entire case of sticks." He wiped his hands on the apron. "I baked a batch this afternoon. I know Hessel is partial to it."

"His favorite."

Ellis hesitated. "With all the trouble at the mill earlier, I thought he'd appreciate a slice or two."

"Trouble?" Greer echoed as a bolt of alarm spiked through her.

Though Greer was kept away from the mill's chaos, she knew the work was hard and dangerous. The yard was cluttered with stacks of enormous felled trees and jaggedly toothed saws. The waterwheel churned constantly, never stopping, even on feast days. Great cogs and stampers whirred, and the gristmill sometimes spat out wayward shards of wood. Accidents happened—crushed legs, sliced hands, punctured sides. Hessel himself could only boast of nine fingers and seven toes, but Greer knew he considered himself lucky. Other men—men like Ellis's father, John—lost far more than that.

"Is everyone all right?"

"Everyone's fine, physically, I'm sure." Ellis tied off the wrapped loaf with a bow of striped twine. "Only . . . the schooner."

Greer remembered the empty Narrows. "They didn't stay long."

Ellis shook his head. "From what I heard, the captain offered far too low a price for the lumber." He stopped, letting the words he didn't say fill in the story's gaps.

Greer pictured how it must have played out. Ayaan's stony silence. Hessel's face red with insult, then rage. "Father wouldn't have taken that well."

Wordlessly, Ellis handed her the bread.

Greer clutched it to her chest; it was still warm from the oven. "I'm sure he'll appreciate your kindness."

Doubt darkened Ellis's eyes.

"Two weeks," she reminded him. "The Hunt is in two weeks, and then everything is done and settled, and it won't matter what he thinks."

Ellis gave a faint shrug, and she wished she could wipe away every bit of wistfulness staking its claim. Melancholy never looked right on Ellis Beaufort. It hung off his features like a pair of hand-me-down trousers, too loose, too short.

But before she could offer any comfort, a roaring wall of sound rang out, thundering over the town and cove like the cry of a monstrous beast. Greer could feel the low vibrations of First Bellows rumble along her sternum. Her ears ached. Her head felt as though it would burst. It lasted exactly ten seconds, then died away.

"One hour till sunset," she said needlessly. She fished a small coin from her pocket and set it on the counter, payment for the bread. "Do you need any help closing up?"

He shook his head. "I'll be fine. Tywynn promised to stop in before Thirds."

"And you'll be at the barn warming?"

"Think it'll still go on? Even with all this?" He gestured toward the window.

"Roibart Andersan would never let a little weather spoil a party."

"Then I look forward to the first dance." He leaned over the counter, clearly intending to kiss her once more.

The scent of browning bread warmed the air between them.

"The sourdough!" Ellis exclaimed and turned before pushing through the kitchen's swinging door.

"I'll see you tonight?"

She listened to the heavy clanks and scrapes of hot metal pans being removed from the oven. He didn't respond, and Greer was certain he hadn't heard her. She marveled at what that must be like.

"I love you," she tried again anyway.

No answer.

With a shake of her head, Greer left the bakery.

When she stepped out from under the promenade's cover, the pitter-patter of raindrops surrounded her in a blanket of deafening white noise. In seconds, she was soaked through.

"Wait!"

Greer stopped and turned, smiling. Ellis *had* heard her after all.

But he wasn't on the walkway. He wasn't on the threshold, watching her go. He wasn't even at the windows.

Confused, she swept her gaze down the promenade, searching for anyone else who might have called after her.

"Starling."

The word was soft and hissed and sounded wholly wrong. Wholly inhuman.

Greer scanned the road.

It was empty.

No one was there.

A tendril of unease unfurled within Greer, its barbs sharp and biting.

"We'll see you soon, little Starling."

3

SECOND BELLOWS—two lumbering rolls of chaos that signaled just one half-hour left until sunset—rumbled as Greer opened the front door, her wool cloak soaked through and rainwater dripping from her dark braid.

Martha Kingston was in the kitchen, wrestling with an eel.

"You shan't get the best of me," she muttered, and cursed at the beast.

The long black body thrashed against the worktable, wriggling furiously to escape her grasp. Martha hissed as the eel snapped at her, drawing blood. Holding the squirming creature down with one hand, she sucked absentmindedly at the wounded finger, then pulled out a mallet. The battle ended with an abrupt, meaty *thwunk*.

"That you, Greer?" the older woman called out, sounding out of breath.

"It's raining hard enough for a second flood," Greer announced, hanging her cloak and satchel from a series of pegs near the front door. She kicked off her boots and shimmied free of her wet stockings. These went on the line before the hearth, joining a pinned set of Hessel's socks and Martha's gloves. She entered the kitchen.

"It'll be snow by nightfall," Martha predicted, picking up a cleaver. Her face was pink from the struggle with the eel, and the short wisps of silvered hair poking free of her bun looked like a saint's halo. The thick blade glinted brightly before sailing in a smooth arc through the air. The eel's head fell free, thudding upon the wooden table. "That'll teach you to bite me."

As if in response, the rest of its body thrashed with angry fervor, a final mimicry of life.

Martha went to work, peeling away the eel's skin from its now flaccid length. It came off in a squelch wet enough to make Greer cringe. "You're late," Martha said.

Greer deposited the loaf of cinnamon bread on the table, careful to keep it from the mess of eel staining the work space. "Dessert is already done. Technically, I'm early." She gave the older woman a quick kiss on the cheek before turning to grab her apron.

Martha eyed the brown paper wrapping skeptically as she pulled innards from the eel's body cavity. "Your father is already in a foul mood—stomping about and snapping all through lunch—he doesn't need additional aggrievements."

Greer brought the apron over her head and adjusted the crossed back. "The schooner didn't really leave without buying the lumber, did it?"

"That it did," Martha said, slicing the eel into short segments. "Hand me the pie dish, won't you?"

Greer crossed to the hutch and stood on tiptoe to reach for the crockery. "But they'll be back, surely. They wouldn't have come all this way just to—"

The older woman shook her head, silencing Greer.

"It's a bad mess they're in," Martha said darkly, as she flattened out the meat with a rolling pin. "I've always said Hessel's temper would get the better of him, and that day has come." She turned to the stove and dropped a pat of butter into the heated cast-iron skillet. It sizzled instantly. "All the more reason to not bring up your day with that boy in front of him."

"I didn't spend my day with Ellis," Greer said, her tone prickling. "I was up past the northern ridge with Louise."

Martha *pfft*-ed a curl off her forehead, as if to say there was not much difference between the two Beauforts. She went on pressing pieces of eel into the pie dish, then threw in shallots, parsley, and nutmeg. "Anything to show for it?"

"There was a whole new area of Redcaps . . . I made a map."

"Someday you're going to run out of world to chart."

Greer certainly hoped not.

As a Steward, Hessel Mackenzie was keeper of the town's records and custodian of Resolution Beaufort's diaries and maps. Hessel kept them locked away in his study.

When Greer was seven, she'd stolen her father's ring of keys and spent an exhilarating night poring over the illustrations of coastlines and waves, wind charts and mountain ranges. The lines they formed, the information they offered, captivated her.

Here was the known.

Here was the not.

Growing up within the unbreakable confines of the Warding Stones, Greer well knew her known. It was the land beyond the Stones—those dark, impenetrable forests and all the dangerous uncertainties they contained—that set her mind racing, that caused her anxieties to spike and her fears to grow. But if she could chart those mysterious depths, bring understanding to their enigmatic wilds, she wouldn't have to be afraid.

The next morning, she created her first map.

It was a poorly drawn rendering of the town's main road. The proportions were wrong, and her lines were misshapen and sloping. But she'd never been more proud.

She set out to chart every inch of Mistaken.

And, map by map, she improved.

She experimented with scale and scope, texture and notation.

Ailie had always praised her endeavors, calling Greer her little scout and urging her to explore new areas. On lazy spring days, she'd pack them picnic lunches and they'd bravely march into the unknown, searching for a stream to follow or a rocky outcrop to measure.

Martha hated their trips, and went on long diatribes about the foolishness of leaving the safety of Mistaken's borders. Shortly before Greer's birth, Martha and two other women had wandered into town, reeling from shock, starvation, and blood loss. They'd come from a small settlement in the north, an outpost along the coast that had been destroyed when a group of Bright-Eyeds attacked, killing nearly everyone.

It had been an arduous seven-day journey for the women, who'd been drawn to Mistaken after hearing whispered tales of a cursed village kept wholly safe from the monsters of the woods by a ring of strange stones. They'd come and stayed within the borders as the sun set, deciding that a life of being penned by those protective stones was far preferable to taking their chances in the wilds.

Martha did everything she could to persuade Hessel to forbid Ailie and Greer's daily wanderings, but when Greer discovered a new grove of Redcaps—a find more lucrative than anything the mill's scouts had come across—the matter was settled.

When Greer was old enough to venture beyond the Warding Stones without her mother, she took her maps and wrote down every bit of the journey, inch by inch. Ailie would study them each night, with a proud smile curving her full lips. Hessel would scan them, making gruff noises of approval as he noted each new Redcap.

Slowly, the vast wilderness surrounding Mistaken became a little more known, a little less feared.

Quickly, Greer had filled her bedroom, hanging her maps over every bit of wall space until they were layered ten deep, the stacks too heavy to be held up by tacks. Every so often they'd fall, fluttering to the floor like so much confetti.

Greer's gaze drifted to the front room, where the new map remained, still tucked into her satchel. "I thought all the new trees would please Ayaan and Father, but . . ."

Martha glanced up from her work, and her dark-brown eyes softened with understanding as they met Greer's. "They'll want to see it. Later. Show them later."

Greer nodded.

Martha removed a piece of cloth covering the dish at her elbow to reveal a mound of resting dough. "Start the sauce, won't you?"

Carrots and celery were at the end of the table. Greer picked up the longest, greenest stalk and held it thoughtfully. "Martha . . ." She trailed off, the question on her lips too terrible to finish.

The older woman grunted as she spread out the dough, urging her to go on.

Greer started chopping the celery into even slices and the steady rhythm of the knife helped set her thoughts in order. "Have you ever heard the Benevolence?"

Martha made a strange *tsk*-ing noise that was somehow both laughter and admonishment. "Did you take a tumble in the woods today? Strike your head on something? What a question."

"No!" Greer set the knife aside, irritation flickering within her. "Not heard *of* them. Heard *them*. Have you ever *heard them*?"

Martha frowned. "Heard them what?"

Greer hesitated. "Speak."

An unbearably long moment spread between them, and Greer wished she could seize her words back.

"Have you?" Martha finally asked, carefully, cautiously. "Heard them speak?"

Greer squirmed under her watchful gaze. "I . . . I don't know. I thought . . . when I was in the woods before, I thought I heard . . . well, I thought I heard something."

"Louise," Martha supplied. "Could it have been Louise?"

"It didn't sound like her. It sounded . . ." She paused, remembering the slippery hiss. "It sounded wrong, somehow."

"Wrong," Martha echoed.

"Not . . ." She sucked in a breath. "Not human. It must have been one of them, don't you think? It's nearly Reaping. They must be somewhere nearby."

"No one has seen the Benevolence since the truce was made, so many years ago," Martha reminded Greer, her cadence worn and familiar. "But they protect us still. That's all we can ever hope for. To wish to see or hear them . . ." She swallowed and shook her head. "We should not seek such things."

"Then was it . . . *them*?"

It made Greer uncomfortable even to speak their name. The Bright-Eyeds were things dredged from the darkest of nightmares, feral monsters of legend and myth turned flesh. Some said they could control the weather, bringing about raging storms and damaging winds. Others said they could change shape, taking whatever form best suited their needs: fangs and claws one moment, winged membranes and talons the next. But everyone agreed that their hunger—for meat, for blood, for utter destruction—was insatiable, and that, should you be unlucky enough to catch their shining eyes, nothing would stop them from destroying everything you held dear.

Nothing but the Benevolence.

Nothing but their Stones.

Martha *tsk*-ed, but she turned with a shudder, as if Greer's question was too terrible to bear.

What frightened Greer most about the Bright-Eyeds was their total silence. She knew they were out there, in the woods, in the trees, gorging themselves with their kills. But she'd never heard them. She, who could hear everything, had never picked up on even a whisper of their passing.

Until today.

Maybe.

"Mama heard things, too," Greer probed carefully.

Greer's memories of her mother were soft and vague and always recalled through a filter of golden, sun-dappled light. A warm smile. A deep, throaty laugh. Her eyes just like Greer's—a dazzling pale gray ringed in charcoal—hair just as dark and wavy, and the same constellation of freckles dotted across one cheek.

She'd been one of the finest seamstresses in all of Mistaken, forever bent over a hoop, tracing rows of stitches across patchwork hues, creating wonders with her strands of colorful threads. She sang while she worked, making up songs that seemed to have no real rhythm or tune. The stories she told were dark and sometimes dreadful, songs of thieves and hangmen, murdered lovers and glittering eyes watching at windows. But, no matter how scary they'd been to young Greer, she'd loved to listen all the same, the terrifying melodies made sweet by the playful lilt of her mother's voice.

Often, however, Ailie Mackenzie would pause, cutting a note short, and tilt her head toward the woods, listening to something even Greer could not hear. Ailie would nod or frown, answering questions no one else noticed, then return to her work and start on a new sad song.

Seven years after Ailie's passing, Martha was the only one Greer could talk about her with. Hessel would brush aside any attempt Greer might make. She found his reticence perplexing: Hessel always had so much to say about everything else.

Martha let out a sigh. "I think . . ."

Before her thoughts could slip free, the final Bellows came. Thirds was three sharp blasts, roaring just as the last ray of sun warmed the horizon. They warned anyone who wasn't back inside the town border that it was now too late. The Warding Stones would pull them home whether they wanted to go or not.

Greer pictured Callum Cairn traipsing down the hillside, leaving his post. She'd never liked visiting the Bellows. The curving horn looked just like the sharp antler of the Biasd Na Srogaig, a towering, long-necked water beast with a fondness for terrorizing loud children to silence.

This was the time of day Greer hated most.

The sun had set, and Mistaken was penned in for the night. No one could venture out beyond the boundary till sunrise.

Greer felt the confines of the Warding Stones tighten around her, squeezing at the hollow of her throat like a noose. She was grateful for the protection they offered, grateful that their magic kept the Bright-Eyes at bay, but, oh, how it chafed.

Just as darkness fell and early night took hold, the front door opened, letting in a string of muttered curses and stomping boots.

Hessel Mackenzie had come home.

4

DINNER WAS a silent affair. Silent for everyone but Greer. She heard every bite and chew, every sip and slurp.

She turned her focus to the slice of pie before her, cutting the pieces of eel into precise, identical segments to drown out the sound of her father's supper sliding into his gullet.

"There's sweet bread for dessert," Martha mentioned. "Cinnamon."

Greer watched from the corner of her eye as Hessel picked up his mug, considering the remaining ale within. "Hmph," he grunted, then drained the glass.

Martha scurried to the kitchen, her own dinner half eaten. Greer hoped she'd be quick to return.

It wasn't that Greer disliked her father—he was her father, she had to love him, she supposed—but she never knew what to say when around him. She always felt, no matter what was on her mind, that Hessel would rather be speaking of something else, to anyone else.

Since Ailie's death, Hessel and Greer had moved through the home as guests in a boardinghouse might, cordial to each other but not strictly certain of whom it was they shared a roof with.

Hessel often seemed bemused by Greer's presence, as though she were a feral creature, wild and untamed, who had wandered in through an open door and wasn't sure how to leave again. Ailie had similarly perplexed him. He'd never known how to reconcile her capricious whims with his carefully constructed world of order and reason.

Whenever Hessel Mackenzie met with something he didn't understand, the only way he could manage the conundrum was to take total control and bend the problem to his will, refusing to give up his grasp until it caved or broke.

Hessel cleared his throat now, his voice grating, as raspy as gravel. "I don't expect I have to ask where the bread came from."

Greer remained silent, certain he wasn't finished.

"Of all the days you had to go and visit that boy." He shook his head.

Greer shifted the cuts of eel across her plate. Perhaps, if she could get them lined up just so, this conversation would go differently. Hessel might not poke and prod her till she wanted to explode. She wouldn't fling out words she only partially meant. It was foolish thinking, of course. One action didn't impact the other. And yet . . .

"I wasn't visiting him," she began, adding another piece to the line.

Hessel's breath puffed, neither a cough nor a laugh, just a sound. A dangerous one, warning Greer into silence.

She swallowed back the rest of her protest and listened to Martha in the kitchen, slicing thick cuts of bread before stabbing them through with a long fork. She heard them toasting near the fire's flames, like a hiss of steam from a kettle.

"I saw Lachlan Davis today," Hessel said, continuing as if he'd been the one talking all along. "Fine lad, very fine. I couldn't ask for a harder-working young man. Has a head for figures, you know. I'm thinking of letting him keep the accounts now. He'll be at the barn warming tonight." He shoveled the last piece of eel into his mouth before adding: "Promised to offer you a dance. You be sure to accept."

Greer pressed her lips together.

Hessel was forever mentioning young men in town, finding endless ways to extol their virtues casually, citing them in a way to make Ellis Beaufort look less by comparison. Whoever caught Greer was assured to inherit the mill one day, and the Mackenzies' land, and the mountain of wealth both afforded. Hessel was hell-bent that his legacy would not pass to a Beaufort, but Greer had fallen for Ellis long ago, and nothing her father did would sway her from him.

Greer wondered if all daughters suffered so in the weeks leading up to the Hunt. She imagined it must be a difficult time in every household, as parents tried their best to tip outcomes in their family's favor, positioning their children for advantageous matches, but she couldn't think of anyone more dogged in his ways or tactics than Hessel Mackenzie.

In truth, she was more than ready for it all to be over and done with. At twenty-seven, she would be the oldest participant hiding in this Hunt. She'd been under her father's roof for so many more years than she'd expected—seven more than she'd wanted—giving both her and Hessel ample time to rub each other raw.

The Hunt couldn't come soon enough.

When Mistaken had been nothing but a settlement, a tiny outpost floundering in a vast and wholly isolated corner of the world, it became evident that if it was to survive, to grow and thrive, many more hands would be needed to carry out the work. Trees needed to be felled, homes needed to be built. The land needed taming and tending. Gardens needed to be planted and maintained. Water sources had to be diverted.

The list of things that must be done was endlessly long.

Too long for the handful of souls who remained trapped within the confines of the Warding Stones.

When Resolution Beaufort set sail for the frigid north, there had been seventy-eight men, forty-seven women, and an assortment of children on board. Those children aged quickly, but it soon became painfully clear, as the town grew, that not every young man was guaranteed a bride.

This seemed to be a problem with no solution. It wasn't as though the men could set out past the Stones in search of a wife. There were no towns within half a day's journey, and though nomadic trappers and wandering hunters occasionally stumbled across the town's border, most knew to leave well before sunset, and few had women in their ranks.

In an attempt to thwart the crisis, the founding Stewards created the Hunt.

Every seven years, all young women over the age of sixteen would set off into the Hunting Grounds—a wide swath of unclaimed land that followed the northern border of town. Each girl would select a spot to hide in until she was found by a searching, seeking lad. Once the girls were claimed, the town would hold a grand group wedding. Each couple would go to their new homestead and while away their first winter together, not emerging till spring. The wives were expected to be heavily pregnant by then, ready to bring forth the next generation.

It didn't always go like that, of course.

There was always someone who'd rather run than hide.

A girl—it was always a girl—determined not to be caught and willing to risk death, would race into the woods, running as fast and as far from Mistaken as she could get. Her body would never be found, hauled off and eaten by the things of the woods with claws and fangs shaper than her desire for freedom.

Mistaken would move past her death without fanfare or mourning, and it was only in the weeks leading up to the next Hunt that her name would be spoken aloud, whispered as a cautionary tale for any other doubtful brides sporting cold feet.

Greer had never had cold feet. She had never had any doubts.

At twenty, she'd scoured her renderings of the Hunting Grounds, searching and scheming for the perfect spot to wait for Ellis.

Then, days before their Hunt, Ailie passed away.

It had been sudden and unexpected. Hessel Mackenzie had stumbled into a sewing circle at the women's gathering house, looking for Greer. She noticed that, though his eyes were not red, his hands were.

An accident at the mill, he'd said. A bad one. So bad they'd placed Greer's mama in a box of knotty pine and nailed the lid shut before she could even say goodbye.

The days that followed had been hazy with grief. Time passed in such an unordered fashion that it wasn't until months later that Greer even realized she'd missed the Hunt. A kindness from Hessel and the other Stewards, allowing her to stay at home and mourn.

Ellis had opted to not take part and patiently waited another seven years.

The wait had not been easy, but it was nearly over.

Soon, Greer would slip into the Hunting Grounds and emerge as Ellis's bride. Despite his blusterings, there was not a thing her father could do to stop it.

Hessel pushed the last of the pie's gravy about the plate, making no motion to finish it. His chair creaked as he shifted, clearing his throat. "I know you and that boy have been . . . close," he began. His tone was different, subdued and conversational.

Uncertain of what he was trying now, she nodded.

"Quite close. And I know that, of all the girls in town, you are his first—his only—choice."

"Yes."

Hessel sighed. "All I'm asking you to remember is that this partnership is for life. This choice dictates your future. And I would hate for it to be tangled up with that boy."

"He's not a boy," she said, daring to disagree.

"He's not good enough for you," Hessel snapped, striking the table. His words were deep and ferocious, a growl you'd hear echoing in a cave just before meeting your end. "He's not who you deserve. Who our family needs. He and his are blights on this town, stains corrupting everything around them. I'll not have my mill, my fortunes, or my daughter sullied by their lot. You will not marry that boy, Greer Mackenzie. I will make certain of it!"

Greer balled her hands, nails digging into her palms as defiance licked her spine. She could no longer bear to tiptoe around Hessel's rages. "You can't stop me. You can't stop him. You ran your Hunt, you had your turn. This is our decision."

Hessel's face darkened, turning sharp and dangerous. His hand raised, and Greer could see its almost-trajectory. It was going to swing hard and fast and strike her right across the cheek. The one full of Ailie's stars. Startled, she pushed herself back against the chair, nearly toppling it. Hessel had never harmed her before; this was new, unfamiliar ground.

Her retreat broke something inside him, giving his action pause.

When he dropped his hand, he looked guilty, although he hadn't touched her.

The house was silent, even Martha knowing to not intrude.

"I need to get ready for the barn warming," Greer finally said.

Hessel bit at the inside of his cheek. "Greer, I—"

She didn't want his apology. She didn't want his explanation. "May I be excused?"

Hessel stared at her for a long, hard moment before releasing a sigh of resignation. "As you like."

The Hunting Grounds

Ailie's Tree

1740

THE GAMBIT BEGAN with a whispered lie, caught and carried on the ever-howling wind.

There were once a boy and girl, close in age, closer even in acquaintance.

Their fathers shared ownership of the log mill, splitting sections of the business in two, as neat as a line drawn across a map. Mackenzie oversaw the yard, the cutting and slicing, the grinding and seasoning. McIntyre hunted the trees, venturing past the marked borders of town, felling the giants, and hauling them back with triumphant swagger.

The boy and girl grew up together. They were playmates and school chums, constant companions and friendly confidants. As they grew older, the boy even fancied he'd fallen in love. By the time they turned eighteen, the year of their Hunt, he was most certain of it.

The girl was not.

The girl had regarded the boy as a close friend, more family than romantic partner.

The girl, you see, had noticed another.

Like a rabbit caught in a poacher's trap, John Beaufort, son of the blacksmith and a member of the town's most reviled family, had become ensnared in her thoughts and heart.

The Beauforts had been pariahs in Mistaken since their patriarch, Resolution, had died, impaled upon the very tree he'd set out to harvest. They now lived along the eastern ridge of the cove, as far from town as the Warding Stones would permit.

But the girl, spotting the lanky lad in his father's shop, had been filled with horrified delight when he, upon catching her open stare, brazenly winked her way.

Weeks later, on a lonely road, they chanced upon each other. She was on her way to the mill, he on his way home. He was smudged black from his day at the forge, sweat-stained and smelling of rank solder. When he smiled at her, gallantly doffing his hat, the girl grinned back, her cheeks as pink as spring petals.

They met again on the road the next day.

And the day after that.

And the day after that, and the day after that, until one of them grew brave enough to suggest they meet in another location, at another time.

As the weeks passed, the pair snatched every stolen moment they could, dizzy with longing and young love.

The other boy knew nothing of it.

So, when the Hunt was finally upon them, when the girl's pink cheeks had grown red, from the cold as much as from John Beaufort's kisses, the boy begged for her chosen hiding spot. He, full of dreams bright and rosy, proclaimed himself to be the one who would catch her.

The girl, full of dreams of John Beaufort, leaned in and whispered the first lie she'd ever told.

Meet me at the hollowed tree in the north field, she murmured, her breath hot against his cheek, driving him nearly mad with want. *I'll be there, waiting.*

The wind snatched those words and carried them away, past the Stones, past the cove, past all of Mistaken itself.

The morning of the Hunt dawned bright with promise.

The boy greeted the morn, his lips wet with anticipation. He was ready. And when the Hunters took to the land, roaming and ravaging the bush, the bramble, searching for their prizes like dogs on the scent,

Hessel Mackenzie ignored their boyish chuckles, ignored their loud mêlée, and raced instead to the north field.

The tree was a towering, barren shell of a Redcap. Spotting a flutter of ribbon peeking from the monster's center, he ran through the tall grasses with all his might. He reached into the hollowed tree with confident, greedy hands. His fingers clasped around the wrist of his prize, and he let out a whoop of triumph.

He'd done it. He'd claimed his bride.

But it was not his beloved whom he pulled free.

He stared in confusion at a girl with eyes as gray as an approaching storm, with hair dark as night. He stared at a girl who was not his Mary McIntyre, but a girl with scattered stars across one cheek.

He stared at her.

She stared at him.

And then she smiled.

And Hessel Mackenzie, the boy who should have had a heart most broken, took his bride in his arms and kissed her.

5

THE BARN WAS warmer than Greer had expected.

The tang of sawdust and fresh paint hung in the air. As one of the largest barns in Mistaken, its construction had been an audacious statement, an earnest hope for good things to come. There would be harvests to store, new animals to house. Bounties were on their way, and the Andersans were ready to receive them.

The air buzzed with lighthearted merriment. After a short, intense summer of tending crops, readying for the harvest and Reaping, and preparing for the dark months of winter to come, everyone gathered now with unusually high spirits, bolstered by the barrels of ale supplied by Roibart Andersan.

Bales of hay, softened with layers of quilts and furs, were laid out in conversational arrangements. Dozens of lanterns and oil lamps gave the cavernous space a happy glow. In the middle of the main floor were long tables heavy with food. Smoked salmon and tender jerky were displayed on ceramic platters. Wooden bowls overflowed with roasted vegetables and late-season berries. An entire length of one table was dedicated to fruit pies and nutty, dark breads.

The storm clouds had rolled away, leaving behind a dazzling night sky, and nearly everyone in Mistaken had turned out. Though most of the women stayed inside, the men congregated in the yard around the ale, refilling their cups and laughing uproariously. Several lads had brought fiddles and pipes and were challenging each other with zesty runs.

For the younger crowd, there was a marked undercurrent to the evening, a pulsing, pressing urge to see and be seen. With the Hunt so near, many were using this night to woo would-be partners while sizing up potential competition. Frilly dresses peeked out from long woolen cloaks. Hair had been slicked and pinned and ribboned. Cheeks were pinched to alluring shades of pink. Everyone was full of smiles and gaiety, as if vying to be the brightest and most dazzling.

All of the good cheer set Greer's teeth on edge; her own thoughts were drowned out by the sounds and shouts of everyone else.

From across the barn, she heard Lotte Morag, a Steward's wife, whisper that she was with child again. Outside, along the far edge of the tree line, hidden by the cover of darkness, came the muffled, breathy moans of two sweethearts fumbling against each other. Beside the bonfire, a group of boys ran through the list of Hunt participants, comparing the girls' looks and the width of their hips. Their conversation was sprinkled with bursts of wicked laughter.

Inside her mittens, Greer's fingers danced with agitation. She longed for a mug of mulled cider. Spirits often helped dull the roar of so much sound. But first she needed to find Ellis. When she was with him, everything quieted, distilling to only the most important of details.

Where was he?

A pack of young men wandered into the yard, and Greer scanned their number. They were led by Lachlan Davis, Hessel's favored suitor.

Greer hadn't liked him in childhood, when he'd dipped the end of Louise's long braids into wells of ink at school, and she liked him even less now. A kinetic energy danced through his short, muscular frame, a caged restlessness that always verged toward mean-spiritedness. With his dark hair and even darker eyes, he reminded Greer of a compact wolverine, endlessly prowling and always on the hunt.

The boys slapped at one another's backs, chests puffed and proud. Their eyes were already glassy from swigs of the whiskey Greer could hear jostling within hidden flasks.

Ellis was not with them.

Lachlan's eyes roamed over the barnyard, intent and assessing. Greer ducked behind one of the thick posts supporting the weight of the loft, but not quickly enough. She wanted to groan as she heard his footsteps.

As Hessel Mackenzie's only child, she knew many had set their sights upon her, hungering after the comforts and wealth the mill brought in and willing to overlook her peculiarities to get them. Over the summer, grand gestures of intent had been made: bouquets of flowers, parcels of ribbons, little gifts of needles and thread, her favorite sweets from the general store.

Greer had refused them all.

"Good evening, Greer Mackenzie," a voice called out, toying and teasing. "You're looking most lovely tonight."

"Oh, Lachlan," she said, turning to face him. "I was just . . . I was just admiring the new barn. It's a marvel, isn't it?" Her voice felt too high. It was obvious she'd been trying to avoid him.

Lachlan peered up at the rafters appreciatively. "Ours will be better."

"Ours?" she echoed, recoiling at his audacity.

A swoop of dark hair fell over his brow as his eyes landed on her. "Oh yes. It will need to be bigger than this one. Much bigger. I have so many plans."

"For . . . a barn?"

"And us," Lachlan added, nodding. His lips turned up and Greer couldn't shake the image of a marten, moving in for the kill. "Never in all my life have I so longed for a summer to end," he admitted. "But it's nearly over. Come first snow, we'll be tucked away in a little cabin of our own."

"A little cabin with an enormous barn," she clarified, deadpan.

He beamed.

"You truly think you're going to catch me, Lachlan Davis?"

He took a step forward, his confidence easy and unearned. "I know I will."

Greer's gaze drifted toward the open doors, where Hessel stood with a group of Stewards. She could hear Ayaan recounting the negotiations with the merchant captain, but her father's focus was fixed squarely upon her. And Lachlan. And the pair they made.

"I spoke with your father at some length today." Lachlan adjusted the angle of his body as though to include Hessel within their conversation, but also using the movement to shift closer to Greer. She could feel the heat of his breath linger in the hollow of her throat. "Did he mention it?"

She shrugged lightly. "He talks about so many young men these days, it's impossible to keep track."

Lachlan blinked, taken aback, before breaking into a snort of amusement. "You're in jest! Good. A wife who can make you laugh will make for a happy home."

He took her hand in his, fumbling around the bulk of woolen mitten. Greer felt the weight of an audience upon her and scanned the barn. There, on the other side of the room, a group of girls studied Lachlan's grasp with unchecked interest, their lips thin with resentment.

She knew Lachlan was considered the best catch of the Hunt, the boy every girl hoped would follow after her with fixed determination.

Almost every girl, Greer thought, squirming free of his brazen touch.

"Have you been practicing?" she asked.

Intrigued, he raised his eyebrows. "Practicing?"

"For the Hunt."

His smile was indulgent. "I've been hunting my whole life. Tracking you won't be too different, Greer Mackenzie."

The truth of his statement left a puddle of unease pooling within her, but she pushed past it. "Then let's try it. Right now."

Lachlan glanced about the barn. For the first time that evening, he looked apprehensive, unsure of his footing. "You want . . . you want me to hunt you . . . here?"

Greer nodded as if she was proposing nothing more than a mischievous dare. "On the day of the Hunt, the girls have one half-hour to hide. Give me five minutes tonight."

"Five minutes," he repeated slowly.

Greer could almost see the fantasies his mind spun. "Would three suit you better? I'm sure other girls would be much easier to track, if you think me too much of a challenge." She nodded toward the group of girls still watching them.

"Five is fine. Make it ten," he said with gallant loftiness.

"Ten, then."

"And when I win?" Lachlan asked, lowering his voice with suggestion. "When I catch my prize, what shall she give me?"

Greer leaned in, lowering her voice. "Anything you like."

His breath caught; his pupils dilated. "Anything?"

"I'd head outside and start the counting if I were you."

He was gone in a clattering of eager footsteps.

Greer turned and spotted a pair of women watching the scene play out with narrowed, disapproving eyes.

"So much goodness," the older one said with a *tsk*, "wasted on such a girl."

Greer longed to throw a pithy retort back at the sour-faced widow, but the clock had begun, and she could feel every passing second. Ducking from their glares, she slipped to the back of the barn and lost herself in the maze of tack rooms and equipment storage. All she wanted was to find Ellis and pull him away from the festivities.

As if he were summoned by her thoughts, she heard Ellis's voice call through the noise of the gathering, as clear as a bell, as unmissable as the Bellows: "Greer."

She turned, thinking he must be behind her, but the corridor was empty.

"Come find me," he continued, and a flush of warmth rushed over her.

They'd played this game throughout childhood, wasting away summer afternoons in sun-dappled meadows. Ellis would hide within the tall grasses and wildflowers and whisper to her, knowing she could hear his every word. Knowing she would always follow after him.

Greer loved that her peculiarity, her ability to hear far and wide, was never a source of bewilderment for Ellis. He never thought it odd, never found frustration with it. He embraced the quirk as readily as any of Greer's attributes, the color of her eyes, the freckles across her face.

Greer searched the stalls and birthing pens, but they were empty, save for piles of fresh straw and a trio of children playing their own hide-and-seek. She peeked in room after room, mindful of each minute Lachlan was counting.

"Wrong level," Ellis whispered.

She looked up, grinning. Heaps of feed bags and hay bales were stored in the upper loft. He must have hidden away in their shadows, watching her progress. Greer found the loft ladder and began climbing. After hoisting herself onto the platform, she pulled the wooden frame up, too, which would stop Lachlan from following after.

Satisfied, she wiped her hands, surveying the shadows surrounding her.

Bales of straw were arranged in towering stacks, turning the loft into a miniature maze. She cocked her head, listening, but the only thing that caught her attention was Lachlan at the fire circle, chatting with friends.

"Where are you off to?" Greer thought it was Callum Cairn who spoke.

"Tired of wasting the night with you lot. I've already found my girl. Might as well go and claim her now. Who needs to wait for the Hunt?"

"Charming," Greer muttered.

The boys hooted with delight. "Who? Who is it?"

"Mackenzie's daughter."

Noises of surprise and disgust followed, each a tiny twist in Greer's heart.

"Greer?" Stephen McNaleigh asked. "She's completely crazy! My old man said she's got the Devil himself whispering his secrets to her."

"So? She's Mackenzie's only child," Lachlan explained. "She'll inherit everything he's got. The farm. The mill. All that money."

Stephen clucked uncertainly. "You'd still have to marry that mad bitch to get at it. I'll take someone like Rose McTaven any day. All I want is a pretty girl to come home to and to come all over."

The boys fell into fits of wild laughter that reminded Greer of the harbor when the white-coat seals were in rutting season. Their coarse antics spurred her to action.

The hatch to the roof was open, filtering moonlight through the square and reminding Greer of Ailie's quilts, stitched together with constellations and stardust.

Greer shimmied up, her boots scrambling to find purchase on the thin rungs. They were nothing but slats of wood nailed to the wall, and for one moment she feared she'd miss a step and come crashing down, alerting Lachlan to her exact location.

But her balance held, and she was soon outside.

The hidden platform was a long stretch of boards, just two meters wide, jutting from the steep angle of the roof. Ellis had laid out a fur and blankets, creating a nest cozy enough to ward off the night's chill.

"You know, when we were building this barn, I couldn't understand why Roibart insisted on leveling out a section of the pitch," he called out in greeting. Moonlight limned him in blue, highlighting the lines of his face and hair. "But this is splendid."

"It is." She squinted over the edge, judging whether Lachlan might be able to catch a glimpse of them. "Do you think anyone can see us up here?"

"Not unless they're all the way at the Andersans' house. Angle's too steep. Tree line's too close. It's the perfect place to hide away." Ellis patted at the spot beside him and nodded toward a brown jug.

"You brought provisions," she noticed approvingly.

"Swiped a few of Widow Sturgette's crowberry tarts, too," Ellis said, gesturing to a nearby basket. "If we're going to squirrel away and watch the stars, we ought to feast like kings."

"I doubt even kings have a view like this," she said, joining him. She pulled a quilt over her shoulders and took a long swig of the cider. It filled her with a pleasant heat, and she bumped her shoulder against Ellis's with familiar affection. "You can see all the way to the Narrows from here," she admired, snuggling against him. "When we have a barn of our own, we should make a hidden spot just like this, just for us. It's beautiful."

"You're beautiful," he confided, running his fingers thoughtfully across the swell of her cheek. "You always are, but tonight . . ." He hummed his appreciation, and there was a look in his eyes that sparked something in the air, sending an electric charge down her sternum. He touched her crown of braids, toying with the sprigs of late-blooming yarrow blossoms she'd woven in. "I like your flowers."

She was inordinately pleased he'd noticed.

"I like you," Greer said, echoing his darkening tone before pressing a kiss to his cheek. "I like you, and I very much like this."

"Are you saying you don't want to join the festivities?" he teased, wrapping his arms around her and pulling her close for another kiss; their lips met for a moment, and another, and another.

"I am saying exactly that, yes," she murmured. She dared a final peek toward the bonfire below. It seemed impossible they wouldn't be caught. In a town as small as Mistaken, eyes were always somewhere, watching, judging. "You're certain no one can see us?"

His laughter was low and rich and so wonderfully warm. "Very. Why? Is there something you want to do up here that you wouldn't want anyone else to see?"

In response, Greer drew her hand across his chest, flicking aside one of his suspenders with a wicked gleam.

Ellis laughed again. "I have no objections to that, truly, but I do want to show you something first." He rolled over to rustle through the basket.

Feeling cold without him, Greer shifted, leaning against the curve of his spine. Her chin fit perfectly into the crook of his shoulder, and she dared to take a quick nibble of his earlobe, knowing it drove him wild.

"Save those thoughts for later," Ellis said, and, with a triumphant flourish, he handed her a folded sheet of parchment. "Here."

"A map!" Greer exclaimed, spreading open the paper. She squinted at the lines in the dark, just able to make out a series of mountains, the dots of towns, the bend of a river unfurling over their laps. "But of what?"

"That's Mistaken," he said, pointing to the bottom corner, near her hip. "And that . . ." He ran his fingertips over the rest of the sheet. "All of that is the land to the north of us."

"North," Greer echoed distantly, her eyes round as she took in the information.

Beyond Mistaken's cove—no bigger than an inch on this rendering and unlabeled, unimportant—was an entire landscape of lines wholly unfamiliar. The seacoast, only ever glimpsed from the top of the Narrows in the very best of weather, spanned the full height of the parchment, impossibly long and full of bays completely unknown to her. Mountains she'd never seen raised to astounding heights. Greer had never beheld anything so wondrous.

"Where did you get this?" she demanded, leaning over to follow an alien river that cut through the land. It didn't look very remote—only a day or two's travel at the most—but, so far from the Warding Stones, it was a journey she could never hope to take.

"Bought it off the captain today when he came to see Tywynn. I thought you would like it."

"I do," she said in a rush. "I love it. I . . ." Greer looked up, meeting his gaze, and her eyes filled with unexplained tears. "I love you."

"I love you," he echoed, and kissed her again.

"This is incredible," she said, turning back to the rendering.

Her heart ached as she studied its lines. Greer knew there were so many things in the world she would never be able to see, but to have such tangible proof of them in front of her gave a unique kind of pain.

She wanted to explore every inch of the map, to experience it all in actual scale, to see the light falling over the impossible mountain ranges, to hear the babbling of the river, to feel the mist off the white rapids. A ribbon of wanderlust unspooled within her, tying its knots around her limbs as if she was a marionette. Her feet itched to go, go now, go and leave, go and learn.

"Can you believe the world is so big?" Greer asked. "That it goes on so far? And farther still, really. This is just where the paper ends." With a touch of reverence, she set the map aside, unable to take in any more.

"It is a wonder," Ellis admitted.

"Do you remember that time we went out to the Narrows?" Greer asked, and a sudden flurry of goose bumps raced over her. She rearranged the quilt so that it spanned across both of them. "When we climbed to the top of the cliff?"

Ellis nodded, shifted, and brought his arm around her, drawing her close. "The Great Bay was so much bigger than I ever imagined it would be."

She nestled against him. "Remember there was that ship out on the coast? It had so many sails on it. And we thought it was going to come into the bay with supplies."

"It was the biggest one I'd ever seen," Ellis said, leaning back against the incline of the roof.

Greer followed, laying her head on the broad plain of his chest. She listened to his heartbeat, lost in the memories of that day. Staring out at the world beyond the Narrows had been like discovering a long-locked door left open. Her imagination had run wild, making her dizzy as she tried to envision what wonders were out there, waiting to be found.

"But it didn't," she went on, sadness creeping in. "The ship. It just . . . went by. It was as if it didn't even know we were here." Her gaze fell back onto the map's corner uneasily. Her entire world, everything she'd ever seen, was rendered there in minute detail. In just one tiny square.

"Two kids perched on a cliff is hardly cause for a clipper to stop," Ellis allowed.

"Not us," Greer clarified, her hand falling on him. "*Us*. The town. Mistaken." She swallowed. "There's a whole giant world out there, and we're not a part of it. Ships sail by every season with places to go and lives to lead, and we're just here."

Ellis studied her. "Well . . . yes."

"Doesn't that ever make you sad?"

He frowned, considering. "Not exactly. It's fun to imagine what that world might be like, but . . . I don't *need* to know. Not really. Everything I need, everything I want, is right here."

"In Mistaken?" Greer asked dubiously.

He let out a snort of laughter. "On this roof. You, Greer Mackenzie, with all your wild wonderings and yearnings, are all I want. You're all the world I need." Ellis pressed his lips into her braids. "And every day I think how lucky I am that, of all the places in the world that you could be"—his breath was hot in the curve of her ear—"you're here, with me."

Greer wanted to give in to his kisses, wanted to sink into the heated bliss of his embrace, but the vast expanse of the map still poked at her, a splinter snagging her attention. "Does it bother you that I do? Wonder? About"—she waved her hand toward the Great Bay—"all that?"

Ellis cupped her face between his hands, pressing more kisses to her forehead, her eyelids, the tip of her nose. "Not at all. I fell in love with all of you." He brushed his mouth across her cheek. "Your traces of stars." He brought her hands up to his lips. "Your ink-stained fingers." He nuzzled at her temple. "All those giant thoughts caught up in that extraordinary mind of yours." He traced down her frame, squeezing at her arms. "You."

Greer tipped her face to his so their mouths met, catching against each other's. He tasted bright and crisp, the first bite of a polished green apple.

The kiss deepened and Ellis grasped her arms, trailed his fingers along the curve of her back, exploring every inch of her as if she were a map to be studied and learned.

"Ellis."

His name hissed from her like a whispered prayer, an oath. Desire flushed deep as Ellis's hands ran over her breasts, palming the curves, before moving to her hips, her thighs. She tugged him on top of her, welcoming his weight. She was pinned and could scarcely draw breath, and it was glorious.

His grip tightened, and she felt his hard length against her. She shifted, letting Ellis's hands roam beneath her layers of skirts, running their way up her legs. He tickled at a spot behind her knees, and her laughter was hushed and breathless. "Stop!" she giggled.

"Stop?" he repeated with innocent amusement, drawing his hands back. Their absence sent a chill across her skin; it prickled her breasts and set her teeth on edge.

"No, don't stop." Greer covered his hands with hers and brought them back across her thighs. "Here."

His grin deepened, dimples winking wickedly. "Don't stop here?" Ellis reached higher, lingering at the top of her woolen stockings. "Or here?" He toyed with the knitted edge, teasing the pad of his thumb against her bare skin. "Or here?" He dared to go higher.

"Definitely there," she whispered, holding back the cry that wanted to tear itself free as he found her center. Nestled away in their heated cocoon, it would be all too easy to forget where they were. All too easy to let out a hungry moan and draw the attention of everyone below them.

Ellis crushed his lips against hers, catching every whimper, stifling each cry.

Greer slid her hands down his chest to tug at the waistband of his trousers. "I need more, I need you," she murmured, echoing his earlier sentiment. "All of you."

As her fingers ran along his length, he released a soft groan that she felt all the way down her middle. She brought her legs up, catching him and curling round his waist.

"Greer, I—"

A scream ripped through the night.

It was loud and long, its pitch ugly as a gut punch, and Greer clasped her hands over her ears as it tore into her mind. They fell apart. The night air washed over them as quickly as an icy wave, dowsing their desire.

In the yard below, the barn warming's merriment hushed with concern.

"Just a fox," Ellis said. His words were meant to be a reassurance, but his eyes flickered with uncertainty.

The cry came again, a jagged ringing off the trees and boulders. Greer fancied she could hear it racing over the water to echo against the cliffs of the Narrows.

She shook her head. "That's not a fox."

Again and again the scream came, breaking up into a maddening cadence that drove into Greer's skull like a hammered nail. The surrounding forest fell silent as its nocturnal denizens paused, attuned to the anguish playing out on the far side of Mistaken.

"Help! Help!" came the voice, clearer now, carried on the night breeze. "For God's sake, someone help us!"

6

"GREER! Where's Greer?"

Hessel's panicked voice rang high above the mêlée as Greer and Ellis crept from the loft. Their caution proved unnecessary. Chaos had erupted, and not a single person gave them so much as a sideways glance. Everyone was clamoring, loud and harried, trying to find unseen loved ones and guess at what had caused the cries.

No one else heard the call for help, Greer realized. *Only the screams.*

As they pressed through the crowd, making their way out into the yard, she felt Ellis pause, unsure if he'd be welcomed. She took his hand with resolute assurance. It didn't matter what her father wanted; Greer needed Ellis with her.

She watched Hessel note their clasped hands, watched his jaw harden, but there were too many other pressing things for him to comment on it. He leaned in, keeping his voice low and hushed. "Can you tell where the cries are coming from?"

Greer was taken aback. Hessel had never spoken of her strange gift, never acknowledged its existence. But now he knew she could help. With a queasy sense of gratification, she nodded. "From the south, out by Cormac Calloway's place?"

The Calloways owned the largest flock of sheep in all of Mistaken. A generation before, Arthur Calloway had allowed the mill to chop down every Redcap on his land, then spent the profits on three sets of rams and ewes, bought from a passing mercantile ship. Now nearly every family in town owned at least one Calloway sheep. Their wool helped ward off the frigid cold, and their mutton made for delicious broths and roasts.

"Someone is shouting for help."

Hessel paled, then turned to the nearby Stewards. "We should take a search party and investigate."

Ellis held up a hand, waylaying them. "You'll need weapons. There've been bear tracks down along the creek."

Michael Morag scoffed. "So late in the season?"

By Reaping, black bears were usually secreted away in their lairs, dreaming of spring salmon.

Ellis did not back down, even in the face of the Steward's scorn. "It's a big one, too. Gil Catasch said he caught sight of it while he was checking traps. It was white."

Greer froze. White bears didn't usually come so far inland—they preferred to stick to the coast, where the ice was thick and their prospects for a meal much easier—but every so often, one would venture along the shores of the Great Bay, making its way to the cove.

They were monstrous beasts, nearly as tall as a man when on all fours, and more than double that when prompted to stand on two legs. The bears were impossibly fast, able to outrace nearly anything, despite their massive girth. A bear so far outside their normal hunting grounds would likely be disoriented with sickness or very hungry.

Greer swallowed back the urge to run home, to flee from the danger like the child she no longer was.

Neither Hessel nor Ellis could be left on their own.

Not in the dark. Not with a white bear roaming the woods. Not when she was the one who could hear it coming.

The air between her father and Ellis grew taut before Hessel finally nodded, conceding. "Roibart!" he called out. "How many rifles do you have?"

THE RACE THROUGH the dark woods to the Calloways' farm felt feverish and surreal. Nothing seemed to play out in linear time. There were cries in the dark and strange flashes of light as everyone from the barn warming took up lanterns and weapons and charged after the Stewards.

Greer caught sight of scythes and pitchforks, broad knives and wooden rifles. Wide-eyed children clung to their mothers' skirts.

As they headed through town, men shouted at sleeping houses, calling for more weapons, more hands, more help. Dazed couples, still dressed in their sleeping gowns and nightcaps, wandered out. They tugged on coats and cloaks and joined the party.

When they reached the Calloway house, nothing seemed amiss.

The group stopped short before the darkened structure, swaying with exhaustion and uncertainty, their whispers and speculation hushing to silence.

Then came the crying. It was faint at first, a wayward kitten wailing for its mother.

Slowly, Greer turned, tilting her head toward the noise, toward the incoherent gibberish, the wet coughs, the strange grunts of pain. Tears pricked at her eyes. She'd never heard such anguish in all her life.

"Father!" she called out, stopping Hessel from approaching the cabin. She could feel the weight of Mistaken's attention fall upon her, as heavy as the hinged bar of the pillory at the center of town. "They're not here!" She licked her lips, wanting to cover her ears as a trembling moan singed them. "They're in the fields. With the flock . . . I think."

Without waiting for the Stewards' command, the townspeople pressed forward, climbing the grassy slope. Ellis fell alongside Greer, gently folding his hand round hers, but she barely recognized him. Her head throbbed and felt hazy, too full of Mistaken's whispers.

As they crested the hill, the whispers died, replaced by breathless gasps and murmurs for mercy. At first, Greer swept her eyes over the field without horror, unable to identify what she was looking at.

It was dark.

The blood made everything darker.

The rest of the group staggered up, brandishing their lanterns and oil lamps, small beacons of light daring to hold back the night's terrors, and she began to understand.

There was a hand.

A hoof.

A foot and something that looked like the back of a man's head. The curved bit of scalp and skull wasn't attached to anything else. It was just there, lying in the field, with so many other similar shapes.

In the center of this mess was Tàmhas Baird. He'd been making the noises. He'd been the one crying and snorting and sobbing as he held on to the partially intact form of Fiona Calloway.

They'd been smitten with each other since Beistean MacIllenass's barn raising last spring, and it was common understanding that Tàmhas would catch her in the Hunt.

Except now Fiona was no more, and Tàmhas could only cling to what was left of her. His mouth was open and moving, but his cries for help had died away, replaced by heaves of grief and the wet sound of air trying to escape from a throat scoured raw by screaming.

He stared at his approaching neighbors with dull incomprehension, eyes glassy and unseeing.

Ellis reached him first. "Tàmhas," he said, gently placing his hand on the young lad's back. "What happened here?"

The bear, Greer thought. *The white bear.*

But as she looked over the field, spotting parts of the Calloways and their herd of sheep, she understood it wasn't that. No bear could cause so much destruction, so much wanton carnage.

This was something worse. This was something far . . .

She looked up, searching the sky.

Had the Bright-Eyeds somehow broken through the Warding Stones? Had they gotten into Mistaken and attacked the Calloways, massacring them and their flock? A single bear could not lay claim to so many kills, but a Bright-Eyed? An entire pack of them?

Greer felt sick, and turned away, wanting to throw up. Why would the Benevolence have allowed this? Why wouldn't they have stopped them? How could they have—

Then she saw it.

Greer froze, studying the line of Warding Stones. Their hulking shapes rose from the earth in craggy cuts of burnished red, cutting across the field like a carving knife through flesh.

The rocks weren't supposed to be here.

Not this far into the field. Not even along this ridge of land.

Greer recognized their shapes instantly. The big one, just beyond where Tàmhas knelt with his broken beloved, was miles off its mark. It had stood watch over Calloway land for generations, but not here. Not in the middle of their pasture.

Greer's eyes swept over the carnage with new understanding, counting each Stone.

The Calloways and their sheep hadn't been attacked.

The Warding Stones had moved.

The Death Tree

1669

THE RECKONING BEGAN not with a whisper, but a scream. So many screams, and the squelch of blood and bone matter. Resolution Beaufort was dead, impaled on the very tree he'd destroyed lives for.

The settlers wanted to leave the body where it lay. They'd wanted to see it rot, never to find rest in hallowed ground. Some uncharitably hoped his soul would suffer the same fate, putrefying in the depths of a most fiery hell.

But the blackflies had come, drawn to congealing blood, and they were hungry.

Once they'd feasted upon Resolution's remains, they turned to the survivors, swarming and biting. Welts raised across the skin of child and adult alike, great swelling pustules of pain. The settlers coated their faces and hands with mud and cried for the body to be removed.

Several of the crew were tasked with burying it within the woods, in an unmarked grave.

By the time Resolution was pulled free, it was late afternoon. The men carried his body past giant stones that stood like sentries along the edge of the tree line, flashing and flickering an otherworldly red.

Deep in the forest, the men began to dig. The sun hung like an overripe piece of fruit as it slowly sank behind a mountain ridge.

The screaming began after sunset.

Malbeck Baird was the only one to return. He stumbled onto the rocky beach, eyes rolling mad with terror, and it was impossible to tell if the blood darkening his clothes was from him or the missing others.

He said they'd been digging.

He said they'd thrown Resolution's body into the pit as the sun set in the west.

Then, he said, the attack began.

Tall, heavyset lumberjacks and sailors alike had been picked up and hurled through the air, not by beasts or monsters, but by wind.

Wind strong and powerful.

Wind that screeched and smelled of lake water and lichen and so much black soil.

The men were tossed about as though they were nothing but a scattering of dried leaves, smashing into trees and boulders, fallen logs and wicked brambles.

The wind had filled with their screams.

Then their gurgled breaths.

Then . . . nothing.

Malbeck's head had struck a tamarack. The tree had scraped away his scalp and sent him into blessed unconsciousness. When he woke, he was in the clearing they'd gone through earlier. One of the flickering stones loomed over him. The remains of the men and their shovels lay in ungainly, messy heaps, staining the tall grass red. The only thing missing was Resolution's corpse. It had been allowed to remain behind.

He told the group how he'd stared at the stones for a long time, trying to put together what had happened, trying to understand. And as he'd stared at their iridescent brilliance, another light had caught his attention.

A pair of bright eyes shining from the darkness beyond the stones.

Then another.

And another.

The falling twilight had made it impossible to see what sort of animal the eyes belonged to, but Malbeck said they were too far off the ground to be those of a stag, and their coloring was all wrong. In dim light, the eyes of deer and other prey shone cool tones of white or green. These eyes were a rusted orange, verging toward red.

Somehow, Malbeck said, he knew these almost red eyes were staring directly at him. They did not blink and they did not come closer, but the lad knew they wanted to. He said he could feel their hunger radiating from them in tangible waves.

Then, in a flash, they were gone.

As the settlers huddled around their fires, frozen with disbelief, they could feel the night press in around them.

They were far from home. Far from help. Far from anything known or certain.

They listened to the shrill cries of unfamiliar birds, the screams of tiny prey meeting their tiny ends, and the footfalls of beasts better off left unimagined.

Some prayed, others cried, and a few stared into the flames with stony resignation, pondering what was to come next.

It had been a mistake to come to this land, that much was certain. But now that they were here, what were they to do?

In the morning, the sun rose over the cliffs of the Narrows, highlighting every bit of debris deposited upon the shore by the night's waves.

There were barrels of tools, somehow undamaged.

Long ribs of the ship's hull.

Strips of canvas from its sails.

Sodden messes too waterlogged to name.

An unfortunate length of a tattooed forearm, ripped clean from its previous owner and crawling with ants.

And a most curious crate.

Resolution Beaufort's swirling initials were carved into its side.

The first mate, Tormond Mackenzie, opened it, cracking the lock with a bar of iron and a grunt of effort.

Inside, remarkably unscathed from their journey across the bay, were papers. Papers and maps, Resolution's diaries, books and charts, and the original explorer's account of his time in this land.

Tormond opened up the leather journal and flipped through the pages.

He spotted maps of the bay, the cove, even the little strip of shoreline where they now gathered. He saw drawings of the trees, those wretched trees that had driven their captain mad with greed and led them here. He read of the explorer's wanderings, of the forests and beasts that stalked the land. He read of his encounters with the people who first lived on the land to the south and with the trappers who had also come from across the sea. He read of the cold, and the flies, and the strange way the explorer had felt pushed about in his travels, as if an unseen presence guided his steps, nudging him in directions he did not wish to take.

And then Tormond Mackenzie read the last lines of the book, written out by a hand heavy with warning.

This land, with all its bounties and promises, cannot be claimed. The consequences of venturing farther prove too great a risk. By all accounts, from nomads both native and foreign, this land has been spurned, though by God or by the Devil, I cannot say. I should have never ventured upon its cursed shores.

7

"THE STONES." Greer sank to her knees. Her voice could hardly be heard above the confused crowd. "The Stones have moved."

Her eyes darted to each of the monoliths.

The Warding Stones were Mistaken's most absolute certainty.

They'd been there before the first settlers had arrived. They'd watched the outpost grow from a floundering band of survivors to a community and town. They affected everyone who came near them.

Occasionally, outsiders would wander across their borders—fur trappers, shipping merchants, people like Martha, fleeing their own villages after an attack from the Bright-Eyes. Should they stay in Mistaken past sunset, the Warding Stones' hold would fall upon them, too, and they could never leave again.

Their grasp was impossible to break.

People tried, of course. Attempting to defy the Stones was a rite of childhood. Nervous, giggling youths would venture past the border just before sunset, only to be swept back by an unseen force, like dust bunnies rooted out from under a bed.

It was harmless fun, for the most part.

But every so often, someone would roam too far. The Stones would always bring the person back, heedless of what lay between the wanderer and the town line. There were the occasional bruises or split lips as people struck trees or stumbled over dips in the ground. Clintock Finley once broke his ankle when his foot snagged on a tree root.

But never had Mistaken seen anything like the Calloways.

In the early days of the town, intrepid farmers, wanting to buy themselves a bit more land, had attempted to pull the Stones down. They'd tried dragging them away. They'd used ropes and chains and teams of cattle. They'd wielded levers and pulleys. They'd even used black-powder explosives.

The Stones would not budge.

Except—now they had.

They'd somehow shifted, cutting the size and sprawl of the land.

Greer could imagine how the terrible scene must have played out.

The Calloways would have been gathering the flock before sunset. They wouldn't have had any worries at all. That part of the forest was well within the borders of town.

Until tonight.

The Stones had moved, herding every living thing along with them. Lambs. Ewes. The entire Calloway family. They must have been carried for hundreds of yards, thrown against trees and brambles, tossed over rocky outcroppings, smashing through streams and into one another.

Greer wondered how it had felt, to lose control of your body, of yourself. She hoped, for their sake, that the first strikes had done them in. She hoped they had not suffered.

Hearing Greer, the townspeople turned from the massacre toward the towering Stones.

Gasps of surprise filled the air.

"Were those always . . . ?"

"Haven't those . . . ?"

"How did they . . . ?"

"Who could have . . . ?"

Ellis knelt beside Tàmhas, trying to loosen the young man's hold on Fiona Calloway. His movements were slow and gentle. With utmost care, he extricated the girl's severed hand from Tàmhas's and laid it out upon the sodden grass.

It didn't look real. It was like a broken curve of pottery, a discarded oyster shell left after a day of shucking. Not a hand. Not a piece of a human who had been breathing and flushed with life only hours before. Fiona was just a few years younger than Greer, with sun-freckled skin and long twists of scarlet hair.

Hanks of that hair now lay strewn around the field like coils of rope.

Bile rushed up into Greer's throat with ferocity, burning everything in its path. She turned her head, coughing and sputtering, as another roil of disgust heaved at her middle.

Around her, the questions began to change.

"How"s shifted to "why"s.

The "why"s grew bolder, increasing from whispers of disbelief to noises of strangled horror.

As the panic swelled, Hessel Mackenzie stepped forward, ready to take charge. He held out his hands, attempting to quiet the clamor, to corral it into submission.

"My friends, a tragedy has occurred here tonight. The Calloways have been a vital part of our community. They were our neighbors, our friends, our family. The loss of . . ."

Here he paused, glancing about the carnage, ill at ease with his calculations.

". . . so many . . . cannot be understated. Cannot be understood. We don't know what caused this, but—"

"It's obvious what caused it," a voice shouted from the back of the group. "The Stones did this. The Stones have moved!"

Hessel's eyes darted to the nearest rock. Its red luminescence danced like a trapped creature testing the limits of its cage, searching for a way out.

When Hessel spoke again, his voice was noticeably cowed, quavering with strain. "It does appear that is the case," he admitted. "But we don't know why. Or how. At daybreak, we should—"

"I'll go."

Greer heard the words ring out before realizing she'd spoken. She sensed those around her turn her way. She could feel the weight of their stares at her back, heavy and uncomfortable.

"I could go." She straightened her spine, trying to bolster her resolve. "I have my maps. I can check the positions of the other Stones against them. If they've shifted, I'll know."

Her father began to shake his head, but Ayaan stepped forward, stopping him.

"What happened here tonight may not be an isolated incident. If other Stones have moved, we need to know where. There could have been others caught like . . ." His gaze fell on Fiona's hand. "We need to understand the new perimeters. We'll need maps. Who else but Greer could do all of this?"

Hessel's gaze drifted over the gathered townspeople as he considered this. Finally, he nodded. "Go at first light. Take others with you. No one . . . *no one,*" he repeated, raising his voice as an order to the entire group, "is to go anywhere alone until we understand what happened."

Two young women beside Greer took small steps back, as if she might reach out and wrangle them into helping her. Others shifted, their gazes studiously looking anywhere but in her direction. Greer glanced to Ellis, and he nodded, a silent promise passing between them. They would stick together, no matter what.

"How?" someone deep in the crowd called out. "How could they have moved?"

Hessel's weary eyes roamed over those gathered, searching for who'd spoken. "I don't know."

"It was the Benevolence, wasn't it?" The crowd parted now, revealing Meribeck Matthews, an older, widowed woman, wrapped in several shawls and a mulberry scarf. "The Benevolence have moved the Stones. They're the only ones with the power to—"

"We don't know that," Hessel said, swiftly cutting off the woman's troubling accusation.

The group swayed, shifting on their feet as the idea settled heavily over them. Faces clouded with doubt. Worry marred the smoothness of brows. Greer didn't want to believe it possible, didn't want to know what it meant that the Benevolence had moved the Stones. Was the truce broken? Was the Benevolence's protection over?

She thought of the map Ellis had bought for her, abandoned in their headlong sprint from the barn's roof and undoubtedly lost. She remembered the river that she would never see, and an echo of her earlier wanderlust rang inside her.

If the truce was over and the border had fallen . . .

Curiosity burning bright, Greer made her way to the closest Stone and raised her head, preparing to test the border. Her heart hammered with an irregular pulse, hope and horror fighting to claim dominance.

Disappointment crushed through her as her hand met with the invisible resistance; it made her fingers ache, break out in a rash of pins and needles, like a limb long fallen asleep and beginning to wake. She leaned against the Stone with her full weight, but it was like fighting against a swell of waves too powerful to swim through. She could go no farther.

"Something angered them," Meribeck shouted, drawing Greer's attention. "Some*one* caused this."

Greer frowned. Only that afternoon, Louise had stalked off, blasphemous notions spilling from her lips, loud enough for anyone to hear. Any*thing*.

This couldn't be Louise's fault.

The events were unrelated. They had to be.

"Please, God, let them be," Greer murmured, her heart aching.

Her words formed into little puffs of breath in the dark, frigid air. They rose up and were carried away.

Away from the gathering.

Away from the field and all its bloody stains.

Away from even the hold of the flickering Stones, traveling out into the great night sky, where they were swallowed up, unheard and unheeded.

8

FIRST BELLOWS SOUNDED just as Greer sank onto one of the long benches of Steward House, flushed and out of breath. There was still one hour till sunset, but all she wanted to do was close her eyes and fall asleep.

She and Ellis had hiked every step of the town's border since daybreak, and her feet throbbed. She was too sore to walk any farther, but not numb enough to forget the pain. Her fingers were smudged black and aching. Her satchel was full of new renderings, new measurements. Still, her work was not done.

Every Warding Stone had moved.

Some had crept in mere yards, as if on tiptoe, hoping the town might not notice their treachery. Others, like the ones in the Calloways' fields, were far bolder.

Greer's mind felt impossibly full. All day long, rumors had flown through the community, carried on the wind, and she'd heard each and every one of them.

They did not surprise her. Imaginations didn't often run wild here. Unable to stray from their small community, the people of Mistaken had learned never to dream of things bigger than their allotted acres.

Those who hadn't been at the Calloway farm woke to the news of the massacre and, predictably, started looking for someone to blame.

It was so easy to point fingers toward Ellis's family.

Resolution Beaufort had damned the settlers, luring them across the sea to this cursed cove, and, generations later, his descendants were still scapegoated.

Beauforts were blamed for any problems that plagued the town, from small annoyances—the swarm of blackflies thought to have been brought on by Resolution's son, Brodie, slaughtering hogs on the Sabbath—to outright absurdity. Once, Melkin Hambright's favorite goat had birthed an entire litter of kids fused together with a solid band of rubbery flesh. He said Ellis's great-uncle Hezekiah had offered to purchase the nanny from him only weeks before, and claimed that the elder Beaufort had cursed both him and the goat when he refused.

Greer rubbed at her eyes, then was startled from her exhausted reverie as Steward Enoch MacÀidh stumbled over her ankles. He squinted at her down the length of his thin, crooked nose. The oldest of all the Stewards, Enoch had been going blind for years and rarely left his cottage, situated just a mile from Mackenzie land; he preferred to putter around the certainties of his farm and to leave the town's affairs to the rest of the council. His presence here only highlighted what a grave situation Mistaken was now in.

He swatted away Greer's apologies, his hand clawed into a gesture of superstitious protection. "I find it impossible to believe that you, of all people, couldn't hear me coming, Greer Mackenzie."

From her seated position, the wide brim of his hat was like a corona of darkness circling his face. He made no effort to hide his scorn. Years before, when Greer was a child of only five years, she'd made the mistake of asking Enoch why she could hear breathy, feminine cries coming from the MacÀidhs' house every time his wife, Iona, was in town at sewing circle.

"Enoch," Hessel called from the front of the room, spotting the confrontation. "It's good to see you, my old friend. Join us."

With a noise of indignation, Enoch picked his way toward the other Stewards.

They were nine strong, patriarchs of the town, each descended from the crew who had sailed to the new world. Though they sat on the council with apparent equal stature, Greer's father, Hessel—grandson of First Mate Tormond Mackenzie—presided over the group with a touch more authority. His was the voice that spoke for the group. His was the opinion all others sought.

He stood at the head of the room now, in deep discussion with the others.

The men were poring over Greer's new maps with great fervor. As Hessel listened, he glanced across the room to meet Greer's gaze. His lips didn't exactly curve into a smile—Hessel Mackenzie was far too reserved—but Greer could sense a glimmer of approval all the same. He was proud of the work she'd done.

The back doors were flung open, and Louise Beaufort hurried into Steward House.

It was a long building, built of spruce and pine. Though large enough to hold every member of Mistaken, the structure boasted only two narrow windows, at the front of the hall. Lanterns hung from the mounted remains of a ship's wheel, casting over the room a dark-amber hue. A single aisle ran the length of the room, splitting the rough-hewn benches apart like a seam.

Greer automatically slid over, making room for her friend, but Louise hesitated, a look of uncertainty darkening her face. With an unhappy twist of her lips, she sank into an empty spot on the back row, joining Ellis.

He glanced from Louise to Greer with a look of wary curiosity before shrugging it away. Greer could see the toll their day had taken upon him. His face was haggard with exhaustion, and a long cut ran red down one cheekbone. The last Stone they'd found had moved into the middle of a bramble of thorns, and it had taken them nearly an hour to break free.

After a long stare at her friend—one Louise pointedly did not return—Greer shifted her attention toward the rest of the room.

The townspeople of Mistaken looked defeated. Dark circles rimmed tired, pained eyes. Noses were red; hands were pale and trembling. One long length of bench was left empty. Normally, it would have been filled by Cormac Calloway and his family. The unfilled space was as jarring as a missing tooth.

A hush fell as Hessel Mackenzie stepped forward and picked up the ceremonial gavel—a cut of polished wood from the very tree that had impaled Resolution Beaufort. Still, he struck it upon the Stewards' table three times, signifying they were ready to begin.

"Friends, I wish we gathered today under better circumstances," he began, his words slow and steady. Greer supposed he was attempting to offer the residents a show of reassuring strength, but his dark undertone sent a chill down her spine.

They didn't know why any of this had happened. Nothing they'd say in the next hour would be anything but conjecture.

"As you know, the Warding Stones have . . . moved."

"How many?" someone in the front row asked.

Hessel released a deep breath. "All of them, I'm afraid. Mistaken's footprint has been considerably reduced. The new borders have cut dangerously across fields and homes . . . fatally, in one instance."

Unbidden memories of last night's pulpy mess rose in Greer's mind, and she winced, wondering that her father could so succinctly sum up the unspeakable tragedy as "one instance."

"While there were no witnesses, we feel confident that the Benevolence was responsible for the movement of the Stones."

"But why?" someone at the far side of the room asked. Greer recognized Tywynn Flanagan's reedy voice, even though she couldn't spot the baker. "Why would the Benevolence do this? We've honored them; we've given our tithes. Things like this happen in other places. Not our Mistaken."

Murmurs stirred, running through the gathered like a dangerous undercurrent.

Tywynn pushed himself to standing, leaning heavily against his cane. "We've always had an understanding with them. We have their blessings, their protection. We're not like those other towns. We've not had such attacks. Our sky has never shattered!"

The room fell into uneasy silence.

Other towns' misfortunes were almost never spoken of in Mistaken.

It didn't happen often, but occasionally bands of frightened travelers would wander into town, emerging from the forest like a gathering of ghosts. They'd come from settlements along the coast, outposts from the north. They were like Martha, survivors of the Bright-Eyed.

As keeper of the records, Hessel had interviewed each refugee, committing their grisly accounts into ledgers.

The attacks were always the same. The Bright-Eyeds would come at night, jagged shadows of chaos descending from the sky in whizzing blurs too fast to make sense of. They struck fast, bringing screams, then silence.

One interminable afternoon when she was small, Greer, tired of being confined inside by yet another winter storm, had sneaked into Hessel's study. With awestruck horror, she'd read through the memories of the attacks, the way the monsters moved with skittering, preternatural speed, the strangeness of their clicking, clattering calls, and the way those sounds mixed with their prey's death rattles.

For months after, Greer's dreams were plagued by nightmares of leathery wings and curved claws. Though they always began the same way—finding herself on the crest of Barrenman's Hill, watching in horror as pieces of the sky fell over the cove, swooping and diving and ripping townspeople asunder—the endings varied. Sometimes Greer, too, was caught and pulled apart, her organs spilling like rain over the town square. Other times she found herself cornered, pressed up against the invisible line of the Warding Stones, unable to escape as the hulking shape of a Bright-Eyed stalked closer, zigging in and out of shadows as if made of the night itself. The worst was when nothing happened to her at all, when she watched from her spot on the hill, moving neither to hide nor to help. An impassive witness, observing the terrible night over and over again without reacting.

The first time she'd had such a dream, she'd raced to her parents' bedroom, crying and seeking comfort. Hessel had told her the Warding Stones would always protect Mistaken, then rolled over and huffed back to sleep. But Ailie, in the dark silence that had followed, had whispered into Greer's hair that she was far fiercer than any creature lurking in the woods.

"It hasn't, it hasn't," Hessel said now, agreeing with the elderly baker, his placations as easy as the rote reassurances he'd given Greer so many years before. Ready to move forward, he held up one of the new maps. "We will post this in the square. It shows the Warding Stones' former positions in black, and the new, marked in red. Study it, and make sure everyone you know has seen it, too. We don't want anyone caught unaware come sunset."

As if summoned by his speech, two more Bellows blasted out, reverberating across the cove like a roll of thunder. Greer pitied Callum Cairn, up on the hill all by his lonesome, with another half an hour till he could join everyone else at Steward House.

"The Calloways weren't caught unaware," spoke up Meribeck Matthews, waiting until the last note died away. "They wouldn't dare go past the Stones so close to sunset, not even for a wayward sheep. They followed the rules, they *always* followed the rules, and still they ended up like"—voice broke—"like that."

The two lines between Hessel's eyebrows furrowed deeper. "Bad luck, certainly. There was obviously no way to foresee that—"

"What if they move again?" the older woman demanded. "What if they keep moving in? In and in, until there's nothing left of the town but a miserable pile of"—her fingers danced in the air like buzzing hornets, swarming around to grab the right turn of phrase—"exactly what was left in that field last night?"

Behind Hessel, Ian Brennigan visibly paled. Other Stewards shifted in their seats, troubled by the full weight of the town's stares. Hessel cleared his throat, and Greer heard a worrying catch at its end. He was rattled. They all were.

"It's easy to worry, to grasp and guess at what might come next, but, Mistaken, we urge you to cast aside such thoughts. After hours of deliberations, the council of Stewards has come to the following decisions." Hessel withdrew a folded scrap of paper from his pocket. "We believe that the shifting of the Stones—an act which has *never* before occurred—was a message from the Benevolence. A reminder."

"A reminder?" scoffed Meribeck. "We've been trapped by them for more than a century—what more reminders do we need?"

"A reminder," Hessel pressed on, "of their presence, yes, but also of their continued generosity. A reminder of what we owe them. We *aren't* like other settlements out in the wilds, fearful of the Bright-Eyes, forever worrying over an attack. We've struck an understanding with our benefactors. We honor them freely."

Greer dared a glance at Louise, but her friend was keeping a pointed stare fixed on Hessel, her face a mask of perfunctory attention. Greer's stomach ached as she remembered the flayed rabbits taken from the forest without a word of thanks, without a gesture of gratitude.

Surely, three rabbits could not have so upset the Benevolence. Greer had left behind tokens, and it wasn't even Reaping. Not quite. Louise could not be responsible for this.

Greer worried over her thumbnail anyway, scratching till the cuticles bled.

Hessel turned the page over and continued reading. "We believe last night was intended only as a warning. But . . . to show our commitment to the truce, to show our appreciation and ensure that this does not happen again . . . we will move up this year's Reaping."

Noises of surprise and alarm rose, spinning into heated conferences as the people talked through the scheduling change. Fields would need to be cut sooner than expected, orchards harvested early, meats removed from their smokehouses before the planned time.

"We understand the enormous amount of work which will need to be carried out," Hessel said, raising his voice to be heard over the growing chatter. "And we sympathize. We will absolutely do our part, working alongside you all, brother to brother as it has always been."

"When?" someone shouted. "When do you propose Reaping to take place?"

Hessel visibly winced. "Tomorrow."

The outcry was so sharp, Greer covered her ears, flinching against the onslaught.

"One day? We had two weeks—now just one day? Impossible!"

Hessel's weary brown eyes searched for the dissenter. "We would not ask this if it was not deemed necessary."

"You ask us to perform miracles!"

The thin line of Hessel's lips thinned further. "I plan to temporarily halt work at the mill"—several gasps rang out—"so that our men may assist however they can. They will help cut wheat, dig up vegetables. They can haul and clean. Pick and prepare."

Tywynn Flanagan raised a shaky hand. "And what happens if the

Benevolence aren't in a waiting mood? The Stones could move again tonight." He glanced at the pocket watch hanging at his waist, calculating the minutes until they'd find out.

Greer glanced out the windows behind the Stewards, doing her own estimates as she studied the purple sky. Twenty minutes, maybe a little longer.

"The council and I discussed such a possibility. Already, we have laid out gratitudes of our own beside each of the Stones, with the hope that our reverence will be noted. Should anyone else like to offer additional contributions, their generosity would be most welcome."

Lachlan Davis jumped to his feet. "As you know, I plan on taking part in the Hunt this year." His gaze landed meaningfully on Greer. "And I have been taking my responsibilities as a soon-to-be husband most seriously. My larders are already well stocked, in preparation for the coming winter." He straightened, drawing up every inch of his squat frame, his chest puffed with pride. "I'd like to be the first to offer additional gratitudes tonight."

From the other side of the room, Elsie Thompson, one of the youngest women who would be hiding in the Hunt, began to clap with adoration.

"Mistaken thanks you." Hessel bobbed his head toward the young lad with warm appreciation, and Greer realized they must have planned the entire outburst, both angling to cast themselves in a good light.

"I, too, would like to offer early gratitudes," Struan Galt announced, his voice cracking mid-sentence, several pitches too high. His ears flushed scarlet, but his eyes burned bright with his eagerness to take part in whatever glory and accolades were being handed out.

"And I!" Kenneth McNamara chimed in, nearly knocking his stool over as he shot to his feet. "I've two ham hocks I can spare, and so many baskets of onions." His eyes darted to a group of young women in the far corner of the room. With audacious daring, he winked.

Tywynn shook his head, unimpressed by the young men's grab for attention. "Gratitudes are the least of our problems. We ought to be figuring out *why* the Stones moved. *Why* the Benevolence is angered. How else are we meant to prevent it from happening again?" Gripping his cane, he turned to face the gathered crowd. "If someone has done something, anything, that might have brought this about, please confess now."

Greer shot a surreptitious glance to Ellis.

His body was still and rigid, like an animal deciding upon fight or flight. His eyes darted about the room as he listened to conversations he was not a part of, scorn and fear clouding his features as he tried to guess where the first strike might come from.

Greer longed to take his hands and race from Steward House. She wanted to pull him to safety, but in her heart she knew it wouldn't make a difference. There was nowhere *to go,* not really. They could flee into the woods as deeply as they wanted, but would eventually have to return, tails between legs, before sunset.

"There'll be none of that," Hessel warned, struggling to carry his voice over the mayhem. He struck the gavel against the table, as loud as a gunshot. "Quiet, now! Quiet, I say!" He hammered again, and a third time for good measure. "We understand the urge to demand answers. The desire to find meaning within such senseless tragedy. But now is not the time for accusations or atonements. Reaping is upon us—a time when we've always come together. We each sacrifice to show our gratitude toward the Benevolence for use of their lands, for holding the Bright-Eyeds at bay. We do this together, united as one. We receive their blessings together, as one. No one man is given more or less than his neighbor. If one falls, we all fall. If one should fail"— he paused, his gaze slowly dragging over every person in attendance— "it brings disaster upon us all. Now, more than ever, we must set aside our fears and do what we must, for the good of everyone. Mistaken, are we in accord?"

Slowly, carefully, heads began to nod.

Lachlan, still standing, looked pleased, as though he'd somehow orchestrated the town's acceptance all on his own. He glanced at Greer, his dark eyes lingering. "Steward Mackenzie—what does this mean for everything else?"

"Everything else?" Hessel repeated, eyes narrowing.

"With Reaping now tomorrow . . . will the Hunt move ahead as well? It has always taken place the morning after."

The Stewards frowned before falling into conference.

Greer looked to Ellis again, and this time he was staring right back. Despite everything, his lips raised in a small smile, kindling a warm spark within her.

If the Stewards *did* move the Hunt, their waiting was nearly over. She would be just two days away from becoming his wife. Greer dared to shoot him a hopeful grin.

Behind the Stewards' table, hands gestured, heads nodded, assents were given. Eventually, Hessel turned.

"It has always been tradition to begin the Hunt directly after Reaping." His words were slow and drawn out, like a spoon pulled through molasses, making it impossible to guess which way the council had ruled. "Given the enormous task being asked of you all, it seems cruel to delay an event so anticipated by many . . ."

For one bare moment, Hessel's gaze fell upon Greer, his expression completely foreign to her. He looked . . . wistful. Maybe even a little sad. Her heart thumped in her chest, and she wondered if his reaction was a show for the town or if he felt it in earnest.

"The Hunt will still take place the morning after Reaping," he announced, pushing away whatever emotion had stilled him. He cleared his throat. "As it has been . . ."

Third Bellows blasted over Steward House, causing some to jump before he recited the four words that always drew every town meeting to a close. ". . . so shall it be."

1669

THE TRUCE BEGAN with a secret journey beyond the Stones.

It had been one month since the storm.

One month since Resolution Beaufort's last breath.

One month since Malbeck Baird had returned after sunset with tales of the bright-eyed monsters and the angry winds that had held them back.

And in that month, trapped between the towering Stones, the survivors had begun to build.

With tools salvaged from the wreck, they felled trees and split logs. They foraged and scavenged and learned to hunt the unfamiliar beasts of these waters and this land. Slowly, bit by bit, acre by acre, the community of Mistaken began to grow.

Structures were erected: platforms and lean-tos, then shelters and small cabins. They sprouted like mushrooms across the freshly cleared cove.

The settlers began to parse through the limits of their new world, growing accustomed to the ebbs and flows of the great Stones. The wind barrier came every sunset—no matter how the days lengthened with summer's approach—then slipped away each morning, allowing unfettered access to the forests' bounties.

Some railed against the restrictions, certain there was a way to break through the wind, to free themselves from the Stones' hold. Each attempt was met with failure.

Others accepted the confines with resigned stoicism and devised a system to warn of the falling night. A bugle—found washed ashore in a tangle of flotsam—was blown throughout daylight's final hour, giving anyone outside the Stones' embrace time to hurry back.

Already, they planned to make something larger, something louder, so that no one could ever miss hearing the bellowed warning.

The settlement was full of plans and preparations, and a council of leaders was selected to ensure that such visions would be carried out with efficiency and order.

Ten men had been chosen.

Ten men began to assess.

Ten men began to write.

They wrote their decisions upon every scrap of spare paper rummaged from Resolution's trunk, passing new laws that made sense in their new world.

When one of the ten spoke out, wondering aloud why the council wanted to focus on growing a town within the strange limitations of the flickering Stones, rather than seek a way out, the other nine laughed.

They'd begun to see their predicament's golden lining.

The bedeviled trees that had so consumed Resolution Beaufort's reason were every bit as remarkable as he'd promised. Merchants would pay premium prices for the lumber, and—according to the ledger found among Beaufort's belongings—they already knew to come. The first ship was due to arrive in a year and had pre-emptively bought an entire cargo hold's worth.

The settlers had eleven months to get their mill running, and the council did not intend for one dissenting voice to slow them down.

Tormond Mackenzie volunteered to venture into the woods first, scouting for groves of the trees. He took great precautions, laying down lines of twine as he traveled, armed with a bow and a quiver of arrows, and always keeping a sharp eye on the sun, anxious to cross the border well before the bugle's first trumpet could sound.

But one afternoon, Mackenzie was running late. The first warning rang out, followed half an hour later by two more. Still he did not return.

As the sky began to shift to red and orange, the council and townspeople gathered near the boundary line, waiting for him. Just before the last of the sun's rays winked out, Tormond Mackenzie burst from the tree line, his eyes wide with wonder.

"I've met them," he declared. "I've met the ones who made the Stones."

Waves of disbelief rippled through the cluster of settlers, and they all drew in to listen to Mackenzie's tale.

He'd been along the western edge of the forest, noting where the prized trees grew thickest, when he felt a change in the air, like currents of wind before a storm. When he looked up, there they stood.

There were four of them, forebodingly tall and indescribably beatific.

He explained how the beings spoke to him with mouths that did not move except to smile. The great ones were pleased that the settlers had washed upon their shores. They had read their hearts and commended their ambitious intentions.

And they pledged to keep the settlers safe.

"These Stones are their gifts to us," Mackenzie said, placing a reverent hand upon the monolith beside him. In return, it flickered a warm vermilion, as if pleased. "They will hold back the monsters with the bright eyes and keep us together."

"Why would they take such interest in us?" the settlers wondered.

"It is not for us to understand why," Mackenzie declared. "Only to be thankful that they have, and to show them our gratitude."

Somewhat appeased, the settlers returned to their homes, brimming with ideas of how to repay such benevolent wardens.

The council of ten remained at the Stones.

The man who wanted to find a way out of the accursed cove railed at Mackenzie, enraged he had not urged the beings to release their grip. He volunteered to go into the forest at first light and find them once more. He pledged to negotiate for their freedom.

The nine others listened with impassive faces but hearts full of grave concern. It would not do to present a divided front to the town. The council knew all too well how quickly whispers of dissent could grow.

So, when Tormond Mackenzie pulled a length of shimmering red beads around the man's neck, they all watched in silent accord.

And when Tormond Mackenzie pushed the man into the gusts of wind that rose along the line of Stones, shoving and breaking him through the barrier, they watched still, wary wonder stirring within them.

Only when the bright-eyed beasts fell upon the man, tearing and biting and feasting and devouring, did they turn and watch no more.

9

THE TOWN OF Mistaken wasted no time preparing for Reaping.

Farmers and merchants and millworkers alike stumbled out into the dark afternoon. Giant braziers were lit, illuminating the fields and orchards so that work could carry on throughout the night.

Greer remained with Martha, plucking the last of their garden's vetchling peas, winter beans, and root vegetables. They piled the bounty on the kitchen table, sorting through every potato and carrot, checking for blemishes, however small. Greer examined each bushel of apples, picked earlier that week, setting aside the shiniest reds, the brightest greens, and packing them into crates with care. Only the best could be used for gratitudes. Especially now.

Neither of the women spoke. Reaping was normally a time of great joy. The kitchen ought to have been full of laughter, songs, and tales from the old country of Danu, Arawn, and the guid folk. Now they worked in silence, their eyes often slipping toward the side yard, where one of the Warding Stones had moved. It was on the far end of the meadow, a mere thousand paces away. It had never been visible from the house before and its wrongness was impossible to ignore.

Greer threw herself into the tasks with abandon, keeping her hands busy, fretting over each leaf of cabbage, every stalk of celery. She hoped that, if she focused hard enough, it would drown out the conversations she overheard from nearby farms and fields. There was so much worry in the air, it turned her mouth sour and sick.

People were scared.

People were angry.

People were looking for someone to blame.

She finished filling her last crate of offerings as the sun rose over the Narrows, highlighting the world with pinks and yellows so lovely it seemed impossible to believe anything was wrong.

They'd need to prepare the pies next. Then the bread. Then cut the smoked meats.

Greer's arms ached as she thought of all the work ahead of them. She hesitated, tracing a finger over a whorl in the table's woodgrain. "Martha? Could I ask . . . the night your town was attacked . . ."

Martha briskly swept the remaining parsnips into a basket. "We need to start on the piecrusts if we ever hope to be done by this afternoon." She *tsk*-ed. "Weeks of work in only hours. I don't know what the Stewards were thinking."

She pulled down canisters of flour, salt, and sugar in quick succession, as if to banish Greer's unfinished question with a flurry of activity.

"What do you remember about that night?"

Martha shook her head. "I've spent almost thirty years trying to *not* remember. I've no desire to dredge it up now."

"I just wondered if you saw them. Then. The Bright-Eyes. Did you see the way it happened?"

Martha's fingers tightened around the sugar. "I did."

"You've never spoken about it."

"No. And I won't now. The world is scary enough without help from me."

Greer licked her lips, wishing she could phrase what she yearned to ask. "I sometimes dream of what would happen if Mistaken was attacked like that . . . They're not dreams, really."

"Nightmares," Martha supplied.

"I can't imagine what it must have been like."

Finally, Martha turned to face her. Her brown eyes seemed darker, guarded. "No. You can't."

Greer squirmed but pressed forward. "Did it feel like this? In the days before it happened, did you know something was wrong?"

Martha considered her question. "No. There was an uneasiness in the air, I suppose—a sense that something was coming—but that was just what life was like then. It was hard and uncertain. Our settlement had no truce with the Benevolence; we didn't even know they were out there. So of course . . . it was terrible, truly terrible, seeing how quickly things can end. We spend so much time working and striving, raising food, raising families, raising a whole town, and for what? In one flash, it can all come undone."

"How did it happen?"

Martha hissed sharply, making it clear she would not talk of the Bright-Eyes.

Greer touched the older woman's back, trying to re-form her question. "I mean . . . in the days after . . . how did the days after happen? I don't see how you move past that. How you just . . . carry on."

Martha shrugged. "There's not much else *to* do. The ones left . . . the ones who were spared or lucky or whatever you want to call it . . . we had to go on. We had to *go*." Martha looked to Greer. "What else could we do? Sit and sob? Close our doors and bar our windows and let the remains of our town fall apart around us?" She shook her head. "No. We left. We moved on. We moved on and found Mistaken." She blinked, lost in memories. "Coming here, seeing the bounties and good fortunes of this town . . ." She sighed. "I'll never forget that. It was like walking into Paradise. You've no idea how good you've had it here. We can't . . . we can't ever forget that. I think all the Benevolence wants is for us to remember."

Greer glanced around the kitchen, looking over their progress. She felt as helpless as a small child woken in the night, seeking reassurance against the imagined terrors of the dark.

The terrors weren't imagined now.

"Do you think all this will work?"

The older woman nodded, then removed a bowl of eggs from the shelf. Flour rose and danced in the morning sunlight as she measured out ingredients.

Greer tried to throw herself into their work, but her unease persisted. "What do you think they want us to remember?"

Martha struck an egg against the edge of the table, and Greer winced at the sudden, brutal crack. The older woman stopped short, peering down at the broken egg. She tossed it to the side, frowning.

Greer's stomach quivered as she spotted the dark, beaded eye and bloodied yolk of the partially formed chick.

Martha cracked open a second egg. "I think they moved the Stones so we'd remember they could."

10

THREE HOURS BEFORE sunset, the town of Mistaken ventured beyond the Warding Stones, their arms heavy-laden with gratitudes. Horses pulled carts packed with offerings too large to carry—bales of fresh straw, bundled swaths of wheat, and half a dozen sheep, freshly slaughtered.

Greer kept far from that wagon. The smell reminded her too much of what she'd seen in the Calloways' field, and she wondered if she'd ever be able to stomach a plate of mutton chops again.

They progressed up a narrow trail that wound through the woods like an unspooled ribbon. The soft glow of their lanterns pushed back the falling afternoon gloom.

Finally, they reached the Gratitude Tree. It had been an enormous Redcap, the biggest in the region, felled during the early years of the town. Its stump was lathed and varnished into a magnificent slab of wood, easily four men long, three wide. Once a season, the Stewards' wives made a pilgrimage to the tree, to wipe it clean of woodland debris and polish its lacquered surface until it shone bloody and bright. It looked like a king's banquet table, straight out of a fairy tale, and was situated perfectly in the center of a vast clearing.

The return to Mistaken would not take as long—not with the

weight of offerings and gifts left behind—but the townspeople were taking no chances. There was a hastiness in the group, a harried pace at which all worked, emptying their crates and casks, lining and arranging the feast across the table.

Roasted ducks and pheasants lined the edges. Pies, cakes, and rich breads studded with dried fruits and nuts filled the gaps, and at the table's center was a suckling pig. It was burnished bronze with spices and smelled good enough to make Greer's mouth water, despite the worry in the pit of her stomach.

When it was the Mackenzies' turn to lay down their gratitudes, Hessel took the lead, helping Greer and Martha arrange their crates of vegetables, their bushels of fruits, their trays of baked goods and lengths of sausages and wheels of cheese. Since he was the wealthiest man in the cove, it was only fitting that Hessel's offering was the most extravagant.

Greer set down the final basket of apples, making sure to place them in a pleasing arrangement. She offered a curtsied bob toward the forest behind the Gratitude Tree and any Benevolents who might be watching the festivities. As she rose, she felt her personal offering crinkle in the deep pockets of her skirt.

Once the gratitudes were laid out, a bonfire would be lit, and every member of the town would cast in one beloved treasure as a final sacrifice.

This year, Greer had selected one of her maps. It was her best, and the thing she was most proud of: a perfect rendering of the cove and shoreline. Its scale was minute but brilliantly detailed, showing each family's home and farm.

Just before heading out, Greer had used the very last of her most prized ink—a rich, iridescent blue that Hessel had purchased off a trader three summers before. The man had claimed that the dark teal mimicked the plumes of a most peculiar bird that lived on the other side of the world in lowland forests warm and wild—a peacock.

When Hessel recounted the story to her, Greer had been overcome with a homesickness most impossible. It seemed absurd to miss a place she'd never see, but there, in the middle of their sitting room, Greer yearned for that land. She ached for it, hungering to see these peacocks with her own eyes. Forever trapped within the acres of the Warding Stones, she mourned a future she'd never have.

She'd vowed to use the ink on only the most special occasions, and had rationed it with sharp vigilance. The glass bottle was nearly empty now, but Greer had dipped in her pen that afternoon and dotted each of her map's Warding Stones—rendered weeks before in their original positions—then scrawled a heartfelt plea across the page.

"We know you're here. We know your might. Return the Stones back to the way they were. Please."

With the very last drop of her most precious ink, Greer had signed her name at the bottom, a blue-stained oath. It was by far the best thing she had to offer the Benevolence.

Beside her, Hessel cleared his throat, snapping her attention back to the present moment. Greer stepped aside and followed her father.

Once their gifts were given, each family joined the others in a large circle along the edge of the clearing, watching the bounties grow. Greer listened to the aged wood stretch and shift under the weight of the offerings, and she dared to hope that this—that all of this—would be enough.

Whatever offense the Benevolence had seen surely must be wiped away by such lavish generosity. The Gratitude Tree had never been piled so high before. It all but groaned under the abundance.

The last families trickled into the clearing, and Greer smiled as she saw the Beauforts. Ellis carried several loaves of bread, and each of the younger children brought handfuls of vegetables. Mary appeared to be present and in good spirits and carried an earthen pot, undoubtedly a stew made from Louise's rabbits. Greer's worry began to ease a little. The Benevolence would get those gratitudes after all.

Louise followed in, her eyes trained low, never once lifting to meet her best friend's gaze. She set a small wedge of cheese onto the table and stepped back, joining the rest of the gathering. The circle was, at last, complete.

Everyone joined hands. Caught between Hessel and Martha, Greer felt too small, like the child she'd never again be.

"People of Mistaken," Hessel said, taking a step forward. Greer's arm stretched out to keep her hold on him. "Good Reaping."

"Good Reaping." Their combined echo was strong and solemn.

"What a joyous time of year this is, when we come together to humble ourselves in this sacred space and give thanks to our merciful protectors."

Greer glanced about the circle, watching how people reacted. After the night in the Calloways' field, she'd never consider the Benevolence to be merciful anythings ever again.

"Let us take a moment of silence as we ready our hearts to welcome them."

The town of Mistaken took a shared breath and closed their eyes.

Greer was never sure what she was meant to do in this moment. How should you ready for visitors who never arrived? But she closed her eyes all the same, listening to the sounds around her.

The Benevolence were near, and this year, more than ever, she wanted to hear them.

She listened to her father's deep breaths and the soft rattle that rasped at their end. She heard the shifting sway of the group and the howl of the wind high above them, a constant drone that never truly died away. It set the tamaracks creaking and ripped the remaining poplar leaves from their branches. There were scratches from a pair of squirrels racing up a spruce, the lumbering shuffle of a porcupine, the patter of martens darting through undergrowth.

There was—

"Starling."

Greer's eyes flashed open.

She searched the circle, scanning for anyone who might have spoken, but everyone had their eyes closed and brows furrowed with concentration. Though she saw some lips moving, their prayers were silent.

"You don't look like much, little Starling."

Certain now that the voice was coming from the trees at her back, Greer turned. Her hands slipped free, rending apart the circle. Though Hessel made a soft noise of confusion, she stepped closer to the forest.

There were spruces, dark and forbidding, and Redcaps grown so twisted that even her father wouldn't dare approach them. Greer scanned their depths, yet found nothing but trees.

"What is it, girl?" Hessel hissed, his voice low to avoid attention.

Despite his effort, others stirred, noticing the interruption. Breaths caught. Whispers rose. Still, Greer remained fixed on the shadows, squinting. Was that movement there, or just a trick of her mind?

"Someone's out there."

"In the trees?"

She nodded.

"But everyone we know is here."

Greer dragged her gaze from the forest. "I don't think it's anyone we know."

Hessel's eyes widened, and the dark worry that had covered him like a shroud since the night at the Calloways' lightened by soft degrees. He looked . . . hopeful. "You heard them? The Benevolence?"

She hesitated. She'd heard something, but was it the Benevolence?

"Greer," Hessel prompted, urgency weighting her name. Reluctantly, she nodded. "That . . . that's wonderful." His eyes raced across the tree line, then he grabbed her hand and returned them to the circle.

Across the clearing, Ellis watched her, face grim with worry. Greer smiled, trying to offer the assurance that she was all right, that everything was fine. She could tell he didn't believe her. She wasn't sure she believed it herself.

"Friends," Hessel began, "these days have been grim. Grim and mystifying. Challenging. It is not possible for us to understand the ways of the Benevolence. To us, their methods seem cruel and incomprehensible, but we must believe they act in our favor. We must believe that they will continue to watch over our cove, protecting us and bestowing prosperous bounties upon all who dwell here. The way they always have. They are close." A sound of mirth escaped him, as if he could not hold back his joy. "They are not faceless gods, far off and uninterested. The Benevolence is here, right now, watching to see what we'll do next."

Murmurs of surprise and confusion rose. Several Stewards dared to approach the trees, trepidation clouding their faces.

"I . . . I see them!" shouted Ian Brennigan. When he turned back, his eyes were bright with wonder. "They've come to show us their mercies."

"Yes! There's one! And another!" Michael Morag cried out, pointing.

Greer tried to see what they saw, narrowing her eyes against the falling light, but there were only shadows. And though she strained to hear the voice, the woods were silent once more.

"They have seen our sufferings. They have seen our pains," Hessel continued. "So now, good people of Mistaken, let us show them our devotion! We must light the bonfire!"

Greer was surprised to see Lachlan Davis come forward, lantern held high. Normally, a Steward performed this most sacred task. She did not doubt that Hessel had bestowed the honor on Lachlan, signaling his great esteem.

Lachlan knelt beside the pile of logs and set to work, transferring his flame to the kindling. The dried grass and twigs caught quickly, casting a warm red glow over the group.

As the fire rose, Lotte Morag started to sing the first hymn.

"As we gather here together, hands and hearts and minds as one," she began, her voice as clear and sweet as a freshwater spring.

The song had been sung at Mistaken's first Reaping, and each thereafter.

"We try ever to endeavor, pleasing Ones whose wills we've done."

Other women took up the next verse, strengthening the old melody with richer altos. The song filled the clearing, haunting and beautiful and so full of hope.

Once the bonfire was fully lit, its orange and yellow tongues flickering high into the dying afternoon, townspeople began to feed their offerings into the flames.

They went alone or sometimes in pairs, but each person had their own moment with the fire, whispering their dearest wishes. It wasn't hard to imagine what was most asked for this year.

When her turn came, Greer knelt alongside the raging heat. She took out her map and smoothed the creases, looked it over one last time. Whispering her wish, she pressed a kiss to the back of the vellum before tossing it into the flames. It was incinerated in an instant, its thin ashes caught in an updraft and carried out into the approaching night.

When all the sacrifices were burned, another song was sung, and then the town of Mistaken returned home, leaving behind their offerings and a bank of smoldering embers for the Benevolence to enjoy.

They all made it across the town line before sunset, pressing a reverent touch to the Warding Stones as they passed.

They stood at the edge of their world, watching the sun dip behind the mountains and feeling its pull in the marrow of their bones. It set without fanfare, and, for one perfect moment, everyone breathed a happy sigh of relief.

The Warding Stones had remained still.

The border had held.

The good people of Mistaken began to cheer. The heavy weight of their worries eased, sloughing off like water from a duck's back, and they celebrated. They danced and jumped and shouted their good fortunes to the sky.

But then, far beyond the Warding Stones, a dark shadow rose, and Mistaken's joy turned into screams.

11

THEY CAME OUT of the trees in the north.
From the clearing, Greer observed, watching the darkness follow the same trail they'd just taken. Though the shadowy mass was thick and absolute, there was a strange undulation within it, the individual movements of thousands, like a murmuration of starlings.

Starlings! she thought, mind racing.

But they weren't birds, Greer noted, catching none of the chirps and calls that would be expected with such a swarm. She closed her eyes, listening; it was unlike anything she'd ever heard before. There was a soft swish of wings cutting through the air, flapping and fluttering, but this was oddly muffled, multiplied too many times.

"What *is* that?" Lotte Morag dared to ask, horror and wonder hitching in her voice.

No one responded. There were no answers. Only dumbstruck awe and rising dread.

The flapping of wings grew louder. How many things could fly so close together, in one huddled mass? It was like a wall of darkness barreling down on them. It was like . . .

It was like her dreams, Greer realized. The way pieces of the sky shattered apart to swoop down over Mistaken and—

The thought that followed was too terrible to finish. "We need to run! Right now!" Greer screamed, startling several children near her. "Run home! Run to safety! You need to—"

But the first bits of the swarm were already upon them, blotting out any remaining twilight with the dense concentration of so very many bodies.

The screams began as townspeople turned to flee, fighting to outpace the intruders, swatting at furred bodies and papery wings when they could not.

"Moths?" Greer had one moment to vocalize her confusion before several of the winged insects fell upon her.

They were large—bigger than both her hands put together, even with all fingers spread wide—and the silvery color of moonlight. Dark stripes ran along the giant wings, and Greer might have found them striking had they not been picking their way over her body with disgusting heft.

Burdened by the roar of so many wings, screams, and wailing, Greer was struck senseless, unable to move, unable to think. Her head throbbed, feeling as if it were about to split apart.

Ian Brennigan's voice managed to cut through the chaos, spurring the townspeople to action. "Get home!" he hollered. "Get home, Mistaken!"

People began to run in all directions, fleeing the onslaught. Some slipped and fell, causing others to stumble, trampling them. The air was thick with confusion and shrieks. It was too dark to see, too loud for reason.

Greer couldn't tell which direction she went; she only knew she had to get away. Stumbling blindly through the madness, she kept her hands out before her, desperate to make sense of her surroundings. More moths flocked to her, batting at her fingers, her face. A jolt of pain shot down her spine as someone ran into her, wrenching her shoulder backward.

"Sorry, I'm so sorry," the person fumbled. "I can't get them off me. Oh God, *please,* get them off me!"

Greer could just make out the figure of Callum Cairn pitching back and forth as he slapped at winged creatures clinging to his coat, crawling over his face, tangling in his hair. He tripped, fell down an embankment, and rolled out of sight.

Greer changed course, heading away from the hill, and struck the side of a granite boulder. Momentarily stunned, she ran her hands over the rough surface before picking her way to the leeward side. She could use the rock's size as protection while the swarm blasted through the valley. If she hunkered low enough, she could be out of the worst of it and figure out her next step.

Greer knew this boulder, knew where it was in relation to the rest of the town. She could picture its position on her maps and, using her internal compass, could visualize how best to get home.

A moth struck the boulder above and floundered down, landing on Greer's head. She'd lost her knitted hat somewhere in the confusion, and could feel the insect's legs tussle through her hair as it fought to free itself. Swallowing the shriek demanding to be set loose, Greer batted at the moth, trying to dislodge it. But it caught on the yarn of her mittens and began to crawl under the sleeve of her dress. Its body was tufted with fur and felt muscular and meaty and so terribly wrong against her sweep of exposed skin.

Greer's screams joined the others echoing across the cove, and, as if in response, the sound of the swarm altered. The muffled swish of papery, powdery wings pitched sharper, like wind cutting across something webbed and leathery. Greer froze as she heard the first volley of clicks and chirps.

Bats!

One dove from the sky, snatching up a moth Greer hadn't even known was on her shoulder. The sound of crunching, struggling bodies filled the air as more bats plunged down, their claws grasping and grabbing.

Greer ducked, crawling across the ground as bits of antennas and twitching legs fell over her. There was a horrible pulse in her head—too much noise, there was too much noise—and she sobbed as she made her slow trek toward the trees, toward home, toward even the smallest hope of safety.

But she couldn't get away from the bats. There were hundreds of them. Thousands. Tens of thousands. It felt as though the entire world was nothing but wings and fangs and claws and teeth.

As the number of moths dwindled, the bats began to turn on one another, lashing out at their own kind. Greer's thoughts filled with the terrible wet sounds of bellies slashed open and wings sheared off. She heard the screams of the smaller prey, their rasping, rustling death rattles as they tried in vain to escape. She heard the screams of the larger bats, triumph roaring through them, victorious monsters of the night. And she heard the screams of the townspeople, of Mistaken, of her very self, as blood fell like rain down from the black night.

SOMEHOW, Greer made it home.

She trudged up the cabin steps on shaky legs before crashing against a porch post. Her clothes were torn and foul with a mess of sticky stains she did not want to contemplate.

The last of the bats swooped overhead, chasing after the remaining prey. Mangled bodies lay in twitching heaps, seized in death torments all across the cove.

Greer didn't understand the waste of it.

None of the bats had fed.

It was not the urge to hunt that had spurred them into going after the moths or their own wretched brethren. The surviving bats had enjoyed themselves, relishing the destruction they wrought, driven by nothing but feverish bloodlust.

Greer ran a weary hand across her face. She knew she needed to go inside, knew she needed to clean herself, but couldn't find the strength. Her head didn't feel right—her thoughts loose and disjointed—though she was unsure if it was from injury or the sudden absence of sound after such prolonged turmoil.

She studied the sky with heavy eyes. Millions of tiny lights pricked the void, occasionally blotted out by a pair of murderous wings. Greer had always thought of the stars as friends, the same dots faithfully shining year after year, letting her know exactly where she was in her tiny corner of the universe.

But now they looked icy and indifferent.

They didn't care.

They couldn't help.

As she watched, soft waves of light formed, streaks of pulsing reds and azure blues. They surged and ebbed and returned, slithering with serpentine grace, undulating in dancing arcs and swirls.

Sky lights on Reaping night.

It had always been considered a lucky sign, a foretelling of good things to come. They should have been beautiful, but now the lights reminded Greer of the flickering caught within the Warding Stones, and she looked away, unable to bear the brilliance.

Why was this happening?

Mistaken had given so much, freely and without reservation.

Why hadn't it been enough?

Greer wanted to cry as she thought of all the work she and Martha had—

Shame burned her as she realized that, in her haste to flee, she'd run without giving anyone else a second thought. The attack had happened so quickly, there'd been no time to think of others, and now Greer felt sick as she worried about all of the people she'd forgotten.

Martha.

Her father.

Louise and Mary and all the Beaufort siblings.

Ellis.

Her stomach pitched.

What had happened to Ellis?

She tried to push away the spiral of anxious contrition. Those moments with the swarm had been utter madness. People running, lanterns smashing. It would have been impossible to find anyone in such turmoil, and Ellis was more than capable of taking care of himself, of his family.

But Martha . . .

"Martha?" she called out uncertainly. "Father?"

She shifted, trying to stand, but the change in momentum was too much for her head. Greer pressed her temple against the post and willed the world to stop turning. Noises came in and out of focus, and she was acutely aware that her hearing had diminished. The world was hushed and still. Such quiet was a sensation she was wholly unused to, and the wrongness prickled at the back of her neck.

People had scattered in all directions to escape the moths. People had fallen. People had been trampled. What if Martha, what if Hessel, had been among them? What if they were lying in the dirt now with broken bones, crying out in agony, and, for the first time in her life, Greer couldn't hear them?

"Get up," she ordered herself, grinding her teeth with determination. "Go find them."

With a groan, she pushed herself to standing and staggered down the porch.

She'd check inside first, then go back into the darkness. She'd search all night if she had to. She'd find a lantern and a weapon to arm herself with, and if the sky was about to shatter down upon them, she'd be protected.

"An ax," Greer decided. "An ax or a kni—"

She stopped short as the very word she was about to say materialized before her, like magic.

A knife.

There was a knife stabbed into their cabin door.

Greer blinked, wondering if her muddled mind was hallucinating. Tentatively, she touched the handle. It was solid and substantial.

The knife was real.

Only after she confirmed its heft did Greer notice that the blade was skewering a bit of parchment to the door. An angry scrawl of letters addressed the missive to Hessel.

Curiously, Greer pulled at the knife, trying the dislodge it, but the blade would not budge. Whoever had left this had used all their might to impale it in place. She debated whether to pull the message free, ripping the paper in the process, to devour the contents for herself.

Everything about the letter felt wrong.

It was the day of Reaping. With so much work to get through, when would anyone have had the time to stop and write a note to Hessel?

And *when* had they left it? Greer was certain it had not been on the door as she and Martha had departed, their arms laden with offerings.

No one would have missed Reaping, especially this year, and no one had been missing from the circle.

She stared at the paper, unease curdling in her stomach.

Who had written this note?

Greer ran her finger along the flap, opening the paper as much as the knife would allow. But it was too dark, and the handwriting too messy. She could only catch quick phrases: "indebted," "the boy," "perdition upon you."

Just as she made up her mind to seize the note, damage be damned, footsteps approached from the woods.

Greer studied the shadowed trees. She couldn't hear anything but the crunch of dried leaves, the snapping of twigs. She couldn't hear the approaching person's breath, couldn't pick out a familiar cadence to the stride. What if whoever had left the note had decided to come back?

"Who's out there?" she asked, throwing her voice into the night. She hated how it trembled.

"Greer? Is that you?"

A broken cry escaped her, and she all but fell down the porch steps. "Father?"

Hessel staggered out of the darkness. He looked terrible. Face ashen, clothing torn. Something had slashed his temple, and red lines ran down his face.

Heedless of his injuries, heedless of her own, heedless of anything but the swell of relief flooding through her, Greer ran across the yard and threw her arms around her father. He held her loosely at first, as if he wasn't sure what to do with this wild thing caught in his embrace, but then pulled her close, fitting her beneath his chin.

"Are you all right? Are you hurt?" he asked, daring to stroke the mess of hair tumbling down her back.

"My head," she said, unsure if he could hear her words with her face buried deep into the wool of his coat. "I can't hear anything . . . not like I usually do."

Hessel pulled away, cupping her face as he squinted, studying. "Let's get you inside. You might have a concussion."

She resisted, looking over his shoulder as if expecting others to emerge from the trees with him. "Did you see Martha? When the attack started I—"

"She's fine, she's fine. She's with Ada Sturgette. Twisted her ankle something fierce. Martha is helping her home." He made a motion toward the cabin.

Greer stopped him again. "Father . . ." She swallowed. "There's a note on the door."

He frowned, his eyebrows drawing together. "A note?"

"Someone left it while we were at Reaping. They . . . they used a knife."

It took her father three attempts to free the blade from the door.

When they got inside, Greer began lighting the hurricane lamps and building up a fire in the cast-iron stove. She expected Hessel to join her, but when she turned, he was already disappearing into his study. The door closed with a firm finality.

"Father?" she called out anyway. When he didn't answer, she knocked on the door, pounding the wood with the side of her hand.

"What?"

Ignoring his tone—harsh, and devoid of any of the concern he'd just shown—Greer twisted the handle and invaded his sanctuary. He sat behind the desk, reading the missive by the light of a single taper. Strange shadows were cast along the shelves of books and journals lining one wall.

She said nothing, waiting for him to feel her presence, forcing him to look up and acknowledge her. A full minute passed. Then another, and Greer finally broke first. "You said I might have a concussion."

He glanced up from the letter, his expression distracted. "What? No. I'm sure you're fine."

"What does it say?"

He looked back to the note, then folded it closed. "Nothing of importance."

"Who was it from?" she persisted.

"No one." He folded it in half again, running his nail along the paper to press it into submission.

"No one used a knife to stab a note of no importance to our door?" She blinked.

Hessel's sigh was pained. "It's nothing for you to fret over. You should rest. You'll need your strength for tomorrow."

"Tomorrow?"

"The Hunt."

Greer let out a humorless laugh. "Are you in jest?"

"We need something to distract from all this . . . unpleasantness. The Benevolence will restore order soon, I'm certain."

"I'm sure the Calloways would love to be distracted from all their unpleasantness," she snapped.

"Greer." His voice was heavy with warning. "For the good of the town, the Hunt will continue as planned. I know it seems callous, but if you only—"

"For the good of the town?" she echoed in disbelief.

"For the good of the town." He tucked the paper into his coat pocket as if the matter was settled.

Greer waited for him to say something more, to say anything at all, but those words did not come. She curled her hands into fists. "I'm going to bed."

Hessel nodded, relieved. "A fine idea. Dawn comes early for us all."

12

THE DREAM BEGAN the way it always did.

It was night, spring now. The air was sweet with newly blooming coltsfoot, lupine, and harebell. The sky was, too, an impossibly vivid velvet, wild with stars and the throaty calls of great horned owls.

Greer stood at the top of Barrenman's Hill, looking down at Mistaken, at the cove it hugged as tight as a comma. Beyond the cove, beyond the Narrows, was the Great Bay, and beyond even that was everything Greer desperately wanted but could not have.

Dots of lights moved across that watery horizon. She knew they weren't falling stars but great ships, full of people, and was struck by the terrifying realization that every one of those many people, on all those many ships, had a life so much fuller than anything she could ever imagine.

She envied the things they'd all seen, and hungered for the things they all knew, and wondered if any of them grasped just how damned lucky they were.

That hunger burrowed deep in Greer's middle, squirming and twisting like a live thing, and when she pressed her hand to her stomach, she half expected it to move, like a babe quickening in its womb.

"Starling," a voice hissed, rushing high above her, nothing more than a rustle of night air.

She glanced up just as the sky came alive with shapes that were neither stars nor the black spaces between them. They shivered and shuddered, roiling with uncanny movement, falling upon the town with flashing eyes, descending into homes, winking out hurricane lamps and tapered flames as the screams began.

Greer stood atop the hill and knew she ought to move, knew she should try to help, but her feet would not budge. They were stuck to the ground, as if caught in a sluice of thick, squelching mud, and she wasn't sure whether to be ashamed or relieved.

It wasn't until a piece of sky landed behind her, plummeting to the earth with all the force of a meteor, that she grew afraid.

Greer looked back and saw nothing but the black of a forest grown impenetrable with mysteries. Then the rusty, reddish shine from a pair of eyes large and set impossibly high off the ground.

A piece of sky.

A Bright-Eyed.

He moved through the shadows on legs strange and wobbling, picking his way toward her, and the sound of his care reminded Greer of the afternoon when a bat had landed in their yard, too sick with the maddening illness to fly. It had traveled through the grass on the tips of toes never intended to be walked upon, its wings folded in jagged angles curious and strange.

That same sort of wings stalked toward her now.

She snapped her gaze back to the town. For all her curiosity, Greer did not truly want to know what this creature looked like. He was certain to be more terrible than anything her imagination could conjure.

"Greer."

He drew out her name with tender familiarity. This was not the voice she'd heard before, the one from the woods and the clearing and the sky. The one who called her Starling.

Goose bumps ran wild over her arms. "Why are you here?"

"Me?" he asked, surprised, wounded, wondering.

"You. Them."

She pointed to a family racing toward the Warding Stones, trying to escape the dark, skittering shadow that followed. The mother—holding her infant son—struck the unseen border and ricocheted back into the nightmare on her heels. Her scream was cut off in a burst of wet splashing. Greer's stomach heaved but she didn't move a muscle, too aware of the Bright-Eyed at her own back and his capacity to inflict the same ending upon her.

"Why is the Benevolence allowing this? Where are they? Why haven't they come?"

Something deep in his gullet clucked like the dry laugh of a loon.

"Oh, Greer." He sounded sad and sympathetic. "You don't know."

"Know what?"

A twig snapped, and Greer felt the creature just behind her now, just shy of the curve of her shoulder blades. The air shifted differently, flowing around two forms instead of one.

Her body, as small and slight as she'd ever felt.

And his . . .

He was so much bigger than her, so much bigger than any one person had a right to be.

He's not a person, she reminded herself. *No matter how much he sounds like one.*

The night breeze stirred, playing over the Bright-Eyed's wings and haunches, his too-large toes and talons. His breath warmed her neck, fluttering the strands of loose hair there, and though Greer knew this was a dream, a dream she'd had so many times before, it felt real. It felt as though she truly was there now, on top of the hill, trapped against this monster.

His sigh sounded as ancient as the earth, as dry as the paper Greer drew her maps on. His response was nothing more than a murmur, a waft of breath caressing the shell of her ear. "No one is coming for you but me."

Something brushed the swell of her cheek, and Greer startled. It had been as delicate as a butterfly wing, as soft as a fawn taking its first tentative steps.

"Close your eyes, Greer," the Bright-Eyed murmured, and she could feel him shift, removing any space left between them. "You don't need to see this."

"Them?" she asked, her eyes flickering over the town, where dark stains splashed over porches and windows, clapboard sidings and wooden walkways. The screams had stopped now, mostly.

"No. Me."

Just before the Bright-Eyed changed, shattering his form into a thousand nocturnal creatures—slithery, blue-spotted salamanders and leathery bats, sharp-faced foxes and those horrible fluttering furred moths—Greer could have sworn she felt a soft press against the nape of her neck, his kiss as swift and tender as the moments after were terrible.

―

GREER WOKE UP gasping for air.

Bedsheets looped around her limbs, tangled and sodden. Her skin was flushed and clammy as the last of the nightmare left her. She pressed a hand over her heart, trying to calm her ragged breaths, trying to still her racing pulse.

Greer's eyes darted around the room as panic bubbled up in her throat, choking her. In an attempt to get her bearings straight, Greer began to recite the list of things she knew to be true, just as Ailie had taught her.

"You are not on Barrenman's Hill."

She nodded.

"The Bright-Eyeds have never attacked."

Another nod. Her heart no longer felt as though it were about to explode from her chest, and she took that to be a good sign.

"The Bright-Eyeds are not here."

Even as Greer said this, it didn't seem as certain a truth as her others. She could still feel the warm imprint of his kiss on her neck. The timbre of his husky voice still resonated in her ears.

"It's the day of the Hunt," she tried again.

That was unfortunately true.

With a final nod, she pushed herself from the sweat-stained sheets.

The morning had dawned so darkly that it still felt like night. Any trace of sunlight was bullied away by snow clouds, and a sparkle of jagged frost coated every stationary thing. Icicles hung in lines of bared teeth, giving the window's view an air of menace.

It's going to be miserable, Greer thought, as she braided her hair.

This was not the way she'd wanted her Hunt to start.

Ailie had told many stories of her own day—of retreating into the hollowed trunk, breathless with anticipation, of seeing Hessel's hand pull her out, and of all the interminable boredom that unwound in the time between. Her mother had spent the long hours scratching elaborate etchings inside the tree, trying to keep her wonders and worries at bay.

But that day had been bright. That day had been warm.

Greer had always imagined squirreling herself away in that same tree. She wanted to find Ailie's drawings and add one of her own, scratching out a hasty rendering of Mistaken while waiting for Ellis. In these daydreams, it was always unseasonably warm, and she'd emerge from the hollowed tree in a beautiful dress of voile and lace, with flowers in her hair, and her cheeks would be pink with fresh love.

There would be no flowers today. And her cheeks would be red and stinging from wind and frostbite. Her dress would be wool and covered away by sweaters and her thickest fur-lined cloak. A knitted hat would cover her braids, and her hands would be too bundled by mittens to sketch anything.

Greer didn't know how to draw Mistaken anyway.

Not anymore.

She turned from the window. "Why are we doing this?"

For the good of the town.

There was a soft knock at the door. Greer turned, expecting to see Martha, but it was Hessel, seemingly summoned by her thoughts. He was already dressed, though Greer doubted that he'd ever gone to bed. She eyed his coat, wondering if the mysterious note was still secreted in its pocket.

Her hearing had returned in slow degrees as she'd tried to sleep. She'd heard him leave the house, his footsteps clattering down the porch, down the walk, down toward town, and Greer had lain in bed for a long while after, guessing where he'd gone.

Before she could find out, sleep had seized her. Then—the dream.

"Good morning," he said. "I . . . I brought you coffee."

Greer supposed he'd meant it as a kindness, something warm to fill her belly before the long, cold wait, but Ailie had warned her of drinking too much, ruefully musing how differently the Hunt played out for the Hunters and the prey.

The men began their morning with a great feast, eating their fill of rich, hearty foods, drinking coffee and tea, and even little nips of whiskey, so that they'd be warm and full of energy for the search to come. But the women needed to remain silent and still. Some would have to wait the entire day to be found and claimed. Greer often wondered how many marriages resulted from a too-full bladder.

"Thank you." Greer wrapped her fingers around the mug, letting it warm her even without drinking.

Hessel shifted his weight uneasily from foot to foot, his size taking up an uncomfortable amount of space in her room. "I imagine you've picked your spot?"

She nodded.

He waited.

A strained smile tugged her lips. "You don't think I'll tell you where, do you? That would hardly be sporting."

"Of course not," Hessel said after a long moment passed between them, as wide as a canyon. "I wish you luck. Today is an important time in a young person's life. I didn't ever . . . I never thought it would come."

She frowned. "Didn't you?"

"It seemed so far off. Ailie always . . ." He stopped abruptly.

"What?" Greer pressed, needing to hear something of her mother, today of all days.

He glanced away. "I found her once in a flood of tears. You and Louise were playing outside, making little dolls out of pinecones or some such. . . ." He shook his head as if those details didn't matter. "She'd been watching you from the window as she worked on a pile of mending. And I noticed she was crying. I thought she must have stabbed herself with the needle or . . ." Again, he paused, ill at ease with the words and phrases used so frequently in the feminine realm. "I asked if she was all right, and she said that that Beaufort boy had brought Louise over. That he'd said something to make you smile."

Greer tried remembering the day in question, but couldn't.

"She said he'd go on making you smile just like that and you'd follow after him. She said she could see it all—that you'd follow him down the aisle, follow him all through life, follow him even into death. She said there wasn't a place on earth you wouldn't follow that boy to."

Greer's heart warmed.

It didn't matter if it was by special sight or mere conjecture. Her mother had been right.

Hessel's thick eyebrows furrowed, and he almost looked ashamed. "I rebuffed it. Told her that was nonsense. That you were nothing but a little girl, still tied to her skirt strings. Told her that you were too good to wind up with some Beaufort. That your Hunt was ages away and it was foolish to be worrying over some imagined . . ." His hands fluttered in the air, fruitlessly trying to grab hold of the right words. He sighed. "But here we are."

"Here we are," she echoed, feeling a stab of pride in her chest.

Like the explorers in her tattered adventure novels, Greer was about to embark on a journey, new and exciting. She *was* going to marry that Beaufort boy, no matter how Hessel had tried to forbid it.

For the good of the town.

Greer hadn't understood what Hessel had meant last night, but now, standing on the edge of this great precipice, her life about to unfold, just like a map, she thought she almost did.

Mistaken was facing dangerous unknowns. Its very air was rife with uncertainty, sour with fear. But in just a few short hours, Greer would have someone to face that fear with, someone to wrap her hand around and hold on to, no matter what was to come.

And that filled her with hope. Hope for miracles and better days. Hope for a future spent with the one she loved. It was hope that allowed a person to keep going on, even as it seemed the odds were stacked against them.

She would have Ellis. And he would have her.

And that was something.

"Father . . ." she began, feeling suddenly inspired. "This *is* a special day."

Hessel nodded.

"Mama always told me so much about the day of her Hunt. Your

Hunt. I . . . It would mean so much to have something of hers with me today. Do you think I might . . ." She swallowed, growing bold. "Could I wear her cape? The velvet one she wore when you found her?"

Hessel's eyes darkened. "No."

"I just . . . I thought that maybe—"

"I said no." His words fell out as flat and heavy as an anvil.

"But—"

"It's gone, Greer. The cape is no more."

Greer knitted her fingers together, feeling cold.

Ailie's velvet cape had been her most cherished possession. It was the same dark hue as a twilight sky and covered with hundreds of constellations, stitched by Ailie herself. Greer had learned how to read the night sky from that cape, wondering over each piece of embroidery as her mother told her the stories behind every star cluster.

Greer had assumed Hessel had stored it away, saving it as a piece of treasure to bestow upon her one day. That he could have gotten rid of it hurt her more than she had words to say.

Hessel seemed to realize his error and shuffled his feet over the threshold, looking contrite. "They'll be starting the festivities soon. We oughtn't be late for that."

Greer nodded, and gave her room one final glance. The next time she stepped foot into it, she'd be a married woman, packing up her girlhood to bring to Ellis's cabin. Their home.

She caught Hessel staring at her with a wistful gaze, as if he was realizing the same thing.

"Aren't you going to try and stop me?" she questioned curiously. "I thought you'd have some last warning, some final plea."

Hessel glanced out the window, considering her words. "No. No, I don't. I know that when the time comes Ellis Beaufort will make the right choice. For him. For you. For Mistaken."

He retreated, leaving Greer behind with an uneasy ache in her chest.

13

DESPITE THE COLD, despite the mist settling in so heavily it might as well have been rain, despite the dread hanging over the town like funeral shrouds, despite *it all,* the girls of Mistaken looked lovely.

The girls were all rosy faces and excited eyes. They wore light capes in alluring shades over dresses short enough for men to sneak quick glimpses of ankles and lace-trimmed underskirts. Heads were left uncovered, so that all might see and admire the beautiful braids and ribbons pinned in place.

Greer pulled her heavy, long cloak around herself more tightly, feeling chilled just looking at them. Hadn't their mothers warned them? Didn't they understand how long they might have to wait? Making her way through the crowd of young women laughing too loudly, brazenly running their hands up the arms of the Hunters, and batting their eyes at whoever paid notice, Greer had never felt so old or tired.

Had she ever looked at Ellis with such swoony, forlorn eyes, with such a fevered intensity of hope and yearning? They'd loved each other for so long and with such equal measure, it was hard to remember.

Her heart hurt for these girls—and they were girls, no matter what the Stewards said—so full of wonderings and wants.

Wanting to be noticed, to be found unique and irresistible. Wanting to be courted and wooed. Wanting for so many things other than the roles they currently played.

Schoolgirl.

Sister.

Friend.

Daughter.

Greer hoped that, by day's end, each of these fresh-faced girls would be found by a lad who would care for her and appreciate all the things that made her her own person, not just the position she'd been assigned. She hoped that they'd find comfort in each other, each having a hand to hold as the Warding Stones shifted and the skies filled with blood. She hoped they'd find the right someones to be with, to stand beside in the face of uncertainty and peril.

For the good of the town.

Mistaken gathered on the edge of the Hunting Grounds, waiting for the Stewards to declare the Hunt begun. A heightened merriment was rippling through the crowd. People laughed and smiled, waved and called out to neighbors. It was as though the entire community had decided to forget the horrors of the night before, if only for this one day.

For the good of the town.

The scent of the Hunters' feast made her stomach growl, and Greer longed to grab a hot biscuit stuffed with thick cuts of hot bacon and sharp mustard. She paused, thinking of the day to come. An empty stomach would be far better than one queasy with too-rich food. Greer took a sourdough roll instead and stuffed it into her satchel alongside a small flask of water.

The young women would be sent first, so they could race to find a spot among the trees and tall grasses, the brambles and thickets. They'd hunker against the cold and begin their wait. Half an hour later, the Hunters would come. They'd roam the woods, the clearing, and the meadows with sharp eyes, searching for their intended prey.

Greer could feel those sharp eyes on her now, acutely aware of every lad taking note of what she wore, of the color of her cape. The lure of Hessel's fortunes could prove hard to resist, even if they had to marry Greer to get it. Their open stares made her squirm. They might be kind, some of them might even be good, but she didn't know anything about these men, and she was certain they couldn't say a single thing of her.

Who would pin their entire future on a virtual stranger?

Men who are not so good, Greer decided. *Men who are not so kind,* she thought, watching as one met her gaze and licked his lips with unguarded suggestion.

Thank God I have Ellis, she thought, feeling guilty and sad for all these other girls who would have to contend with the likes of these hungry men.

But where *was* Ellis?

Where was Louise?

Greer studied the tables, packed with Hunters eating their gluttonous fill and the girls who didn't know any better. Neither of the Beauforts were there, or in the crowds gathering farther off.

The Stewards had said Louise was to run . . . Where was she now?

A crack of gunfire ripped the air open, signaling the young women to make their way to the start of the Hunting Grounds. The flags flanking the gate waved lazily.

Greer looked about wildly, trying to find Ellis. Where had the morning gone? She'd thought they'd go over their strategy one final time and steal a quick kiss.

But the crowd was too thick, and she couldn't see him anywhere.

She did, unfortunately, spot Lachlan Davis.

"See you soon," he mouthed to her, smiling wickedly.

With a shudder, Greer joined a group of girls who looked as nervous as she felt. Now that the moment was here, bravado was stripped away, and smiles began to wobble. Some had to be all but pulled from parents who called out final words of encouragement and good wishes.

Still Greer scanned the crowds, desperate for any sign of the Beauforts.

She needed to see Ellis—just once—before the cannon fired. She needed to see his smile. She needed to find Louise.

Hessel Mackenzie and the other Stewards made their way to the front of the crowd, climbing a platform that had been hastily assembled at dawn.

"Good morning," Hessel began, his voice booming in the cold, crisp air.

Greer tried to duck to the back of the group, anxiety spreading in her chest, but several of the younger women gave her horrified looks, as though ignoring the Stewards, ignoring her own father, was a crime. With resignation, she turned back to the front. The Beauforts were there, in the crowds, somewhere. They must be.

"It has been more than one century since our forefathers came to this land, arrived at this cove, and—caught in the grip of the Warding Stones—settled Mistaken. It has not been an easy road. At times, it's felt impossible to go on. It would be easy to give up, to say that the work is too hard, that our unusual circumstances are too severe. But we never have. Mistaken has always been a community of forward thinkers. We do what we can, and we do what we must. We carry out this Hunt, daring to believe that, in another century, our town will still be here, blessed and thriving."

Cheers rose, first from the Hunters, then from their quarry, and finally from the rest of the town. Women clapped and men whistled, and through all their celebration, Greer searched for the Beauforts.

Where *were* they?

"And so, good townspeople of Mistaken, I declare the thirteenth Hunt now officially under way! Ladies, I wish you good hiding, and, lads—even better luck!"

After a playful wink from Hessel, the town's cannon fired, from its place high atop Barrenman's Hill. Greer covered her ears, wincing as the blast ripped through the air. It deafened everyone, leaving the group dazed.

"Go on!" the Stewards urged, waving their hands to spur the girls into action. "Your time has begun—go on!"

"Greer!" a voice shouted over the chaos, and her heart brightened.

She fought her way round girls who raced by, heading into the trees, wanting to find the best spots first. There were too many bodies jostling in too little space, and for a moment, Greer feared she'd be dragged away. Men pressed forward as the girls left, watching their progress with hungry eyes.

But then there he was, right beside her. Ellis swept her into a tight embrace.

"I'm sorry I'm late," he said, struggling to be heard over the mêlée.

"I was so scared I was going to miss you, and there's something I need to—"

"It doesn't matter; you're here now," she said, cutting him off as her mouth found his. The kiss was long and sweet and exactly as she'd imagined it would be. She cupped his cheeks, reveling in how good it felt to kiss him in public. Though the Hunters would claim their prey all throughout the afternoon, here and now, she'd openly declared hers. "I love you, Ellis Beaufort."

Greer was surprised to see tears prick his eyes. Ellis pressed a long kiss to her forehead; his fingers ran over her face, her arms, as if he were trying to memorize every bit of her.

"You need to hide," he urged. "Find the best spot you can, and stay there. Don't move, don't make a sound. Don't let anyone find you."

"Not till you," she promised.

He smiled but it looked off, smaller than it should. "Not till me. Go!"

Startling into action, Greer made her way to the gate and ducked through the opening. She dared one last glance back at Ellis.

"Come find me," she whispered.

The Hunting Grounds were a long strip of fallow fields, untouched forests, and, at their very end, a vast meadow of tall grasses and wildflowers. Greer would need to run at full sprint to make it to Ailie's tree before the Hunters were released.

As she plunged into a patch of brambles, she heard the voice once more, and it stopped Greer dead in her tracks.

"What are you running from, little Starling?"

She shook her head. Thorns clung to her skirts and cloak, trying to snare her in place, trying to hold her so she would be easy prey for the first Hunter passing through this thicket.

"Leave me alone," she snarled, fighting to free herself.

"We don't run from anyone," it persisted.

"Enough!" she growled, eliciting a gasp from the thicket to her right. Greer squinted and saw the concerned eyes of Madeline Montrosse peeking from the foliage of a tea bush.

"Are you unwell? You look . . . strained."

Mad.

Greer knew what she meant to say, and Madeline wasn't wrong.

What else would you call it, shouting at people who weren't there, on the one day of your life you were meant to be as sneaky and silent as you could?

Mad indeed.

"I'm fine," Greer assured her. "Just . . . all these brambles."

Madeline stared at her in stony silence before disappearing back into the leaves. "I can't believe, of all the girls in town, Lachlan chose you."

Greer wasn't supposed to have heard that aside and certainly shouldn't have responded, but her blood was racing high, and she felt bold and brash. "I can't, either. Happy hiding, Madeline."

Greer followed the creek bed as it cut across the deepest part of the forest, winding its way to the farthest reach of the clearing. Over the years, she'd drawn so many maps of the Hunting Grounds, she had her path memorized. She knew every turn to take. She knew where every step should fall.

Up ahead was the clearing.

The trees parted back, revealing the weak gray light of the morning. There were too many clouds in the sky for her to tell what time it was, and Greer wondered how long she'd been fighting her way through the wood's tangles.

There would be another cannon blast to signal when the Hunters were set loose.

As she raced across the open field, her heart pounded heavily in the center of her throat. There was a bad stitch in her side, and she felt as though she couldn't draw full breath.

She needed to hurry, needed to find the tree before—

The cannon fired. With her sharp ears, Greer caught the whoops of the men as they took off.

Ailie's tree was just ahead: an ancient, wizened Redcap stretching into the sky like a drowning man fighting to free himself from a torrent of waves.

Everyone in town knew never to touch a Redcap unless you had on thick leather gloves. The stinging sap would burn for days, causing rashes of bubbling hives and yellow, weeping pus.

It was the perfect spot to hide.

Decades before, a bad storm had blown into Mistaken. Winds had torn roofs off homes, pulled tree roots straight from the ground, and sent giant boulders down hillsides as though they were nothing more than a child's marbles. Rain had poured so heavily it had turned the town into a muddy sluice that took weeks to dry out.

And the lightning . . .

Ailie had been little more than a girl when that storm had rolled through. A girl out picking blackberries, caught by surprise when the sky had opened up with its torrent of fury and fire.

The Redcap tree had been struck seven times. Ailie had watched in horrified awe as that heavenly fire burned up every bit of sap from the tree, leaving it a scorched shell.

Days after the storm, Ailie had returned to the tree, marveling at how well it looked, amazed how the lightning had carved out a hollow spot hidden straight down the center of the trunk, perfect for hiding.

When she'd run her fingers over the burnt bark, they'd come away clean. No burning sap, no stinging welts.

Ailie decided then and there that, when she took part in the Hunt, this was where she would hide.

Greer approached the jagged Redcap now and circled it to find the hidden entrance. The opening was high up the tree's trunk, a nearly imperceptible slit in the blackened bark.

She grabbed at a branch and prayed the old tree would still support her weight. Bits of bark peeled away, and twice Greer nearly lost her grip. But then she was up, nearly ten feet off the ground, and peering into the dark shaft.

She shimmied into the hollowed space. With all her layers, it was a tight fit, but once she pulled her hood over her face, she would be completely undetectable from a Hunter's eyes. She settled into the snug enclosure and willed her breathing to slow. She'd made it. She was here. She just needed to wait for Ellis.

Greer didn't like it in the tree.

Though the space was large enough for her to hide in, it wasn't comfortable. The wood was hard and unforgiving, and she could already feel a wave of numbing pins and needles consuming her left foot.

Sounds from inside were strangely muffled, and yet too close. She listened for the Hunters, wanting to find Ellis's footsteps among them, but couldn't hear anything past her racing heartbeat.

It was impossible to sense how much time had passed by.

A minute? Ten? An hour? Three?

Once her eyes adjusted to the dim light, Greer found her mother's etchings, the constellations of stars and flowers she'd drawn while in the hollow, waiting for her Hunter to come. Greer traced her mittened fingers over the little calendulas, marveling at the detail and care Ailie had managed in such confined surroundings.

Greer leaned back as best as she could, trying to release the tension building between her shoulder blades.

How long had she been in this tree?

It seemed like hours.

She feared it was only minutes.

Greer started counting to herself, wanting to keep an accurate calculation of the minutes going by, but the numbers got too high, and she missed a second, then three. She tried again, only to be startled from her count when an enormous cormorant landed on the branches just above the tree's opening.

It was a large bird, the biggest she'd ever seen, solid black save for its wickedly hooked golden beak. It turned its tufted head with rapid movements, surveying the clearing with eyes that looked nearly human. Greer stared with fascination, marveling that the creature didn't seem aware of her presence.

Until it was.

With another shift of its head, the cormorant peered down into her hiding place, bright eyes meeting hers with a direct and uncomfortably frank stare.

The tilt of its head made it seem confused, as if it was trying to parse out what a human was doing up so high in its domain.

"Hello, little Starling," it said—the bird's beak moving as the voice in her head spoke. And then it dove, talons outstretched, and aimed directly at her face.

Greer came to with a gasp, choking back the shriek that wanted to burst from her chest.

It was a dream.

It had only been a dream.

How long had she been dozing?

Wanting to cry as she moved, stretching stiffened muscles and numb limbs, Greer took a quick peek out the tree's slit.

More clouds had rolled in while she'd slept, making it seem as though it was already twilight. Greer shook her head, scanning the sky for even a speck of the sun. There was no way she'd slept away the entire Hunt. She couldn't have.

It wouldn't have taken Ellis that long to find her. He knew she was going to be in the clearing. He knew exactly what tree Greer had planned to hide in.

He should have been here by now.

He should have come.

Unless . . .

I know that when the time comes Ellis Beaufort will make the right choice.

Her father's words echoed in her head, and Greer wanted to howl.

Suddenly it all made terrible sense.

Louise's absence earlier.

Ellis's now.

Her father had done something. Done something to Louise. Done something to make Ellis choose.

"No!"

She covered her mouth with horrified alarm. The word had slipped from her so quickly, and, given the strange way that sound played in the hollow of the tree, she had no way of knowing who might have heard her.

Cautiously, she rose until her eyes were just over the edge of the opening. It was hard to make out much of anything.

The sky was even darker now.

Sunset had to be only minutes away.

She'd somehow slept an entire day, and *why hadn't Ellis woken her?*

Why hadn't he found her?

What had Hessel done?

Greer nearly wept as a figure, tall and lanky, made his way out from the tree line.

It was him.

That was Ellis.

Her heart thudded as she waited for him to reach her. Greer wanted to push her way free of the tree and run to him. She wanted to throw her arms around Ellis and claim him for herself, rules be damned.

But she stayed where she was, frozen in the depths of the hollowed Redcap. She had to remember that this was Ellis's moment as much as it was hers. He, too, had waited seven extra years for it. She would not rob him of his opportunity to find her.

She pinched her cheeks, making sure she'd look flushed and rosy, a bride awaiting her groom.

She waited.

And waited.

Where was he?

She nearly rose up again, wanting to see exactly where he was, but she knew, she *knew*, that if she did that he'd be right below her, and she'd startle him and ruin the moment.

Fingernails digging into the fleshy meat of her palms, she waited.

She waited until she could bear it no longer.

Too much time had passed.

One peek couldn't hurt. Maybe she could feign a birdcall, something to snag his attention and set him on the right path.

Greer pulled herself up and squinted over the edge once more.

Ellis was . . .

She scanned the darkening meadow.

Ellis was gone.

Greer fought to stand up, feet scrabbling for purchase along the smoothed hull of the tree. She twisted about in the tight space, checking the meadow behind her.

No Ellis.

She turned north, where a pair of Warding Stones dotted the farthest edge. A flash of light caught her attention, but it didn't come from the Stones. It came from something just before them . . .

Greer blinked, unsure of what she was seeing.

Ellis had gone past Ailie's tree. He'd gone right by it, heading for Mistaken's border. He was over two hundred paces from her.

What was he doing?

"Ellis!" she dared to shout, heedless of any Hunters who might be nearby. "Ellis, I'm back here!"

She could hardly feel her feet as she climbed out, all but falling from the tree. When she pushed herself up, struggling to stand on legs as shaky as a newborn foal's, she saw Ellis had looked back and spotted her.

She waved as a wide smile broke across her face.

Ellis returned her wave, but not her smile.

It was a strange gesture, one that looked far more like a farewell than a greeting.

Greer frowned and started to make her way to him. He shook his head and held his hand out, now a warning, an order to stay put, to stay back, to stay away from him.

Ellis's lips moved, but, for the first time in her life, Greer could not hear him.

"What?" she shouted, confused and trembling.

He repeated himself, and though she still could not hear his words, she could read his lips. *Don't follow me.*

For one dreadful moment, the heavy clouds parted, revealing the last sliver of sun as it slipped under the mountains to the west. Greer watched in horror as the sun sank, winking out like a candle blown. She heard the three rolls of the final Bellows. And somehow, impossibly, she watched as her beloved stepped over Mistaken's border, breaking through the Warding Stone's hold, and headed into the unknown wild, completely unscathed.

"Ellis!" she screamed, and charged across the clearing.

A giant gust of wind picked up as she approached the border. Greer tried pushing her way through it but could gain no purchase. It howled all around her, throwing grit into her teeth and eyes, and she felt as if the world was coming apart, but when she stumbled back toward the meadow, all was quiet. All was still.

"Ellis!"

She shouted for him over and over. She tried again to fight the wind, desperate to find the spot where Ellis had somehow slipped through. Tears fell, clogging her throat and blurring her vision, making it impossible to see. When her legs gave way, because she was too spent to hold her grief upright any longer, she sank, striking the ground with her misery and rage.

What had he done? And *how*? And—

Greer's chest felt torn open, as if a wild animal had ripped her ribs apart before devouring her heart in one callous gulp.

She pulled her knees to her chin, burying her sobs into the swell of her skirts.

When a hand fell on her shoulder, squeezing it with warm strength, Greer's breath caught.

He was back. Ellis had come back.

"I hate to say it, but I am impressed. You really did make me search all day."

Greer pushed the tears from her eyes and gasped.

Standing over her, his hand now clutched round hers with possessive might, was Lachlan Davis. His face was flushed with triumph. "Caught you."

Greer blinked with incomprehension.

There was no way Lachlan was with her now, claiming her as his.

There was no way Ellis had crossed through the Stones' hold.

Not after sunset.

Not today of all days.

None of this could be.

And yet, somehow, it horribly was.

A dark shadow swooped overhead, and both Greer and Lachlan reflexively ducked, fearing another swarm.

But what flew through the sky was so much worse.

It was massive, wings spread wide as it circled over the forest beyond the Stones, like a vulture waiting on carrion. It scanned the area with dark intensity, and Greer could see the exact moment it found what it was looking for. She heard its quick intake of breath.

"Farewell for now, little Starling," the Bright-Eyed murmured, then drew its wings into a tight dive as it silently began to stalk after Ellis Beaufort.

14

Greer stared at the forest Ellis had ventured into after somehow breaking the Warding Stones' hold. He'd wandered away, and the Bright-Eyed had swooped after him, leaving a trail in the brush that was wide and ragged, like a mouth snarled with screams.

Greer wanted to scream as well.

How had Ellis gotten past the Stones? It was a certain impossibility. No one could leave Mistaken after sunset.

But he had.

She'd seen him do it.

"Did you see that?"

Beside her, Lachlan's voice was hushed with awestruck horror. Dragging her eyes from the tree line, Greer glanced at him, then their hands, still worryingly knotted together. She'd never seen Lachlan so stricken, stripped of his confidence and ease. Everyone in Mistaken treated him like a god, imbued with strapping charisma too powerful to ignore.

Now after seeing a Bright-Eyed, Greer knew she would never again think of Lachlan as the apex of anything.

"Was that ... what ... what was that?" he whispered, sounding like a little boy woken in the thrall of a night terror. His hand trembled, tightening painfully around hers. She tried to loosen his grasp, but it was as if an iron vise had clamped around her.

"Lachlan," she prompted. "Lachlan, your hand."

He didn't hear, his focus still sharp on the trees ahead of them. Greer had seen that look once before when hunting with Hessel, a doe sensing their approach, frozen with anxious vigilance. A sheen of sweat broke over Lachlan's brow despite the cold.

He's just realized he's not the predator but the prey.

"Lachlan," she tried again, pushing herself to her feet. She needed to break him from his spiraling thoughts. They needed to act fast if there was any hope of saving Ellis.

Ellis.

Just the thought of his name stopped all momentum. Her heart ached, and she wanted to burst into tears. How had this day gone so dismally wrong? They should be at Steward House, starting the Joining Ceremony, becoming husband and wife. But she was here, with Lachlan Davis of all people, and *how had Ellis gotten past the Stones*?

She yanked at Lachlan's arm, jerking him from his tortured reverie. "We need to go. We need to find the Stewards. We need a plan."

"A plan?" Lachlan repeated slowly, doubtfully. "A plan for what?"

Disbelief colored her laugh "To form a search party. To go after Ellis."

Even as she said it, Greer knew it wasn't happening.

Not tonight.

Not until dawn's rays broke the horizon and the Warding Stones' hold loosened.

As if hearing her thoughts, Lachlan stepped toward the Stones, dragging Greer along with him. "How did he do it? How did Beaufort do it? Is the boundary gone?" With his free hand, he reached out, feeling at the invisible wall.

Greer shook her head, wincing against the inevitable onslaught. "It's not, it's still there, it's still—"

The wind rose up, hitting them like an explosion of thunder. They were cast back, nothing more than leaves caught in a storm. Lachlan tried again, choosing another spot. Again, the wind howled. Again, they were thrown. Again and again and again and again.

"Stop it!" Greer howled, bruised and bloodied. Every bit of her ached, and she wanted to scream at how stupid he was. "The line is still there. It's not going to let us through, no matter how many times you run at it!"

"Then how did he do it?" Lachlan snarled, whipping round on her. "I've never been able to cross over that damned line, not once in my life, but then fucking Beaufort somehow does it? How? *How?*"

"I don't know!" Greer admitted, fighting tears. "You saw it happen. He just . . . He stepped into the forest. No wind. No barrier. He was just . . ."

"Gone," Lachlan supplied the word she would not say.

"Yes."

He turned back to the forest, fresh horror growing over his face. "Do you suppose *it* can cross the line, too? The Bright-Eyed? If Beaufort could, then . . ."

A shudder ran through Greer.

Lachlan fell to his knees as he struggled to draw breath, finally releasing his hold on her. Greer surprised herself by kneeling beside him. She rubbed circles across his back, recalling how Ailie had so often done this for her, talking Greer through times when the world felt too loud, when all the sounds and noises threatened to rise up and overwhelm her.

"Breathe in through your nose, out through your mouth," she coached. His chest sounded wet and ragged, and he trembled beneath her touch.

"It can't be, it can't be," he whispered, over and over, until the words ran together, bleeding into one long stream of panic.

Greer pressed against his curved frame as she tried to catch his eye, tried to give him something to focus on through the haze of dread. "What? What can't?"

When he finally looked up, something in his stare made her insides curdle.

"If the Benevolence let that thing go after one of us—even if it was a Beaufort—then Mistaken's truce must have broken."

15

It took Greer nearly an hour to drag Lachlan out of the Hunting Grounds.

Darkness had claimed the sky, and, without a lantern, navigating their way through the brambled wood was nearly impossible. Lachlan was no help, leaning so heavily against Greer's side it was a struggle to keep him upright. She wondered if he'd slipped into shock, if seeing a Bright-Eyed had somehow jarred his mind loose.

Finally, Greer spotted the bright dots of dozens of lanterns, lined up just beyond the gate, warming the area and holding back the night. It seemed the entirety of Mistaken was waiting for them.

"I see something!" cried the small voice of a child. "They're coming! They're coming!"

As they approached the fence, Lachlan staggered forward, caught on a tree root or perhaps his own foot, and grabbed Greer. "What was that? Is it the monsters?" he gasped, sounding panicked.

Greer tried to shove him away but his hold was firm. "Stand up," she hissed. "We're nearly home. Nothing is after you."

"Greer?" Hessel cried out, lost somewhere in the sea of glowing lights. "Is that Greer?"

"And Lachlan . . . I think." Greer recognized the alto of Imogene Davis—Lachlan's mother.

Hessel fought his way to the front, swinging open the gate. "They're back!" he confirmed, sounding happier than Greer could ever recall. "Are you both all right? When Third Bellows sounded, and you'd not come back . . ."

The words left unspoken pricked at Greer.

"We're all right," Lachlan said, even as his grip tightened.

"No," Greer began. "Ell—"

Hessel clapped his hands, drawing the town's attention. "The last of the couples have returned. Our Hunt is at an end!"

Greer looked sharply to Lachlan, still clutching her arm. Sensing the weight of the town's eyes upon him, he'd straightened, and his hold now looked more protective than needy. She turned to her father, protest bubbling from her diaphragm. "We are not a couple. He did not claim me!"

Hessel slapped a proud hand across Lachlan's back. "Well done, son."

And Lachlan . . . smiled.

Greer gaped as the curve of his mouth deepened into a wide grin. More men stepped forward, offering out handshakes and their congratulations. It seemed their adoration for the town's favorite son overrode any reservations they held for Greer.

"Lachlan didn't find me," she reiterated, raising her voice. "Lachlan, tell them. Tell them what we saw!" He ignored her. "Father," she said, turning to Hessel and pulling him from the crowd. "Something horrible happened out there. Ellis is gone."

For one terrible moment, Hessel did not react. He only stared at her, listening for more, as if her words were not news but confirmation.

He knows. He already knew.

"Gone?" Hessel finally asked, carefully schooling his tone.

"Just after Thirds, Ellis crossed over the border and went into the forest," she said anyway, wanting to watch him hear it. "He wasn't thrown back."

"That's not possible."

"I thought that, too, but it happened all the same. And then . . ." Greer paused, her throat tightening as she remembered the thing in the sky that had followed. "And then a Bright-Eyed went after him."

She expected him to deny it. She expected him to say she'd misunderstood or imagined what she'd seen. Hessel surprised her by doing neither.

"You're certain? It was a Bright-Eyed?"

Lachlan, suddenly aware of Greer's absence, turned to join them. "I saw it as well. It went after Beaufort."

Greer marveled at Lachlan's composure, as if he'd not spent their return journey cowering from every strange noise, every looming shadow. He pantomimed the Bright-Eyed's girth, the width of its wingspan, then curved all his fingers, approximating talons.

It had four toes, not five, Greer silently corrected, remembering when she'd first seen it swoop out of the clouds. *Not two.*

"Well." Hessel let out a long breath. "Beaufort made his choice."

She let out a short, choking laugh. "What choice? No one just leaves Mistaken. Not after sunset."

Hessel frowned at her outburst. "It must have happened *before* sunset. The Bright-Eyed took him *before* Third Bellows." His tone was even and reasonable, as though they were disputing nothing more than the price of wheat at market.

Greer shook her head, anger filling her jaw and urging her to snap and bite. "No. No. That's not how it happened. Ellis left after the Bellows. I saw him. I heard the last horn, and he stepped over the border, and the Stones did not throw him back. And the Bright-Eyed . . ." She shuddered. "The Bright-Eyed didn't take him. It stalked after him. Ellis is still alive! Lachlan!" She looked to the young man, waiting for him to confirm what they'd seen.

Instead, he rubbed cloying circles across her back. "She has a right to be upset." Lachlan glanced to Hessel. "It was all terribly confusing."

She squirmed against the patronizing strokes. "Get your hands off me."

"The sun had set, and it was so cloudy," Lachlan went on. "So many things going on. Ellis being snatched up. Me claiming you." He tried to take her hand, but she jerked from his grasp. "It's no wonder she's confused."

"That's not how it happened, and you know it!" Greer snarled. "Ellis is out there, in the woods now, with that Bright-Eyed tracking him. He needs help."

Hessel made a sound of disbelief. "How exactly do you propose we offer it?" He gestured toward the hill behind them, up to where the Bellows lay. "As you say, it's after Thirds. *We* can't cross the border. Not as Mr. Beaufort did. Apparently," he added.

Greer clenched her fingers. "At sunrise. We need to go after him at sunrise. We should ready our packs now. Food and water and medical supplies. Ropes. Weapons. Maps!" she exclaimed. "I'll get every one I have, and we'll divide them among the search parties."

Hessel's expression softened, turning to pity. "If what you saw was truly a Bright-Eyed, then there's no need to go after the boy," he said, picking his words gently. "There won't be anything left to find."

"He's not dead!" Greer said, bristling.

She didn't think he was dead. She couldn't imagine a world in which he was dead.

I'd know if one half of my heart had stopped beating. I would.

"Then where is he?" Hessel asked, looking around the crowd as if he expected the young man simply to step forward. "The Bellows have sounded; the sun has set. If the boy was alive, he would have been tossed over the town line. Those are the rules. So where is he?"

"He's out there!" Greer shouted, pointing toward the forest. "Somehow. He's out in the wilds, and we need to help him. Please. Someone must believe me." She scanned the cluster of people gathering to listen. Their faces ranged from curious to indifferent to skeptical. Her hope withered. She would find no assistance here. "Fine. I'll go after him myself. I'll—"

Greer stopped short as she caught sight of one of Ellis's brothers, standing at the outer edge of the group. His freckled face was shadowed with worry.

"Rhys!" she exclaimed, and pushed her way to the boy. Even as she grabbed hold of his upper arms, she knew she was using too much force. He looked terrified, not of the situation, but of her. Greer tried to rein in her rising panic. "Where is Louise? Is she all right?"

Wildly, Rhys glanced around, trying to find help, but no one stepped in to save him. "She . . . she's at home. Taking care of Ma."

"She was supposed to be in the Hunt. Why wasn't she in the Hunt?" Greer demanded.

He shrugged helplessly.

"When did you last see Ellis? When did—"

"Greer." Hessel's hand fell heavily upon her shoulder. "You're scaring the lad. Leave him be."

"Why didn't Louise hide in the Hunt? You said she must, but then she didn't. She didn't, and now Ellis is gone. It doesn't make any sense. None of this day has made any—"

Hessel made a gesture, and Ian Brennigan and Michael Morag stepped forward to break her hold on the younger Beaufort.

"Let me go!" she demanded, thrashing against the Stewards, trying to catch her father's gaze. She knew she was making a scene, making the situation so much worse, but no one would listen to her. "You spoke to Ellis; I know you did! What did you say to him? What did you *do*?"

Hessel clucked, shaking his head. He looked toward the rest of the town, his face unreadable even to Greer. "It has been a long and strange evening. In light of the . . . unexpected events of the past few days . . . I think it best to hold off on the Joining Ceremony until tomorrow afternoon. Let us meet at Steward House before sunset, to celebrate the blessed union of so many happy couples." He nodded, as if convincing himself as much as the group. "We will meet tomorrow, Mistaken."

"Tomorrow?" Lachlan repeated, sounding on the verge of pouting.

Hessel turned to Lachlan. "Don't worry, son. She's exhausted and not thinking clearly. She'll be ready for you tomorrow."

16

To Greer, the lock's tumblers fell in place as loudly as thunder. She tried the handle anyway. She tried shaking it, rattling it loose, but the Mackenzie cabin had been made of felled Redcaps, and the study's door was thick and strong.

"You can't just lock me in here!" she shouted, slamming her palm against the wood. "Let me out!"

"This day was too much for you. You don't look well. You need rest, food. Martha will . . ." Hessel stopped short and sighed. "I . . . I'll get you something."

Even through the door, Greer heard his footsteps retreat to the kitchen. She heard him speak to the Stewards. She listened as they discussed her claims, trying to piece them together with the lies Lachlan had told.

"And she saw the boy die?" Enoch MacÀidh asked. "We're certain of it?"

"It was too much for her mind, poor girl," Hessel affirmed. "She needs to be kept somewhere safe, where she can't harm herself. I'd have Martha keep watch, but she's still at the Sturgettes' house. I couldn't think of anything better than . . ." His voice trailed away, as he undoubtedly glanced toward the study with trumped guilt.

"Ellis isn't dead!" Greer howled, banging on the door. It stung, but she hit it again, wishing it was a Steward's face, and again for good measure. "We need to go after him. We need to . . ." In a nauseating rush, her adrenaline drained away, leaving Greer as hollowed as a cored apple. "He's not dead."

Exhaustion made her head spin, and she stumbled away from the door, sank into the chair behind Hessel's desk, and rubbed her eyes. Her lashes were full of grit and dried tears. Only hours ago, she'd been in Ellis's arms, happy and hopeful and kissing him before the start of the Hunt.

How had everything gone wrong so quickly?

She had no doubt Hessel would hold her here until tomorrow's Joining Ceremony, but what then? Would Lachlan try the same? Would he keep her under lock and key, penning her in place like an errant sheep?

Greer's eyes flashed open and scanned the room for options.

She stared at the door, wondering if she could pick its lock. She was certain she could align the mechanism's tumblers just so, listening to them clink into place, but that wouldn't help if the entire council of Stewards were in the cabin. Even with the element of surprise, there were too many of them; they were sure to overpower her.

There was a window in the study, but it was heavily paned with lead tracings, and Greer didn't think she'd be able to shimmy her way through the frame, even if she could find a way to break the glass quietly.

"There must be something," she muttered, drumming her fingers on the side of the chair.

The room was littered with ledgers and journals, papers and maps. One entire wall was lined with books, crammed like silvery fish in jars of pickled brine. Each tome's spine was stamped with the mark of the Stewards, indicating town records, accounts of events and meetings. They would be no help to her at all.

A little woodstove took up one corner of the study. It was unlit. Could Greer feign a chill and dash out while a Steward was occupied with the kindling? Her escape played across her imagination—she'd race through the garden to the trees, where she'd hide till sunrise, then cross the border to Ellis.

But Greer's boots, hat, and cloak had been stripped from her as she'd entered the house. She couldn't possibly grab them all before being intercepted.

Frustrated, she slammed her fist on the edge of the desk, rattling Hessel's wells of ink. She hit it again, just to revel in her minute act of defiance, but stopped short when her ears caught the soft click of something opening. Something near her feet.

Curious, Greer slipped from the chair and knelt on the floor. Her pounding had released a catch, revealing a small door hidden within the desk's footwell.

She paused, cocking her head toward the door, worried that her clattering might have drawn attention. She waited for approaching footsteps, but, deep in conference over the day's events, neither Hessel nor the other Stewards seemed aware of her at all.

Greer reached into the hollowed space and felt about blindly. She tried to not imagine a horde of spiders lurking in the darkness, ready to skitter up her arm. The hidden section seemed to run the entire length of the desk, and she had to stretch to reach its end, where she just barely touched the edge of something small and wooden. With a grunt of effort, she managed to grab it and bring it into the light.

It was a box, narrow and long and covered in intricate carvings Greer did not understand. She used her thumbnail to flip it open and blinked against a sudden burst of light.

The inside was a disordered mess of leather cording and bits of dazzling sparkles. When Greer pulled one of the strings free, she realized they were pieces of jewelry, necklaces and bracelets. But, rather than diamonds or emeralds, rubies or pearls, or any of the other precious gems Greer had read of but never seen for herself, the baubles were woven clusters of beads. Each one shone and sparkled with the same otherworldly luminescence as the town's Warding Stones.

She scooped them out, let them tangle through her fingers. The pieces looked familiar, stirring a whiff of a memory, but she couldn't fully grasp where or when she'd seen them.

With the box emptied, Greer noticed that a bit of its lining was flaking free. She toyed with it, picking at the edge, as she wondered over the mystery of the stone beads. She knew they must be important—why else would Hessel have hidden them away with such care?—but she couldn't begin to sift through their significance.

It wasn't until the box's entire lining had pulled away that Greer realized it wasn't a bit of decorative paper at all but a clever cover, concealing a small journal, only a few dozen pages thick and tiny enough to fit into the palm of her hand. Setting the jewelry aside, Greer opened the book. Its spine cracked with brittle age.

She scanned through the pages, eyes glossing over the old-fashioned script as she tried to discern its meaning.

The book was a list, made up of three columns: one for years, one for names, and the last enigmatically labeled as "Effects." The handwriting changed over time, and Greer had to squint to make out some of the notations. But when she turned another page, she instantly recognized Hessel's spidery scrawl take over.

1754: Catriona Belfour.

In the "Effects" column, Hessel had jotted a series of symbols, geometric shapes hexed through with various slashes. Neither they, the name, nor the date meant anything to Greer. She knew of the Belfour family—they owned a parcel of land to the south of the Mackenzies' farm—but there was no Catriona among them.

She looked at the entry on the next page.

1761: Agnes McKintney.

Greer sank back on her heels, thinking. She had a few memories of the older girl, but they were vague and hazy. Though she could picture her at the blackboard in the schoolhouse, strawberry-blond hair pinned into careful braids, Greer couldn't remember the last time she'd seen Agnes or even thought of her.

Questions piled up, like stones forming a house, and she frowned, looking over the dates with fresh eyes.

1761 had been a Hunt year, the one Greer was first meant to have been in. Who had caught Agnes? Greer ticked through as many of the Hunters as she could remember, but each had found some other bride. Agnes had not been found. Agnes had not been caught.

So where was she now?

As Greer tried to wrestle memories from that murky, grief-shrouded year, she turned the page and caught sight of the list's final entry. Everything within her stopped.

1768: Ellis Beaufort.

She studied the curls and loops of her beloved's name, jotted down in Hessel's familiar hand.

Ellis Beaufort.

Why would her father have written his name? What did this list account for?

Catriona and Agnes are gone, and now Ellis is, too.

Greer looked from the book to the pile of jewelry, trying to piece it all together. They were connected somehow, but she was too exhausted to see it. She rubbed at her aching forehead, and as her hand fell away, the memory came to her.

In the clearing, as he'd waved farewell, Ellis's wrist had glinted, a flickering of light she'd ignored at the time because she'd been so intent on catching his eye. But there had been a telltale flash of red. She was sure of it.

Ellis had been wearing one of these bracelets.

She let this idea sink in, mulling over its implications.

Ellis had been wearing one of these bracelets when he'd crossed over the boundary line, after sunset, and the Warding Stones had not brought him back.

Hessel had a whole box of these bracelets in his study, secreted away with a list of missing people. A list of missing girls, then Ellis.

Which meant . . .

"Oh, Father," she whispered. "What have you done?"

17

BY THE TIME Hessel returned to the study, bringing Greer a tray of food, pale-gray light had begun to brighten the horizon. Greer had already returned everything, tucking the box back into its hidden drawer.

Everything but one piece of jewelry.

She'd selected a necklace, hiding it beneath her dress and sweater. The cord was long, and the beads hung between her breasts, a cold mass that felt uncomfortably present against her bare skin. Greer had the terrible notion that the flickering might shine through her layers of wool.

"I thought you'd be hungry," Hessel said, setting down the tray of cold cuts of smoked venison, a hunk of bread slathered with too much butter, and a mug of cider. She noted he hadn't brought a knife or fork.

Greer reclined in the great leather chair behind the desk, her legs kicked irreverently over one arm. Hessel remained standing, clearly waiting for her to leave the chair, but she stayed put, eyes fixed on the partially open door. Had his hands truly been so full, or was this an attempt to see if she'd run?

After a beat, Hessel took the smaller chair. "You don't look like you've slept at all," he continued, as if this had been his intended arrangement all along.

She remained silent.

"You should try to rest before the ceremony." Hessel cleared his throat, unnerved by her stillness. Greer had never seen him so disquieted before, so eager to fill a void. "For what it's worth . . . I am sorry about the boy, Greer. It's a terrible loss for his family." Hessel sighed. "And for you, I suppose . . . in this moment. But you'll see. Things like this always happen for a reason." He nodded, and she wasn't sure whom he was assuring. "For a good reason."

Anger simmered just below her sternum, radiating down her limbs, and she had to press her arms tightly to her chest to keep from lashing out. "For the good of the town?" Greer scoffed.

Hessel's eyes brightened, until he noticed her sarcasm. "You don't see it now, but yes."

Greer sat up, placing her feet on the ground as she leaned toward her father. "Why wasn't Louise at the Hunt?"

It was Hessel's turn to fall silent.

"The Stewards denied her request to sit it out. They said she had to hide. But then *she* spent the day at home, and *Ellis* somehow stepped out into the wilderness after sunset. Why? *How?* What did you do?"

"I?"

"Who else? You set it all up. You forced him into some sort of bargain. Louise could stay with Mary if he . . . if he—what?—didn't come find me?"

His gaze fell, and Greer knew she'd guessed right. She studied him as though he were a stranger. He felt like one. She knew he disliked Ellis. She knew he wanted someone different for her. But she hadn't thought him capable of . . . whatever *this* was.

She willed the tears pricking at her eyes to not fall. "Do you really hate him so much?"

Hessel considered the question. "I don't . . . I don't hate him. But I will admit . . . I was cheered it was Beaufort who went into the woods yesterday."

She felt the heaviness of the beaded necklace against her chest. Hessel didn't know that she knew of the jewelry, that she'd figured out what the baubles could do. "You were cheered?"

He blinked.

"You knew he'd go into the woods?" she tried, pressing for a response.

"Of course I did."

She shook her head. "But that's impossible. Crossing over the border is impossible."

"Not as impossible as you think." He glanced toward her. "You're a clever girl; I always thought you'd put it together."

She waited.

"Haven't you noticed there's always someone who doesn't come back from the Hunts?"

Agnes, Greer remembered with ferocious clarity. *Agnes never came home.*

Memories of other girls surfaced. Girls who had to be forced into the Hunting Grounds. Girls who'd screamed and scratched. Girls who'd claimed they'd rather die than be caught. "The girls who run."

Hessel frowned but nodded. "They usually are girls, I suppose. I . . . I wanted to wait till you and Lachlan were more settled into family life, once he was ready to take on more responsibilities, to join the Stewards, but . . ." He sighed, as if it couldn't be helped. "What do you know about the truce?"

Greer felt herself shrug. "Only what the Stewards say."

"Enlighten me."

She shifted uncomfortably, and recited the story with rote efficiency. "When the settlers arrived . . . there were all sorts of dangers. The wind and the flies, the cold and the ice. There were predators—wolves, white bears, wolverines. Lynxes and cougars. The Bright-Eyes. But then the Benevolence came, and the founders saw how powerful they were. They begged for their help, and the truce was struck. They promised to give us their protection."

They trapped us here.

Greer didn't say those words aloud but couldn't stop them from darting across her mind, like a sneaky mouse racing along the baseboards.

"And in return we give them?"

She furrowed her brow, incredulous that he wanted her to answer such a question. "Our gratitudes. The harvests at Reaping."

Hessel's stare was as heavy as a thunderstorm. "Anything else?"

Greer studied his desk as if it might have the answer, then gasped. "Not anything. *Some*thing. Some*one*." Her stomach lurched, feeling sick. "They want one of us. A sacrifice."

Hessel made a sound of surprised pleasure. "I knew my estimation of you was not misplaced."

"What do they do with them?" Greer asked. She could picture the story play out, following her father's hints as clearly as a line on a map. "The Benevolence—what do they do with all the girls who run?"

Hessel had the decency to look uneasy. "It's not as if anyone has ever come back to tell the tale."

"Do they give them to the Bright-Eyeds?"

"I don't know."

"Do *they*? Do you tell those girls what they're running to?"

"Of course not. They're already willing to forfeit their lives. They get what they want, and we do as well. It's a perfect arrangement." He brushed at the knees of his trousers.

"It's barbaric."

"It's necessary," he corrected flatly. "If the founders hadn't agreed to this one little thing, we wouldn't be here. There would be no Stones. The Bright-Eyeds would have hunted us off within a fortnight. One life every seven years for the safety of the town is a payment small indeed."

"You think he's dead," she realized. "Ellis."

Hessel weighed out his response. "You truly saw a Bright-Eyed?"

She nodded. He made a sound of disappointment, but she understood it was not for Ellis.

"Will it count? His sacrifice? If the Bright-Eyed got him before the Benevolence could?"

Her father looked at a loss for words.

"He's not dead," Greer decided. "I'd feel it if he were. Here." She touched her chest and could feel the shape of the necklace beneath her fingertips. A plan began to stir, deep in the recesses of her mind. It wasn't entirely formed yet, but the foundation was being laid, piece by piece, brick by brick.

She had the necklace.

She had her maps.

She just needed . . .

Greer frowned. There was so much she needed. So much she'd be unable to source stuck in this room.

A sound caught her attention then, the padding of footsteps soft and sly. They were too light to be any of the Stewards, too surreptitious. Someone had slipped into their house and was sneaking about.

Greer waited for Hessel to hear the intruder, but he just stared, mulling over her words. She wondered at his oblivious ignorance, and for the first time, instead of envy, she pitied him: how terrible to go through life so completely unaware of what was truly going on around you.

"Perhaps he's not," he finally allowed. "But if Beaufort is alive now, if he somehow managed to survive a night out there, it's only a matter of time. As you said, there's the wind and the cold, the wolves and the bears. The Bright-Eyes."

Greer caught a sharp intake of breath, the clap of fingers over someone's mouth to stifle a whimper. She recognized the pitch and instantly knew the footsteps belonged to Louise.

Louise was here.

Greer's mind raced, putting the last bit of her plan together. How could she let her friend know what she needed without giving her presence away?

"Ellis is alive," she said firmly, more for Louise's benefit than Hessel's. "He's alive, and I'm going after him."

Her father's laughter was short and dark. "He's gone. You need to let him go."

Greer shook her head, seeing a slim chance. "I just need a bag. I'll fill it with my maps, and food and water, and then I'll go after him. You won't have to send anyone with me. I'll go alone."

"You're not going anywhere except down the aisle of Steward House to wed Lachlan Davis," Hessel snapped, his patience waning.

"That. *That* is where you are going. And *this* is where you'll stay till then."

He stood up so abruptly that the wooden chair beneath him clattered over.

Greer heard Louise dart away to keep from being caught. She wanted to cheer as she heard her friend slip out the front door, undetected. She prayed Louise was on her way home, already sorting through what Greer would need.

She narrowed her eyes at Hessel. "I'd rather risk every creature in the whole of the woods than spend even one night as Lachlan's wife."

Cheeks burning with anger, Hessel left the room, slamming the door behind him.

18

Steward House had been hastily decorated with swags of cut greenery and late-blooming yellow poppies. Clusters of candles nestled between the arrangements, and their flames danced as the matrons of Mistaken bustled back and forth, putting final touches on the hall before the ceremony began.

Greer watched them work with Hessel's arm tucked painfully tight around hers, as he and the other Stewards gathered in the entry. With a brightness so fervent it seemed false, the men chatted of the Hunt and the matches made, and tried to guess which couples would have the most agreeable winter. She tried to ignore the playful ribbing and knowing glances directed at her father.

Just behind them were the brides-to-be, each wearing her finest dress and clutching at a sprig of pin cherries. An identical bouquet had been thrust into Greer's hands as she'd entered, along with a handkerchief. Greer absently wondered how many of the tears that were about to fall were ones of joy.

The Hunters clustered close together at the front of Steward House. They'd formed a circle and were all smiles and laughter and hard slaps across one another's backs as they waited.

In between the girls and grooms was the rest of the town. Everyone in Mistaken was expected to attend each Joining Ceremony, pledging to support the new couples as they could, offering helping hands and plenty of grace during the often fraught first year of marriage. Nearly every seat was filled; the benches were packed and overflowing with families and well-wishers.

All but one.

The last row of Steward House, used by generations of Beauforts, was conspicuously empty.

Greer stared warily at the bench while picking apart her nosegay, showering the floor around her with green-needled confetti.

Where were the Beauforts?

At home, grieving Ellis's disappearance, most likely.

But where was Louise?

Greer's entire plan—her stupid, untested, ill-thought plan—was predicated on Louise's understanding her veiled message and packing a bag.

But what if Louise hadn't understood?

What if she had thought Greer mad with her own grief? Louise didn't know what Greer had seen. She didn't know that Ellis had been able to cross the boundary unscathed. She didn't know that Greer could now do the same.

Greer touched the necklace beneath her dress, doubt creeping in.

What if she was mistaken, and the beads didn't work, didn't do what she'd only assumed they must? What if she managed to free herself from Hessel and flee the Joining Ceremony, but was still sent right back into town as sunset fell?

The piling uncertainties scraped her raw, and she scratched at her hands, feeling as if they were breaking into hives.

Greer glanced toward Lachlan, catching him in uproarious laughter, his mouth hanging open, showing too many teeth. He looked carefree and careless, and why shouldn't he be? By all accounts, he'd won. He'd caught his intended and was about to marry the wealthiest, if craziest, woman in town.

Greer's itching fingers balled into fists.

She was not going down that aisle.

Not to him.

Not to anyone who wasn't Ellis.

She'd rather take her chances against the Warding Stones, against the cold and the wolves, against every creature within the woods, even the Bright-Eyes.

She'd rather die first.

As if he could sense the threat to his impending happiness, Lachlan's attention drifted across the room, searching for and finding Greer.

"Good Stewards," he called out, his voice rippling with a self-satisfaction that infuriated Greer, "shouldn't we get the joining under way? We lads grow anxious for the wedding night to come!"

The grooms all laughed, and a scattering of the townspeople joined in, too. Several brides dared to smile, even as they flushed bright red and glanced nervously at one another.

"Of course, of course," Ian Brennigan said. "We all remember such heady eagerness and would hate to prolong your anticipation any longer. Mackenzie, what say you?"

Greer felt her father freeze and heard his breath catch. He was responsible for carrying out the ceremony, but, to begin, he'd need to leave Greer with the rest of the brides, unattended.

She tried to remain as still and impassive as possible, even as her heart began to race, knowing she was on the edge of the precipice.

It didn't matter if Louise didn't show. Greer had on her boots and her warmest cloak. She had her hat and mittens. She had her necklace. She'd make do.

Resolve strengthened her stance.

She could do this. She *would* do this.

Even so, she released a silent sigh of relief as Louise ducked in through the doorway, her younger sister, Norah, close at her heels. Louise guided her through the crowd of brides, all but shoving her to their row.

"It seems your family bench isn't altogether full, Louise Beaufort," one of the Stewards behind Greer noted.

Louise, just about to sit, stopped short and turned to face their group. "No, Steward Wresling. My brothers Rhys and Riley are at home, taking care of Mama. She is, understandably, too distraught to join us."

"Distraught?" Michael Morag echoed. "But this is a happy day."

If Louise was upset about having to explain her family's tragedy, to lay it bare and exposed to the whole of the town, she did not show it. She allowed her hazel eyes to meet the Steward's without shame or anger. "Because of Ellis. Because he disappeared yesterday. Because you all believe him dead."

The room fell into uncomfortable silence.

"Mama's grief has brought her to the point of hysteria, and we thought it best to keep her at home, to avoid creating a scene. Like this," Louise added flatly. "However, if you'd like us to fetch her, so that she, too, might pledge support to all these joyful couples, I can certainly send Norah home. Steward Mackenzie will have to speak rather loudly, though, to be heard over her wailing."

The Steward swallowed. "No. No, I don't believe that will be necessary."

Point made, Louise took her seat beside Norah, her movements deliberately slow and unhurried.

Greer stared at the back of her friend's head, wondering at her thoughts. Louise's neck swiveled as she scanned the room, giving a stern look at anyone caught whispering about her family. Before turning her attention to the front, Louise glanced over her shoulder and offered a discreet nod to Greer.

For a moment, the anxiety plaguing Greer dimmed. One part of her plan had fallen into place.

Hessel tightened his grip around her elbow, as if branding her with a silent warning. "I'll see you at the end of the aisle," he promised, speaking loudly enough to sound like a proud father. Only Greer heard it for what it really was—a thinly veiled threat.

She resisted the impulse to throw out a final retort.

Instead, she met his eyes, wondering if this was the last time she'd ever see him.

Once she found Ellis—and she had no doubt she would—there would be no need to return. With their beaded jewelry, they could go wherever they wanted. Nothing would stop them from wandering to the coast and finding a ship. Greer thought of her bright-blue ink. They could venture there, to that faraway land, and see the peacocks for themselves. Their beads meant that the entire world had suddenly opened to them. Greer felt dazzled by the prospect, enchanted, beguiled.

She just needed to escape Mistaken first.

So Greer said a silent farewell to her father and joined the group of brides, trying to appear as innocent as she could.

Hessel looked as though he were about to say something, looked as if he'd somehow guessed her plan, knew that she'd stolen a necklace, knew what she planned to do with it. But Ian Brennigan slapped at his shoulder, ushering him to the front so that the ceremony might begin.

Greer bided her time, waiting to see what Louise had planned.

Hessel drew the room's attention, welcoming all who had gathered. He commended the couples waiting to be joined and reminded them of their sacred marital duties—to each other and for each other and for the good of the community.

"For the good of Mistaken," the townspeople repeated when prompted, and Norah Beaufort immediately burst into tears.

"How can anything in Mistaken be good now that Ellis is gone?" she sobbed, throwing herself upon Louise, her smaller frame heaving.

"Oh, Norah," Louise began, rubbing at her younger sister's back. "We talked about this, didn't we?" She glanced up as the weight of the room's stares fell upon her. "I'm so sorry. It's just . . . this is all so fresh, so raw."

"He's gone!" Norah wailed, her voice screeching in pitch. "He's gone, and they wouldn't even look for him. Ellis! Ellis!"

Snot bubbled from the youngest Beaufort's nose, and tears streaked her cheeks.

Greer's heart ached for the young girl, and for Louise as she tried to pick her sister up from the bench. She bent in all the wrong angles, too heavy an object to stand on her own.

"I'm so sorry," Louise stammered, all but falling over as Norah began to flail, tossing herself this way and that, trying to escape her sister's grasp. "I think . . . I think it best . . ."

"I think it best you get her home," Hessel said, overriding any suggestion Louise had been about to make. "Under the circumstances, perhaps your family should offer their good wishes in spirit only."

Louise nodded, face scarlet with embarrassment. "Norah, come with me. Norah, *please!*"

But the girl was past the point of reasoning, well beyond propriety. She'd dropped to the ground, a dead weight that Louise could not lift. She pitched back and forth with such fervor that not a single person stood to offer assistance, wary of touching such concentrated grief.

"Norah," Louise tried again, grabbing at her sister's arms and yanking her from the row.

The young girl was a mess of petticoats and stockings. Several women clucked with disapproval, swatting at their husbands and sons to cover their eyes.

Greer stepped forward and, heedless of her fine wool skirts, knelt beside them.

"Norah, it's Greer," she tried, and swerved to avoid being struck by a wayward limb. Norah's wrist caught her cheek anyway and all of the crowd, even Hessel and the Stewards, gasped at the violence of it. "We're taking you outside now, but you need to help us, help Louise."

"No one helped Ellis!" she shrieked, flopping onto her back, her eyes scrunched and streaming.

"Someone get her out of here!" Lachlan exclaimed, annoyance heating his face. "She's ruining the ceremony."

"Sorry," Louise called out again. "I'm so sorry."

Greer left her bouquet on the floor and struggled to scoop Norah into an upright position. Once the girl's arms were around both her and Louise's shoulders, they shuffled into the fading afternoon.

Only once Louise had pulled the door to Steward House firmly shut did Norah straighten, a wicked grin spreading over her face. "Did I do very well?"

Greer hugged the small girl, pressing a kiss to the top of her head. "You were magnificent!"

"There's a bag packed for you along the fence to the Hunting Grounds," Louise said as they crossed into the side yard. "I tried to think through everything you'd need, but there was so much I didn't know."

Greer threw her arms around her friend, imparting her gratitude with the tight squeeze. "You are a wonder! I knew you'd understand! Thank you!"

"Do you really think you'll be able to find Ellis?" She murmured her doubt quietly into Greer's shoulder, keeping her voice too low for Norah to overhear.

"I do," she promised. "I will. I know he's still out there."

Louise looked unconvinced. "Before sunset? I don't understand . . . How will you—how did *he*?"

The door to Steward House opened and Michael Morag peered out. "Greer, they're waiting for you. You'll have to get your sister home yourself, Louise. The ceremony is starting now."

Greer gripped her best friend's shoulders, wishing there was a way to say everything she needed to. But there was no time. There was only—

"Now!" Norah shouted, giving away the ruse with an excited cry. "Run now, Greer!"

19

Greer took off in a sprint and raced across the empty field bordering Steward House.

"Hessel!" Michael Morag called, shouting into the building. "She's running!"

Greer laughed at the sounds of confused commotion as Hessel began issuing orders and Stewards and grooms alike hurried to grab their coats and gloves. They stumbled out of Steward House like a pack of hunting dogs set loose on a fox, baying and howling, hungering for another chase, nearly salivating with cruel excitement.

Greer only dared to glance over her shoulder once, and spotted Louise and Norah cheering her on as the men ran her way. Louise jumped into Lachlan's path, waylaying him as he tried to duck around her.

At the far edge of the field, Greer slipped into a line of tall grasses and made a sharp turn, hoping her pursuers would be too distracted with the thrill of another hunt to notice her change of direction. She wove through tangled thickets and brambled copses, pulled toward the Hunting Grounds like a fish on a hook.

Louise's pack was along the perimeter's fence, mostly obscured by a pile of leaves. The dark canvas bag was full of pockets and straps. Greer pulled it free and hefted it onto her shoulders. It was lighter than she'd hoped, but she had no time to take an inventory of what Louise had rustled up. She'd sort through it later, once she was over the border, once the sun had set and she was no longer being followed.

For now, she slipped through the gate and headed toward the meadow and the Warding Stone she'd watched Ellis pass yesterday.

The air was filled with the sounds of the Hunters. They spread out, breaking into smaller groups. The woods slowed them down, as they combed through the underbrush, scanned twisting thickets, and peered with discerning eyes into the canopy for branches sturdy enough for a girl to climb.

Greer fought back a snort of laughter at their unimaginative assumptions. She wouldn't run from the Joining Ceremony only to hide away like a cowering sparrow. She was escaping. She was breaking the hold Mistaken had on her, had had on them all since the day they were born.

The meadow was up ahead.

The easiest way through would be straight across, but the space was wide open, with no tall grasses or shrubs to hide in. She'd be spotted the moment she stepped out into the field, so she took the long way around, stopping every so often to pause or double back, trying to cover and obscure her trail as best as she could.

She heard Hessel's puffed breaths as he fought his way through the mire of dried creeping vines, the twisting grasps of wisteria stretching along the forest floor like the wires of a poacher's snare. He'd ventured into the woods with several other Stewards and barked out occasional orders, snapping and biting, his fury evident.

Greer had no doubt she'd be able to avoid her father's furious blustering.

But Lachlan Davis . . .

Try as she might, Greer could not pick out his footfalls from the others combing through the woods. She knew he was an experienced hunter, celebrated each season for his sharp skills, his sly methods. He always brought back the biggest bucks, the most pheasants or rabbits or beaver. His family's larders were full of salted fish, of smoked jerkies.

She could not afford to underestimate him.

The sky was heavy and dark when she reached the northern edge of the meadow and finally dared to enter the open space, cutting toward Ellis's point of departure.

She expected to feel a marked difference as she slipped by the Warding Stone. There was always a catch as one left Mistaken, a slight tug as if the border was calling them back, trying to lay its claim. This was felt deep in the bones, a poking at the marrow, a prodding sensation that you were going the wrong way, leaving the safety of the known.

But, wearing the necklace, Greer didn't feel a thing. She went into the dark woods five yards, ten, then twenty, and though she knew sunset was quickly approaching, falling unseen behind a bank of steel-gray snow clouds, her heart didn't quicken with fear. There was no anxiety, no worry. She was not scared of being in these woods. She was not fearful of the night to come.

Ellis's trail was easy to spot in this virgin wood. His heavy boots had left clear marks in the soft ground, and every so often there were snapped twigs in the brush, signs that he'd pushed his way through.

As she went on, the terrain grew rougher, rocky and steep, and after a few minutes spent fighting her way up the angled slope, Greer was panting, her dress warm and damp beneath the thick wool of her cloak.

"What in the Devil's blazes are you doing, Greer?"

She startled at the sound of his voice, as shocking as a gunshot. Lachlan.

"It's nearly sunset—you're going to get us killed," he went on, climbing the embankment as easily as if it were level ground.

Greer kept her eyes low. Ellis's footprints were harder to spot here, and she needed to concentrate. "Go home, Lachlan."

"Not without you," he said, picking up his pace until he was on her heels. He reached out and grabbed at her cloak. "We need to hurry if we're going to get across the border before Thirds."

"You do," she agreed, struggling to wrest herself free of his grasp. "You should. You still have time to turn back. Just go, Lachlan, please, before you get hurt."

He let out a laugh of disbelief. "You'll be tossed back, too."

"I won't," she promised. She didn't have the breath to explain.

"Damn it, Greer." His fingers dug into the underside of her forearm, so hard that Greer could already feel bruises beginning to form. "You're going to get us killed, you stupid girl," he snarled, tugging at her.

"I'm going after Ellis. Save yourself while you still have time."

His molars ground together as he fought to pull her back, back from the hill, across the border, and down the aisle.

"Come on," he snapped and grabbed at her waist. Even with Louise's pack and her heavy winter clothes, Lachlan was able to hoist her over his shoulder as if she were nothing more than a cask of ale, a sack of flour, a lamb on its way to slaughter.

"Let me go!" she ordered, all but screaming as she thrashed against him, kicking out and striking his chest.

"You've already made me a laughingstock. All winter, I'll hear how my bride raced off for the wilds rather than join me on our wedding day. I'm not walking away from this empty-handed."

"I'm not your bride," Greer protested, flexing and squirming and doing everything she could to make Lachlan realize she was not worth the effort. If only she could get free of him. If only her feet were on the ground. She'd drop the rucksack and run.

Sunset couldn't be far off now.

He let out a cry as her knee struck his clavicle. Off balance, his equilibrium thrown, he staggered, careening back toward the ground, taking her with him.

They landed hard, in a heap. Greer scrambled to free herself from under his heavy weight.

"Stop running!" Lachlan demanded. He rolled atop her so that she was pinned in place, unable to flee, unable to fight as he pressed into her ribs and the jut of her hip bones. "Everyone warned me. They said I was making a mistake, setting my sights on Mackenzie's mad bitch of a daughter, but I didn't listen. I thought I knew better. I thought your father's riches would be worth it."

He seized hold of her leg, fingers clamped around her ankle as tight as a vise, and began dragging her down the slope. She twisted, trying to flip to her stomach to protect her head. Lachlan was hauling her down without regard for any rocks or underbrush. She grabbed at anything she could in an attempt to stop him.

His hand came out of nowhere and fell across her cheek with a heavy slap. "You're going to be worth it. I'm going to make all this worth it."

Greer blinked, seeing stars. She'd never been hit before, not in childhood horseplay, not in a schoolyard tussle, not even in the dangerous moments of Hessel's darkest anger. That she had now, by this brute of a boy she was trying to help, made her want to howl.

Fiery anger kindled in the pit of her stomach, smoldering and sharp. It licked its way up her spine, crackling with such an intense, heated pressure that she bared her teeth, loosened her jaw, and let her rage rip its way into the world.

The effect of her scream was immediate.

All around her, trees pitched backward. Small branches were ripped from their trunks, leaving behind fresh wounds of green wood. The air turned visible, rippling into a tight series of waves that shot from her, racing toward the horizon and taking hold of anything in their path.

Struck in the chest, Lachlan went somersaulting down the rest of the hill, tumbling over himself as he was thrown back through the woods, back through the brambles, all the way back across the town border.

He landed in a heap and did not move.

Her voice, pierced so sharp and completely deafening, tore past the Warding Stones and spread over the town of Mistaken. She could picture the scream rocketing to the Great Bay, across its waves to the coast, and out to sea.

She clapped her hands over her mouth, and the sound died.

The seconds after the scream were filled with the most profound silence Greer had ever known.

It was as if the entire world listened with bated breath, cringing and cowering as it waited for what would come next.

She couldn't hear the calls of Hessel or the Stewards, the sounds of the search parties, or the rustles of forest creatures that they stirred up. There was no birdsong, there was no chatter of small beasts. There wasn't even the whistle of the ever-present wind.

There was just . . . nothing.

Then came the notes of Third Bellows, three long blasts announcing the end of another day, the start of another night. Even they sounded cowed, dwarfed by the immense magnitude of Greer's anger and pain.

The Bellows sounded, and the sun set, and Lachlan did not move.

The Bellows sounded, and the sun set, and Greer remained on the far side of the Warding Stones.

Feeling as if her head were stuffed with goose down, Greer picked up her pack and stood.

Movement on the far edge of the clearing caught her attention. It was Hessel.

She saw him see her. She saw him see Lachlan.

As he hurried to the young man's broken body, she turned away with disgust. Let them have each other.

Greer studied the climb ahead of her. She was facing a forest painted unfamiliar by the shades of falling night. In the dark bruise of twilight, she could just make out the tracks of her beloved.

She set off after them, and did not give Mistaken a single backward glance.

PART II

THE WILDS

I am rather inclined to believe that this is the land God gave to Cain.

—JACQUES CARTIER,
   upon first seeing the cliffs of Labrador

20

Night descended swiftly in the woods.

Without the lights of nearby cabins, candle tapers, and oil lamps, without bonfires and hearth embers, the darkness fell over Greer and was not pushed back.

Even the moon and stars hid from her, obscured by an ominous blanket of clouds that smelled like the promise of snow.

"Please don't," Greer beseeched the sky.

Snow would cover every trace of Ellis's tracks. He'd already had an entire day's head start. How could she follow a trail she could not see?

Before the last trace of twilight expired, she stopped and opened the pack.

Right on top, as if Louise had anticipated exactly what Greer would need and when, was an oil lantern—blessedly full—a piece of flint, and a small hatchet. Lit, the lantern's golden glow pushed back the night and allowed her to continue after Ellis's prints.

"Follow his footsteps," she said, speaking aloud. Her voice sounded strange and muffled, as if she'd caught the echoes of something trapped in a deep well. The scream had done something to her ears. She prayed it was temporary.

The Bright-Eyeds weren't the only creatures she needed to worry about in these woods. Wolves and grizzlies roamed here. Lynxes and great horned owls. That white bear Gil Catasch had seen. How could she keep herself safe from such predators if she couldn't hear them coming?

"Doesn't matter," she muttered, coaching herself with firm tenacity. "Just follow Ellis's tracks. Just find him."

If she kept her eyes trained on the ground before her, if she kept her focus on this one task, Greer wouldn't have to think about why her ears were both ringing and terribly numb. She wouldn't have to remember how she'd felt when that scream had ripped free of her throat, of her chest, of her very soul.

She wouldn't have to think about how it had picked up Lachlan and shoved him back, back, back, how its potency had caused everything around her to retreat, as if she was a destructive force of nature, as if she was the very wind itself.

And she certainly wouldn't have to think about how still Lachlan had remained once the scream had stopped.

No.

Hessel was with him. Lachlan was fine.

Maybe.

And Greer had Ellis's tracks to follow.

She would keep her mind focused, and only after she found him would Greer allow herself to remember the way Lachlan's leg had stretched away from the rest of his body, its angle so terribly severe.

She winced. "Follow the trail. Just follow the trail."

Without the moon, it was hard to tell how much time had passed. Her lantern threw out only enough light for her to see paces ahead of her, and she began to feel she was passing by the same series of trees, again and again.

Was she going in circles? What if Ellis's path was nothing but a giant loop, doomed to be repeated over and over until she found him sprawled facedown, dropped dead of exhaustion or torn to bits?

"You're not going in circles," she told herself, as if putting the words out into the night would be enough to make them true. "Keep going. Ellis did."

Greer held out the lantern, brandishing its light as far as she could throw it, and studied the surrounding forest with sharp, discerning eyes.

The uniformity of the pines made her feel as if she were caught in an illusion, like the time she and Louise had lined up two mirrored plates so that their reflections echoed back and forth in an unending cycle, a break in logic and reason.

She'd never seen these trees shrouded in such moody nocturnal shades before, and her throat caught at the singular beauty of the moment. Freed from the Warding Stones' grip, she, Greer Mackenzie, was witnessing something entirely new, that no one in all of Mistaken could lay claim to.

Overcome with a dizzying sense of wonder, Greer dropped to her knees, reached out to the tree nearest her—a black spruce—and bowed her head. For an uneasy moment, her words would not come, too entangled in her lingering sense of guilt that she'd not thought to start her journey with a prayer.

As she waited for the right ones to surface, she closed her eyes and sank into the moment, acknowledging its marvel. She hoped that the Benevolence would feel her reverence, understand her thankful heart, and bless her.

"Guide my steps and keep them swift," she whispered. "Keep the Bright-Eyes far from me, and please"—she squeezed the bark of the spruce, trying to impart the earnestness of her plea—"*please*, keep Ellis safe and bring us together again soon."

A sharp whistle cut through the canopy overhead, and Greer opened her eyes to look up. The sound was high and keening, enough to even break through her muffled fog, but unlike any birdcall Greer had ever heard. She froze, remembering the bats that had come on Reaping night.

"Just an owl," she promised herself. "It's just an owl."

Another cry pierced the night, but this time Greer recognized it.

It was a wolf's howl, coming from somewhere to her south. At first there was just one, but then another joined in, and a third, then a fourth. A whole pack. Their notes lingered in the icy air, the mournful pitches sending shivers of fear down Greer's spine.

She pictured them poised on the edge of a cliff, surveying their kingdom with wide chests and massive paws, heads full of yellow eyes and sharp teeth.

Trappers who had wandered into Mistaken, becoming caught within the Warding Stones, had said the wolves around their cove were different from the ones they'd hunted before.

They grew bigger. Meaner.

But the thing that scared the trappers most was the wolves' intelligence.

"Certainly smarter than me," Baptiste Moreau had once warned, seated at a campfire while Mistaken celebrated a Hunter's Moon.

Lachlan had scoffed it off, saying that—by his estimation of Baptiste—that wasn't a lot.

Giving the tree one final touch, Greer set off, quickening her pace.

She hiked for hours. Her knees throbbed, and the pack's straps were just uneven enough to cut welts against her shoulders. Her eyes ached from squinting against the lantern's light.

Still, she went on.

She stumbled up more embankments, tripped over unseen tree roots and leaf-covered rocks.

Only when she came upon the remains of a fire circle did Greer pause. She studied the area, hungry for details. The campsite looked fresh and undisturbed. Ellis had stopped here, this small clearing edged in fallen logs, and built up a fire. His prints were all over the ground.

Greer spotted a bower of branches, its shape formed too perfectly to have been tossed there by the wind. Several limbs were propped upright, creating a protective lean-to. Ellis had made this nest and rested here, sleeping upon a bed of pine needles.

She knew she should press onward, knew she would be able to catch up with him sooner if she didn't stop. But the bed looked so tempting, and the remnants of his fire invited her to set it ablaze once more. He'd already done the work. She just needed to create one small spark.

Only once the fire was going, its flames big enough to warm Greer's chilled limbs, did she begin to look through the rest of her pack.

Besides the flint and hatchet, there was a loaf of bread wrapped in brown paper and twine, as if Ellis had just brought it home from the bakery, and some sort of jerky—Greer sniffed and guessed it might be venison. There was a small set of cooking tools—a pot, a plate, a metal cup—and a canteen of water, already filled. Greer took a long, grateful swig. Squashed at the bag's bottom was a cache of clothing, including a spare set of mittens and a heavy flannel shirt. It was a dark blue-and-green plaid, her favorite of Ellis's. She removed her cloak and slipped the shirt over her dress. It was far too big, but felt soft and warm and smelled of Ellis. She snuggled in its comforting familiarity for a moment before throwing her cloak over it.

The rucksack's inner pockets contained a small knife, a compass, and—to her great delight—an extra set of socks. She scrunched her fingers into the plush wool, smiling as she imagined Mary knitting these, wholly unaware that Greer would one day use them to go after her son.

As exhaustion set in, Greer fell into the bed of pines, stretching. She shifted back and forth, trying to find a comfortable position. She would rest for only a few hours, and then head out.

Something rustled beneath her.

Her eyes flashed open, and she rolled over, pawing at the branches.

There, nestled in the greenery, was a folded square of paper.

As she flattened it open, Greer's breath caught.

It was a map, the one Ellis had gotten off the merchant captain only days ago. The one Greer assumed had been lost forever in the chaos of the barn-warming night.

Ellis had saved it.

Ellis had taken it with him.

And, against all likelihood, Ellis had used it to leave her a note.

She scanned his penciled words with hungry eyes, devouring each syllable. It felt as if he was speaking directly to her. She could almost hear the rich warmth of his baritone.

Greer,

I hope that one day these words will make their way to you. I hope they bring you comfort. I pray they do not cause grief. I have ventured off into the northern wilds to serve as a sacrifice for the Benevolence. I do this for the town, yes. For the people of Mistaken, certainly. But more than anything, I'm doing it for you. The Stewards have explained everything to me, the way the pact with the Benevolence was formed, what they expect of us, and all the terrible dangers that can come when our side of the bargain is not met. Don't mourn me, Greer. I go willingly. I go for you. All I've ever wanted was for you to be happy and loved and safe. You've always had my heart. Now you'll have my protection, too.

I'm leaving this here because I know you well enough to be certain you'll come looking for me. I want you to find and read these words, and then I want you to turn around and go home. Don't try to save me from my decision. It was freely made, freely given.

I've written this on a map to show that, though it might feel as though we're worlds apart, here on this paper it's only a matter of inches, just the spread of a hand. I take comfort in imagining that I will be able to hold out my hand and feel yours reaching, too.

Be happy, Greer, and, please, after you read this, forget me. Forget me and live the best life you can. For both of us.

Ellis

Hot tears welled in Greer's eyes but fell cold, freezing in the icy air and sobering her thoughts. She read through the letter once again, then a third time, trying to lessen the sting of his words with repetition.

He didn't want her going after him. He told her to turn tail and go home. Told her to forget him. As if that would be so easy. As if she could simply choose to exist without her other half.

"I can't, Ellis." Her whispered breath steamed around her in the frosty air. "I can't forget. I will never give up. I'm coming for you."

She turned her attention toward the map, squinting as she tried to place where she was now. Mistaken was in the lowlands, sandwiched between the Great Bay and the start of the Severing Mountains. Their elevation rose gently at first, then by leaps and bounds.

Worry quickened within her. If Ellis was headed into the mountains, it would be nearly impossible to follow him. She had no snowshoes, no ropes, no spikes for her boots. Could she catch up with him before he ventured past the foothills?

On a good day—traveling through areas of the forest that she knew—Greer could cover twenty thousand paces, if she left Mistaken's border the moment the sun rose and slipped over it again just seconds before Third Bellows sounded. But Ellis did not often go on these expeditions with her. Ellis would not know these woods. He would be moving slower, searching for the best path, drawn toward . . . what exactly?

She thought of the great black-and-white geese that flew overheard with the changing of seasons. Even before experiencing a migration, they were pulled south, following an urge, ancient and unescapable. Did Ellis feel that now, that tug toward the Benevolence?

She took out the compass and looked into the darkness where the red arrow pointed. Ellis had said only a matter of inches separated them. Wistfully, she reached out her hand, wishing it was that easy. Greer squeezed her eyes shut and imagined his hand stretching to hold hers, too.

For one wondrous moment, it felt as if fingers wrapped around hers, as warm and big and enveloping as Ellis Beaufort's heart, and Greer sobbed, knowing it was only her imagination.

"Ellis?" she dared to ask anyway, and tightened her grip, wanting to hold on to this phantom trace of him forever.

Horrifyingly, the fingers around hers squeezed back.

With a gasp, Greer's eyes flashed open, but her hand was as empty as the sky above.

21

GREER WOKE TO a world of blinding white.

Snow had fallen as she slept, nestled away in her layers of wool and pine boughs. The fire had gone out, doused by either the falling flakes or Greer's inattention.

She sat up, muscles aching in protest.

She needed to get the fire going again.

She needed to eat.

She desperately needed to relieve herself.

Stumbling from her makeshift bed, Greer found a spot downhill and squatted.

The clouds had cleared after dropping their inconvenient drifts, and the sky was a soft silver, heralding the approach of a new day. The snow wasn't particularly deep, but it covered every trace of Ellis and would make tracking him nearly impossible. She considered it a small favor that the snow would make it just as hard for Hessel to follow her.

If he was following.

If he hadn't thoroughly washed his hands of her after yesterday.

After the scream.

In the cold light of this stark morning, Greer had nothing to distract her thoughts from that scream. Taking a deep breath, she pushed out the most ferocious noise she could. It was a cross between a snarl and a growl, but it was nothing compared with the deafening blast that had torn out of her yesterday, setting the world to tremble and throwing an entire person a quarter of a mile back.

How had she done it? Where had it come from? She'd never felt anything like it within her before: an all-consuming, all-powerful, indignant righteous rage. Greer couldn't have held it in if she'd wanted to, and in that moment, she had very much not wanted to. She'd wanted it out, wanted it free to push and shove with more force than she'd ever been capable of. She'd wanted to be heard.

But it wasn't natural.

It wasn't right.

If everyone could scream like that, the world would descend into chaos. It would end in a fury of sound shaking the very core of the earth apart.

Dark thoughts pounded in Greer's mind.

What was wrong with her, that she could make such a mark with only the quiver of her voice?

No one else could hear like she could. No one else could scream like that.

Greer wished Ailie was with her. Ailie, her mind only ever half rooted in the here and now. Ailie, always dreaming up stories and sad songs in which anything was possible, in which the sound of a girl's voice could bring a mountain down.

Greer wished she could nestle into the crook of her mother's shoulder and whisper all these terrible worries. Ailie would laugh and press a kiss her to her forehead and assure Greer that everything was fine. That Greer herself was fine. She'd have an answer for it all.

Without Ailie, Greer returned to the campsite, stewing in her worries. She ate a few bites of the bread and a little of the jerky. Her stomach protested, but she ate anyway, knowing she'd need energy for the day to come.

As she ate, she studied the map.

There was a river a little way from where she estimated she was. The muffled haze in her ears had faded in sleep, and Greer could pick out the soft rush of water some miles away, its current too fast to have frozen yet. It would make sense for Ellis to have gone toward that.

Without a map—his own left for Greer—the river would be the easiest landmark to locate.

She traced the river's path northward, following the way it cut through the foothills, winding down from the mountains. Despite everything, a thrill of delight shot through her as she imagined hiking its length. Every step she'd take on this journey was one step farther from Mistaken, farther from anything she'd ever known. She'd catch up to Ellis, and then . . .

Her fingers spread across the width of the map, wonder stirring her blood.

They could go anywhere. See anything. See *everything*.

They could find what lay beyond the edge of this map, and the map after that, and the map after that. They could explore the entire globe if the fancy struck them. They'd have their beads and they'd have each other. Nothing would stop them.

Greer repacked the bag, but slipped the knife into her skirt pocket. She kept out the map, too, and clutched the compass with a fierce grip.

Ignoring the lingering ache in her shins, Greer stood. She was ready.

It wasn't until she turned to stamp out her fire that she noticed the tracks in the snow.

They were on the far edge of the campsite, as if whoever—whatever—had made them had wished to remain in the shadows, away from the fire's glow.

They were big.

Bigger than the pads of a lynx or a wolf. Bigger even than the tracks Greer had once seen of a rogue grizzly bear, and those had made dinner plates seem small.

Like the marks Greer had noticed in the woods with Louise, these prints boasted only two toes. She followed their progress around the campsite, gnawing at the side of her cheek as she took in the muddled mess of them near the lean-to. Here, the marks were pressed in deeply enough to mix with the earth beneath. Whatever made these tracks had stood there a long while, swaying from foot to foot.

It watched me sleep, she realized hollowly, her throat tightening with dismay.

This creature had stood scant feet away from where she'd rested, and she—the woman who heard absolutely everything—had not noticed.

Greer remembered the strange sensation she'd felt last night, when she held out her hand, hoping to feel Ellis also reaching for her. Fingers had slipped around hers, squeezing tight—she was certain of it now—but it had not been the hand of her beloved.

"Who's out there?" she called loudly, boldly, the way you were supposed to when confronted by a predator. You were supposed to make them think you were every bit as strong and powerful as they were. You were supposed to convince them that you could put up a fight. You were supposed to show them you were not to be messed with.

Far from home, with nothing but a little dagger and a dull hatchet, Greer did not feel formidable. She did not feel strong or—in that moment, staring at the tracks beside her exposed lean-to—particularly brave. But she would not give that away. She could not let the creature—Benevolent or Bright-Eyed—suspect.

So she hoisted her pack and set out for the river.

22

THE SUN ROSE into a day so blue it was almost painful to take in.

It was bracingly cold, and the wind whipped through the pines, stinging the exposed skin of Greer's cheeks, but she pushed on, checking her compass, checking the map, and keeping her ears sharply attuned for the roaring rush of the river.

Without clouds to obscure her view, she could chart the sun's arc and guess at the time of day, allowing her to mark her pace as she ventured deeper into the woods.

They were far busier than she expected, so late in the season. Squirrels raced through the canopy above her, hurrying to gather the last nuts and berries of the year. Snowshoe hares darted in and out of thickets, leaving soft tracks to mark their progress. White-tailed deer crept on impossibly long and slender legs, their liquid eyes startling as they caught sight of Greer.

Every hour or so, Greer would pause to drink from the canteen, quenching her thirst before refilling the flask with handfuls of snow. It would melt as she hiked, ensuring she never grew dehydrated.

During one of these breaks, she took a moment to remove her pack and stretch out on a length of fallen tree. She rolled her shoulders back and forth, letting her spine flex and crack. Satisfied, Greer reached down for her canteen, then shrieked as she caught sight of what she'd grabbed instead.

It was a length of white bone. A jaw, studded with teeth. She pitched it far from her, and it landed in a clump of ferns.

"Just a deer," Greer reassured herself. "It was just a—"

She glanced down, looking for the rest of the skull. Hot bile filled her throat, its sudden bite stinging at her sinuses, as a pair of empty eye sockets stared up at her.

They were forward-facing and so terribly round, not at all like those of a deer. A hollowed heart-shaped hole was positioned beneath them. Greer absently reached up to feel at her own nose.

Human.

It was a human skull.

"Ellis," she gasped. Her heart ripped in two, unable to take the sudden rush of pain that filled it. She couldn't draw breath, or think straight.

Her hands fluttered toward the skull, unsure of what to do. She wanted to reach for it, reach for *him,* but the gesture felt macabre and obscene. So she stared down at it, studying the curves and ridges of bone, the cavernous holes where eyes should have been.

Ellis had had such beautiful eyes.

"I'm taking you home," she promised, her voice cracking. She ached to cry, but the tears would not come. "Mary will want to . . ." Greer bit her lip. How would she ever begin to tell the Beauforts?

Greer stared forlornly at the area around her, trying to determine where the rest of Ellis was. As terrible as it would be, she'd need to gather everything she could and take him back to his family, back to Mistaken. She could not bear to leave him here alone.

A few yards away, in a sprawling mess of hobblebush, she spotted the rising curve of a rib cage. The vine was tangled through the bones, and Greer paused, taking in the way it had spiraled around several of the ribs.

Even in the heat of summer, the hobblebush would not have spread so quickly.

She searched the area again with fresh eyes, taking in all the details she'd missed when she so quickly jumped to the wrong conclusion.

The bones were the color of aged parchment, sun-bleached and picked clean. There wasn't a trace of muscle or tendon remaining. There was no blood. This had not happened recently. This could not be Ellis.

The skull stared up miserably, as if pleading for help. Greer turned it away from her, unable to bear the blank gaze, and gasped as she noticed the two thick lines running across the arc. They were scored in deep, slashes of unimaginable strength.

What could carve into bone like that?

"Who were you?" she asked the skull, even as the answer came to her.

This was one of the girls who ran. One of the girls who'd picked death over a life of enforced matrimony. One of Mistaken's sacrifices.

She'd been fast, to have gotten so far. She must have been incredibly brave and fearless. Greer envisioned her racing through the undergrowth, skirts kicked up, braids flying, hell-bent on freedom. But then . . . her ending was too grim to bear imagining.

Greer could see evidence of it all over the clearing. There was a long femur, shattered to splinters; ribs scattered like confetti; when she dared to glanced up, she saw a section of vertebrae dangling from the branches of a tamarack, looking too much like links of sausages hanging in a smokehouse.

Greer didn't know if she'd ever known this girl. Her clothing had long since rotted away. She didn't know if she'd ever sat beside her in a sewing circle, if they'd skipped rope or played jacks in the schoolyard. She did not know her name or family, but she did know that this young woman, whoever she was, did not deserve what had happened to her.

If the world was good and just, Greer should have lovingly gathered these bones and taken them back to Mistaken. Allowed her family to bury and mourn her. Allowed her to be remembered with love.

But the sun was past noon, and the shadows were already growing long, and somewhere out there was Ellis, and he was alive, and he needed her more.

Greer collected what she could of this poor girl, reuniting pieces of her body. She covered the remains with gathered stones, creating a mound of fist-sized rocks, and then sat back on her knees, examining her work.

"I'm sorry this happened to you," she began. "I'm sorry you thought there was no other way. I'm sorry for your last minutes. I hope they were quick." Greer frowned. "I don't know if you knew what would happen . . . if you knew your death would be payment for our truce . . . but . . . you've helped to keep Mistaken safe. 'Thank you' doesn't seem enough, but . . . ."

Greer touched a stone, wishing there was more to be done, knowing there was not.

With reverent silence, she put on her pack and continued north.

23

THE SOUND OF the river was maddening.

All day long, Greer had listened to its rushing susurrus, but she had yet to come across a single sign of it. She checked the maps and then the compass again, uncertainty creeping in and souring her stomach. She'd always prided herself on knowing exactly where she was on any given map, but here, in this unfamiliar land, she felt lost.

She *was* lost.

"Perhaps the scale is wrong," she muttered, not wanting to admit her predicament. A faulty cartographer was easier to blame, even if it didn't fix the problem. "I'm not at the river yet because the measurements are off."

When she spotted a rock formation rising through the canopy, she dumped her rucksack at its base and began climbing, eager to see above the tree line. So far up, she should be able to survey the land, see its entire sprawl as if she were a bird in flight, and find that damned river.

When she reached the top, Greer wanted to cry.

There was so much land between her and the mountains, so much wild space full of dangers unseen and unimaginable. It was desolate and vast, so much bigger than anything she could have ever guessed, peering at the world from the cliffs of the Narrows.

How could such a small corner of a map span so wide?

The impossibility of ever finding Ellis crashed over her.

She felt like a fool. Setting out into the wilds, she'd been so full of certainty and confidence. She'd pictured reaching Ellis in record time, easily able to double her pace over his, ready to take his hand and save him.

Every bit of that fantasy now made her cringe.

She'd been so naïve. So stupid.

But she wouldn't be any longer.

Greer held out the map before her, lining it up with the view of the mountains as she saw them now, and attempted to do the math. She counted trees, converting their numbers to yards, the yards to miles, and then she looked at the map again and pinpointed where she was.

The river was not far, half a day's hike, maybe less if she pushed herself.

Greer took one last look, studying the miles of wilderness, looking over the trees and ravines, the starting foothills of the mountain range, over the snowcapped behemoths themselves. She cupped her mittened hands around her mouth and cleared her throat.

"Ellis!" Her cry echoed like a gunshot.

She fancied that the wind was on her side, and imagined it taking her words straight to Ellis's ears. He'd stop in his tracks, eyes wide with surprise, and turn.

"Ellis Beaufort," she tried again, wishing with all her might that she could summon the power that had magnified her scream before. "Can you hear me?"

Seconds ticked by, filled with the chatter of a flock of birds who were hiding somewhere in the trees below.

"Ellis!"

Nothing still.

"I'm coming for you!" She shouted her promise to the sky, to the trees, to anything that might be listening.

"Why?" came a voice, came *the* voice, somehow here with her now, even in the middle of this stretch of solitude. That awful, impossible voice.

Greer startled, then scanned the forest floor below. Nothing stirred. She looked through the branches around her. Was it roosting in a tree?

"Where are you?" she demanded.

"Here," it answered, sounding as if it was off to the west. "Here." The voice came from the east. "I'm right here," it whispered, sounding as if it were only steps behind her, its lips nearly brushing the fine, downy hair of her ear. Greer could feel its breath across her skin but would not give it the satisfaction of turning to look. She understood it would not be there.

"Are you ever going to show yourself?" she dared to ask. "Or do you just mean to creep around, whispering your little asides till I drop over from exhaustion?"

"Be careful what you wish for, little Starling," it hissed, and Greer recalled her dreams and the creature who'd backed her up against the Warding Stones, making her watch as the town of Mistaken was torn apart. She remembered the slashes scored deeply into the skull of that unknown girl.

"I'm not scared of you," she lied.

"Oh, little Starling," it sang, arcing over the sky, swooping past her on wings unseen. "You should be. You will be."

"Where's Ellis?" she demanded. "Is he safe?"

Its laughter was dark with amusement. "Are you?"

Greer let out a cry of frustration, and though it lacked the scream's power, it was enough to startle the nearby birds. They exploded from the tree, and Greer wasn't sure whether to laugh or cry.

They were starlings, their small bodies sleek and dark as they sliced through the air like bullets, flying circles around her.

Instinctively, she covered her head and ducked low. She could hear each of the starlings' heartbeats, fast and panicked. The murmuration seemed to expand, then shrink around her, whizzing by, as images were quickly formed, then lost. Despite the sheer multitude of bodies flying through so small a space, they never ran into one another, they never struck Greer.

She dared to raise her head, squinting through the chaos, and wondered if she could climb down from the perch. Surely, the birds wouldn't follow her into the depths of the forest. They needed room to fly en masse, they needed space and open air and—

Greer frowned, spotting something on the ground below her.

It was still, mostly hidden in the shadows of the trees, but then took a concerned step forward, standing upright on two legs.

It was a person.

She blinked in disbelief even as her heart hopped high in her throat. "Ellis!" she exclaimed, trying to be heard over the rustle of a thousand starlings. "Ellis, I'm up here!"

Heedless of the birds, Greer hurried to climb down the rock, but with all the lichen and ice and snow, she slipped, skidding over the edge. She fell into the starlings, and for one moment, she had the strange notion that they would save her, that she was one of them, and that they would come together and spirit her away to safer ground. Her feet would land as softly as an autumn leaf, and she would race to Ellis while the flock of starlings cheered for her, for them, for their new life of freedom and love and—

The ground raced up to meet her, faster than she could have imagined.

24

Greer woke sometime later to the impossible sounds of a crackling fire.

Bits of wood sparked and popped, and she could feel the embers flush her cheeks, her chest, her body, all the way down to her fingertips and toes.

She kept her eyes shut, certain it was a dream, certain she'd seriously injured herself in that stupid, thoughtless fall, and that she was actually lying in a snowbank, delirious with blood loss and exposure to the cold.

Men at the mill told stories of getting turned around in the woods, of wandering with shoes wet after fording a creek, and of the phantom tendrils of heat that would wrap around their limbs, causing them to remove more clothing no matter how cold it was, no matter how strange it seemed. Then they'd pull off their shoes, revealing toes shriveled and blackened into stumps—if there were even toes left behind at all. The onlookers would shriek with dismay and glee before solemnly promising to never wander too far into the woods, to keep to Mistaken's knowns, to always respect the power and uncertainty of nature.

Greer had never made such promises. She knew herself too well, knew she would forever be drawn into the wilds, knew her curiosity could never be sated. It would take far more than the cautionary tale of a missing toe to keep her from roaming.

But now here she was, far from home and so grievously injured she'd conjured up an imaginary bonfire to trick her mind into accepting what was happening to the rest of her body.

She wondered how long it would take to die, if she was close now.

It must be soon, Greer reasoned. *The great unknowable end.*

It was a surprisingly comfortable way to die, ensconced in a cozy world of fanciful heat. There was no pain, no fear.

"Are you awake?" asked a voice, tearing into Greer's reverie, and the fear came then, dousing her with an icy shock so surprising she sat up, eyes flashing open.

There was a blaze after all, a very well-made one, much bigger than her campfire from the night before.

What time was it?

The sky above was dark but not quite fully. The air had a soft, velvety quality, stained a rich navy, not black. The sun had set, but twilight hadn't yet turned to dusk.

"Who are you?" Greer asked, squinting to make out the figure sitting on the opposite side of the fire.

His face was obscured by waves of heat and dancing shoots of flame, but Greer could see that this man was not Ellis. He sat taller, stretched wider, and took up space with more confidence than Ellis would have dared.

Dark eyebrows hooded over equally dark eyes. If Ellis Beaufort was autumn—warm and burnished gold with laughter and heat—then this stranger was winter itself, harsh lines, sharp shadows, and the eerie stillness that grabbed hold of the world after a deep snowfall.

"Who are you?" Greer repeated, tilting her head to see through the flames. She caught a glimpse of sharp cheekbones, a long nose, and a thin mouth.

"How's your head?" the stranger asked instead of answering her. "You took quite a spill. I've never seen starlings attack like that."

"They weren't attacking. I slipped."

I slipped making my way down to you, she wanted to add, but it didn't seem right to blame this stranger for her accident, not when he'd clearly tried to help her, building this fire, covering her with a blanket she only now realized she'd sunk her fingers into. It was wonderfully warm.

Beaver pelts, she thought absently, feeling the soft and bristly fur against her skin.

Her bare skin—

In alarm, Greer searched the campfire for her mittens. Had she lost them in the fall? A quick inspection showed that her fingers were fine, without even a trace of frostbite, but she couldn't hope to continue her journey without them.

"You fell into a snowdrift," the stranger said, missing nothing. "Your mittens and cloak were soaked by the time I reached you. They're drying there." He jerked his chin, gesturing toward a fallen log where her articles of clothing were laid out with thoughtful care.

Only then did Greer realize her cloak had been removed. Squirreled away under the furred blanket, she'd not suffered its absence.

"Thank you," she said stiffly. "I . . . I'm Greer."

The stranger nodded.

A feeling of unease spread over Greer. She'd studied the map until its lines were imprinted across her memory. She could recall each bend of the river, every small lake, every rocky crag. There hadn't been a dotted town, a settlement, or even a trading post marked anywhere near Mistaken. The closest sign of life was the village of Kennebrinlette, and that had been miles away, nestled at an inlet on the coast. Greer hadn't been able to make out even a glimpse of the ocean from her vantage point before she fell.

So where had this stranger come from?

And how, with so many untold acres of wilderness, had he come across her just as she needed help?

"I suppose I'm quite lucky you saw me," she began, straining to keep her voice even, to not show fear.

He grunted in acknowledgment, then picked up a long stick propped beside him and poked at the fire, pushing a log toward the middle of the inferno.

"I didn't think there were any settlements this far inland," she tried again, trying to avoid framing her curiosity as an actual question.

"No?" he asked, finally speaking.

"Or north," she prodded.

His expression changed, slipping into the smallest of smiles. "We certainly are north."

Greer shifted, pretending to stretch, while letting her eyes roam, searching for her belongings. Her cloak and mittens were on the log, and she spotted her rucksack, laying on its side just out of the stranger's reach. She wondered if he'd gone through it while she'd been unconscious. Running her hands over her body, she was relieved to find she still wore the beaded necklace, but was alarmed when she realized her knife was missing.

Had the stranger removed it?

Or had it been lost in the fall?

Gingerly, she touched the back of her head, feeling at the goose egg, which ached with a pulsing, tender throb. She was surprised to find there were no wounds, no lacerations.

"No blood," the stranger spoke, noticing her examination. "That's good. You've no idea the kind of creatures out here that would be drawn to the scent of your blood."

"How lucky," she said, echoing her earlier sentiment.

He nodded. "I imagine you've got quite a headache, though. How's the rest of you feel?"

Greer pushed herself up, testing her limbs, while surveying the camp and the stranger who'd remained so well hidden behind the flames.

He wore buckskin trousers and an impressive pair of furred boots. They lashed up his calves, coming nearly to his knees. His coat was enormous, the wool worn shiny in spots. Though it was cold enough for Greer's breath to puff in a frosty haze, the stranger wore no hat, and his hair was shorn close to his scalp, far shorter than the men of Mistaken wore theirs. It was fuzzy, like a peach, and a brown so dark it was nearly black.

"I think I'm all right," Greer decided, scooping up her cloak. She was surprised to spot her knife on the log, hidden by the drying garment.

"That was beside you," the stranger said, gesturing again with the tilt of his chin. "It's a wonder you didn't land on it. That would have been a nasty stab."

"With lots of blood." She smiled, slipping the knife back into her pocket.

"That's a terrible place to keep it," he observed. "You should have it sheathed against you. Easy to remove, hard to lose. On your calf, maybe."

Greer nodded as if it were possible to produce such an item magically, simply because the stranger said she ought to. She grabbed her mittens and eyed her pack.

He hoisted it to her. "I'm no thief."

The bag thudded against her chest, and she scrambled to catch it. "I didn't think you were," she said, but she retreated quickly to the far side of the fire, giving him a large berth while allowing her to keep a close watch on his movements.

He shrugged as if her obvious safeguard didn't bother him in the slightest, and it was the nonchalant expression on his face that made Greer decide to be bold.

"Are you a trapper?"

"I suppose you could say that," he said, responding in a way that made it seem like he'd answered her question even if he'd not.

She nodded toward his boots. "They're very fine," she observed. "Caribou?"

"Grizzly. Same as your blanket."

Her eyebrows rose with genuine surprise. "You hunt grizzly?"

His lips rose.

"I've never seen one in person, only their tracks," she admitted, regarding him in a new light. "But I've heard stories of how big they can get, how ferocious and fast."

He leaned in as if about to impart a grave confidence. "The secret to hunting something so ferocious and fast," he began, "is to always be a little more ferocious."

Greer's smile felt small and weak. "How long was I asleep?"

"You were unconscious," he began, drawing out the word to mark the distinction, "for a few hours. Two or three."

"Still twilight, then," she said, glancing to the sky.

"This time of year, there's more night than day . . . Does it really matter what part of it we're in?"

Greer supposed it wouldn't to someone who was not from Mistaken. She wondered what it would be like, not to feel the ticking by of every hour, not to be held captive to the comings and goings of the sun.

"The night is terribly pretty, though," the stranger allowed, his gaze lifting to the stars, a half-smile tugging at his mouth.

For one terrible second, his eyes flashed a faint red, reflecting the firelight like the shine of an animal.

Greer startled, but when the stranger shifted, the illusion was gone. She massaged the back of her head, wondering if something had been damaged after all. Bursts of light were supposed to signal a concussion, weren't they? Greer wanted to ask the stranger, but hesitated, unwilling to show any sign of weakness.

"Are you hungry?" she asked instead, fumbling with the flap on the rucksack. "I've a bit of bread and jerky. We could share."

It was a generous offer, especially since she knew how little there truly was, but the man shook his head.

"I set a few snares while you were out." He cocked his head toward the shadows. "I'll see if we had any luck." As he stood, his gaze fell heavily on Greer. "It would be incredibly foolish of you to try running off in the dark while I'm gone. There are all sorts of things in these woods that would be upon you in a heartbeat."

"But not you?" she guessed, sounding braver than she felt.

Another half-smile. Another strange trick of eye-shine that Greer longed to believe was in fact a trick. "Not me," he agreed, then slipped into the trees.

25

THE STRANGER RETURNED with a pair of snowshoe hares, holding the rabbits by their haunches, necks snapped, paws dangling.

He hadn't been long, maybe only ten or fifteen minutes.

In his absence, Greer had gone through her pack, searching for evidence that he'd taken something from her meager possessions. Nothing had been touched, and she found he'd refilled her canteen with fresh spring water. The solicitous gesture irked her for reasons she could not name. She'd wanted to think badly of him, certain his presence was a danger. It was irritating to be proved wrong.

She'd briefly considered leaving, but the woods were pitch-black, and the crackle of the fire was comforting. She'd figure how to extricate herself in the morning, when her belly was filled and the light had returned. Still, she kept the knife close at hand.

To show she could be helpful as well, Greer set to work melting handfuls of snow in her little stew pot, then threw in a scattering of stinging-nettle sprigs. The tea was steeping as he returned.

The stranger hoisted his catch high, letting her inspect the bounty.

"It looks like the Benevolence was on your side," she admired.

He furrowed his brow, as if not understanding her.

"The Benevolence . . ." she began, but stopped. He did not recognize the term. "They . . ." Greer felt too tired to explain. "You brought back a very good catch."

"Suppose you'll want them roasted?" he asked, nodding toward the fire.

She laughed. Belatedly, he joined in, and Greer had the strangest sensation that it had not been a joke.

"I've made tea, but I'm afraid I only have the one cup. Do you have one in your pack?"

Greer had noticed his lack of supplies as she worked around the camp. There'd been no bag, no pack. It seemed completely improbable that a man who hunted grizzlies would wander into such impenetrable wilds without some sort of kit.

He'd need weapons at the very least—bows and arrows, knives, a rifle with powder and bullets—but she'd wandered a wide circle around the camp—gathering nettles, she'd reasoned as her conscience listed guiltily—and hadn't seen anything.

Oddly, the missing kit reassured her. She wasn't the only one quick to distrust.

She stared at him now with innocent eyes, waiting to see how he'd respond.

But the stranger shook his head. "Never been much for tea. You go on and drink up."

She blinked. "Don't you want something to warm you, after your long hunt?"

He laughed. "It wasn't that long."

"But you must be cold. Take the cup first. We can share."

The stranger only took the rabbits behind the log for cleaning. Greer saw a quick flash of silver as he removed a knife from some hidden sheath.

He made quick work of the hares, stripping the fur in long, clean swaths before flaying out the body and removing the organs. He skewered the limbs on a branch and set them roasting over the flames.

"No fancy herbs or salts," he said, more observation than apology.

"It smells wonderful all the same," Greer said, shifting beneath the thick heft of her cloak and hoping the stranger couldn't hear the rumble of her stomach.

They settled back into their spots at the fire circle, Greer sipping the bitter tea while the stranger roasted the rabbits, turning the sticks every so often. Though he seemed content to sit in silence, the inside of Greer jangled, anxiety thrumming and building in her, until the question she longed to ask came bursting out.

"Are you really not going to tell me your name?"

He frowned. "I don't recall doing anything to give you such an impression."

"I told you mine, and you didn't offer yours in return."

"You never asked." For the first time since they'd met, a full smile crossed his lips. It was wide and toothy and just a touch lopsided. "Well. Won't you?"

Greer opened her mouth but laughed with disbelief, unable to form the words.

He stretched out his legs, warming his feet before the fire, clearly enjoying his moment of triumph.

"Oh, kind sir, won't you tell me your name, please?" she tried, her tone sweet but long-suffering.

"Finn," he said without preamble. "Noah Finn."

"Noah," Greer repeated, testing its feel.

"Finn," he corrected. He inspected the meat, tapping at a leg. Unsatisfied, he returned the rabbit to the fire. "You know, you haven't said what you're doing so far out here. Inland. In the north," he parroted, and the corners of his eyes crinkled.

"You've not asked," she countered.

He laughed. "Greer Mackenzie, what in the Devil's blazes are you doing out here, so far from the shores you call home?"

Her first impulse was to join his good humor, but the laugh caught in her throat with the sudden, horrible realization that she had absolutely not told him her last name or where she'd come from.

Greer stared at this stranger—and it didn't matter that he'd finally shared his name, he was a stranger still—wondering how best to proceed. She was in the middle of the wilderness, alone with a man she knew nothing about. A man who somehow know more of her than he had any right to.

Even if Ellis somehow knew exactly where she was, somehow knew she needed help, he'd never come to her rescue in time should something sour with this stranger called Finn.

Greer was on her own.

"Running away from home." She threw it out lightly, mischievously, as if she'd not noticed the disturbing intimacy he'd given away. "Isn't that how all good fairy tales begin?"

He glanced about the trees and, again, she spotted that eye-shine. "Are we in a fairy tale now, do you think?"

She shrugged, though she felt as if she was picking her way across a treacherous spring river. One wrong step and the current could take hold, washing her to peril. "How long have you been out here?"

"Long enough."

"It's strange, I've never felt such solitude as I did today, but you were so close, exactly when I needed you."

"Lucky thing."

She nodded. "Perhaps there are more people in the forest than I first thought. Have you seen many on your travels?"

"Not many."

"There was a young man heading north earlier, perhaps a day or two ago? Tall, auburn hair?"

Finn shrugged and took the skewers out. "Done, I think."

"His name is Ellis? Ellis Beaufort?"

He made a helpless expression. "You hungry?"

Greer accepted a stick. "Thank you."

They fell into silence, though Greer's head was full of meat tearing, teeth sinking deep.

Finn tore through his allotment, barely bothering to chew the tender meat. He ripped the flesh from the bones with gusto, swallowing quickly before going after another bite.

Though she'd not eaten much since leaving Mistaken, his voracity made Greer queasy. She ate two of the haunches before her stomach revolted, unable to take any more.

"You want the rest?" she offered, handing over the stick.

He bobbed his head, stretched to take it from her, and went to work on the remainder of the rabbit, biting and swallowing and biting and swallowing until the meat was no more.

"We should dispose of the bones, right?" Greer asked. "A ways away from the fire? To keep predators from coming close?"

Finn considered this. "I can if you're worried."

"Aren't you?"

Wordlessly, he shook his head.

"You said it yourself, there are so many things in the forest."

He shrugged but stood, shucking off the great wool coat he wore.

"What are you doing?" Her question came out sharper than she meant.

He turned, holding out all the bones. She tried to not notice the shine of grease coating his fingers.

"I though you wanted me to get rid of these?"

"I mean your coat. Aren't you freezing?" She did a double take at his hands. "You're not even wearing gloves. Or a hat."

"I've always run hot. And it's not so bad tonight."

Greer's breath steamed around her, and it wasn't until she began to pay attention to it that she realized Finn's did not.

"Take my coat if you're so cold," he offered, nodding toward the discarded garment. "I won't be long."

Again, he slipped into the trees, leaving Greer alone at the campsite. She had the strong impulse to throw on her pack and run. There were too many things about Noah Finn that alarmed her.

His eyes.

His strange warmth.

The way he somehow knew her last name, knew she'd come from a town along a shoreline.

She wanted to get as far away from him as she could. Her thumb twitched against the strap of her bag, itching to pick it up. But she stayed still, stayed seated, stayed in the inner glow of the fire and the safety it offered.

There were grizzlies.

And the wolves she'd heard the night before.

And the Bright-Eyes.

She couldn't forget the image of those two-toed tracks she'd discovered circling her camp earlier that morning. Or the voice. That sly, singsong voice that had followed after her, teasing and taunting.

Though she didn't fully believe that this fire, however big and bold it currently seemed, was enough to keep away such a monster, it felt safer here than out in the dark and the cold.

So Greer stayed put and waited for Noah Finn's return.

26

Only . . .

Noah Finn never came back.

Lost in her thoughts and worries, Greer didn't notice the passing of time, the way the bruised sky finally turned over into the black of actual night.

It wasn't until a shooting star raced by, streaking across the void, that she noticed the dark, noticed she was still alone.

Greer stood and left the fire, daring to wander to the edge of its glow.

"Finn?" She took another step into the pines, hesitating to raise her voice, lest she catch the attention of something large and wild hiding in the trees. But when he did not answer, she felt forced to. "Finn? Are you out there?"

Nothing.

"Finn!" she yelled once, a sharp, loud bark. A command to be answered.

There was no response.

"Damn everything."

Greer studied the faint highlights of his tracks in the snow, their edges barely limned. She plodded after them until she came upon a mess of bones, the remains of their dinner. They were cast in a heap, as if Finn had dropped them there, with no intent to bury them.

"Finn?" she tried again.

His silence grated on her nerves.

She stepped around the mess of rabbit and started to charge after him, but then stopped, realizing she'd gone the wrong direction. There were no footprints to follow. Turning back to the bones, she searched the area for more of his tracks, but the only ones she saw were those that led from the campsite.

Then they just . . . stopped.

She circled around, certain she'd simply missed them, but there was just the first set and the bones.

She recalled how the Bright-Eyed had drifted on currents of air high above Ellis. Her mouth dried and fear closed her throat. Greer didn't think she could call out Finn's name even if she tried.

A swoop of air stirred through the canopy, sounding just like the muscled flap of a pair of very large wings. Greer bolted back to the camp, back to the fire.

She hoped that Finn would be seated at the fire, that he'd somehow doubled back without her catching sight of him, without her hearing. He'd give her a dry look of amusement as she explained her foolish worries.

But the fire burned without an audience, and his great wool coat was still thrown haphazardly over the log, waiting for its owner to come retrieve it.

Greer wandered from the fire again, this time going in a different direction, one without footprints to follow, because somehow, inconceivably, Noah Finn did not feel the cold, and Noah Finn's breath did not fog in the air, and so maybe it was possible, maybe it was stupidly and improbably possible, that Noah Finn had wandered off in this direction without leaving a trace.

He hadn't, of course.

Just like he hadn't gone north or east or toward the rushing sound of the river off in the distance.

Greer roamed as far from the fire as she dared, searching and scouring for any sign of the trapper, but there was none.

Only when a lone howl rose up, eerie and wavering and setting the hairs on the back of her neck on end, did Greer return to the circle, this time for good.

The wolves were back.

Greer imagined what she must look like to the creatures of these woods, to any wolves, or bears, or mountain lions. To a Bright-Eyed swooping overhead. A little speck of a human next to a little speck of light, ready to be swallowed by the surrounding void of darkness and teeth and claws.

I need protection, she thought, and, even in her mind, her voice whimpered.

Greer pawed through Noah Finn's coat, hoping to find something larger than her knife, and cursed when she discovered nothing but empty pockets.

Her eyes fell on the mess of innards he'd left behind just past the circle of logs. He'd cleaned the hares well and with an expert hand. The organs lay on the snow like glittering rubies.

Without hesitation, Greer scooped them up and raced to the pile of bones. She lay out the remains of the hares, arranging them in an artful offering, and prayed that the Benevolence would hear her and come.

"With . . . gratitude and . . . thanks, I leave these . . . tokens as an offering for . . . thee," she recited, out of breath and tripping over her words. "May they be of good use . . . and bring you great pleasure. Please . . . protect me now. Keep me safe through this night . . . and on my journey."

Another howl rose, sounding closer now, and Greer was horrified to see how her hands trembled.

"And, please, keep Ellis safe . . . bring us together again," she added before flying back to the fire.

Sometime between rescuing her and disappearing into the night, Noah Finn had gathered up a mighty pile of branches, and Greer threw them onto the fire now, letting the flames rise high. Too high, probably, but if the stranger was still out there, if he was alive and had not been scooped up by the sneaky voice that persisted after Greer, she wanted him to be able to find his way back.

Back to the light.

Back from the wolves.

Back to her.

Recklessly, Greer tossed another branch onto the flames and picked up Noah Finn's coat.

She could hope for his return, even while pragmatically acknowledging that its heft was far warmer than anything she had. She slipped her arms through the sleeves and buttoned up the front. It hung off her frame as if she was a child playing at dress-up, but it made her feel safer somehow, as if it was a suit of armor, not just tattered wool.

She laid her cloak over the ground and sat, pulling the bear blanket over her lap, and began her vigil.

She would stay awake, waiting for Finn to return. And if the dawn broke and he had not, she would say a prayer for his soul, douse the fire, and continue after Ellis.

She couldn't afford to lose sight of her mission. Finn's disappearence had shown her just how terrifyingly fast the wilderness could strike.

She would let the fire burn all through the night, high and bright, a beacon calling out to anyone who might need to see it.

In the morning, as the sun painted the sky soft in shades of gray, as the cold winter winds howled through the firs, gusting and tousling their branches until everything inside her mind turned to a hush of white noise she could not escape, Greer ate a small breakfast. She packed her rucksack and set off into the woods once more, Noah Finn's coat on her back.

As she went past the spot where she'd laid out her offerings, she noticed that the area was clear, save for the bloody stains on the remainder of the melting snow. Whatever had come to feast upon her gratitudes had not left a single footprint behind.

GREER SPENT THE MORNING following the sound of the river, climbing up and down embankments, always heading toward the rushing water. As the elevation rose, slowly, gradually, the landscape shifted. Trees were no longer plentiful and didn't grow to astounding heights. The ground beneath her hardened, turning rocky and treacherous, and her feet bore the brunt of the unforgiving terrain.

By midday, they were in agony, and her joints had begun to ache as well. Her knees felt swollen, and the tops of her ankles throbbed.

She stopped to adjust her boots' lacing. The bows had come undone, and she'd nearly fallen, catching her stride on the loose leather cords. Her pack swayed precariously as she bent over, threatening to pitch her down the steep incline, like an ungainly turtle.

Greer double-knotted her laces and got ready to straighten. She pressed her hands to the ground, and was about to shove back with all her might, letting the momentum of the heavy rucksack work in her favor, when she spotted a sliver of footprint, just beyond the spread of her fingers.

She instantly recognized the shape of the track and almost fell over, letting out a sound of surprised relief. Ellis's right boot had a crack in the inner middle of its sole, where the tread had worn thin and split.

His footprints cut sharply through the trail she'd been taking, and with the thin, rocky soil, she'd almost missed it.

"Ellis?"

How old might these tracks be? It hadn't snowed since her first night in the woods. When had he come through?

With a groan, Greer removed her pack, allowing her aching shoulders to have a moment of respite while she stretched and drank deeply from her canteen. She ate a bit more bread, looking down the trail Ellis had come from. He'd been much farther west, and she wondered what had drawn him that way after his first night's campsite.

Hessel had implied that the sacrifices were whisked away after setting foot over the border, but here were Ellis's tracks, miles and miles from Mistaken.

He'd walked here. On his own.

There were no prints accompanying his, no guide to show him the way. Did he know where he was going, or was he simply acting on instinct?

And the Bright-Eyed . . .

Was it stalking him still?

―⁓―

SHE FOLLOWED his tracks for the rest of the afternoon, until they led her to the river.

Greer let out a whoop of excitement.

It was wider than she'd expected and looked deep. Its dark waters frothed with little white-tipped eddies. The current was surprisingly fast.

Greer stood along its bank, acutely aware that the sky above her was beginning to dim. Hidden behind a scattering of slate gray clouds, the sun was sinking with dangerous speed toward the horizon.

Another day gone, and Greer still hadn't found Ellis.

Her eyes shifted back and forth along the riverbank as she tried to plan out her next move. Ellis's tracks were at her feet, and there were more on the other shore, as if he'd merely hopped over the offending rapids with a great leap.

Perhaps it wasn't as deep as it looked.

Greer poked through the undergrowth, looking for a long stick. She leaned out as far as she dared—falling in so close to sunset, with no campfire prepared, would be a death sentence, no matter how effectively Noah Finn's coat kept away the cold—and stabbed the branch into the swirling depths.

In an instant, the water swallowed it up all the way to her hand and jerked the stick away with terrifying strength.

There was no way Greer could ford this river on foot.

"How did you do it, Ellis?" she muttered, walking up and down the bend, trying to spot his trick.

Eventually, she gave up, resolving to work it out in the morning. There had to be a series of rocks hidden just beneath the rapids' surface. She'd see them when the sky was bright and would cross them when the day was warmer.

Till then, she needed to find a spot to set up camp.

Downstream from Ellis's tracks was a little berm, sloping up from the river's edge. The ground was softer there and less rocky. She searched the area for other tracks. It wouldn't do to set up along a game trail, but this one seemed clear enough.

Using the last of the day's light, Greer searched for kindling. Once her fire was going, she opened the pack and withdrew her cloak and the blanket Noah Finn had left behind.

She'd tried to not think of him throughout the day, tried to not wonder if he had family somewhere who would notice his disappearance, who would miss him. She tried to not conjure theories on where he'd come from, where he'd gone, and how it had happened. She tried, she tried so hard, not to remember the way his eyes had caught in the campfire, the faint red glow of them. She hadn't known a person's eyes could shine like that.

But even that had not been able to save him.

He had to have been taken by a Bright-Eyed.

There'd been no other prints in that clearing save his and Greer's. Whatever had stolen him away had come from the sky, swooping and snatching like an owl after a marmot.

She couldn't imagine the strength it would take to pull a grown man from the ground. It made her think twice about wandering off to look for juniper berries for some tea.

Greer scanned the skies overhead but saw nothing. The clouds were thick and low, and she worried that another snowfall would come and cover up Ellis's tracks once again.

Across the river, up along the ravine, small flickers of light caught her attention. For a moment, she thought it was fireflies, dancing in a grove of trees. But their time of year had long passed.

So why did she see lights now?

It was a pair of dots, there one moment, then gone the next, then appearing farther downstream, then up again. Almost as if . . .

She remembered Noah Finn's eye-shine with a sudden, queasy recognition.

. . . something was pacing back and forth.

Something was watching Greer.

Pretending she hadn't spotted them, she took one of her collected sticks and poked at the bonfire. She waved at the smoke, as if a breeze had blown some in her eyes, and shifted seats, giving her a better vantage while hiding behind the wall of flames.

Greer watched the eyes; they shone a bright amber.

They were high off the ground, at least six feet, and moved back and forth with an easy grace. There was no stumbling, no dodging around tree roots or dips in the land. The languid repetitiveness reminded Greer of the feral cats allowed to roam the mill's outbuildings to keep down the population of rodents who might otherwise nest in the wood chips.

Greer wanted to believe it was a deer drawn to her fire, or even a bear, standing on its hind legs as it decided whether she would make an easy prey. But a bear would lumber back and forth. And a deer wouldn't pace.

Greer was certain it was the creature who'd been following her. The creature taunting her. The creature with two toes.

A Bright-Eyed.

Despite the cut of the wind and the air's chill, Greer felt a bead of nervous sweat trickle down her back. Last night, she'd made an offering to the Benevolence, and whatever had taken Noah Finn had left her in peace.

She had no such gifts or gratitudes now.

Greer rummaged through her pack, looking for something, anything that might appeal to the Benevolence. The last of her bread was already stale, and the remaining jerky looked so meager, she feared they'd be more insulted than honored to receive it.

When she hazarded another glance toward the trees, she noticed that the Bright-Eyed was now stock-still, its amber-orange eyes shining directly at her, watching with interest.

"I see you," she began, startling herself as her voice broke the air. She had not known she was going to address it, had not planned on acknowledging its presence. But the words fell out easily. Even more surprising still was her tone. She sounded bold and confident. A woman without fear.

It blinked but said nothing.

"Were you in the woods last night? What do you want from me?"

The eyes shifted, disappearing for a moment.

"Answer me! I know you can!" Greer shouted, smacking her mittened hand against the stump she sat on.

The Bright-Eyed's gaze flashed in her direction, then lowered; it was crouching down, readying to race toward her, on four legs, not two. It took off, leaping skyward, and the air filled with the sound of flapping, leathery wings. It caught a gust of wind and sailed even higher still. Flying over the tree line, its dark shape was visible in stark relief against the gray light of the dying afternoon.

Greer's breath caught as she saw just how big it was, saw the curve of its massive wings and dangling limbs. Its muscles were lean and sinewy—a monster built for speed and strength. Curved talons, inches long, hooked out of bony toes with too many joints.

Those toes—fingers?—were now headed toward Greer as the Bright-Eyed drew in its wings, turning itself into a streaming bullet, diving with lethal speed.

Greer ducked toward the protective heat of the flames, but the Bright-Eyed still grazed by, snatching at her hat.

It let out a high, keening whistle, mimicking the pitch of the wind. Slicing by for a second pass, it came close enough that Greer could smell it, musky, with a wild tang that reminded her of peat moss and bog water.

Though it zipped by too fast for her to make out its face, Greer could feel its eyes on her all the same, sharp and appraising. She could hear the low chuckle rumbling in the back of its throat, its laughter like a loon's tremolo.

"You're such a long way from home, little Starling," it murmured, diving in once more to spin around her, a confusing cyclone of membrane and limbs. Its long claws reached out and swiped at a loose lock of her hair, shearing it off.

Her scream tore up her middle as she balled her fingers into fists. She bared her teeth against the force of the cry's fury, and sent it out into the world.

It was just as loud as it had been before. Like a meteor smashing into the earth, it displaced everything around her, causing whole trees to lean away. Rocks and the gritty pebbles of the riverbank were cast back like scattered marbles. Even the river's current was affected, as waves sloshed up the opposite bank before carrying on downstream. Greer could see the air around her ripple, sending out compact waves of sound.

And the Bright-Eyed . . .

It tumbled from the sky, pitched off-kilter by the surge, rolling over itself as it plummeted. It struck the ground on the far side of the fire with a tangible thud, nearly knocking Greer from her feet. It remained flattened and still until the last note of her scream faded, and for one long, worrying, yet elated moment, Greer believed she had killed it.

She took a tentative step toward the heap of flesh and claws, but it suddenly flexed, staggering to push itself up. Greer gaped at its inverted joints, at the way the forearms jutted at angles extreme and so very wrong. It reminded her of the furry, too-muscular front legs of the wood-nymph moths that liked to lay their eggs in Martha's buttonbush.

The Bright-Eyed scuttled down the riverbank, obviously dazed but keeping a careful distance from Greer. Gaining confidence, it tested its wings, opening their great expanse again and again, and Greer had to squint her eyes against the dirt kicked up in their wake.

It swooped back and forth in lazy circles as it recovered, riding the air currents like a scavenging bird of prey. Finally, it landed in a tree branch on the far side of the river, shaking the whole Redcap. With it nestled in the thick branches, all Greer could see were its shining eyes and the curved arc of its wings.

"You're full of surprises, little Starling," it mused. "We would do well to remember that."

"We?" she asked, willing her voice to not quiver. The scream had left her feeling scraped completely raw. Her head reeled, dimming the world to a horrible muffle of indistinct sounds. But she sensed a new wariness in the creature and wanted to capitalize on its uncertainty while she could. "Are there many of your kind here?"

Its laughter was deep and wet, and Greer wondered if she'd managed to hurt it, if those visible sound waves had damaged something soft and fragile and important inside. Or perhaps the Bright-Eyed had been injured during the fall.

She fervently hoped for broken ribs.

"More than you'd guess, little Starling."

"Why do you call me that?"

"Why does it bother you?"

Greer could feel it baiting her, trying to get her to scream again. "It was my father's nickname for my mother."

The words were out before she even realized she recalled such a thing. For all their fights and her mother's melancholy, there had been happy times between her parents. Hessel would softly tease Ailie about the scattering of freckles across her face, about her hair, pitched in moody shades of night, calling her his Starling.

The creature blinked at her, unsurprised.

"How would you know that?"

"How do you think?" Its response came infuriatingly fast. It didn't need space to ponder, time to think. It went straight for the answer most guaranteed to inflame Greer.

"You watch us, obviously," she began. "But how? The Benevolence keeps you away. The Warding Stones hold you back."

"Do they?" it wondered aloud.

"Don't they?" she threw back, pulling out her necklace and brandishing the beads.

The eye-shine tilted, studying the stones, studying her. "So, so full of surprises."

"Why do you want Ellis?" she demanded.

"Why do you? He's no longer yours. He chose to leave."

"He was forced!" Greer protested.

The Bright-Eyed shook its head, revealing a quick glimpse of a snout, wrinkled and boxy, and thin lips flexed around a mouth full of fangs. "The sacrifice always goes with a willing heart. That has always been the way."

"What do you do with them?"

"What don't we?" The Bright-Eyed smiled so broadly its serrated teeth winked out of the darkness, and Greer's heart sank.

Overhead, the clouds began to drift apart, revealing a sliver of moonlight.

From somewhere in the woods, alarmingly nearby, a familiar howl rose up, and both Greer and the monster glanced toward the sound.

The Bright-Eyed tipped back its head and let out a similar cry, eerily vulpine but somehow bigger, somehow more dangerous.

The wolf fell silent, clearly cowed.

Greer wanted to laugh. She wanted to cry.

She'd seen the damage wolves could bring. Steward Kinship's entire line of sled dogs had been torn to pieces by a rogue male and his mate. The sounds of the attack had haunted Greer for weeks afterward.

But this wolf, the alpha of its pack, had immediately turned tail, ceding its territory and place as top predator.

"Where is he going?" she asked, drawing back the Bright-Eyed's attention.

"The wolf?"

"Ellis."

"Say you do make it to my mine, what then? Do you truly believe two puny, fragile creatures such as yourselves could really best my Gathered?"

"Yes," she said quickly, too quickly to decide if she meant it or not.

The Bright-Eyed let out a snort of laughter, sounding stronger than before. "I hadn't thought you'd be so humorous, little Starling. How we've underestimated you."

"Yes," she said, keeping up her wall of bravado. "You have."

"Your scream did catch me off guard," it admitted, swaying from foot to foot. The branch creaked heavily. "That won't happen again."

Without warning, the Bright-Eyed sprang forward, crossing over the river with talons outstretched. Before it reached Greer, it exploded into hundreds of smaller creatures. Furry moths and swooping bats. Barred owls, barn owls, and great horned beasts. They fluttered around Greer in a dizzying dance of absolute chaos, swooping and scratching and driving her mad with their clicks and screeching, before scattering into the night.

—

GREER STARED UP at the sky, unable to sleep. Before settling into her nest of fur and pine boughs, she'd built up the campfire to a towering inferno, letting the flames keep watch. She felt confident the Bright-Eyed wouldn't come back that night and was mostly convinced it had scared away the wolves, but Greer didn't want the light burning low. She couldn't bear the thought of waking to absolute darkness, not after she'd seen what the Bright-Eyeds truly looked like. Not after seeing what they truly could do.

Everything around her now seemed suspicious.

Were those soft hoots across the ravine actually from a saw-whet owl, or had the Bright-Eyed returned, mimicking their calls as it had the wolf? Flickers of eye-shine, set low to the ground, appeared to belong to a male fisher out on a hunt, but what if they weren't? What if a part of the Bright-Eyed that had burst free was spying on her? The night felt full of eyes, and Greer squirmed in her makeshift bed.

She'd expected to fall into a stupor of exhaustion, but instead she watched the starry sky, feeling something amiss. Sleep would not come, no matter how she wished for it.

Greer thought through the day: waking to find Noah Finn hadn't returned, exulting over Ellis's tracks, meeting the Bright-Eyed, then releasing that scream . . .

She felt as though she'd overlooked something, something important that needed to be noted. It prickled at the back of her neck, so persistent she finally rolled over and sat up.

There would be no sleep for her.

Greer stood and stretched and set to work making tea. It was hours before sunrise, but she wanted to be prepared to face the river at first light. She studied the map while the juniper sprigs brewed, following the river's line until she spotted a quirk in its bend that looked just like the one in front of her now.

Greer was about to set aside the map, ready to fill her mug, when she caught sight of three unexpected words halfway up the first mountain range on the paper.

Sandry Mining Company.

She frowned, remembering. The Bright-Eyed had said something about Greer making it to its mine. She scanned the map once more, searching for any other mining settlements.

There was only Sandry.

The Bright-Eyeds must be using the old mining camp as their . . . Greer paused, uncertain of what to call it. Roost? Den? Lair?

Whatever it was didn't matter.

Greer had located where Ellis was headed.

And as soon as the sun rose, she was going after him.

28

GREER GLARED AT the swirling eddies before her. The river seemed even more swollen than it had the day before. Fallen leaves raced by at alarming speeds. The footprints on the opposite bank mocked her, and, for the thousandth time, Greer wondered how Ellis had managed to cross the frigid water.

She scratched at the back of her scalp. After her encounter with the Bright-Eyed, Greer hadn't been able to find her hat. She felt all right in this moment—the day was surprisingly warm—but she knew she would miss it dearly as she began her climb to Sandry.

She checked the map, studying the river's winding bends. There was a spot downstream where the water briefly split into two, the halves veering sharply away from the other.

There's an island, she realized. *Cross there, then go back to Ellis's tracks.*

It took nearly an hour to reach the little spit of land. There was a scattering of boulders spanning the southern edge of the river, nearly twenty feet across. Greer guessed she could use them as a bridge to get to the island. From her vantage point, the water running along the north side looked shallower, the current easier to ford as well.

Taking a deep breath, she began climbing the first rock. It was hard work, scrabbling up the porous, slick surface. The rucksack tugged at her back, taunting gravity. Though it didn't take her long to reach the top, she was already out of breath.

It wasn't a far jump to the second—three feet, maybe four—but that boulder's surface was full of uneven crags. Greer worried she might catch an ankle and skid over into the river below.

Saying a quick prayer, she took as much of a running start as she could and leapt.

She landed hard, and the weight of her bag wanted to keep going, knocking Greer to her knees as she clung to whatever handholds she could find.

Three rocks left.

Greer spanned the gap between the second and third with a precariously wide step.

Now in the middle of the river, she took a moment to admire its winding length. Murky water raced by, sending little waves sloshing up as if to grab at her.

She frowned as she caught sight of movement downstream. A long, serpentine shadow approached, fighting against the current. It was massive, longer than the carts used at the mill to haul trees, and nearly wider than the timber itself.

As if sensing Greer, it slowly ascended from the water's depths, showing off a muscular back, mottled blue and gray, the color of a stormy sky. Rows of lethally barbed scutes lined its body, giving the giant sturgeon an otherworldly, mythical air. This was a dragon come to life, truly an ancient creature of legend and horror.

She froze, watching its formidable body glide past her with undulating grace. Despite the season, when most of his brethren would be found in the warmer waters off the coast, this sturgeon was headed upriver, for purposes unknown. Greer could only stare after it in slack-jawed wonder before it submerged with a seductive swish of its tail.

She kept her gaze fixed on the swirling water but did not see the sturgeon again. Unease spread within her, like a stain of wine traveling across a pristine tablecloth. The span to the fourth rock was the widest she'd need to cross, and Greer eyed the rushing water warily. If she fell short, she'd be swept away and that would be it, there'd be nothing left of this journey. There'd be nothing left of her.

Greer played with the straps of her bag, wondering if she could throw it all the way to the riverbank, which would allow her to jump with less weight and more control. The shore looked too far, but she thought she could at least get the bag to the next boulder. It was large, with a mostly level top.

"It's not that hard," she muttered, coaching herself. "Just take off the bag and toss it."

She double-checked that the map and compass were inside Finn's coat pocket before letting the rucksack slide from her back. She tested its heft, swinging it back and forth as she estimated how much strength she'd need to get it onto its mark.

With a grunt of effort, Greer hefted the bag across the gap.

As it sailed through the air, she held her breath, watching and waiting to see where it would land. Her heart caught as she noticed the lantern dangling from the canvas loop. The glass sparkled in the sunlight, looking achingly lovely before it struck the rock and shattered. A burst of broken shards sprayed across the ledge.

She swallowed hard, trying to push down the warnings firing through her bloodstream, screaming that this was a bad idea, a very bad idea, maybe the worst one she'd ever had, and—

She leapt.

In her haste, Greer overestimated the jump and fell onto the shards of glass. Though her boots protected her from the wicked edges, she landed clumsily, her foot slipping and catching on the rucksack. In a tangled mess, both it and Greer went sliding off the boulder, plummeting into the waters below.

The current hit her with all the force of a battering ram, and it took Greer a stunned moment of agonized disbelief to understand why she hadn't been swept away.

A fallen tree was jammed between the last two rocks, and her pack's strap had snagged on one of the branches. Greer clung to the bag with all her might. Her arms trembled as she fought to stay above the water's surface. She sputtered for breath, kicking hard against the roaring rapids, trying to pull herself onto the log. It was slick with lichens and a slimy skin of autumn leaves, and no matter what Greer did, she could not find purchase.

The water was bitterly cold, squeezing her chest with such ferocity that even when she could kick above the surface, she couldn't find a way to draw air into her lungs. The pulsing, pounding slosh of the waves never stopped. There were always more, hitting her in the face, filling her ears. They flipped Greer from side to side, and her stomach heaved from the relentless motion.

Instinctually, she called out for help, using what breath she could to scream. If she was going to drown in these watery depths, she wanted to meet her end fighting. The current rippled, pulling her under, and she swallowed an enormous mouthful of river water. She choked, gagging on the brackish cold, only for more water to rush in through her nose, burning her sinuses.

Greer thrashed and, for a horrifying moment, she couldn't tell which way was up. The world was nothing but a verdigris haze. She tried one direction, then the next, smashing her head against one of the boulders. Dark stars filled her vision, and she was certain this was the end.

But the current slacked, and she bobbed to the surface, gasping for air.

A disconcerting warmth began to spread down her arms. Its phantom shimmers started in her fingers, so white and bloodless they were beginning to turn blue. It spread down her arms, surrounding her elbows with the unpleasant sensation of a sleeping limb beginning to wake. Pins and needles prodded at her, making their way to her shoulders and spreading across her core.

The cold, she thought with alarm. *It's so cold I'm beginning to feel hot. Too hot. Too cold,* she corrected. *It's too, too cold.*

Along with the prickles and the paradoxical heat came a terrible sleepy sensation.

Greer fought to keep her eyes opened and focused.

Too cold, too cold, too cold . . .

Her body felt deliciously heavy, as if she were covered in a pile of quilts and goose-down blankets.

What if I just let go?

It would be so terribly easy.

Just a release of her fingers, just a final glimpse of the sky.

She pictured her body floating downstream, tossed about like driftwood, and it looked so peaceful, so dreamy. For a moment, she flexed her fingers, wondering if she had the strength simply to surrender.

Ellis.

Her lethargic brain conjured up one last daydream.

Ellis was in the foothills of the Severings, surrounded by a vast and unforgiving landscape. He looked utterly spent and defeated. And somewhere in the distance, trailing behind him, caught high on currents of air, out of sight, was a Bright-Eyed.

No!

The vision startled her to action and, with the last of her strength, she kicked, launching herself at the log. She squirmed and thrashed, and hauled herself up. Her body fought Greer every step of the way, threatening to roll off the side, moving with stagnant slowness as if she were already nothing but dead weight. Finally, she centered herself on the log and collapsed in an exhausted heap.

Icy water streamed down her face, and Greer couldn't tell if it was the river or her tears. She let out a laugh that might have been a sob. She was alive. She'd not given up.

But she needed to get moving.

She could already feel a delicate layer of frost building over her clothes, could feel her limbs wanting to remain inert.

"Move!" she growled. "You have to move!"

With a heave, she pulled her bag free and threw it over her back.

Greer shuffled inch by inch toward the next boulder, certain the tree would give way and send her to a watery grave.

When she reached the next stone, she let out an aching whimper of relief. She wanted to cheer, but there was still so much more to do, so much farther to go.

Her thighs screamed as she pushed, hefting herself onto the rock. It was too smooth, without grips, and she clawed her fingers against the stone, cracking nails as she fought to hang on. When she was finally off the log, Greer flopped onto her back, her spine curved over the bag, and stared at the sky, heaving for breath.

The cold was setting in, its claws sinking deep. But there was only one more section of river to cross, and then she'd be on the island. She just needed to keep moving.

Greer rolled onto her side, looking at the little spit of land.

There was a trio of birch trees, their leaves long fallen and lying in moldering piles along with spirals of papery bark, the perfect thing for kindling if her flint was still dry.

Greer would have to stop and build a fire. She could not continue with wet clothes, and, though the delay grieved her, she felt so grateful to be out of the water and alive that she didn't care.

"One more jump," she promised, but didn't like the sound of her voice. It was thick and froggy, her throat scraped raw from screaming against the icy water.

Greer tried to sit up, and the world around her spun.

Too cold, too cold, it's still too cold . . .

She listed forward and, for a horrible, panic-stricken moment, thought she was going to keel back into the river. But she flung her bag, blessedly tossing it high onto the shore.

Using the last of her strength, she jumped off the rock.

She knew instantly something was wrong.

She hadn't gotten enough height.

She hadn't gotten enough distance.

Greer found herself back in the river, being pulled downstream away from the island, away from her supplies. She tried to swim, tried to fight it, but there was no resisting the current. It pulled her, tugging her down, down, down—until, suddenly, she was up, torn from the river.

She'd been scooped from the water, scooped from certain death, by a Bright-Eyed. It carried her over the island, grabbing at her rucksack, and all the way across the river, but the cargo proved too much, and suddenly they were both falling, tumbling down from the air, and landing in a heap.

Greer grabbed at her head, certain it was bleeding, though she couldn't remember what she'd struck it upon. She whimpered as her hand came away wet and red.

The Bright-Eyed struggled to untangle itself before collapsing with a painful groan. The last thing Greer saw it do, before unconsciousness seized her, was spread out its wings, covering her in a protective layer of heat.

―

WHEN SHE FINALLY WOKE, night had fallen, and the sky was a riot of colors, flaring brightly, fanning out in two streaks of green and purple. They moved in perfect unison with each other.

Sky lights, she thought fondly, and felt to make sure the beaded necklace was still secure.

The morning came rushing back to her, and she sat up with a gasp.

Crossing the river.

The slip.

The fall.

The Bright-Eyed.

Carefully, she pushed herself up, wincing with every flex of muscle. Pain radiated from her temple where she'd struck it trying to find her way out of the current's hold.

The sky lights continued moving in identical precision, and Greer rubbed at her eyes, certain she was seeing double. She worried that something important in her mind had been jarred out of place, but the colors shifted once more, becoming a single spiral, tinged pink.

Greer let her gaze fall from the sky to take in her surroundings. She blinked against the darkness, unable to understand how she could see the trees around her so clearly. It was obviously night, and the moon was nothing more than a sliver, but it felt as bright as day.

Even though it made her stomach curdle, Greer turned her head, rotating right, toward the river, then left, where the Bright-Eyed should have been.

In its place was a great blaze of fire, crackling and warm.

That's why I can see, she realized dully.

Her thoughts were plodding and slow. It felt impossible to tie concepts together, and she was certain the injury had done something terrible to her head.

On the far side of the fire sat a figure.

"Oh," she murmured with incomprehension.

"You're awake."

"I think I have a concussion. Or . . . something," Greer admitted, wanting to retch as her sense of equilibrium careened, making her see things that were not there, things that could not be there. She closed her eyes, praying that when she opened them, things would seem normal again.

She opened them wide and cursed.

Because there, on the opposite side of the fire, sat Noah Finn.

29

"I CAN EXPLAIN everything," he said, leaping to his feet as he saw her look of recognition.

"You're dead," she said, staggering to her feet. Greer held out her arms, listing heavily to the left. She swatted at him even though he stayed back, giving her a sizable berth. "I saw you die." She frowned, seeing him in double. "Saw . . . See . . . I didn't see. Not exactly. But you died. In that clearing."

He shook his head, and even that motion made her queasy. "I can see why you'd—"

"See," she interrupted, fixated. She could feel herself bogged in the mire of her thoughts but was powerless to escape. "I see."

"Your head . . . You need help."

"I don't need anything. *You're* dead."

"I'm not," he promised.

Greer had so many words that wanted to come out, but they were tangled and twisting, piling up in her mouth. She could pry just one free, and its simplicity felt like a victory. "How?"

Finn took a step closer, but stopped when Greer flinched. "You're certain you want to know?"

She wasn't, but she nodded anyway.

He sighed and, with a helpless shrug of his shoulders . . . changed.

Greer gaped, unable to say anything, unable to put words to what she witnessed, unable to even gasp.

Noah Finn was there and then was not.

In his place, towering above her, was a Bright-Eyed.

It wasn't the same one who had attacked her last night. Greer noticed differences, both subtle and overt. The Bright-Eyed who'd gone after her along the river had stretched out its talons, showing off four long jointed toes ending with razor-sharp claws. Finn—her mind balked to use such a label, but wasn't sure what else to call him—had two claws missing.

Two toes, he has two toes, Greer realized, matching them with the prints she'd seen, first on the hunting excursion with Louise and then at the camp on her first morning in the wilds.

"It was you," she said aloud. "You've been following me all this time."

"Not always," he refuted, and his voice was so different now, rounding deeper as it filled a chest cavity so much larger than Finn's had been.

Than Finn's is, she corrected herself, and her head spun with the utter conundrum of Finn as a person, alive and not dead, and Finn as a Bright-Eyed, hulking over her now.

As if he noticed her discomfort, he shivered, his entire body shaking with tremors, and changed back to his former appearance.

"You're a monster," she accused unnecessarily.

He sighed. "You're not well. Let me help you," he said, starting toward her again, and she nearly tripped over herself in an attempt to retreat.

"Stay away from me. I have . . ." She fumbled in her skirt for her knife, but it wasn't there.

"I didn't take it," he said quickly. "You lost it in the river. I told you that was a terrible place to keep it." He shifted on his feet, working his way closer without taking actual steps.

"You've been following me, watching me," she said, countering his movement as she circled the fire, trying to keep the flames between them.

"Yes."

Greer let out a snort of disbelief. "That's all you've got? 'Yes'?"

"What should I say?"

"You should . . ." A wave of vertigo washed over her, so strong it nearly brought her to her knees. Her head was disconcertingly heavy, and it felt almost impossible to remain upright. A sharp whine rang in her ears, growing in intensity until it was as if the Bellows were going off in her mind. "You should . . ." She clutched her head and wailed. "What did you do to me?"

"Nothing! The rocks . . . You fell . . . You need help." He held out his hand, stepping closer.

Greer didn't want to take it. She didn't want anything to do with him, but another round of unsteadiness seized her, and she grabbed him to keep from pitching forward.

With more care than she would have given him credit for, Finn helped ease her onto a log. She pressed her fingers against his steadying arm, wondering at the flesh beneath his sleeve. It felt so terribly human.

With gentle touches, he moved her chin, tilting her head to look over the gash with appraising eyes. "Tell me how you feel."

"Angry," she admitted, and he had the audacity to laugh.

"I mean your head."

"It hurts."

"Can you be more specific?"

"No." Greer knew she was being childish but was past the point of caring.

He sat beside her, and she wanted to cringe from the utter normality of it. He didn't feel monstrous. He felt like a man.

"No one knows you can do that," she said, the conversation feeling strange and surreal. "In Mistaken. There are so many stories about the Bright-Eyes, but . . . none of them say anything about . . ." She paused, unsure of what to call the transformation. "That."

He said nothing, but the silence was heavy enough to seem like a response.

"You saved me," she went on, studying the fire. "Twice now."

"Yes."

"Why?"

He shifted, uncomfortable. "I can toss you back, if you mind it so much."

She saw the joke for the deflection it was. "It doesn't make sense."

Finn frowned. "I wouldn't have let you die. I'm not a monster," he began, and Greer found the strength to laugh. "I'm not."

"I know the stories about your kind. The towns you've attacked. The people you've killed. What but a monster could do that?"

He bristled. "Those towns weren't an amusement."

"What, then?" she demanded.

He looked away. "We needed food."

In all the accounts she'd read, in all the stories Martha had told, never once had it been said that the Bright-Eyeds were feeding.

This made it better. This made it so much worse.

"You were hungry."

His eyes shifted to her. "Yes."

Greer studied his hands. His fingers were long but not unnaturally so. The nails were short and blunt, cut all the way to the quick. Still. They were powerful hands, hands capable of striking someone down, of snapping someone's neck. And she could not forget how fast he'd turned, shifting from Finn into something capable of so much more.

"Are you hungry now?"

He did not laugh. "Are you?"

She was, but said nothing.

He nodded. "You should feed."

She hated his phrasing. Hated the way it made her sound nothing more than an animal, a wild, mindless thing set only on filling herself.

"Rest," Finn went on. "You'll feel better after both."

Greer wanted to protest, to say she felt fine. She didn't want to give this Bright-Eyed any reason to think her smaller and weaker than she already was. But her head ached, and the words would not come.

"You saved me today," she began, unsure of where her sentence was going, "but last night, the other one . . ." She didn't know how to complete the thought.

Finn tipped his head to one side, and Greer was struck with the familiarity. It was something she did so often the gesture was written into her muscles.

He's listening.

Greer found herself cocking her head to the woods, too, trying to hear what he heard.

After a beat, Finn shook his head. "She will not bother you tonight."

Surprise made her dizzy. "She?"

Greer had not stopped to consider the Bright-Eyed's sex, but if pressed, she would have guessed male. It had been so aggressive, so cruel and callous. She couldn't articulate why, but learning it was a female gave Greer an odd sense of betrayal.

Finn stood up.

"Where are you going?" she sputtered, suddenly fearful he would leave her. He was a dangerous creature, but a known one. She could not say the same for the other.

He gestured toward the woods. "You need to eat. Whatever was in your pack is ruined."

Greer watched the trees behind him and said nothing.

"I will come back." His promise was a reassurance, not a threat.

"And she won't?"

Finn shook his head, and his eyes flashed, shining orangish red. His secret had been there all along, only she'd not understood it.

She blinked hard as another wave of vertigo struck her, gripped the log, held on tight. Her head felt as if she was careening to one side, but Greer knew she'd not moved an inch.

Finn snatched the canteen from the mess of belongings she only now noticed he'd set out to dry. He disappeared down the embankment.

Greer stared at the flames. Her mind was congested with thoughts too big to hold, too impossible to fathom.

"Drink this while I'm gone," Finn said, suddenly returned. He pushed the canteen into her hands.

Greer looked up at him, and for a terrible second, he split into two—her vision doubled. "She really won't come after us tonight?"

He nodded.

"How do you know?"

"I'll be with you, and we don't hunt our own kind."

30

THERE WAS A peculiar taste to the water, brackish and dark, reminding Greer of the time a woodchuck had drowned in the well at the mill. It had been nearly a week before anyone had discovered the unfortunate rodent.

Though the water in her canteen tasted like that now, Greer was too parched to care. She drank in great gulps, swallowing it down quickly before she could register the strange taste.

When she'd emptied half the canteen, she paused and set it aside, taking stock of everything.

Her knife was lost.

Her lantern, shattered and gone.

Her bag and all the supplies it still contained . . .

Greer glanced at the rucksack. It was so close, only just beyond the fire, but it felt miles away. When she tried standing, she immediately sank back down, the motion too much for her head. A thin sheen of sweat formed across her upper lip, and she absently wiped it away before studying her fingers.

Fingers, she realized. It took her a moment to realize why this was such a singular thought.

Her fingers were bare.

Her mittens . . .

She looked across the camp Finn had set up, searching for them, searching for evidence that he'd removed her clothing to dry before the fire, but saw nothing of the sort. She still had on everything she'd worn when she fell into the river, but the clothes were dry now.

Greer didn't like that. She didn't know what it meant, how it had been accomplished. Could Finn have stripped every wet article from her, let it dry, and dressed her again, without her stirring?

Under all her layers of cotton and wool—her chemise and undergarments, her dress and sweater, Ellis's shirt, Finn's coat—she squirmed uneasily. She peeled off the coat, looking for evidence of tampering, but found only relief.

It's so hot.

So late in autumn, the thought was absurd. It rang wrong, like a fiddle out of tune, but that didn't make it any less true.

Greer picked up the canteen again and drank deeply, still ignoring the taste. She kept swallowing till it was empty, and even then she held it straight above her, trying to catch every last drop.

It was still far too warm, and some distant part of her muddled mind wondered if she'd developed a fever, but her head actually felt a bit better. She gently touched the wound; the bleeding had stopped, and the swelling wasn't as bad as she'd initially feared.

Greer's eyes fluttered closed.

She desperately wanted to sleep, but couldn't get the image of Finn as a Bright-Eyed out of her mind. She couldn't believe she'd missed so many of the signs that he was something more than a trapper, something much more than a human wandering through the woods.

That eye-shine.

The way his breath had not stirred the air around him.

The way he'd known her name.

Her eyes opened and looked skyward.

She wasn't sure how much time had passed since Finn left, but it suddenly felt too long. Had the other Bright-Eyed returned?

"We don't hunt our own kind," he'd said, but what if she saw Finn's acts of rebellion—saving a human twice over—as justification? What if she was out there right now, circling him?

Greer tilted her head, listening to the far forests for any sign of Finn.

A sense of uneasiness swept over her as she mimicked his gesture.

Greer licked her lips. She felt as if something important was on the tip of her tongue.

All her life, she'd known she was different from others in Mistaken. It wasn't just in the things she heard, but in the way she felt, too.

The Warding Stones were revered as a circle of protection, holding back the terrors of the wilderness and keeping the residents safe from harm. But Greer had felt their presence like a collar around her throat—a necklace far heavier than the beads she currently wore—holding her back, keeping her tethered to a place that could never be big enough to satisfy her.

They were a pen, a cage.

Ailie had said something similar once, when Greer had been young, too young to truly remember.

There'd been a satchel on her parents' bed, the big one that Greer now used for all her mapping excursions. Ailie had been filling it as if preparing to go on a trip.

Even as Greer remembered this, she knew that couldn't be right. Where would Ailie have gone? She strained, trying to recall what had actually been going on. Had her parents had a fight, and Ailie planned to stay somewhere else until their tempers cooled? They had had a tempestuous relationship—often raising their voices, breaking crockery, smashing plates, hurling glasses—and the house would be filled with Ailie's tears afterward.

There was nowhere in Mistaken that Greer could go to escape the sounds of Ailie's sorrow.

On the day when Greer had seen the satchel, her mother had been filling it, not with clothes or food, but with bits of Greer—a box of her baby teeth, locks of hair she'd tied with old ribbons. As Ailie packed, she'd whispered a litany to herself, repeating it over and over, like a prayer.

"They're just stones, you cannot be contained, they're just stones, you cannot be contained."

Even if Greer didn't remember the circumstances of that day, her mother's words were etched across her mind like initials set in silver. The echo of them circled through her bloodstream like a heartbeat.

You cannot be contained.

Greer pushed herself up gingerly, expecting a rolling churn of nausea and vertigo, but there was none. Still thirsty, she swiped the canteen and picked her way down to the river, leaving Finn's coat behind.

She refilled the vessel and drank. The water was clearer now, tasting of cold minerals and thawed snow. In moments, it was empty, so she filled it again. And again.

Her stomach ached, bulging and round and fuller than it had been in days, but she still could not get enough. Going straight to the source, Greer leaned over and sucked up the water like an animal, guzzling it down.

When she'd drunk all she could and was satiated, she sat back on her knees and wiped her lips. She stared across the river, looking at the land she'd come from, the forest she'd crossed. She looked up the hill, back to the fire, to where Finn would soon be returning.

She had no delusions that she was safe in his presence. He was a Bright-Eyed, and that should have been enough to make trust completely impossible, but, worse still, he was a Bright-Eyed who had repeatedly saved her, proving he acted with reckless unpredictability.

Greer couldn't let down her guard. But she also couldn't afford to run away from a dinner she had not had to hunt herself. Despite the gallon of water sloshing within her, her stomach still rumbled with hungers unfulfilled.

She turned to refill the canteen one last time but stopped short when she caught sight of her reflection. The water rushed by with too much speed for a perfect reverse image, but she could make out the dark shape of her frame, and the pair of eyes shining back at her with a faint red glow.

She stumbled back from the water's edge, spilling the canteen all over herself. The water splashed everywhere, soaking into her boots. She winced, ready to feel the icy grip of wet toes in the frigid outdoors, but such pain did not come.

Greer looked through the forest with wild eyes, noting piles of frost-covered leaves, spotting little daggers of icicles hanging from tree limbs. It was below freezing, yet she longed to tear off her clothing, feeling as if it were a sweltering summer day.

Numb, she trudged up the hill to await Finn's return.

—

GREER HEARD Finn's approach long before she saw him. He was still in human form, walking upright on boot-clad feet, carrying another set of hares with snapped necks.

"You look better," he greeted her.

"Do I really?" she snapped, standing.

She saw him note her flicker of eye-shine. He stopped short. Though not a single muscle moved in his face, she could tell he was pleased. After a pause, he held up the rabbits. "Hungry?"

She was across the fire circle in seconds, moving faster than she ever thought possible. She charged at Finn, leaping at him like a mountain cat going for the kill, and they fell to the ground, Greer atop him.

She gripped the collar of his shirt with balled fists. "What did you do to me?"

31

Greer's fury rose as Finn smiled.
She'd never struck anyone before but now felt the urge to take her fist and hit him until his smile was bloody.

"You changed me!" she spat, tightening her hold on his shirt, and shaking him.

Part of her expected *him* to change now, turning into the fearsome creature she knew he was. She expected him to change and fight back, devouring her whole before she could even begin to defend herself.

But he didn't.

He only lay there, looking at her with the most infuriating expression painted across his face. He was amused. He was . . . pleased.

She did hit him then, balling her hand into a fist and striking his shoulder with a growl of frustration.

"Oh!" It was like smacking a stone wall. Greer cradled her hand to her chest, wondering if she'd broken bones.

Finn propped himself up on his elbows, making Greer uncomfortably aware that she still straddled his lap. Immediately she rolled off, settling back on her feet, ready to run even as she acknowledged there was no place to go. Where could she run that he wouldn't track her? How could she outrace a Bright-Eyed?

She couldn't, so she stayed put.

"What did you do?"

Finn's gaze was serious and searching. "I only strengthened what was already there."

She felt her stomach lurched, suddenly nauseated. "Strengthened?"

He blinked. "Your mother."

"What . . . what about her?" Greer felt compelled to ask even though she feared she already knew the answer.

Finn frowned, remorse coloring his expression. "Greer . . ."

"Say it."

He sighed. "Your mother . . . Ailie," he added tenderly, "was just like me."

His words rang with truth, but Greer shook her head anyway, wanting to deny it, wanting to hold on to one more moment in which she could believe it wasn't possible. "No. She couldn't be. She grew up in Mistaken. Everyone would have known. Her friends, her . . ." She stopped, about to say *family*.

Ailie had had no family. Greer had guessed she'd been an only child and that her parents had died young. Neither Ailie nor Hessel ever spoke of them.

"We're her family," Finn said, following Greer's unvoiced thoughts. "When she stepped out of that tree, all those years ago, she rewrote everything. She became part of Mistaken, as if she'd always been there. And the townspeople—all of them, even your father, *especially* your father—believed it."

"How do you know about the tree?" It wasn't the question she wanted to ask—it wasn't the important point—but Greer fixated on the detail. If she could catch him in a mistake here, maybe, somehow, all of the other things he'd said could be wrong, too.

"I saw it."

She shook her head again. "Impossible. That was nearly thirty years ago."

Silently, he watched her.

In the quiet, Greer's mind filled, piling up questions and accusations, protests and words, words, so many words. But when she finally spoke, only one fell out. "How?"

Finn tilted his head, trying to follow. "How did I—"

"How did *she*—how did she . . ." Greer let out a growl of frustration. "The Warding Stones keep the Bright-Eyes away. She couldn't have lived within them."

"Not without being in a great deal of pain," he agreed. "The stones do repel us, chafe us something fierce, but if we choose to set aside our skin, it's bearable, for a time."

Greer made a noise of disgusted horror. "Set aside your skin?"

Finn nodded. "She would have had some sort of clothing . . . it would have been precious to her. It held all her might, all her . . ." He made a gesture with his hand as if the word eluded him. "Shedding away her power would have allowed her to live within the Stones. It would have allowed her to become like them."

Like me, Greer wanted to say, but she no longer knew who—or what—she was. A memory sparked. "There *was* a cloak. She kept it in her hope chest. I tried to put it on once . . . It was so beautiful . . . But she tore it from my hands before I could. She said it was too fragile for a little girl to play with. When I went poking through the trunk later on, it wasn't there."

"She would have found a new place to hide it."

"But it . . . it didn't look like *skin*. It was so fine . . . covered in embroidered constellations and little stitched forests. It was the prettiest thing I'd ever seen."

Finn looked wistful. "You're one of the few who would have seen it that way. She'd enchanted it. No mortal eye would have thought it special. But you . . ." He tapped at her temple before sliding the pads of his fingers down her cheek to cup her face. "You have your mother's eyes. Her ears, too."

Belatedly, she shied from his touch, using the motion to feel at a lobe, even though she knew it wasn't the shape Finn was referring to.

He offered her a sympathetic smile. "You hear things, yes? Things that, if you were a mortal woman, with mortal ears, you wouldn't."

She swallowed down her denial.

"See the frost?" he went on, easily, as if this were not upsetting everything Greer knew about herself or the world around her. "It's cold out tonight."

Faintly, she nodded.

"Yet here you are, bare-headed, without coat or mittens, socks wet and starting to freeze." He pushed back the sleeve of her sweater and ran his fingers over the length of her forearm, coming to a stop at the delicate skin of her inner wrist. "There's not so much a ripple of gooseflesh on you."

Involuntarily, Greer shivered, then flushed, knowing her reaction had nothing to do with the temperature around them. "I *am* cold," she insisted, hastily pulling down the sleeve. "If it wasn't for the fire—"

"You're not as cold as you think, Greer Mackenzie. You're never as cold as you believe you are."

"Say I believe you," she began slowly, reluctantly, looking at the fire, the trees, the frost. Anywhere but him. "Say any of this is true . . . what does that make me?"

"Special," Finn answered readily, without hesitation. "So very special." A loud rumble came from her stomach, breaking the moment, and he laughed. "Let's get these rabbits roasting."

Greer watched him break down their bodies, pulling off skins, pulling out organs. There were so many things she wanted to ask him, she scarcely knew where to begin.

"My eyes," she started. "I saw them in the river. They've never looked like . . ." She swallowed. "I've never seen them shine like that. What did you do?"

Finn kept his attention on the hares. "You were hurt."

She waited for him to say more, but he remained resolutely focused on his task. "I was hurt. I was hurt and what?"

"I took care of it, took care of you. The only way I know how." He glanced meaningfully at his hands. His fingers were stained with blood.

Greer recalled the strange taste of the water in the canteen. The canteen Finn had refilled. She focused on his hands, his bloody hands, and the kerchief she only now noticed was knotted round his wrist.

Ailie had told her so many eerie tales from their homeland across the sea, stories of selkies and each-uisges, caoineag and Ghillie Dhu, but the most nightmarish of them all were the Baobhan Sith.

Those fables raced through her mind now. The blood drinkers were beautiful and strong, able to shift their appearance and control the desires and temptations of their prey. They were wily and fierce, with little regard for the humans they went after.

Had Ailie been telling her stories of the Bright-Eyes?

Of herself?

"Blood," she guessed, and her throat flexed, fighting the urge to retch. "You fed me your blood."

"And you feel better." Finn ripped the hind legs off one of the hares, not bothering with a knife. He skewered the set, then handed Greer the stick so she could begin roasting. "Your vision has cleared. Your headache is gone."

"Yes, but—"

"If you'd known, you wouldn't have drunk." It wasn't a question.

"Of course not."

"Well. Good, then. It worked."

"Good?" she repeated. "Not good at all. You took away any choice I had!"

He dragged his attention from their meal, flashing eyes meeting hers. "There was never a choice to make. You're one of us," he said with long-suffering patience. "Your blood is our blood. Mostly. Ailie fed you hers for years without you being ever the wiser."

Greer stared at the fire. It looked too bright now, and she shifted her gaze away, to the shadows of the forest. Only . . . they weren't as shadowy anymore. She could see into them, see details that should have been impossible.

The etching of frost on a leaf half a mile away. Individual feathers on a screech owl perched high in the tree line. The subtle play of moonbeams too weak to have ever been noticed.

She now could see as well as she could hear, with alacrity and a keen edge.

And when she looked up to the stars . . .

Greer gasped.

"They're beautiful, aren't they?" Finn asked. His head tipped up and he smiled.

For a long moment, they watched the stars spin, radiating a luster too perfect to put to words. They danced and sparkled, surrounded by pulsing glows that seemed to chime like the tinkling of a bell.

"Why would my mother do that? Do any of this?" she asked softly, feeling the last of her resistance ebb away. She didn't doubt that Ailie was exactly what Finn said, which meant that Greer, too, was exactly what Finn implied. "Why would she leave the Bright-Eyeds and live as a human?"

"For you." His stare was long and solemn. "You've no idea all the things she planned for you. The things she wanted and dreamed."

"But you do?"

"Mostly."

Again, that word. She waited for him to go on.

He sighed. "Having children can be difficult for us." He jabbed another stick through the second hare. "They're born small, weak. Most don't survive their first day. But if one of the parents is human . . ." He trailed off, gesturing toward Greer. "Ailie needed a strong bloodline."

"Why?" Greer challenged. "It wasn't as though . . . She never even told me what she truly was."

"Who," he corrected sharply. "Not what." He clicked his tongue against his palate. "She was going to tell you. When you were old enough, strong enough. Ailie was going to start training you so that when you finally returned home you'd be ready."

"Training?" Disbelief colored her echo. "As though I'm a soldier! Training for what?"

Finn let out a laugh of genuine surprise. "To kill her."

32

THE SKEWER FELL from Greer's hands, dropping into the fire, but she didn't notice until Finn was beside her, swiping up the meat.

"Kill her?" she echoed with horror. "Kill . . ." She gulped.

Finn tapped at the hare. "A little undercooked, but I think you'll find that better now."

"Why would I kill my mother?" Greer demanded, every word falling like thunder.

"Because she was the sovereign."

Greer could only stare blankly.

"Because she was dying," he tried again.

Now she laughed. "She wasn't."

"I promise you, she was."

"Was she sick? Father said there'd been an accident, but—"

Finn stopped her. "Ailie was very, very old. It's a wonder she was able to have you at all. Remember." He paused. "Our kind can take on any form we need to." In a flash, Finn's face shifted into a dozen iterations of himself, going middle-aged before allowing his cheeks to round into the soft fullness of childhood, then turning into an old man. He transformed from man to woman, girl to boy, even becoming something that almost looked like her mother, but a terribly, terribly wrong version of her, a wizened crone, ancient and exhausted.

Greer grabbed his arm to stop him from making the old woman turn younger. She couldn't bear to have any form of her mother with her now. "Finn, stop!"

He let out a little shudder and returned to himself once more. "Do you see?"

Greer nodded unhappily. "So . . . she was older than she looked. But why would she need someone to kill her? If she was so old . . . couldn't she just . . . wait?"

Finn looked pained. "Yes, but . . . no. It doesn't work that way. Not for a queen. She has powers that we just . . . don't. The only way a successor can inherit the full power of a sovereign is to kill for it. The fights are brutal. Ailie knew the next leader—her challenger—would need to be strong. Strong enough to defeat her and hold so much power, strong enough to lead the Gathered. She knew a child strengthened with mortal blood would be up to such a task."

"Me," Greer said, summarizing everything with one small word.

"You," he agreed. "But . . . when Ailie left, the woman you saw last night—Elowen—declared herself sovereign and no one has dared to challenge it."

Greer shrugged. "Then you have a queen."

Finn sighed. "Elowen may say she's sovereign, but that doesn't mean she has the power for it. Not truly."

Greer considered this. "When Mama died, it was an accident. No one killed her, so her powers wouldn't have transferred . . . Where did they go?"

"She cast them off when she went to live with the mortals. They'd be in her skin, her cloak," he added. "Ailie's velvet cloak."

Her face fell. "I haven't seen that in years. Father said . . ." Greer trailed off. What *had* Hessel said? "It doesn't matter anyway. The cloak is gone. You have a sovereign. So . . ." Her fingers twisted together.

Finn regarded the fire for a long moment, so deep in reflection she could practically hear his thoughts grind. "What do you know about bees?" Greer shrugged helplessly. "When a hive is in danger of losing their queen, nursery bees will favor some of the eggs in their care, feeding them a special kind of jelly to make sure those bees are born queens. But a hive cannot have more than one sovereign. When the new queens are born, the old will seek them out and exterminate them."

Greer's blood ran cold with understanding. "Elowen is going to try to kill me?"

Finn nodded, his expression grim.

"But . . . I don't want to kill *her*. I don't want her place."

"You might someday. And she won't wait till you change your mind. That's why she took the boy. She's drawing you out, forcing you to fight on her ground."

Greer froze. "Took the boy? Ellis?"

It didn't make sense. Hessel had sent Ellis out as a sacrifice for the Benevolence. The Bright-Eyeds had nothing to do with it.

Did they?

Greer recalled the deep slashes carved into the skull she'd found in the woods. She thought of the Bright-Eyeds' talons, how they were just the right size, more than capable of inflicting such damage. She thought of the Bright-Eyed who'd been there, waiting for Ellis to cross the border, ready to follow after him.

The Benevolence were giving the Bright-Eyeds the sacrifices. There was no other explanation. But it was too terrible and too unwieldy a thought to process; Greer slammed it to the back of her mind, to return to later.

"What happens to Ellis once everything is over?"

"I suppose that depends on who wins." Finn brought the snow hare to his mouth and took a ferocious bite into its side. Though patently not cold, Greer shivered.

"Elowen will kill him," she guessed. "Feed on him."

"She could make him her consort," he offered, talking around a mouthful of meat.

"Against his will?"

"She can be quite beautiful when it suits her."

"But Ellis loves me." Though these words were so small and simple, they held everything.

Finn said nothing as he continued to eat, chewing through tendons, snapping and grinding bones, wholly indifferent.

Greer could scarcely believe what she was about to ask, but she saw no other choice. There would be no reasoning with a Bright-Eyed, no way to assure or make promises. "How would I fight her? How do you kill a sovereign?"

He shrugged. "I've never seen it myself. Ailie had been queen since before I was made."

"Made?" she repeated.

"I wasn't always this way," Finn admitted. "I was like you, once." Here, he laughed. "Well. No one has ever been quite like you. But . . . mortal."

"You were human?" She was aghast.

He nodded.

"What happened?"

"Elowen."

She waited for him to explain.

"She turned me. Gifted me her blessing."

"Blessing—blood," she clarified. "She fed you her blood?"

Finn nodded.

"How much?"

"I wouldn't know. No one ever explained it to me. Ailie was very adamant that our numbers must remain small. When Elowen made me . . . it was an uncomfortable time for the Gathered."

"Do you remember what you were like . . . before?"

He chewed thoughtfully, taking his time. "It was many, many years ago."

Greer sighed, exhaustion settling in. Too much had happened in too short a time. Her mind felt stretched full, unable to hold any more. Wearily, she pulled the rabbit from her skewer and ate, mulling hard.

She so desperately wanted not to believe him, to deny everything he'd told her.

But she'd seen him change before her very eyes.

And, even more, she remembered how her mother had been.

There'd always been something of the uncanny in Ailie Mackenzie.

Her sad, wistful smiles, the distant glint in her eyes, the way it sometimes felt as though she was in two places at once.

Her mother was a Bright-Eyed.

Sovereign over them all.

"Did my father know? About what Mama was? About what I . . . am?"

The revelation didn't sit right with her, didn't make her feel good. Greer was uncomfortably aware of the wild blood running in her veins now, of all the differences that set her apart.

"Who," he corrected again. "Who you are."

Greer dipped her head, unsure if it was in shame or contempt.

"I would guess not. Eat," he urged, nodding toward the meat in her hands.

Greer took a bite, then another, relying on rote movements to swallow, then bite again. "I don't know how to fight," she admitted. "Not against someone like her. Like you," she added, listening to him crunch apart bones with minimal effort. "You say I'm like you, but I'm not. I can't change. I'm not big or vicious. I can't fly. I can't even cross a river without drowning."

"You'll think of something," he reassured her.

"So you . . ." She stopped to consider her words. "You want me to win? To kill Elowen?"

"It's what our queen wanted. Our lives serve her pleasures."

"But you're here, helping me now. You saved me. Twice," she reminded him. "Did Elowen tell you to do that? To help the poor little mortal so that she could rip me to pieces in front of all her court?"

"Not that queen," Finn said softly.

"You're still loyal to Mama," she realized. He bobbed his head. "And me by extension."

His eyes darted away, as if she'd guessed something he hadn't wanted known. "Yes."

"What do you think will happen when we get into the mountains? Truly?"

"I think luck will be on your side. I think you'll prevail."

"And then?" Greer removed the second leg from the skewer. She tore into the meat, eager to fill the hole of doubt and fear growing in her. "What happens then?"

"You'll become queen."

"Of monsters." The thought filled Greer with unfathomable dread.

Finn's eyebrows furrowed, wounded. "Of your people."

Greer's gullet lurched. She wasn't one of them. Not truly.

She still felt like herself. Mostly.

Herself and a little something more.

She pushed aside the notion, even as she felt her blood stir, intrigued and eager to explore that tiny, treacherous word.

Mostly.

What differences lay in who she'd been and who she was now? She amended her thoughts. Who she'd always been.

"I wouldn't know how," she said softly, wanting to wipe away his hurt but feeling she was only making a bigger mess of it.

"You'd have me."

"As an adviser?"

She didn't know why she asked it. Nothing he could say would make a difference to her. She only wanted to get to the mines, find Ellis, and run. Run from these monsters, run from this alarming legacy she didn't know how to accept.

I'm still me.

Mostly.

"As your consort." His admission was soft and hushed. The hope held within it was too painful for her to bear.

They stared at each other, and the seconds between them seemed to stretch, growing into an interminably loud silence with every breath that went by. Abruptly, he pitched his stick into the fire and stalked away from the circle, away from Greer. "I'm going to get more wood."

Before Greer could stop him, before she could say anything, he was gone in a flicker of shadows and suffering.

1740

THE BEGINNING OF the end began with a pattering of hooves, echoing their way from the wide sea, impossible to ignore.

The queen was aging.

She could feel the end's approach in every corner of her body. In her bones, growing thin and brittle. In her blood, circulating slow and sluggish. In her heart, beating softer and less steady.

The queen had years and years ahead of her, so many decades a mortal mind might think her invincible, impermeable to time and decay, but she could hear death's steed, riding closer, closer, ever closer.

Every day the queen heard his approach, and every day she studied her small court, fearing for them. They would need a leader. Someone strong and fierce, someone clever and ruled by logic. None were up to such a task.

Least of all Elowen.

Impulsive, brash Elowen.

It had been a mistake to change her. The queen knew that now, all too well.

So, without a suitable replacement, the queen began to plan.

She would go into the world and allow a mortal man to claim her as his bride. She would have a child with this man, a child stronger than any of her Gathered, blessed with the wild blood of a sovereign and a mortal's temperance.

Most of the Gathered wept and begged her to not go, but Elowen watched on with flames of wounded anger burning in her eyes. Still, the queen could not be persuaded. She promised she would return with a daughter. She promised she would bring home their new queen.

Her mission did not sit well with the queen's guard. He had watched over her since joining the court, when Elowen had foolishly made him, and had become the queen's protector and friend. The aging queen was fond of the young guard. Before she left, she promised he'd one day win her daughter's heart, and serve as her consort for generations to come.

The queen set out for a little village on the edge of a vast body of water. She pulled off her magic skin, worked it into a beautiful cape, and took her mortal form, young and luminous and lovely, with a scattering of stars across one cheek. When she looked just right, she hid herself in a hollowed trunk and waited for a young man to come and claim her.

While she waited, she drew patterns on the inside of the tree, crying tears of sadness and discomfort. She missed her kin. She could feel the bite of the Warding Stones trying to repel her. But she would not be moved. She needed her daughter to be born here, in this world of pushings and pulls. She needed her to stand firm, without bending or breaking.

When a hand finally reached in, she took it and allowed a young man to pull her out of the tree and into the center of his world. It didn't matter who he was, only that she'd fooled him. She fooled the town, too. They believed that she was one of them, that she'd always been there, part of their community, part of their life.

They were wed that night, and only a few weeks after, the queen felt his seed take root. She felt her womb quicken, heard a second heart beat inside her, and knew, without a doubt, it was a girl.

And the queen was pleased.

She was pleased when the girl was born and came into the world looking just like her, pale and dark and covered in stars.

She was pleased as the girl grew, full of joy and smiles but also depth and stillness. It made the queen proud, seeing the woman she would become, knowing she would make a fine sovereign.

But then, one day, the queen was not pleased.

She watched her daughter notice the neighbor boy, saw the way she smiled at him, heard her laughter, gentle and soft, and knew that, despite all her careful planning, he would be her undoing.

She prepared to leave, eager to take her daughter into the wilds and save her from the disastrous curve of the neighbor boy's smile. As she gathered her things, she paused at the box of her daughter's baby teeth, counting their pearly number, and remembering when each had fallen out. It had not been that long ago. Her daughter was so very young.

Too young, the queen realized. Too young, and not at all prepared. She needed to be older, wiser, and stronger. The queen put away her bag and went back to waiting, watching, and listening to death's approach.

Years passed.

On the day when the hoofbeats of death grew too loud for the queen to hear anything else, she pulled out her hidden cloak. They needed to escape the village, and it had to be that afternoon.

The girl had grown and, as predicted, had fallen in love with the neighbor boy. The queen knew they planned to wed. She knew her daughter's heart would break. She knew the patient young guard would heal it.

Bundling up her cloak, the queen was about to set off after her daughter when the door to the cabin opened, revealing the silhouette of a man.

He stepped into the cabin, lunging for the cloak, and the queen's eyes went wide with surprise.

Death had arrived for her at last.

33

THE DREAM BEGAN the way it always did.
    Night.
    Spring.
Barrenman's Hill.

And the jagged, jittery shapes that were not the night, were not the sky, but were somehow just as big and ancient as both.

Greer felt the stirring of shadows behind her, felt his approach, just at the shapes swooped down from on high, descending over the town, like locusts, hungry to feed.

"Finn." This part of the dream was new, knowing his name.

"My sovereign."

The screams began, ragged and raw and piercing through her heart.

"How do I stop them? How do I stop this?"

She felt him step closer to watch with her, his chest brushing the line of her shoulder blades. From the periphery of her vision, Greer saw the tips of his wings curling overhead, as tall and forbidding as a sentinel.

"Why would you want to?" His breath stirred the air across her neck, his whisper hot in her ear.

"They're going to destroy everything."

"They already have," he countered, and she suddenly realized they were not talking about the same thing. "Do you know how many trees have been cut for that mill?" Finn went on. "How many ragged wounds have been gouged into the earth for ore? Do you hear how she cries?"

Greer watched a winged figure fall out of the night and rend Michael Morag apart. The wind shifted, bringing the tang of blood. She thought she shook her head but wasn't sure. Everything felt hazy to her, lit in a dreamy filter that let her catch every moment of Mistaken's end.

"It's better like this," Finn said. He traced a finger along her, starting at the nape of her neck, letting it fall down her spine.

In the dream, she didn't think of Ellis. In the dream, there was no Ellis, just Finn and the way his simple touch made her breath catch.

The end began with the turning of the winds and the whispered slice of wings unseen.

She blinked, wondering where such a thought had come from.

"What will happen to it? To Mistaken?" she asked, nodding toward the village. A flicker of orange licked through the windows of Gil Catasch's stables. A Bright-Eyed had plummeted into it, knocking over a lantern before knocking over Gil himself.

"Does it matter?"

Finn was so close his lips caressed the curve of her ear, and though Greer knew that behind those lips were rows of serrated teeth, fangs monstrous in their size and shape, she leaned in to him, wanting to feel more.

"Will they turn them?"

"Only as you command. The Gathered will not offer their blessing without yours."

Greer imagined what it would be like to rule over the people of Mistaken. She pictured her father, face full of fury as he realized his place in this new order. She thought of Mary Beaufort, cursed with an eternity of confusion and fear; of Louise, who'd never believed in the Bright-Eyes anyway. What would she think if she became one herself?

It would be terrible, but would it be worse than if they were gone entirely? She ran her tongue over the edges of her teeth, choosing their fate.

"None should change," she decided, shocking herself.

She glanced back. Finn, now in his human form, nodded with a courtier's deference. Curiously, Greer reached out and cupped his cheek, feeling the stubble across his face and the unnatural heat which radiated off him. When his eyes flashed toward her, his eye-shine was feverishly bright. He nuzzled against her palm, luxuriating in her touch, before pressing a kiss to its center.

She wanted to be surprised but found she could not.

His lips were dry and warm. He moved them lower, flirting with the soft skin of her inner wrist. His teeth grazed over the blue veins pulsing beneath, and she wondered, should he sink them in, what would her blood—human but not, human only mostly—taste like?

Greer turned, fully facing him. He ran his hands through her hair, threading fingers around the loose locks, gently tugging the ends, and tipping her face to meet his kiss easily.

"How I've waited for you," he murmured across her mouth, opening her lips with his. His tongue swept through, dancing over hers, running along the ridges of her teeth. "Waited for this."

"For me?" she asked.

He nipped at the corner of her lips, smiling as she matched his movement.

"You," he affirmed, and pulled her to him, fitted her frame against the length of his. Finn's hands swept down her back, fingers spread wide so as not to miss a single inch of her, as their mouths ravished each other's. Her spine arched and his mouth wandered lower, ripping open the buttons of her bodice to press hot, wet kisses down the column of her throat, tasting the hollow between her clavicles, before finally, finally, reaching her breasts.

Greer closed her eyes, wanting to savor each sensation, delight in every thrill he drew from her. His hands felt as if they were everywhere, all at once, holding and grasping and kneading, pressing and prodding and claiming her as his. He was rough yet reverent, possessive and resolute, and absolutely confident that every gesture he made brought her pleasure.

And because this was a dream, and because there was no Ellis, Greer allowed herself to be pulled down, laying herself bare before Finn, before the sky, before all of Mistaken, burning in the distance.

∼

SHE WOKE WITH a gasp and wrenched herself up.

The flames burned lower now; the logs were broken apart into a bank of red embers.

Finn had returned while she'd slept and was lying on the other side of the fire, eyes closed.

She studied his sleeping form with the nightmare—had it been a nightmare?—still fresh in her mind. His face was relaxed, his brow unfurrowed, unworried. She had the terrible urge to run her thumb along the line of his cheek to see if he was as warm as in the dream, but pushed the thought away.

It would be foolish to deny that he was handsome.

Of course he's handsome, Greer thought irritably. *He can choose to look like anything he wants. Why wouldn't he try to draw me in, to entice?*

Entice . . .

She remembered the way his mouth had roamed her skin, how he'd licked her throat and nipped at her flesh, softly, with the edges of his teeth, then softer still, following with kisses and murmured appreciation.

Against her better judgment, she allowed herself to slip into memories of the dream, basking in the heat of his stare, his possessive hold. Desire gripped her, curling through her middle, snaking to her mind. Her breath quickened as she remembered the husky warmth of his voice whispering, "My sovereign," as he'd plunged into her.

It was a cold slap, ripping the haze away. Greer had no desire to rule over anything, but something in the way he'd said those two words tempted her, making her feel powerful and alluring and—

Greer shoved the thought away.

No.

She loved Ellis. She loved their life and the dreams they'd planned with all her heart.

She was not a queen.

These thoughts, these desires, were nothing more than passing fancies, bits of an overheated imagination. They were an uncontrollable wisp of wondering, a chance for her mind to sort through all the things it couldn't in the harsh light of day.

She was not the Greer from that dream. The one who'd impassively watched the Bright-Eyes destroy her town, her family, her friends. If that was happening here and now, she'd do anything in her power to stop it, to stop them.

Wouldn't I?

She felt her stomach squirm uncomfortably, painfully aware of how many seconds it took to answer herself.

Of course I would.

So it did not matter that she still felt the sensation of Finn running his hand down her side, grasping the curve of her hip as he filled her. It did not matter that the memory of his eyes smoldering into hers aroused her even now. That was a dream. Not real life.

Finn was not Ellis.

Finn was not hers.

Finn did not matter.

The only thing that did was getting to Ellis.

Greer would do whatever it took—push through untold miles of wilderness, climb a mountain, face Elowen and a court of her creatures—to save him. She would even travel with Noah Finn, ignoring the way his presence churned up everything she thought she knew and understood about her life. She needed his help, needed his knowledge. She needed his—

A cry echoed in her mind, a heady rush of insistent needs being fulfilled. She remembered, too, how he'd cried out, giving in to his desires, seizing hold of hers. She shook her head, casting away the unwanted remnant.

"You're awake."

Finn's words startled her. Greer hadn't realized he was up, staring at her through the haze of heat waves.

"Good morning," she began, uncertain of where they stood after his abrupt departure, after his potent admission.

He made a sound of reciprocation and stretched. Greer was determined not to notice the way the hem of his flannel shirt rose, revealing a stretch of taut, tanned skin. She glanced away, to make sure of it.

"How are you feeling?"

She felt along her scalp. There was no bump, no bleeding. It didn't even feel tender. "Better."

"You look it," he observed. "Slept well? Pleasant dreams and all?"

Their eyes met, and Greer was overcome by the uncanny knowledge that Noah Finn knew exactly what she'd dreamed.

"I . . ." She blinked. "I don't remember."

"Pity." He shoved himself from the ground with a groan that so perfectly echoed the sound of his release that she flushed. "You sure you're feeling better? You look . . . piqued."

In a skittering instant, he was beside her, his wrist on her forehead, the back of his hand testing the heat of her cheeks. He was close, too close, close enough that she was overcome by his scent, that wild blend of green growing things and musky warmth. It was all Greer could do to stop herself from grabbing his shoulders and pressing her mouth to his. How quickly she could pull him atop her. How quickly she could let him sink within.

What are you thinking? she wondered, wholly bewildered, horrified beyond measure.

What set her thoughts to such passion? Why was her blood so quick to race?

Blood, she realized, and wanted to laugh. It wasn't her blood but his. His blood, inside her, turning her wild and wanton. He'd done this. Beguiled and bewitched her. All with that damned blood.

Her fingers clenched, and she had the terrible urge to scratch at her skin, slice it open, cut across veins, and let his blood pour free of her. She could feel its otherness pulsing through her, seizing hold of her impulses, tempting her to ruin.

"Sunrise is coming," she said instead, nodding toward the faint lightening of the sky. "We should get going."

He froze, every muscle in him going still. "We?" he finally asked. "We are going? Together?"

Greer wanted to say no. She wanted to say no and cast him and every trace of her wild wantings to the horizon.

But she nodded. "You've been following me for days. It seems silly to stop now."

Finn's mouth curved, his grin as every bit as wicked as it had been in the dream. "Oh, Greer Mackenzie, I've followed you for so much longer than that."

1761

THE LONGING BEGAN with a bit of silk ribbon and the sound of sobs echoing through windswept trees.

The queen was dead.

The guard had felt her passing with an acute slice through his center. Her absence was sudden and glaring, a jarring hollow, a carved wound.

The moment the loss was realized, he took to the sky, leaving behind his lonely cordillera roost to race toward the little scrap of land where the queen had lived for two decades. He passed over the mine, his old home, where Elowen and the false court now reigned. His wings carried him down, across fjords and forests, lakes and marshes, until he came to the village.

The guard could feel the town's ring of protection even from so high overhead. The Stones formed a perfect barrier, a thick line nearly impossible to cross. Within the rocks were sharp scatterings of iron deposits, which held him back, pushing him away like a compass needle gone wrong, pointing anywhere but true north.

But even as he felt the Stones cast him aside, he was drawn closer, pulled along like a wave toward the moon, like salmon to spawning grounds, like moths to a flame.

He needed to see her.

The queen's daughter.

He needed to see this one small part of Ailie that still existed in the world.

Greer.

The guard flexed his wings, catching a draft to circle the town border, feeling for her. He was in luck. She was in a clearing outside the Stones, a spot he knew well. Ailie had often taken her there as a young girl, for leisurely afternoons, for picnics and play. He'd even joined them on occasion, shifting into small animals sure to delight a child: a curious hare, a spotted petrel, a large-eared ermine.

Now he swooped down soundlessly, falling through the forest, thinking which form to take. He'd watched Greer from afar for years and knew all the ways the queen's blood worked within her.

The stars across her cheek.

Her curious mind.

Her sharp ears.

As he approached cautiously, he shifted to a sleek, smaller body more suitable for creeping through tangled brambles on silent paws. He let his fur grow gray and dusky, the better to hide within the shadows.

At the edge of the clearing, the wolf paused, unable to take another step. Now that he was here, so close, he wasn't sure what to do.

The queen's daughter was crying, sunk down on her hands and knees, as great sobs racked her frame. Her anguish filled the air. The pitch and power of her sorrow withered the last of the autumn's wildflowers, curdling their petals to husks, and leaching color away from the tall grasses till the entire meadow was a sea of amber and brown. Even the clouds above seemed to respect her mourning, turning dark and somber. Too consumed with her grief, she did not notice.

The guard swished his tail through a cluster of formerly yellow arnicas, overwhelmed with wonder. The blooms were now shriveled and black. That Greer could have done this with only the register of her voice . . .

Had she bested her mother, assuming the sovereign's powers?

The guard didn't think so. Ailie wouldn't have wanted the duel here, so far from their roost, from the court. And Greer's countenance had not changed. He saw no telltale flash of eye-shine as she looked to the sky, howling.

This power, this remarkable power, was hers and hers alone.

The guard longed to go to her and let her pour her sorrows onto him, but he couldn't move. His body trembled against warring impulses.

Before the queen left, she'd made the court swear a new oath of fidelity, promising to remain faithful no matter how long her return might take. Elowen had promptly broken it, going off to serve her own desires before Ailie had even reached Mistaken. But the guard had not. He could not. He'd hold fast to his sovereign's commands until her final plan was carried out.

Only . . .

He no longer knew what that plan was. He'd counted on the queen to take Greer from Mistaken, to bring her to the mine, to tell her everything. He wasn't supposed to meet the queen's daughter here, when her grief was open and raw, when she didn't know the truth of who she was, of what she would become.

He stood watching now on uncertain ground, terrified of taking a wrong step. He wanted to howl with frustration. *Why* had the queen waited so long? *Why* hadn't she explained? *How* could she have left him with this impossible decision?

If the guard stepped out now, full of stories of courts and crowns, he'd frighten Greer, ruining any chance that she'd ever take her place as sovereign. She'd never leave the Stones again, content to keep herself in their security and in the arms of her mortal suitor.

The guard knew all about his human rival. He'd caught passing glimpses of him as he sailed high over the cove. He'd heard the queen's whispered assurances that it was a phase, a fling, a small moment of Greer's life that would never amount to anything.

Still, he regarded this boy with suspicion.

And where was he now, when his sweetheart, the girl who was supposed to mean more to him than any other in the world, was falling apart, cracking under the weight of unspeakable grief?

Greer burst into a fresh set of tears, the pitch of her agony growing higher, and the guard cowered against such might. He had to do something. He couldn't bear to witness this distress, and shuddered to think what chaos her voice might cause if it wasn't stopped.

The song fell out of him before he was even aware he'd thought of it.

It was a lullaby, a very old one.

The queen had always been full of music and melodies, sad songs of lost loves and bittersweet ends. Songs that made you forget what you were meant to be doing as you paused to listen, beguiled by the haunting beauty of her lilting notes.

The guard had watched this happen to both the Gathered and mortals alike. He watched Greer now, her sobs stuttering to a stop as she caught the first strain of his mimicked notes. Her bright-gray eyes were large and luminous as they swept over the edge of the clearing, looking into the trees. When they passed over the guard, his breath caught, and he stopped the song.

"Mama?" There was so much hope contained in that one anxious word that the guard's chest ached and he could not continue.

The queen's daughter pushed herself up and approached the forest. He wondered if he'd somehow made a noise that had given his location away, or if she, too, felt the unmistakable link they shared.

The guard didn't know what inspired it—if it was the queen's will or his own heart—but he knew he could travel the whole expanse of the frozen north, flying thousands of miles to its distant rocky shore, and always find his way back to her.

Greer.

He knew the sound of her blood. Its racing cadences were as familiar to him as his own. He knew each and every one of her bends and curves, from the way her eyes lifted as she smiled to the full swell of her lips, and the angular shapes her fingers made as she drew, holding on to charcoal nubs. From afar she had dazzled him, bewitching his heart, holding captive his thoughts, so that all he could see was their shared future.

They would reclaim the court, and Greer would take her place as the rightful sovereign. The Gathered would leave behind these mountains and go north, go west, go wherever their wanderlust led. They would see wonders.

But first, he'd need to—

A twig snapped underfoot, pulling the guard back to the here and now. She'd gotten so much closer. His ears perked, and their movement drew her attention. When she spotted him, she let out a short gasp.

The guard swayed from side to side, unsure of what to do. He whined softly, praying she'd understand he was not a threat. Again, the queen's daughter surprised him. With slow, careful movements, she knelt into a gathering of reeds, her eyes never leaving his.

"Mama loved wolves," she began, her voice wavering and raw. "Did she . . . did she send you to me?"

The guard ducked, an assent, a reverent bow. He wasn't sure how she took the gesture, but one corner of her mouth rose, in a faint smile.

"She died today," she went on. "And I know she's gone, I know she's not coming back, but . . . I could have sworn I just heard her singing." Her laugh was barbed and bitter. "I feel like I've gone mad."

She hung her head low, and a dark lock of hair tumbled from her braid. Everything in the guard ached to shift, so that he might be the one to tuck the strands behind her ear, so that he might be the one to push aside her tears. They fell unchecked from her swollen eyes, and she hugged her arms tightly around her body.

The guard could feel time pass, slipping over their shared moment like water droplets racing off the wings of a duck. The sky grew darker, and the woods readied for the coming night. Crepuscular animals awoke in their burrows. Owls stirred. Crickets and katydids broke into song. But the queen's daughter didn't notice.

It wasn't until a great bellowing roar rolled down from the hill inside the Stones that she stirred. She blinked hard, realizing the time, realizing what the horn meant.

"I . . . I have to go. Father will be . . ." Her voice tightened and dropped away. She looked at the guard. "I wish I had a gratitude to give you." She searched the clearing, absently fiddling with a length of silk wrapped around her wrist.

The guard instantly recognized the starry knots and stitches. The queen had sewn this ribbon. With gentle movements, he edged closer to her, nudging at the bracelet with his snout. Greer took in a sharp breath, but he did not smell fear, only wonder.

"Would you . . ." she began, then laughed with soft incredulity. "Would you like this?"

He lowered his head, showing he meant no harm, and remained as still as he could as she removed the ribbon and tied it loosely around one of his front paws.

"Thank you for staying with me," she whispered before daring to trace one finger along the curve of a toe. Then she brushed over his claws and jerked away, tightening her hand into a fist.

"Greer!" a voice shouted, breaking the moment. Both of them snapped their heads toward the Stones, instantly alert. "Greer, where are you?"

The guard's ears flattened.

It was the boy.

"I have to go," she apologized, pushing herself from the ground, pushing herself from the guard.

He wanted to call out to her, to stop her, to keep her here with him. "Stay!" he wanted to cry.

But she crossed the clearing, returning once more to the hateful Stone, caressing its surface as she passed by. Her fingers brushed along its luster in unconscious routine, and Finn closed his eyes, imagining it was him she touched instead.

34

THEY SET OFF at sunrise, Finn leading the way.
Greer had expected him to follow the winding riverbank, but he plunged straight into the forest, without even a glance at her map. Heeding his internal compass, Finn roamed the terrain with ease, and it was all Greer could do to keep up. He slipped through the tangled undergrowth with preternatural grace, always a dozen or so steps ahead of her, making any attempt at conversation impossible.

If she was being honest, the grueling pace was a bit of relief. Her head was muddy with thoughts and worries, and Finn's clip stamped at least some of them into an exhausted silence.

Still, all the hiking in the world couldn't make her forget the way he'd looked at her last night before slipping into the woods. It couldn't erase the dream, and the way it kept repeating through her mind. She'd felt so connected to him in it. Not just in the physical way the dream had played out, but in the familiar intimacy of their conversation. They'd been two people well acquainted with each other, comfortable and at ease, and Greer was surprised to find how much she wished for that now.

Ellis, she reminded herself. *You have that ease with Ellis.*

But . . . did she?

Before the Hunt, before this journey, she wouldn't have hesitated to say yes, to shout it from Barrenman's Hill, to let the entire cove know that she loved Ellis Beaufort with all her heart and always would.

And she still did.

But her heart . . .

She knew things now about that heart, about the blood it pumped, that would certainly give Ellis reason to wonder about—if not outright question—her loyalty. She wasn't the girl he'd fallen in love with. In truth, that girl had never existed. Not even mostly.

What would Ellis think of all of this, of her new self? What would his family, his mother, Louise? Louise would be horrified, her best friend become the very monster she didn't believe in.

It was all too terrible to bear.

When Greer began her journey, she hadn't thought about the Beauforts. She'd only envisioned Ellis and herself, armed with their beaded charms and dizzyingly in love, heading out into the world for adventure and exploration. She wanted to laugh at how naïve she'd been.

Ellis was a good and responsible man. He cared deeply for his family and would never let them come to harm. That he was out here now, wandering through the wilderness as a sacrifice for the town, was proof of it. He was trying to appease the Benevolence, offering himself so that they would continue to hold back the Bright-Eyes.

Greer stopped in her tracks, as a new thought seized hold of her.

Bright-Eyed blood ran through her veins. She wasn't one of them, not exactly, but would the Benevolence note such a distinction?

Her eyes, now so sharp and keen, flickered through the trees surrounding them, searching, searching for any sign that they might be near.

"Greer?"

She glanced up the hill. Finn had noticed she'd paused; half a dozen yards from her, he looked back with concern.

"We're almost to the top of the ridge."

"Yes." She swept her gaze over the forest again, certain one of the Benevolence was about to step out from the shadows and tear her to bits.

"Are you all right?"

No.

"Yes," she repeated instead.

Finn studied her. "We can rest once we've reached the edge."

She stayed planted, shifting the weight of her pack while peering through trees and pockets of undergrowth. She wasn't even sure what to be looking for. If the Bright-Eyes could shift and mimic their surroundings, it only stood to reason that the Benevolence—by all accounts, more powerful and clever—could do the same. She could be looking at a whole horde of them right now and she wouldn't know.

Before, such an idea would have comforted her. She would have felt protected and safe. But now . . . did her faithfulness matter anything to them? Her gratitudes and gifts? Her prayers and pleas? All her life, she'd tried so hard to honor and revere them. Did they care at all about the veneration of an enemy?

As the hairs on the back of her neck rose, she turned and hurried after Finn.

THE LAST STRETCH UP the ridge was the worst.

The embankment was so steep, Greer all but crawled up it, grabbing at rocks and exposed tree roots to help pull herself along.

"A few more yards," Finn called out, already at the top.

Greer knew he'd meant it as encouragement, but in the moment, it seemed like an executioner's sentencing. Her dress clung to her in a sticky, sweaty embrace, and her pack seemed determined to flatten her into the earth. She'd lightened it before they set out it, casting aside anything ruined by the river, but it now seemed to have doubled in weight. Tripled, even. With a great heaving breath, Greer pressed on, gaining a scant number of inches.

For the first time that day, Finn approached her, shuffling back down the hill with infuriating ease.

"Here," he said, holding out his hand.

"I can do it," she insisted and wished her words had been infused with strength instead of coming out in such a deflated gasp.

"Greer," he insisted. "Give me the pack, at least."

With the giant rucksack gone, she did find it easier to scale the rest of the ascent. Finn stayed with her the whole way, remaining blessedly silent as she fought her way up. When they reached the top, Greer sank down, drawing in great heaping gulps of air. So far into the foothills, it was thinner, and she felt she had to take in twice as many breaths.

Beyond the ridge's crest rose the first of the Severings, looming over the valley like a watchful god. It was bigger than anything Greer could have ever imagined, sprawling out for miles and rising high into the clouds. It was rocky and forbidding, full of sheer walls and jagged crevasses. Some trees edged along its base like a skirt, but they petered away as the mountain grew, revealing a deadly world of rock and ice.

"There's a road up to Sandry," Finn said, as if reading her mind. He pointed to a spot roughly halfway up a series of crests. "It's pocked and overgrown, but it will be easier than this."

Greer couldn't believe such reassurances but didn't have the energy to voice her doubt.

"Water," he instructed.

She unlooped the canteen from the rucksack's straps and pulled out the cork stopper. "You first," she said, offering it to Finn.

Surprised, he took a few swallows before sinking down to the ground beside her and handing the canteen back. "It *has* been a hard climb," he said, as she drank deeply.

Greer wiped the back of her hand over her lips and let out a small sigh. "Has it? You look like we've been out on a leisurely stroll."

He smiled. "Trust me, it has. Flying would have . . ." He shrugged; their differences could not be helped. "Do you need more?"

Wearily, Greer took another long swig from the canteen.

"No, I meant . . ." Finn nodded toward his wrist.

"Oh," she said, her gaze falling to the strip of cloth covering the spot where just last night he'd ripped open his flesh for her. She spotted another bit of fabric beneath the makeshift bandage and squinted, struck by a strange sense of uneasiness.

"I think it would help." He unwound the bandage, ready to offer more of his blood, more of himself, and revealed a dark strip of silk.

Greer snatched his wrist, bringing the bracelet in for closer inspection.

It had been seven years since Greer had seen the ribbon, and though it was tattered and frayed, its once-bright colors now faded into hazy hues, she would have recognized it anywhere.

"Where did you get this?" she whispered.

Finn took a breath, but before he could answer, realization washed over her.

"It was you," she said. "That day in the clearing. You were the wolf." She looked away as an uncomfortable heat filled her cheeks. How foolish he must think her, falling for his ruse, actually believing her dead mother had sent a sign just for her.

"I didn't want you to hurt alone."

The simplicity of his admission made her glance back, daring to meet his stare. "You knew when she'd died?"

He nodded. "I felt it. Here."

He raised his hand—the one wearing her mother's ribbon—and touched his chest, gesturing to his heart.

Like a fish caught on a line and pulled to shore, Greer leaned in, reaching for the bracelet. She traced a finger over it and felt the heat of his skin beneath the worn silk.

"It was the best gratitude I could think to give," she said, admiring her mother's stitches, still dazzling and perfect even after so many years. "I'd thought . . . I was so grateful to have you there. I'd cried for so long and . . ." She glanced up, startling at how close their faces were. But she didn't back away. "You stayed with me. That whole afternoon."

"It was as much a comfort for me as it was for you."

Greer studied his profile with fresh eyes, recalling his earlier words. Here was proof of just how long he'd followed after her, watched over her, but for reasons Greer could not put into words, it did not bother her. In fact, it . . .

"Do you want it back?"

His voice was less than a whisper, brushing across her ears with husky intimacy.

Greer withdrew her hand. Part of her did, longing to have this small scrap of Ailie with her as she ventured into the mines. The other part of her warmed as she realized how long Finn had held on to it. She liked knowing that a little part of her had been with him, too. "No. I gave it freely. It's yours."

"I don't have many possessions," he admitted, "but it is my most treasured." His gaze fell on her. "When Ailie died . . . it felt as though part of me had as well. But being there, with you . . . you helped ease that ache."

Unable to stand the weight of his eyes upon hers for another second, she looked away, peering out over the valley, then gasped. "What *is* that?"

Below them was a wide basin, the last level swath of land before the Severing Mountains began to rise. It was littered with great piles of debris and wreckage. Tall, broken timbers jutted from messes of fallen bricks and torn-apart roofs. It had been a town once, quite sizable, but now . . .

Nature had begun to creep back and reclaim the once settled area for its own. Saplings stood in the middle of roofless structures. Remnants of cabins and other buildings were covered in green moss and gray lichen. She could pick out what had been the main thoroughfare, several large buildings, shops, a blacksmith's forge, stables. This had been a bustling, thriving community, at least a hundred families strong.

Greer pulled out her map and searched for anything that would indicate what this disaster had been. "Was that Laird?"

"Once," Finn confirmed.

"What . . . what happened to it?" she asked, already knowing the answer. Greer had read survivors' accounts, she knew Martha's stories, she'd seen it play out in her dreams.

Finn shifted, sensing a response wasn't needed.

"How many Bright-Eyes were there?"

"Here?"

Greer thought she nodded.

He kept his gaze trained on the scene before them. "Two."

Two.

Two creatures had unleashed this much damage and devastation.

Decades had gone by since the massacre, but Greer fancied she could still hear the echoes of Laird's screams hanging in the air, ringing off the crumbling structures, seeping from the bones of houses long emptied of inhabitants.

"Well. Three, I suppose, at the end." Finn scratched at the back of his neck. "This was where Elowen turned me."

"This was your home?" Greer was aghast. He nodded. "How long ago did this happen? How many people were killed?"

He shrugged, unbothered. "I don't remember."

Greer thought of the hares she'd eaten, the eel Martha had baked into a pie. Cuts of venison, rashers of bacon. She wouldn't have bothered to remember them, either, and her gut twisted with shame and disgust.

But when I eat a slice of ham, I don't slaughter every hog in Mistaken.

She spotted a pale length of bone curving down from the remains of a rafter, and winced. It was part of a rib cage. Greer looked away, not wanting to imagine how it could have ended up there.

"We'll need to get to that," Finn said, pointing toward the hill on the other side of the village. Greer could just make out the remains of a road, still traced faintly into the earth like a nearly healed scar. It led up into the mountains, up to Sandry.

"This was where the miners lived," she murmured, piecing everything together. "With their families . . ."

She studied Finn, wondering if he'd had a family then, a mother and father or a wife and children. He shrugged again, unconcerned, and his lack of interest made her heart ache.

"Were you a miner?" she pressed.

"I don't remember."

"You lived here. Surely, there must be something."

Finn frowned. "I . . . I probably was. My feet . . . There must have been an accident, before I turned. Some of my toes were crushed. They still are." His gaze flickered up to the mountains before them. "Do you think the mines could have done that?"

She thought about his two-toed prints. "It's possible."

He nodded, as if the matter was settled, then reached out his hand. "It's steep."

Greer stared at his proffered fingers. They were long and thin, rough with calluses, and looked so terribly human.

She considered her own. Ailie, in a fit of bloodlust, had torn apart an entire town. That same blood flowed through Greer's veins. She remembered the entirely too-still form of Lachlan Davis, laying in a broken heap at Mistaken's border. She'd done that, with just the power of her voice. What would her hands be capable of?

She studied the stitches of Ailie's ribbon and the tight series of knots she'd tied with her own hands, overwhelmed by a sense of bewilderment. She felt too human to side with what she knew lurked beneath Finn's exterior. But she herself was too monstrous ever to return to Mistaken. Where did that leave her?

"Greer?" he prompted, stirring her from the tortured reverie.

She glanced behind her, staring down the hill they'd climbed as if she could see all the way back to Mistaken, and then Greer slipped her hand into his and followed Noah Finn into the remains of Laird.

35

THEY TRAVELED ALONG the center of the road. Burnt-out shells of buildings rose on either side. The ground was littered with shards of glass and the broken bits of so many lives. Greer spotted the cracked face of a porcelain doll. Its body was long gone, and the toy seemed to regard her with an accusatory stare, as if Greer were personally responsible for its missing limbs.

In a way, she felt she was.

"It's so quiet here," she murmured, and her voice seemed to hang too long in the untouched air.

She'd expected the town to have the same white noise as the forest—claws scurrying up trees and feathers flapping, birdsong and pattering from the game trail—but there was nothing here. Even the wind seemed far away, shying high above them, unwilling to touch the forsaken remains.

"You look troubled," Finn said, watching her from the corner of his eye. Greer had dropped his hand the moment they were on level ground, but he kept finding ways to reach for her, helping her around rubble, steadying her on a slippery bit of ground. Like a lover. Like a consort. "These people would be long dead, even if Ailie and Elowen hadn't come."

It wasn't exactly true. The original miners would be gone, but there would have been others, descendants and new settlers. This town would have been thriving had it not been for the Gathered. There would not be this wide and gaping nothing.

They passed by the remains of a small cabin. A crumbling wall held up a column of bricks that had been a hearth. From the shadowed depths came a crack, the sound of weight snapping a branch in two, and Finn and Greer froze, their heads swiftly turning in unison to the source.

A pair of dark, limpid dots stared from the gloomy mess. They were wide and unblinking, the eyes of a white-tailed deer. A doe.

Finn's stomach let out a gurgle of emptiness, breaking the moment.

In a flash, the doe sprang from the ruined cabin and bounded away. Finn started after it, then stopped short, glancing to Greer. She could feel his expectation, but he said nothing.

"You're hungry," she realized. Still, he waited. "Don't let me stop you."

"Follow the road through town to the first crest," he said, pointing. "We'll meet there. I'll save you the best parts," he promised before changing forms as he crashed through the trees after the doe. Greer heard a rush of air as his wings burst from him, and she alternated between admiration and horror. How much of his blood would she need to fly?

Feeling impossibly earthbound, Greer continued through the deserted town.

Most of the remains had been pulled apart long ago, stolen by scavengers or washed away in bad weather, but every so often, Greer caught sight of a length of femur, the wide scoop of a scapula. She even saw a tiny skull peeking from the depths of a gnarled Redcap. Its bleached surface looked like the face of a barn owl. Greer lowered her gaze to her feet, vowing not to look up until she was well outside of Laird.

Even though she knew the brutality had played out long ago, Greer's chest ached with dread and guilt. This town was not so different from Mistaken, but there'd been no protection from the Bright-Eyes. They'd had no Warding Stones.

Why should one town be blessed with such favor, such privilege, while so many were not? Greer knew her father and the Stewards would say they'd been selected because of their goodness, their moral superiority, because they'd taken the initiative to make a truce with the Benevolence.

Had Laird not done so? Or Saint Agnabath? Or any of the other dozens of towns Greer knew had been attacked? It seemed like the grandest stroke of dumb luck to be born in a place like Mistaken, trapped but safe, cursed but protected.

Instinctively, she worried at the beaded stones round her neck. Tears pricked at her eyes as she felt the collective crush of so many lives torn apart. How could the Benevolence have allowed it to happen? If they'd blessed Mistaken, why not the other settlements, too? The people within the Warding Stones were no better than these miners. They'd had lives and loves, families and dreams. Shouldn't that have mattered?

As she picked her way over a split and moldering cask of ale, a sound caught her attention, drawing her from her dark thoughts. Slowly, she turned. Though she was certain she'd heard the soft padding of footsteps, she saw no one.

Greer narrowed her eyes and took another step.

Faltering just a half-second behind came the sound. She tested it again. And again.

Whatever followed her only moved as she moved, making it next to impossible to determine where the watcher was.

Greer glanced down the road. She only had a few hundred feet before she'd pass the last of the buildings and escape Laird, before she'd be in the wild once more. She decided to press on.

It came again, a rustled creeping, and Greer tried her best to not imagine the worst.

From the periphery of her vision, she spotted movement slipping in and out of the shadows. It darted though the space between buildings so quickly, Greer almost believed her eyes were playing tricks on her.

"Elowen?" Greer dared to ask, even though she didn't think it was the Bright-Eyed. She wanted to make her presence known. She wouldn't hide or skulk, even if that might have given her the element of surprise.

No one answered.

Without thinking, Greer ducked into the crumbling remnants of a cabin. The open space was littered with broken chairs and debris.

"She went that way," a voice whispered outside, catching her attention.

She kept low, hiding under the remainder of a windowed wall before carefully peeking over its top. Two figures crept along the back side of the road, dipping in and out of the ruins, clearly following her. One was dressed in loose, beaded leather pants and a heavy furred cloak. Its hood was pulled up, obscuring his face. And the other . . .

Greer paused, instantly recognizing the wool coat.

She nearly fell over herself in her haste to flee the hiding spot.

Her joy echoed off the empty remains of Laird as she shouted his name. "Ellis!"

36

THE FIGURE TURNED, and her hope plummeted.

This was not Ellis.

It was a girl, not much younger than Greer herself. Her skin was a rich copper. Her dark eyes were wide with fear, like those of a deer catching the scent of a nearby predator.

With dismay, Greer looked again at the coat's sleeve. Yes. There, near the elbow, was the patch she'd sewn on after a spark from the bakery's ovens had singed the wool. She'd carefully darned the hole over, even embroidering a tiny heart into the sleeve. She'd teased that Ellis could take her love with him wherever he went.

Except her heart was now here with this stranger, and Ellis was not.

"Where did you get that coat?" Greer demanded, forgoing any attempt at civility as she braced herself for the worst. She couldn't imagine a scenario in which, with winter fast approaching, Ellis felt compelled to give up his coat.

The two strangers stood motionless.

"Do you . . . do you speak English?" Greer asked, heart faltering. There were a few groups of hunters and nomads from the south who occasioned through Mistaken, looking to trade. They never stayed for long, knowing to cross the town's border well before sunset.

The stranger took a step back, eyeing her warily. Her mittened hands clutched at the gaping collar. The coat was far too big on her small frame. "It was an even trade; I didn't steal it."

"A trade?" Greer repeated, trying to temper her flare of irritation. She had the overwhelming urge to grab the young girl and shake her. She could feel herself lean into the motion but held back, alarmed by the dark impulses that festered under her skin, ever since Finn had slipped her that canteen of blood. She licked her lips, trying so hard to slow her thoughts, to hold back her urgency. "I just . . . I've been searching for the man who wore that coat. When did you trade with him?"

The stranger looked to her companion, as if wondering how to answer.

He wore a furred cloak and was far older than the girl. His eyes were lined and weathered. Wide streaks of silver ran through his long black hair. The girl had so many similar features that Greer thought she must be a granddaughter.

"Yesterday," the man finally answered. "We were checking traps along the river, and he wandered out of the trees."

"He was full of hunger," the girl interjected. "Delirious with the pains of it. He gave me the coat in exchange for a meal. When I tried to give it back, he wouldn't take it. He said he owed me more than he could ever repay."

That sounded just like Ellis, stubborn and proud to a fault.

"How did he look? Was anyone else with him?"

The pair exchanged a glance that Greer could not read.

"I've been looking for him for days and have been so worried," she pressed. "Anything you could share, no matter how small a detail, would be so welcome. Even if it . . . even if it sounds upsetting. I can handle it. Please."

The older man shifted, looking uneasy. "How do you know him, this man? Are you kin?"

Greer nodded eagerly, hungry for information. "Yes! Well, nearly. We're to be wed. But . . ." Greer's words faltered, losing their momentum.

The granddaughter opened her mouth, ready to say something, but apparently thought better of it and looked away, uncomfortable.

The man offered a small wince of remorse. "It would be best to forget him. He is gone."

"Gone?" Greer repeated, trying and failing to draw breath.

"Bewitched," he intoned. He toyed at a strap of leather around his throat, studded with metal beads and woven wires, and mustered an expression of sympathy for Greer. "You won't see him again. The Fire-Eyed Ones will have had their way with him by now. I'm sorry."

"The Fire-Eyed Ones," she echoed.

The older man nodded. "Evil spirits that walk the earth, always looking to feed. They can look like you or me but are not." He frowned, as if searching for the right words. "You can always tell their true nature by their eyes," he went on. "They burn like flames, like animals in the dark."

"My grandfather thought you were one at first," the girl admitted, looking sheepish.

"Oh," Greer said, uncertain of how to deny it, thankful it was daylight. She had no idea how long Finn's infusion would affect her and couldn't imagine what would happen if these strangers should happen to see her eyes flash.

"But now we know you're not."

"You do?"

The girl pointed at her throat to a necklace that looked just like the one her grandfather wore. "The iron keeps them back. It . . ." She frowned, searching. "It wards them away. You would not be so close now if you were one of them."

"But that man you are with," the grandfather began. His thick eyebrows were drawn to an almost solid line, concern evident on his face. "He is not a good man. He is not even a man at all."

"I know," she admitted reluctantly.

"You know what he truly is?"

Reluctantly, Greer nodded. "We call them the Bright-Eyes."

He looked surprised. "You know this, yet you travel with him?"

"I need his help."

The set of the grandfather's jaw hardened. "Then I think you do not know the Fire-Eyed Ones at all. If you did, you would not trust them. You would let your beloved go and not follow after."

Tears pricked at Greer's eyes. "I can't. I'm not . . . I'm not leaving him out here. Not with them."

"Where is your protection?" he asked, unmoved. "What weapons do you have?"

Greer hesitated, unwilling to admit that she was alone without so much as a pocketknife. "I have wards," she began, pulling out the beaded necklace. They inspected it with narrowed eyes, unimpressed. "And . . . other things."

The granddaughter's expression darkened. "You have nothing. The Fire-Eyed Ones are a pestilence that cannot be stopped. They've eaten nearly everything the land has. Elk, caribou, musk ox. Even the white bears are no match for them. They go after the sturgeon, plucking them from the waters like minnows. You cannot fight beasts like this."

"I don't want to fight them," Greer said, feeling foolish and small. "I just want to save Ellis—the man you met."

The girl made a snort of dismissal.

"Tell me about your beads. I've never seen anything like them," the man said, gesturing to her necklace.

"I'm not sure where they came from," she confessed. "I think maybe the Benevolence?"

"Benevolence," he repeated carefully, as though it was the first time he'd ever said the word.

Greer paused, wondering what they would call them. "The ones who keep the Fire-Eyed Ones away. The Benevolence is like . . . their minders? Their wardens?" With curved fingers, she pantomimed a circle of protection.

The older man shook his head. "No one holds power over those spirits."

"They do." She explained how Mistaken's settlers had made the truce, how the Stones the Benevolence gave them repelled the creatures but also held their people to the same stretch of earth. The strangers looked horrified. "Without the Benevolence, how do you stay safe?"

The grandfather glanced at the buildings around them. "Our people wander, following the earth's gentle tugs. It has been many years since we were so close to these mountains. It is much changed here. The Fire-Eyed Ones have reshaped the land, reshaped everything. Patterns and rhythms that have held since the rivers were created no longer make sense. They've broken down, they're breaking apart."

"The Bright-Eyeds weren't always here?"

He shook his head. "They arrived with the white men from across the sea. They come from your ancestors' world, not ours." His eyes shifted, leaving hers to study the trees just beyond the broken buildings. "I often wonder what that world must be like, to have created so many kinds of monsters."

Greer frowned, uncomfortable with the implication. She'd always assumed the Bright-Eyeds were of this new world, part of its vast landscape, as ancient as the mountain themselves. But if not . . . had a settler from across the sea unknowingly brought them over?

Not them, she realized with horror. *Ailie.*

Ailie had been sovereign then. It would have been her on the ship.

What had prompted her mother to leave behind her homeland and venture into the unknown? She pictured her clinging to the sides of a great schooner, her wings folded into tight, serpentine lines, like a lamprey suctioned onto prey. How had no one noticed her? Perhaps she'd masqueraded as livestock, or a member of the crew itself.

Greer imagined her mother stepping off the ship, regarding the wilds before her. She could feel Ailie's hungers stirring, insatiable appetites wakening. She glanced around Laird's remains. This was what those appetites and hungers had brought.

"Forget the boy," the older man advised. "Forget the monster you travel with, return home, and pray your mighty Stones keep their power."

"What about you? You're not safe out here. Where are your people?"

The girl began to answer but her grandfather silenced her with a sharp look.

"She's not one of them," she protested.

"She was *with* one of them," he hissed. "We cannot risk trusting her."

"That's fair," Greer allowed. "Though I truly mean you no harm. I'll leave now. Not for home," she added in a rush, seeing the grandfather's face begin to relax. "I'm not going back without Ellis."

His expression dimmed. "Then I fear you will not be going back at all." He placed a hand on his granddaughter's shoulder. "Leave her to her mad endeavor."

The girl nodded, and they turned to leave.

"Safe travels," Greer called after them, wishing it with all her heart.

The girl looked back, offering a small smile. She paused, indecision flickering over her face, then ran to Greer, ignoring her grandfather's protests.

"Food wasn't the only thing that man traded his coat for," she began in a whispered rush. "He asked for protection. He said he was in great danger. Grandfather doesn't know, but I gave him my knife," she admitted. "My iron knife," she added meaningfully.

The older man reached them and pulled the girl away without another word.

Greer watched them leave before turning to her own journey. She could feel a small flicker of hope kindle inside her.

No matter what Elowen had done to bewitch him, Ellis knew he was in danger.

But now he had a weapon.

Now he was prepared to fight back.

37

WHEN GREER FINALLY ascended the crest, sweating and winded by her climb, she was surprised to find Noah Finn was not there.

She dropped her pack and peered over the land below with shielded eyes. So high up, she had an excellent view of the valley, but couldn't see any sign of him. She glanced up the mountain behind her and saw only trees.

It seemed impossible for her to have beaten him.

She cupped her hands and shouted out his name. Her voice ricocheted off rocks and the ruins of Laird, but after the echoes died, the air fell still, her call unanswered.

Greer pulled out her canteen and took several swallows of water, wondering and waiting.

So far into the foothills, the sun felt closer here, but it was a cold, pale light that fell on her. Snow was coming. Greer could feel the storm's approach with a dull ache in the middle of her bones. It was a big one, and she wouldn't be surprised if, by morning, they were buried under layers of white.

As Greer took another drink, she studied the way the road snaked back and forth, quickly rising in elevation. Long ago, miners would have used it to haul their equipment and supplies up the mountain before returning with heavy carts of harvested ore. Greer didn't doubt the hike would be exhausting, but one she should be more than capable of doing on her own.

Only . . .

She swallowed hard.

She had no idea of what to expect when she got to the mine. She'd assumed Finn would be with her, coaching and encouraging, lending a hand if necessary. Greer couldn't imagine taking on Elowen without him.

Greer rubbed her hands over her arms in a flurry of adrenaline as apprehension and doubt set her skin to gooseflesh.

What was she doing?

What was she thinking?

The strangers had been right. This was a mad endeavor. One that would undoubtedly get her killed.

Greer looked over the valley again, searching for Finn. She paced across the ledge. She could wait, burning up precious hours of daylight, and they could go up together, the way it was supposed to happen. Or—

"Starling," the voice came down from the mountainside, ringing and resonant.

Greer whipped around, but the only thing moving was a bank of clouds rolling in. The snow was closer than she'd thought.

"What are you waiting for, Starling?" Elowen called out with a surprising lightness. "Come find me. Come find your love."

Greer's jaw tensed so hard that her molars ground together. She knew Elowen wanted to bait her into doing something stupid and rash.

"I know you hear me," Elowen went on. "You hear everything, don't you, little half-wit? Why don't you answer?" Her laughter sounded like the trickle of a brook, lilting and musical. "Answer me, Starling. Go on."

Resolutely, Greer sat atop her pack. She sipped at the canteen again, staring forward as if taking in the view.

"Answer me!" Annoyance rumbled in Elowen's voice. Its reverberations vibrated through Greer's body, making her clavicles feel as though they would shake apart.

"I will when I have something to say!" Greer snapped and when she spoke, her words sliced through the very land around her, shaking trees and rocks in equal measure.

Elowen fell silent, retreating, and Greer watched with fascination as little pebbles skittered down the slope beside her, jarred from their stasis by the residual echo of her voice. Even as her head throbbed, she felt a strange wave of pleasure in having created something so tangible.

Absentmindedly, she rubbed at her chest, feeling where Elowen's words had sunk in. Though they'd hurt Greer, they didn't seem to have affected anything else. Another stone, the size of her thumbnail, rolled downhill, leaving behind a squiggling wake.

Finn had said Ailie knew her daughter would be strong, stronger than even a mortal turned Bright-Eyed, but Greer hadn't believed it. She couldn't change her appearance, transforming into whatever suited her fancy. She couldn't leap into the air, knowing wings would catch and hold her. She was not strong, not in the way Finn and Elowen were.

She reached out and traced the rock's path.

But her voice had done that.

Elowen's had not.

Greer remembered the moment she'd screamed Elowen out of the sky, the rolling thud as she'd smashed into the earth. She remembered the way the trees swayed and the river shifted.

She'd done that.

Perhaps that was the only weapon she needed.

The clouds were well and truly settled in, low enough that Greer felt she could reach out and touch them. The storm would soon be upon her.

She had no more time to wait.

She had no more time to waste.

Finn would have to find her on his own.

Greer stood and slung the pack over her shoulder.

"I'm coming, Elowen," she said, not with a scream, not with a shout. Just a whisper she had no doubt the Bright-Eyed heard every syllable of. "I'm coming for you."

INSTEAD OF FOLLOWING the miners' road up the mountain, Greer kept to the forest running alongside it. Though Elowen obviously knew she was on her way, the road felt too open, too exposed for travel.

Snow had begun to fall. The flakes were thick and heavy, quickly dusting a layer of powder over everything and reducing the world to a palette of grays and whites.

The woods were littered with strange piles of debris: large swaths of metal railing curved into impossible shapes, wheels and cogs and levers and so many things she couldn't identify, all torn apart, useless and rusting.

Iron, Greer realized, passing a giant spool of cable that was nearly as tall as she was.

This was iron machinery from the mines. When the Bright-Eyeds had taken the caverns, they must have ripped apart anything left behind, casting it down the mountain, exiling the cursed metal as far from them as they could.

The forest had begun to reclaim the space, covering the detritus in creeping vines and determined saplings. Greer thought about taking something with her, but even the smallest pieces weighed too much, and grasping the metal for only seconds was enough to make her own palms break into itchy discomfort. She shuddered to think how the creatures had stomached removing so many pieces themselves, and wondered why they simply hadn't chosen a different spot to roost.

Greer wondered if she might somehow lure Elowen here and use her voice to impale her upon a ragged piece of railroad track. She smiled—picturing how Elowen's limbs would flail like those of a pinned insect—then stopped short, wanting to cast the horrible idea from herself. Since she drank Finn's blood, her mind no longer felt entirely her own, too easily prone to thoughts of dark desires and violence.

Greer closed her eyes and tried to wipe it clear of everything but Ellis.

She imagined how good their reunion would be, how she'd feel like herself again, secure and whole, because the other half of her heart would be back.

She drew a deep, centering breath, then opened her eyes and gasped.

There, just up the embankment, as if summoned by her thoughts, was Ellis.

He was holding his side and walking with a strange sort of hitch, favoring his right leg as he hop-walked down the road.

Greer wanted to race to him, wanted to crash into him and throw her arms around his neck. She wanted to pull him to her and cover him with a hundred kisses. A thousand. She never wanted to stop kissing him. But she held herself in check, remaining hidden in the shadows of the trees, certain this was a trap.

The wind shifted, hurling snowflakes into his eyes, and he tucked his arms tightly around his frame.

Even from so far away, Greer could see his shivers. "Stupid coatless boy."

She glanced up the road from where he'd come, waiting to see a flash of eye-shine as Elowen stalked after him. But Ellis staggered through the snowstorm all on his own. His labored breathing filled her ears. There was something terribly wrong about it, a heavy wetness that shouldn't have been there.

He stumbled again, pitching forward to land hard on his knees, and Greer couldn't take it any longer. She burst after him, already slipping free of Finn's coat.

"Ellis!"

He looked up, squinting into the trees, frozen with fear. For a long moment, he stared at her, motionless and without response. Then she was beside him, putting the coat around his shoulders, cupping his face as she pressed her forehead to his. He blinked slowly, once, twice, as if wresting himself out of a dream, a trance, a nightmare. He gasped. "Greer?"

She laughed, throwing her arms around him.

It took him a moment to return her embrace. "What are you doing here? What are you—how are you—"

"We need to get you out of this cold," she said, and ran her hands over his arms, trying to generate warmth. Tears of happiness welled in her eyes as she felt the tangible, solid heft of him.

"Are you really here?" he asked, his voice hushed with wonder.

"I really am," she promised. "There's more shelter in the trees. Let's get off the road."

"You've been here before," he accused, protesting her lead. "You were, but it wasn't you. They made me . . . *She* made me see all kinds of things that weren't here."

"Ellis, I promise you, it's me. I'm real and I'm here and I'm getting you off this mountain."

He released a rush of air that sounded like a sob. "It's really you?"

Greer nodded and pressed a quick kiss to his forehead. "Come on."

She hoisted him to his feet. He leaned heavily against her, and slowly, gently, Greer led him into the woods. Returning by way of the road left them too exposed, too vulnerable. They'd take cover in the trees, resting for a moment while she sorted Ellis and his injuries out, then they'd try to reach Laird by nightfall.

"Where's Elowen?" she asked, once they'd found shelter under the boughs of a thick fir. "Why isn't she coming after you?"

Ellis sighed, sounding impossibly exhausted. "She's gone."

"Gone?" she echoed and peered toward the road with disbelief.

He nodded. "I took care of her. I . . . I . . ." His sentence dissolved into a wretched cough that sounded as though his body was tearing apart.

"Ellis!" Greer exclaimed, drawing him to her. "Get this on all the way, fasten it up," she chastised, helping him into Finn's coat. She rubbed her hands along his body, trying to stir some sort of heat into his limbs. He felt cold, so cold, a block of ice, his body immobile and so . . .

Greer stopped her ministrations.

. . . bloodless.

"Ellis . . ." she began cautiously, unable to hold the concern from her tone. "Did she bite you?"

He frowned. "Bite me?"

"Did she"—she licked her lips, now noticing all the things about him that looked so terribly wrong—"did she feed on you?"

Ellis winced. "I don't think so. I don't . . ."

But he pawed at his side again, and Greer gently lifted the sweater. Horror stole her breath away.

The left side of his body was mottled with bruises, punctured with bites. She could read the violence across his skin as easily as lines on a map. There were so many different sets of teeth marks, some wide half-crescents, showing the impression of every tooth, some nothing but the pointed stab of incisors. Greer shuddered as she imagined these mouths roaming over Ellis, drawing out his blood, painting their lips red with it. Her hands balled into fists, and if Elowen had been beside her now, Greer could have cheerfully ripped her teeth out.

"It didn't hurt," Ellis said, an attempt to reassure her, but his voice was too high and breathless. He let out a laugh. "Much."

Greer looked up just in time to see Ellis draw back his mouth into a smile, revealing his own teeth. They were long and needle-sharp, like those of a northern pike, like a set of daggers, like—

Ellis lunged at Greer, knocking her over as he tried to sink those teeth into the crook of her neck.

"Ellis, stop! Ellis, get off me!"

Her legs thrashed as she tried to dislodge him, but he was so much bigger, so much stronger. His hands wrapped around her wrists, holding them down as he pressed his face to her throat, snapping and trying to find purchase. When Greer felt the points of those wicked teeth graze her skin, she did the only thing she could think of and screamed.

The sound roared from her, flinging Ellis across the clearing. He struck a piece of machinery hidden in a thicket of thorns. There was the horrible sound of something wet squelching violently open, then a gurgle of blood and breath, mixing together in ways they were absolutely never meant to.

Too scared to move, Greer pulled her knees to her chest, burying her head in her arms. She didn't want to see what she'd done. She covered her ears, jamming her fingers painfully inside, but nothing she did could mask those sounds.

A howl of despair ripped from her, setting the ground around her to tremble and startling a roosting flock of nuthatches. They took to the sky with shrieks of dismay that seemed to echo everything screaming in Greer's soul.

She'd come so far, endured so much, to have it end like this.

Ellis, turned.

Ellis, killed.

By her.

By the one who loved him most. By the one who had done everything she could to save him.

The irony was too cruel to bear.

So she let out the pain, shaking the world apart, wanting to hurt it as much as it had hurt her. She screamed past the ache and the fury, tearing into her grief with bared teeth and balled fists. She screamed until she could no longer draw breath, until the sound of her voice choked everything inside her and black stars filled her vision. Her head listed heavily, weighted with too much pressure, too much angst.

Just before she passed out, succumbing to the welcomed promise of oblivion, Greer opened her mouth and screamed again.

38

GREER CAME RIPPING out of the silent aftermath in a rush of colors too bright and sounds far, far too loud.

She opened her eyes, wincing at the blinding white outside her shelter. The storm had not let up as she'd slept, tucked away in the compassionate embrace of unconsciousness, and the snowdrifts now piled high enough to make hiking out of the forest without snowshoes next to impossible.

From beneath the shelter of the fir tree, she watched as flakes the size of silver coins rained down like shooting stars. She heard each one land upon its fallen brethren, growing their number, multiplying into a frozen army intent on immobilizing her.

Greer blinked, curiously removed from the scene. All her focus had been on reaching the camp, on reaching Ellis. Now that he was dead, what was she meant to do?

Part of her thought about rolling back over. She could let the snow cover her in a blanket too heavy to move, too deep to breathe through.

It didn't matter to her now.

But she was thirsty, and the whole of her throat ached, red and flaming and flayed apart by those screams. She blinked again, wondering what to do.

"Water," she decided. She could barely push the word from her. It sounded like a bird's egg, small and fragile and so impossibly easy to break.

She felt the same way.

With a groan, she sat up and instantly regretted it. Her head spun, as if she'd spent the night downing cup after cup of Steward Bishop's lauded juniper spirits.

She reached blindly through her pack, searching for the canteen. It was a quarter full, and she guzzled back most of it in one long swig, crying in relief as the water cooled her throat. She swayed slightly, thinking through what must happen next.

Though the storm raged around her, sitting on the frozen ground with only Ellis's flannel shirt over her clothes, she did not feel the cold.

Ellis.

It had all gone wrong so terribly fast.

Greer wanted to forget every moment of it. She wanted to erase those last horrible seconds, his mouth at her neck, his gasps for life as the iron impaled him. She only wanted to remember him as he'd been before. Warm and human and wholly hers.

She crawled out from the shelter, dragging the rucksack behind.

She needed to see him once more. Even if it was just the smallest glimpse.

She needed to say goodbye.

Greer stood on shaky legs, trying to get her bearings in this new world of white. Snowflakes landed on her eyelashes, brushed her skin with cool, indifferent kisses, then fluttered by unmelted, unchanged.

How much of me is left unchanged? she wondered, holding out her bare hands, catching the flakes, studying each starburst, taking in every filigreed point. It didn't seem like there was much of the old Greer left at all. Uneasy, she let the snowflakes fall from her.

She turned to her left and spotted Ellis. Wind had pushed the snow into deep drifts around him, completely covering his corpse. She paused, playing out different scenarios in her mind. She imagined brushing aside the snow for one last look, taking in all the damage both she and Elowen had inflicted. Or she could walk away, leaving him behind forever.

Which version would hurt least?

After a long, drawn-out moment, Greer stood on tiptoe and pushed away the snow. A shock of disbelief welled within her and, even though it hurt, she threw back her head and laughed.

The figure that had attacked her, that she'd killed, impaled upon the jagged point of a cart's handle, was not Ellis. A Bright-Eyed, one she hadn't seen before, had masqueraded as her love, but in death, its body had begun to revert to its monstrous state, muddling features into a nightmarish chimera of body parts. Half its face still looked human, a shard of dark eyebrow and copper-colored skin. Greer wondered if this Bright-Eyed had belonged to the same people as the girl and her grandfather in Laird, before its turning.

Whoever the poor soul had been, it was most assuredly not Ellis.

But it wasn't Elowen, either. The set of its now milky eyes was too wide, its body far too tall. Greer stared up at its gruesome visage, the curled snout with black bristles, the ears as cavernously large as a bat's. She'd never seen a Bright-Eyed so still. For the briefest moment, she pitied it.

"I did it. I killed one," she whispered with surprise. Laughter bubbled up within her.

"Greer?" Finn's voice broke through her elation, startling her.

She turned, catching footfalls. Through the white noise of the snowstorm, they sounded distorted and far away, even as she spotted him trudging up the hillside.

"Finn! Look!" she exclaimed before it occurred to her that perhaps he would not be as overjoyed to see the corpse. "It attacked me, but I stopped it!" she added, hoping he'd understand.

Finn squinted against the driving snow, studying the motionless body behind her. His eyebrows raised, impressed. "Salix, one of Elowen's fiercest guards. Besting him is no small feat."

A flush of pleasure warmed her cheeks. Greer's fingers curled; she craved his praise even while acknowledging the horror of what she'd done. She turned from the dead Bright-Eyed. "Where were you? I waited for as long as I could, but the storm—"

He waved aside her explanation. "Plans changed." He indicated a length of rope held over his shoulder. She couldn't see what trailed behind him, but she could hear the soft swoosh of snowshoes.

"Finn?"

With a sigh, he stepped back, revealing a dark huddled shape. "Greer."

The voice was rendered almost too hoarse to recognize, but Greer would have known its gruff formality anywhere. "Father?"

39

GREER STARED DUMBSTRUCK at the sight of Hessel Mackenzie. She'd never expected to see her father again, and now he was here, with thick ropes tied around his wrists, and being led up the mountain like a pack mule.

"Why is he . . . ? How did you . . . ?"

"Found him outside Laird," Finn said, giving the rope a firm yank.

"Let me go," Hessel hissed, his tone too low, and dangerous given his current position. "Greer, some assistance, please?"

"What are you doing here?" she demanded instead.

"I'm bringing you home."

A snort of laughter burst from her before she could stop it. "Are you in earnest? You can't still think I'm going to marry Lachlan." The idea was so absurd, she laughed again.

"Lachlan is dead," Hessel snapped.

"I'm sorry to hear that." Greer waited for the rush of guilt to come, expecting it to crash over her like a summer storm. It didn't. "I never wanted to hurt him. Truly."

Hessel's gaze darted to the dead Bright-Eyed behind her. His thoughts were so easy to read that she reddened. He didn't believe her. He honestly thought her capable of such monstrous acts, of such wicked intentions.

Because you are, sang Finn's wild, wily blood. It felt hot in her veins, scalding the rest of her, burning away the remains of who she'd been before she'd consumed it.

"If you're not planning to drag me down the aisle, what are you after?" she asked, her tone harsh as she tried to cast away the troubling thoughts.

"You don't know what you're doing out here. You've no idea the mess you've wandered into."

Greer raised an eyebrow, back bristling. "Do you?" She glanced to Finn. "Does he know you're—"

"Yes, yes, he's one of them," Hessel said, talking over anything Finn had been about to say. "It's fairly evident."

"What about me?" she snarled, wanting to wipe away every trace of his arrogance. "Or Mama? Did you know what she was? What that makes me?"

Hessel's intake of breath was all she needed to hear. "I didn't at first."

Greer turned away, unable to bear the sight of him. He'd known, and never told her. He'd never even hinted at it. All those times he'd snapped and scolded, frustrated by her unusual abilities, every time he'd made her feel less instead of more. He could have explained it to her, helped her understand, but he'd chosen to keep it secret. He'd let her flounder and stew in anxiety, worried she was mad, worried she was broken.

"I should think you'd be happy I left. One less secret for the great Hessel Mackenzie to keep. It must be terribly difficult; there are so very many of them."

"You found my hidden drawer." It wasn't a guess. "I thought that might be the case. When Lachlan was thrown back. When you weren't."

She turned, narrowing her eyes. "*I* threw Lachlan back. Before sunset. The Stones had nothing to do with it."

Hessel nodded, looked grim. "Every soul in Mistaken heard that scream. We covered it up, of course. There was an attack. Lachlan died, valiantly trying to save you. It was all terribly romantic."

Finn rolled his eyes. "We're wasting time. What should we do with him?"

"I suppose you found the second drawer as well," Hessel went on, ignoring the Bright-Eyed. "Read all about your mother." He shook his head. "I should never have left you alone in my study."

"What second drawer?" Greer questioned, unsure if she was stepping into a trap.

"The one with Resolution's journal."

Greer frowned. "That's at Steward House."

"His final journal, yes," Hessel allowed. "I have his first."

Against her better judgment, Greer's interest piqued. "It talks about Mama? How she got here? When she arrived?"

"Resolution's second voyage, yes," he confirmed.

Greer ran through everything she'd been taught about the founding of Mistaken, about the settlers' journey across the sea, but the scenario felt wrong. It didn't make sense. "Mama was with the founders?"

Hessel shook his head. "No. Beaufort made three trips to the new world. Ailie was with him on the second."

"Three voyages?" she echoed with confusion.

"Three. When Resolution first stepped upon these shores, he discovered that Albert Crowley, the young explorer who'd told him of the Redcaps, had lied. Crowley had promised that no one but Beaufort knew of the trees, but by the time they arrived, a mill was already up and running, with another four being readied. Beaufort was so furious, he murdered Crowley."

"Murdered?" she gasped. "But the accounts all say Crowley left, going south."

Hessel gave her a withering look, as if aghast by her naïveté. "Accounts written by Resolution himself."

"So . . . none of our stories are right. Nothing the Stewards have taught us has ever been true."

Her father chewed on the inside of his cheek before answering. "The truth isn't always right. And, sometimes, the thing that *is* right, the thing that makes everything else possible, isn't true."

Greer frowned, adding this troubling idea to her bits of gathered knowledge. She turned them over in her mind, like colorful chips of a mosaic, twisting and trying to parse out what image they'd create. "So Mama stowed away on Resolution's ship."

"Stowed away?" Her father let out a short bark of laughter. "She didn't sneak onto it, if that's what you're thinking. He brought her here in shackles!"

Finn's head snapped toward Hessel, horrified. "Shackles? Ailie would never—"

"You can read the whole sordid story if you don't believe me."

"In a journal, left behind in a hidden drawer, miles from here," Finn pointed out. "How convenient."

Hessel shrugged, unbothered by the Bright-Eyed's scorn. "Resolution was born in wild country, steeped in magic and folklore. The Beaufort farm bordered a wide heath. One night, when he was a young lad, his father foolishly remained working in their barn after dark. Resolution never saw him again."

Greer raised her eyebrows, waiting for her father to explain.

"There were creatures out on that heath. Everyone knew to hide away in their homes before sunset, before the uncanny could come. Demons and Devils, things of nightmares and myth. Gray Trows, who walk backward, determined to kidnap the first maiden they stumble across. Silent Cù-Sìth, stealthily racing across the land, ready to devour. The Nuckelavee with its venomous breath, poisoning crops and animals alike. But none were as monstrous as the Betwixt."

"Betwixt?" she echoed.

"Something between man and monster," Finn murmured slowly, as if dredging up a long-buried memory. "My nan told stories of them. They could change form at will, and drank the blood of their victims." His eyes fell on Greer, looking uncertain. "I'd forgotten her stories . . ."

Greer turned to her father. "What happened next?"

"After her husband died, Beaufort's mother moved their family far from the heath, into the city, where the wild things dared not follow. Years passed, and Beaufort became a man of business and schemes. He met Crowley. He went to the new world. He came home, feeling wounded and betrayed, and went back to that heath to set a trap for his father's murderer, painting it with his own blood. And it worked. He caught Ailie."

Greer let out a strangled sound of disbelief. After seeing Laird and knowing the devastation her mother was capable of, it felt impossible for Greer to imagine her being captured by Resolution Beaufort. "Why would he trap her?"

"He saw the mills already built, the mills being planned, and he couldn't stand it. He wanted this world's riches for himself alone. He needed someone—something—that could stop everything, quickly. Permanently."

"If he set Mama loose, she'd attack, and the mills would shut down," Greer summarized, working through the steps Resolution must have laid out in his journal. "His would open without competition."

"We're still the only mill along the whole of the coast with Redcaps," Hessel said with pride.

Her stomach churned, slick and oily, in her disturbance at how corruptible men could be in pursuit of the elusive promise of wealth. "That's diabolical. And so terribly stupid. The mill wasn't guaranteed to be a success, and how did he know Mama wouldn't turn on *him*? There wasn't yet a truce. How did he know the Benevolence would come to his aid? To the town's aid?"

She saw a look pass between her father and Finn.

"What?" she demanded.

Finn's expression turned to pity. "Greer . . . there is no Benevolence."

She blinked, certain she'd misheard.

Hessel cleared his throat. "When the first Stewards figured out what Resolution had done, they came up with the story of the Benevolence and the truce. They told everyone in town, making it so big, so grand, it would have to be believed, to be taken as a truth."

Greer felt numb. "Why?"

Her father sighed. "It was meant to be a comfort. The settlers were alone. They were scared. They had no way of returning home. They needed one small thing to be all right, one thing they could hang their hopes upon. Tormond Mackenzie concocted the story as a mercy."

Greer questioned the mercy of telling a group of desperate survivors such a fantastic lie, but a bigger thought troubled her. "If there is no Benevolence . . . if there never was a truce . . . where did the Warding Stones come from?"

"The rocks have always been here, dotting the land. But the magic comes from the old world, from Beaufort himself. After his father died, he became obsessed with learning all he could of the uncanny, of the occult. Before setting Ailie loose, he charmed the stones, casting a protection spell over them to hold back her kind, to keep future settlers safe within the cove. But Beaufort's words were wrong and too specific. He didn't live long enough to see how he'd damned everyone unlucky enough to see a sunset within Mistaken."

"We truly are a town of mistakes," she murmured. "Why would Mama have gone along with any of this? Surely, she was stronger than Resolution. She could have escaped or—"

"I think she was intrigued by the idea of a new world, a new continent to see, to explore, to feast upon," Hessel mused. "She had an insatiable hunger for *more*. That didn't stop when she came to live in Mistaken, when I pulled her out of that tree. Did you know she bought nearly all the books we have? When merchant ships would dock, she was always the first to market, ready to see their wares, see what new things she could consume." His expression softened. "There is so much of her in you, Greer. The good parts, I mean. You have those hungers, too. Your wanderings, your maps. I . . ." He shook his head, discarding his next thought.

"What happened to her?" Greer asked softly, surprising herself. Every bit of Hessel's story spawned a dozen questions within her. Questions that might never be satisfied. But this one could. "The day she died . . . you said there'd been an accident at the mill. But . . . Mama almost never went to the mill."

"It was only a few days before the Hunt," her father began.

The wind shifted, pelting a blast of snowflakes at them. Greer leaned toward Finn. She wasn't as cold as she ought to be, but she did miss the comforting weight of his coat.

"I came home and discovered she was leaving. At first, she denied it, but when I tried to stop her, she changed. She was there and then she wasn't, and in her place was this . . . this *thing*. I'd never seen one of them before, but I knew exactly who she was. What she was." His eyes grew distant. "She said she had what she needed"—Hessel glanced toward Greer but didn't entirely meet her stare—"and that she was leaving, returning to her mountain, returning to her kind. And then she took out this mess of briars and berries . . ."

"You killed her," Finn guessed, his voice so full of sorrow. "Before she could put on her cloak, you killed her."

Greer's mouth dropped open. She didn't like her father most days. She knew he wasn't a good man, knew he was rarely an honest man, but she'd never considered him capable of murder.

He didn't respond.

"Father?" she prodded.

"Yes." He didn't elaborate any further. He didn't need to.

Greer's hand shot to her lips, covering the gasp that wanted to escape. She wasn't sure if she was going to plead for more information or cry.

"Before I . . . Before she . . ." His sigh was shaky. "She told me what she'd done. Why she'd done it. I know all about how you're supposed to take her position, how you're meant to replace her. And that's why I'm here. To take you back. You're not one of them, Greer. You know nothing of their ways, of what they're capable of. You belong in Mistaken, with your people."

"She's just as much a part of us as she is of you," Finn disputed, his eyes flashing as the remaining light began to fade from the late afternoon. A curtain of snow obscured him until all Greer could see was that bright glow.

Hessel laughed. "She's nothing like any of you."

Greer glanced toward her father, and his breath hitched sharply. He'd seen her eye-shine.

"What did you do to her? What have you . . ." Hessel stopped and shook his head. "It doesn't matter. Let me and my daughter go."

A dark laugh barked out of Finn. "Why the Devil would I do anything you want? You killed our queen. You killed *her mother*. You have no power here." To prove it, he jerked hard on the ropes binding Hessel's wrist. The force pitched the older man to the ground, making his knees crack against icy rocks.

Hessel remained bent over, breathing heavily. "I have it," he whispered. "I know where it is."

"What?" Finn tilted his head with a curiosity that made him look like an owl contemplating his next meal.

"Ailie's skin. The brambles or cloak or whatever it is you call it. She said it was where her powers were kept. You'd want that, wouldn't you? It's important? Important to your . . . kind?"

Finn narrowed his eyes.

"Take my daughter and me back to Mistaken. Return us there safely—without a touch of harm befalling us—and it's yours."

Finn looked at Greer, shifting only his eyes. "Have you seen it? Ever? Anywhere in your house? At the mill?"

"Not since I was little. Not since Mama . . ." She swallowed, hardening her expression. "Not since you killed her," she threw at Hessel.

"It's there," he promised. "I kept it where no one would ever come across it. Hidden so that no one would ever suspect what I'd married."

Finn ignored the insult. "How do we know you didn't burn it? Toss it out to sea?"

"He wouldn't have," Greer decided. "He's too much of an opportunist. He'd know it might one day become useful."

"And it has," Hessel pointed out. "Take the offer, boy. You know you can't resist it."

Finn's eyebrows furrowed, as though he might be truly considering it.

"Finn!" Greer exclaimed, horrified. "I'm not going back to Mistaken. Not without Ellis."

He grabbed at the crook of her arm, pulling her aside. "You need that cloak," he hissed through clenched teeth, his breath fervent and hot in her ear. "All of Ailie's powers are in it. You'd have what she had. You'd be queen without question. Even Elowen would have to concede that. She'd back down. Immediately. You wouldn't have to duel. You wouldn't have to fight. There'd be no need to—"

Before Finn could offer another point of persuasion, he was yanked back, his shoulder nearly pulled from its socket as the rope he held was torn away.

Hessel was gone—snatched high into the tree line, where he fought against a Bright-Eyed captor.

"Where's the cloak?" Elowen demanded, holding him in her clutches, her great wings barely visible through the curtains of snow.

"Leave my daughter alone and it's yours," Hessel gasped, thrashing his legs through open air in a vain attempt to find purchase. The leather cords of his snowshoes snapped, plummeting the footwear into the darkness below. "I don't care who has it. I'm not picking a side."

"Tell me where it is and I won't pick your spine out through your mouth," Elowen countered.

"There's no need for violence," Hessel protested, his knuckles turning white as he clawed at her grip. "Just stay away from Greer. Please," he added, his tone softening even as his struggles doubled. "Leave her out of all this."

Elowen contemplated his offer. The force of her wings threw blinding pellets of snow. "No," she decided, and hoisted him higher, bringing the soft flesh of his throat to her mouth. She sank her teeth in deep, then jerked away, ripping out his vocal cords to stop the screaming.

"No!" Greer cried out, racing across the clearing as a curtain of her father's blood rained down. It splattered her face and soaked into her clothing, saturating everything with a slick, coppery heat.

Elowen flapped her wings, gaining elevation as she continued to feast. Hessel, unable to speak but not yet dead, squirmed against her deadly embrace, losing his pack in the process. He floundered, attempting to push the queen from him. But she was too strong, focused on her meal with an unbreakable concentration. Soon his head lolled to the side, and Hessel Mackenzie moved no more.

Elowen soared off into the night, bubbling with dark laughter, and leaving Greer and Finn behind in a drift of red, steaming snow.

40

GREER STARED AT the patch of sky where her father had been.

She'd gone numb, stunned at the speed and ferocity with which Elowen killed. By the time Greer realized what was happening, it had been too late.

Nothing moved now but the falling snow. Elowen was long gone. Hessel, too. Still, Greer couldn't tear her attention from the sky, certain that, if she just kept watch, they'd come back and everything would somehow be undone.

"He'll come back," she mouthed to herself. "He has to come back. He can't be . . ."

Father is dead.

The thought was loud and forceful, ringing in her head, and she frowned. The words didn't sound right, as if they'd fallen in the wrong order.

Father . . . is . . . dead.

She thought them again, then again, but the repetition did nothing to help them make sense.

Hessel Mackenzie had been a force of nature, bending everything around him to his will. He'd been respected, revered, even feared. How could such a giant of a man meet such an inglorious end?

Father . . . is . . . dead.

Shadows moved through the curtains of snow, and Greer's heart leapt high, beating its hopeful cadence painfully in the center of her throat. When she spotted the gray face of a boreal owl, she turned from the sky.

Hessel Mackenzie was not coming back, and it was foolish to pretend otherwise.

Finn was suddenly beside her, standing too close, and she didn't know where to look, wasn't sure what to do with her hands or her arms, and then his fingers were at her jaw, tipping her gaze to his, demanding acknowledgment. Eye-shine met eye-shine as he studied her, concern worrying at his face.

"Greer," he prodded, and touched her cheeks, holding her face with gentle, tender pressure.

She knew what he was doing, knew he was trying to clear away her fog of disbelief. She knew all of this, and still wished him gone. She wanted to be alone, wanted to have the space to think and grieve and . . .

Her eyes welled.

Greer didn't want to be alone, not truly.

She wanted to be wrapped tight in the arms of someone who knew her, who loved her. Someone who understood the complicated tangle of emotions knotting her chest. She wanted the comfort of history and steadfast consistency.

She wanted Ellis.

She could picture him with her now, the sad smile that would mar his face, the heft of his frame as she leaned against him, the trail of his fingers along her back, tracing endless patterns. She'd done the same when John Beaufort had passed, running nonsensical shapes across Ellis's shoulders, allowing him space but reminding him she was there.

Carefully, Greer cupped her hands over Finn's to lower them away. She caught sight of Ailie's ribbon, still tied around his wrist. It was stained dark with blood. His skin was sticky with it, and hers was, too, and she dropped her hold, overwhelmed by the coppery tang.

Hessel's blood was everywhere.

Now that her focus had been taken from the sky, it was all she could notice. It steamed in the snow beneath them. Dripped down from tree limbs. It coated her hair, her face, and, despite the absolute horror of being painted in her own father's blood, her stomach panged with a curious hunger.

Greer nearly retched in disgust, and the tears that had threatened to fall began to now.

Even if Ellis was here, she suddenly doubted that he would know her, that he would understand anything going on inside her.

How could he, when she couldn't make sense of it herself?

"We should clean you up," Finn murmured, wiping at one of the rivulets running down her cheek. He studied the red coating his fingertips before instinctively sucking them clean. Greer turned her head, unable to watch. Her chest tightened, fighting the urge to scoop up a handful of red snow for a taste.

This is wrong, this is so very wrong, her thoughts shouted, urging her to move, begging her to flee. Her throat flexed, her mouth watered, and it was all she could do to remain still as Finn bent down and traced a long line across her cheek with his tongue.

She fixed her gaze upon Ailie's ribbon.

It was Finn who'd been with her after the death of her mother, who'd known she was hurting, who'd known she needed comfort, who'd needed it himself, and it made sense that he was here now. It felt right. It felt fated.

Finn understands this, she realized. *He understands you like this. The real you. The one Ellis would never.*

And he never would.

He'd pull Greer from this madness in a heartbeat. He'd tell her to fight against the strange, dark impulses tugging at her limbs. He wouldn't see that the blood had been spilled, that it couldn't be returned, that it wasn't doing Hessel any good any longer, and . . .

Finn's blood roared in her veins, silencing doubts, urging her to action. It wanted her to stay. Wanted her to tilt her head and meet the mouth that roamed over hers, teasing, tasting. It wanted the blood he offered, wanted his touch to push away the sorrow and death and let her feel life.

Finn's lips were at her temple, his kisses reverent as he cleaned her, cleansed her, anointed her into something she didn't understand but suddenly wanted to.

It would be so easy to give in to the seduction of that blood. Too easy, really.

Releasing the last of her trepidation, Greer kissed him back. She tugged him toward her, hungry for the feel of his body against hers. A growl of pleasure caught between their lips, and she wasn't sure if it had come from him or from her.

His hands moved lower, caressing her breasts, bunching the fabric that separated her body from his. He tugged at the collar of her sweater, kissing the hollow of her throat before his teeth raked over the length of her collarbone.

He was going to bite her, Greer realized. He was going to feed on her, feed on himself, because his blood was within her, and if he took in her blood, mixed with his . . . that would be it, wouldn't it? She'd no longer have a foot in both camps, no longer belong to both sides and yet neither. There would be no more "mostly"s. She'd have turned.

Her head swam, dizzy with desire; she was reeling with wants and worries.

It felt impossible to stop, the culmination of everything Ailie had wanted for her. It was inevitable, two streams merging into one river, waves pulled ashore by the tug of the moon.

I'm sorry, Ellis.

Greer froze, wondering at her thought. It had sounded so small, so fragile. The last of who she was without Finn's blood guiding her. Was she really about to let it go, to let it wink out of existence?

"Stop!" she cried, and Finn startled away. They stared at each other, mouths open, breaths panting hard and fast. His face was flushed; his eyes dilated. Greer didn't doubt she looked every bit as wanton. "I can't."

Finn raised an eyebrow. "Can't?"

She shook her head. "That's not me. That's not who I am."

"Oh, Greer . . . it could be."

She hesitated, then shook her head. Somehow, in the muddled wilderness of Finn's blood, Greer found that voice again. It was small and powerless, but it was hers, and she seized it with a hold that would not be broken. "No."

Finn sighed, resigned. "You're really going after him?"

"Yes." She swallowed. "Your blood changes nothing."

He turned away, his figure as still as a statue. The silence between them was just as stony.

The snow continued to fall, dusting their shoulders in a limn of white.

Greer looked to the road, picturing it rising higher and higher until it reached the mines. "I know that you probably don't want to help me now."

After a long moment, Finn glanced back. His face was tight and unreadable. "I don't . . . but I will. I'm not leaving you alone against the Gathered."

The thought of him on her side cheered her more than it had any right to. She offered him a smile, small and tenuous. "What do we do now?"

"We could set up camp here tonight. If you need the rest."

"No," Greer decided, her refusal sounding every bit as flat as she felt. "I'm tired of camps and fires. I just want this to be over."

He grimaced. "I wish we'd never learned of Ailie's cloak. It would be the thing that would change it all. But it's in Mistaken. Somewhere."

There was no good answer, no right choice. Every bit of confidence she'd gained after slaying Salix had been stripped away. Elowen had moved so fast, killed with such ruthless efficiency. Greer couldn't imagine matching that. They needed the cloak. But there wasn't time.

She looked around the clearing, wondering if there was anything she might use as a weapon. Her eyes landed on a dark shape partially obscured in a snowdrift. "Father's pack!"

She trudged over and pulled it free, surprised by its heft. Unbuckling the clasp, she removed wrapped smoked meats, a wedge of hard cheese, a flask with contents so strong it made her eyes water. There was a canteen, a map, extra gloves, extra socks. She kept unpacking, pulling out item after item.

Greer thrust her whole arm in, searching for a pistol, a knife, *any-*

thing, but stopped when she brushed over something impossibly soft. She frowned, wondering that Hessel had thought to bring something so insubstantial with him.

She pulled, and a ball of velvet embroidered with sparkling threads as bright as the cosmos tumbled free. It spread open across the snow, shimmering with an otherworldly luster.

"Is that . . ." Finn stepped in to examine Greer's find.

Hessel *had* packed a weapon. The best one in his arsenal.

"Mama's cape."

⁓

"YOU SHOULD PUT it on now," Finn said, repeating the refrain as they readied for their final ascent.

Greer had transferred anything useful from Hessel's bag to hers, and now sat on a fallen log, tightening the makeshift straps of Hessel's broken snowshoes.

Ailie's cloak was folded over her arm. She couldn't yet bring herself to put it on, but also couldn't bear to release it. Ailie had warned her never to play with it, and now, as it brushed against her, warming her side, Greer knew why.

The velvet radiated a power strange and difficult to understand until it was held. It was like looking into a pond choked with brackish water and spindly weeds. You couldn't see through its depths, but you could sense things moving below the surface, things with keen eyes and powerful tails, things with jagged fins and pointed teeth.

Greer didn't really believe the cloth would spring to life and harm her, but she had the irrational thought that it might try. She wondered if the cloak recognized her, if it could feel Ailie's blood in her veins. When she put it on, would it rebel, chafing against a foolish girl who was decidedly not its owner?

But if it *did* take to her . . .

Greer shuddered as she imagined being wrapped in the dark energy she felt. Finn's blood had already changed her in so many ways—what would a concentrated dose of Ailie do?

Would she be able to shift her form?

Would she be able to fly?

Both seemed beneficial against Elowen, but uncertainty kept Greer from pulling the cloak on and finding out.

"Maybe you should wear it." She turned to Finn, ready to foist it upon him, but froze at the last moment, holding it close to her chest instead with a possessiveness she wasn't entirely sure she felt.

Finn looked up in alarm. "It's not mine to take."

"But it could be, couldn't it? You could wear it, and then you'd be king," she reasoned.

"That's not how it works. The queen is sovereign. The king is only her—"

"Consort."

The word fell between them like shrapnel.

Finn cleared his throat, looking acutely uncomfortable. "Yes."

"What does that mean, 'consort'? Would you be"—she paused, grasping for the right word—"a partner?"

"Protector," he corrected. "Someone to stand by your side, to help when the need arises." He looked away. "A lover. A confidant. A husband."

"Oh." Greer swallowed, and an uncomfortable heat flushed over her chest. She'd thought as much, but it was another thing entirely to hear the words said aloud.

From across the clearing, Finn stared at her, motionless save for the flick of a finger worrying at his thumbnail. In a flash so quick she scarcely saw it, he skittered to her and knelt in a snowdrift, impervious to the cold. Heat radiated off him, warming her in turn, and when he reached for her hands, she did not pull away.

"I know it's not the path you pictured for yourself. I know I'm not the man you imagined beside you."

"You're not," she confirmed even as she allowed his fingers to tangle with hers.

He nodded, accepting the statement with downcast eyes.

She leaned in, trying to draw back his attention. "But that doesn't mean . . ." She stopped, unsure of the words she wanted to say or why she even felt the compulsion to give them. She didn't owe him reassurances. And yet . . . "If things had been different . . . if I'd met you first . . ." Greer shook her head, acutely aware of the cruelty of her attempt. "I can't. I don't want to be sovereign. I just want to get Ellis, and then we'll leave and never bother the Gathered or interfere with Elowen. I'll swear it to her. There needn't be any . . . Things don't have to end like that." She pointed to the dark stains spreading across the snow. Even the rapidly falling flakes couldn't cover the garish evidence of Hessel's final moments.

"Elowen won't take that risk," Finn warned.

"What if I give her the cloak, as a sign of my sincerity?"

"You can't!"

Surprised by the force of Finn's outburst, Greer dropped her hold of him. "Why?"

"Elowen isn't meant to be the sovereign! She's done things Ailie would never have sanctioned."

Greer felt her shoulders rise into a shrug. "But isn't that her choice? If I became . . ." She swallowed down the word, unable to even say it. "I'm certain there are things I'd do that Mama wouldn't approve of."

Finn sighed, raking his nails through his short hair. "You don't understand."

"I don't," Greer agreed. "Which is why I shouldn't have the cloak. I don't know the Gathered. I don't know your ways. I don't even—"

"I know you," he snapped, silencing her. "I've watched out for Ailie—for you—for *years*. I saw her middle swell. I heard the first cries you took. I watched you grow, watched you become the woman you now are. I'm telling you, Greer, you're our sovereign."

"I'm not," she protested.

"Your mind is so sharp," he argued, "your spirit so curious. You look at huge, unknowable things and you sort through them with reason and skill. You make the obscure understandable. Like with your maps. We need that. We need you."

Despite herself, Greer felt a thrill stir as she dared to wonder. Could she lead the Gathered? With Ailie's powers and Finn's might, she could rule as sovereign. And with Ellis at her side, made king, made like her . . .

She shook her head. She could never do that to him.

"Elowen can't be all that bad," Greer began, chewing at the inside of her cheek. "Mama turned her for a reason. She must have seen—"

"She craves human blood."

Greer glanced to the large swath of red staining the snow before she could stop herself. "One could say the same of you," she pointed out not unkindly.

Finn growled in frustration. "It's not like that . . . *I'm* not like that. Not usually. You've seen me eat other things. It's possible. But Elowen . . . Human blood is all she wants. Since she's taken over, there have been so many more attacks. And she's careless, turning more and more. The court is enormous—bigger than Ailie would have ever allowed—and they're feeding only on human blood. It changes us, gives us different strengths. You saw how they shifted those stones . . . Resolution's wards won't hold them back forever."

Greer remembered the barn warming, the massacre at the Calloway farm, and let her understanding of that night shift. There was no Benevolence to have moved the Warding Stones. It had been the Bright-Eyeds. Elowen.

"And now she wants to venture south, where there's more to feed on. More settlements, more villages. More people. It's a foolish move. It risks exposing us, and there's no reason for it. There's plenty of game here, game in the north. We could wander for thousands of miles and not come across a single person. Our secrets would be safe."

Greer started to refute it, started to tell him everything the hunters in Laird said, the way the Bright-Eyeds' presence had shifted the landscape, taking too much, devouring everything in their sight. But she stopped short, her mind catching on a small detail she'd only now just noticed.

"Finn . . . you said it was just Mama and Elowen who'd attacked Laird."

He nodded.

"How big is the Gathered now?"

He stared at her, unblinking. "I . . . I don't know. I've been away for so many years, watching over you and Ailie. I . . ." He swallowed, the line of his jaw hardening. "At least a dozen. Probably more."

She gaped at him.

Two Bright-Eyeds had annihilated Laird. Now there were over a dozen. She couldn't fathom the destruction such a number could unleash. She sank her fingers into the plush folds of the cloak, her mind reeling.

The girl and her grandfather and the rest of their people.

Louise and Martha and all of Mistaken.

Towns she'd never heard of.

People she'd never met.

They were all in danger. It wasn't enough to kill Elowen. It wasn't enough to take her mother's place and attempt to bring in an age of reason and moderation. She'd felt the dark stirrings of the Bright-Eyeds' wild blood within her. Such abominations could not be allowed to exist.

She needed to destroy them all.

She needed to end everything Resolution Beaufort had begun.

Greer released a long, shaky breath and threw her pack over her shoulders. "All right. I'm ready to meet the Gathered."

41

It was nearly midnight when Greer and Finn rounded the final bend. A splintered sign spanned the road, welcoming all travelers to the Sandry Mining Company. It had once been bright with color, but after so many harsh seasons without care, the paint had faded and peeled so badly the words were nearly illegible.

The storm had temporarily eased, clouds parting to allow moonlight to brighten the abandoned site. With her newly enhanced vision, Greer could see each of the camp's remaining structures with crystalline detail.

The site was . . . rough.

Decades of neglect had taken their toll. Greer wondered what the miners had dug for, what precious resources they'd hauled out of the mountain before the Bright-Eyes had attacked, putting a stop to operations.

A scattering of buildings bordered a work yard: an office and bunkhouse, a fenced pen for horses and pack mules, a blacksmith's forge, and several other smaller shacks Greer couldn't identify. They were all falling apart, with caved-in roofs and broken windows, so thoroughly covered in moss and mold it seemed the forest was swallowing them whole. Behind Sandry was the vertical face of the mountain, looming over the camp like a sentinel. At its base was a large opening, braced by heavy timbers and stones: the entrance to the mine itself.

Greer felt a wave of gooseflesh break over her as she studied its darkness. It seemed to be alive, a sentient, knowing thing that watched her with equal interest.

The ground going into the tunnel was scarred with pockmarks and nearly impassable. She recalled the lengths of tracks discarded throughout the forest below. The Bright-Eyeds had torn them up, cast them out, and never bothered to repair the mess. Who cared for roads when you could fly?

Hidden in the shadows of the stables, Greer and Finn waited, scarcely drawing breath as they listened to the sounds around them.

Nothing stirred.

She'd expected to see some evidence of the Gathered: sentries posted, an aerial watch drifting soundlessly on air currents above, flickers of eye-shine roosted in nearby trees.

But there was nothing.

"Where is everyone?" she whispered.

Finn gestured toward the mine's entrance, then flexed his hand, indicating a steep decline, a lower depth. There would be dozens of shafts, and even more smaller corridors splitting off the main thoroughfare, a veritable maze. They'd talked through what Finn remembered of the mine as they'd hiked and had agreed it would be best if Elowen could be drawn out into the open.

Greer was excellent at finding the lay of the land, at tracking her way through regions uncharted, but a mine was different. She'd have no landmarks, no frame of reference. There would be no sun or stars to guide her way.

It would be just her and the dark.

And the Gathered.

Finn tapped at Ailie's cloak with meaningful insistence.

She bit the side of her thumb, worrying her teeth back and forth against the skin as she studied her mother's cloak, watching the way it shimmered in the moonlight.

The fabric felt wrong in her hands, wrong in this place. It was too lovely and too fragile a thing, a dew-dotted spiderweb, the first skim of hoarfrost on a pond.

"Greer," Finn all but growled, his whisper hot in her ear. "Put on the damn cloak."

"Where is Elowen?" she hedged. "Why is she waiting?"

"Why are you?"

It was an impossible question to answer. She knew with utmost certainty that putting on the cloak would alter her forever. Nothing—no matter how strong a case Finn made, no matter how Greer accepted its benefits and inevitability—could tempt her to hasten that moment.

"Is that a Starling I hear?"

Elowen's voice echoed out of the mine, and Greer sank against Finn with relief. Elowen had made the opening gambit, and they could sit back and decide upon the next move. Beside her, Finn drew a finger to his lips—a warning, a reminder.

From deep in the tunnel, a pair of flickering eyes approached the entrance, coming out of the darkness like fireflies.

Other Bright-Eyes appeared. Two walked upright, flanking Elowen, while the eye-shine of some was positioned impossibly high off the ground. Distorted bodies crawled along the ceiling with a curious scuttle, picking their path with hooked claws at the joints in their wings. They emerged upside down, their necks snapped at nearly impossible angles to scan the yard.

Just like bats, Greer thought, as she got her initial glimpse of the Gathered.

At first glance, every creature looked the same—pallid skin, luminescent and riddled with dark veins; shoulders so hulking and muscular they curved the spine; arcing, membranous wings; cavernously large ears; faces truncated with too many teeth—but as Greer studied the motley tableau, she noticed the differences. Tufts of feathers, tawny as an owl's; skin brittle with scales and patches of molt. Some had tusks, others horns.

She counted five, then six, as Elowen stepped into the moonlight, her eyes as sharp as those of a fox.

Greer's breath caught as she saw the smaller figure nearly hidden, tucked away in the curve of the Elowen's wings. She hadn't seen him in the tunnel because he cast no eye-shine. He was still wonderfully, wholly human.

Ellis.

Everything in her wanted to race to him, but a swift shake of Finn's head held her in check. They remained in the shadows, watching, waiting.

One of the Bright-Eyeds beside Elowen surveyed Sandry's remains, his massive tusks swinging from side to side as his orange eyes took in the yard. "There's no one here," he announced, his voice deep and gravelly, a veritable nightmare.

"I told you," Ellis said, sounding exhausted. "She's not coming. She's trapped in Mistaken; she can't leave, she wouldn't follow me."

"Why isn't he back in the roost with the others?" questioned the tallest of the guards. "He shouldn't be out here."

"I want him to see this," Elowen snapped. "I want *her* to see him."

Along the rock wall, one Bright-Eyed snorted; his slitted eyes were wary, mistrustful. "See what? You *said* she was near." He gestured to the empty yard. "Where is she?"

"That's no way to speak to your sovereign. We all heard the voices," the tusked guard growled. With a powerful sweep of his wing, he pushed Ellis from the group. Ellis stumbled forward, slipping in the snow; he landed on his knees with a painful crack. "Find her," the guard demanded.

"There's no one to find!" Ellis spelled out, each word drawn long with fraying patience. Impossibly, he retreated toward the Bright-Eyeds. "This is pointless. It's freezing. I'm going back in."

"Stop him," Elowen ordered, and the two guards stepped together, blocking the tunnel.

What are you doing, Ellis? Greer wanted to shout, but Finn gripped her arm, waylaying her before she could even think to move.

He shook his head, his meaning clear: *Not yet.*

"Stop these stupid games," Ellis went on, taking another faltering step toward the guards. "I came to you as a sacrifice. Willingly. For Mistaken. Eat me or turn me or do whatever—just end it."

"Shut him up," Elowen hissed, and the tall Bright-Eyed swung at him, striking Ellis across the face with the long length of his winged forearm.

Ellis staggered back, losing his hat.

Greer had knitted it for him just last winter. She'd used the finest wool, carding and cleaning out every bristle and burr before spinning the fibers and dyeing the skeins. Seeing that reminder of home, that proof of their lives before all this, strengthened Greer's resolve. She wanted to go back to that—to a version of that—and never again have to worry about dark shapes falling from the sky.

Ellis clutched at his face, muffling a groan. Greer could smell the tang of fresh blood and knew his nose had been broken, even before drops of red dotted the surrounding snow.

The Gathered snapped their collective attention toward the blood, their sudden longing fierce and palpable. From high above, the smallest Bright-Eyed began to skitter down the rocky face of the cliff, drawing closer. Its eyes were large and rapturous.

Greer started forward, wanting to warn Ellis, wanting to stop the bloodshed before it could begin, but Finn's fingers dug in deep, holding her in place.

"Wait," he mouthed silently.

Then the Bright-Eyed was gone, hidden somewhere among the boulders clustering against the mountain's face. But Greer could still hear him, hear the rasp of his dissent. "The mortal is right. We've watched for days, and the girl hasn't come. I'm sick of such stagnancy. I want to hunt."

Elowen sighed. "And you will, when this is over. We'll return to the cove and destroy those damned Stones. We'll drink the town dry, but first we need—"

"No, now!" he yowled, racing out of the shadows.

Finn was on her in an instant, one hand cupped over Greer's mouth to stifle back her cry as a lynx sped toward Ellis, haunches long and paws massive, a feral bloodlust winking in its eyes. As much as she wanted to thrash free, Greer slackened against Finn, understanding that the element of surprise was their greatest asset.

Before Greer was even aware she'd moved, Elowen was across the yard, intercepting the cat. It began to shift back into a Bright-Eyed, growing larger, its spine lengthening and flexing like a snake. But before the transformation could complete, Elowen snapped its neck and tossed it over her shoulder, discarding it as though it were nothing more than a game bird.

The Bright-Eyed landed with an ungainly thud, a monstrous tangle of limbs and wings, now wholly motionless. The remaining Gathered swayed uneasily, their eyes darting from Elowen to their fallen kin.

The tusked guard made a motion toward the dead Bright-Eyed, but Elowen's snarl stopped him short. "Farrow?" he called out instead. In the following silence, his eyes narrowed. "You killed him!"

Elowen whirled around, meeting the eyes of her court, her face contorted with fury. "And I'll do the same to any of you who goes after the boy."

With disgust, the tusked Bright-Eyed stalked into the tunnel, throwing muttered curses under his breath.

"Laithe! I did not dismiss you! Get back here or I'll—" Elowen started after him, but stopped short, a look of uncertainty playing across her vulpine face.

"Already set to kill another?" Ellis asked, sneering up at her. He turned to the others. "How quick she is to throw you all away. She exiled the first only hours ago . . ."

Salix, Greer thought, remembering the Bright-Eyed she'd killed. She wondered what he'd done to make Elowen cast him out. Perhaps her court wasn't as loyal to her as Finn had feared.

". . . then this poor sod," Ellis went on. "And now she threatens Laithe. Are you going to stand for this? Are you going to let her kill the lot of you?"

Elowen's nostrils flared, and even from across the yard, Greer could hear her teeth grind together. She growled at the tallest Bright-Eyed, snapping her orders in a language Greer did not know.

He offered a short bow before reluctantly turning in to the dark.

Greer could hardly believe her luck. Just three Bright-Eyeds remained outside the mine. Success was still uncertain, but she felt a wash of relief as the numbers began to tip toward their favor.

Then Ellis began to laugh.

It sounded like broken glass, its edges sharp and dangerous, dark with loathing and teetering into madness. He paced about the yard like a feral animal, caged and raring for a fight. As he approached the stables, his eyes fell on Greer.

Time seemed to freeze, catching the breath in her chest.

Ellis had always been an open book, and Greer watched the wide range of emotions tumble across his face. Disbelief and wonder, love and worry, fear, and—finally—horrible realization.

Greer saw the exact moment when Ellis understood what her presence here meant. What her presence here made her. His eyebrows furrowed, and his eyes grew wet with welling tears. He pressed his lips together, and she wasn't sure if he was fighting the urge to cry or to scream.

For a long moment, they simply stared at each other. Greer drank in every detail of him, the exhausted circles under his eyes, his ruined nose, the mouth she hungered to kiss. Ellis stared back, saying so many things with his eyes that he could not speak aloud. But then he disappeared into thoughts Greer was not privy to. His expression darkened, and a stab of fear staked through her middle.

"I love you," he mouthed, offering one small smile. Then Ellis whirled back to the court, slipping out the iron knife secreted in the sleeve of his sweater. He hurled it toward the Bright-Eyeds, his throw powerful and precise. It sailed through the air, flipping round like a silver spinner, until it struck Elowen, stabbing her directly in the hollow of her throat.

42

THE MINING CAMP erupted into chaos.

Elowen staggered back, pressing talons over her neck, trying to stanch the bubbling wound. Instantly the remaining Gathered went on the defensive: The two smaller Bright-Eyeds plummeted down from the cliff wall to protect their injured sovereign. One knelt over her, mopping at the blood, applying pressure, and screeching as loudly as a nest of cicadas. The other took a wide stance, enormous eyes darting from structure to structure, looking for other threats.

Hearing their cries of rage, the taller guard returned. Startled, he scanned the scene, trying to determine what had happened. When he spotted the knife, he dived at Ellis, wings spread wide to sail over the uneven ground.

"Get Ellis, we need to get Ellis!" Greer cried, leaping from their hiding spot.

She charged across the open space. Finn shifted form and swooped in after her. He tackled the guard midair, and they tumbled down together, rolling in a dizzying flash of bared teeth and claws and wings.

For a split second, Elowen's eyes met Greer's, sharp and seething. She tried speaking, but air whistled over her damaged vocal cords, and her words came out like nails across slate. Then Greer was with Ellis, and she pulled him to his feet. She pressed a quick kiss to his lips, mindful of his broken nose, all too aware of the Bright-Eyeds at their back.

He reached for her, looking dazed. "What are you doing here? How did you—"

"We've got to run," she said, tugging him toward the forest. "Hurry!"

The guard Finn was fighting broke away from their brawl and circled after Greer and Ellis.

Greer swung her rucksack at the Bright-Eyed and slammed a blow to its side, but it recovered quickly, striking her across the temple so hard she fell backward, seeing stars. A high pitch rang in her ears, and she groaned, struggling to rise.

"No!" Finn cried, skittering toward her in a flash.

As he inspected her wound, Ellis went after the Bright-Eyed. He managed to land a punch to the monster's jaw, but was knocked back as the tall guard lashed round. Ellis was thrown behind the moldering remains of an outbuilding, crashing through a post as if it were a stack of blocks.

"Finn, you have to get him out of here," Greer pleaded.

He shook his head, gently prodding at her temple. "I'm not leaving you."

"We can't do what we need to with him here. Get him to safety, please."

High over the camp, the tall Bright-Eyed roared with triumph before tucking his wings close, diving after Ellis.

"Finn, *please*!"

With a frustrated curse, Finn darted behind the building and grabbed Ellis by the scruff of his neck. He strained to lift both of them skyward, his great wings beating for all they were worth, kicking up snowflakes and bits of grit. Greer squinted, trying to follow their path.

"Stick to the plan!" Finn shouted to Greer before heading south.

"No!" Ellis howled, fighting and flailing. "You can't leave her! Greer, you have to run! You have to . . ." The forest snatched away the rest of his words.

She watched them go, wishing she could follow, but the snow was too deep and they were too fast and she'd never be able to outrace . . .

She froze, suddenly aware that the commotion behind her had silenced.

Dreading what she was about to see, Greer turned.

Every Bright-Eyed's gaze was fixed upon her.

She could feel blood trickling down her face, and saw how their eyes tracked each drop. Her mouth dried. Her stomach rolled over. It was a terrible thing to face another creature and realize you were so much smaller, so much less fearsome, and so very much alone.

She wanted to take a breath, to cry, to plead, to *something*, but couldn't. Couldn't think, couldn't move, couldn't do anything but—

The cloak.

Everything inside Greer screamed at her not to put it on. She saw Ellis's face, his look of sorrow and understanding, his pity. If she wore it, she would no longer be the woman he knew, the woman he loved. It would change her in ways she could not predict.

But it would save him.

Recklessly, she unfurled Ailie's cloak, letting its fullness flutter free. It sparkled under the moonlight, the metallic threads dazzling and as bright as the stars overhead.

"The sovereign's mantle," whispered the tall guard, cowed by its luster.

"Get it," Elowen managed to gasp, stabbing her knobby, elongated finger at Greer.

"This?" Greer held out the cape as if she might actually hand it over.

Elowen's eyes burned, smoldering with contempt.

With a burst of reckless laughter, Greer bundled the cloak beneath her arm and took off running, heading into the forest. She didn't dare look back; the Bright-Eyeds would be on her within seconds. There was a hiss of orders from Elowen, and Greer heard the rattle of blood across the wound.

"Thank you, Ellis," she murmured, darting into the tree's shadows.

She'd planned to make a large circle, swooping back toward the camp, but the Gathered crashed through the undergrowth, moving slower than expected. Their giant wings did them no favors in the dense woods, and Greer began to envision a scenario in which her stupid, ill-thought-out scheme might actually work.

But then she heard the footfalls.

They came from her right, the sound of padded paws dancing over the snow. She heard the pant of an animal racing after her at lethal speed. She saw the swish of a tail, long and tufted and nearly white.

The tall guard had shifted, giving himself the sleek body of a wolf. Greer caught sight of yellow eyes just before it lunged, jaws snarled wide.

She ducked, pivoting her direction, and the wolf skittered past, sliding into a snowbank. It rolled, flipping over to find its prey, but Greer was already heading back toward the site. She raced through the rubble as fast as her snowshoes would allow.

The yard was empty.

That surprised Greer. She'd assumed that the Bright-Eyes would chase after her, temporarily leaving their sovereign behind. But the spot where Elowen had lain was empty, save for a smattering of blood and something else, something small and precious, cast aside in the chaos and forgotten.

The iron knife.

It stuck out of a snowdrift, its flat edge reflecting moonlight and drawing Greer's attention. The handle had been carved of bone, but even so, her skin prickled as she pulled it free, uncomfortably close to the iron. How it must have burned Elowen as it sank in.

Greer whirled back with the knife drawn, ready for the wolf.

But it was gone.

An eerie stillness fell over the site. Nothing stirred. Nothing breathed.

Greer scanned the area, keeping a sharp watch on the sky, wary of an attack from above.

When a great horned owl fell from the darkness, too big to be anything but one of the Gathered, talons stretched forward to gouge her eyes, she was ready. Dropping Ailie's cloak, she slashed at the owl with the knife and caught the bird across its belly. It screeched once, sounding so much louder than an owl had any right to.

Innards spilled free, steaming lengths of intestines falling into the snow. When the body hit the ground, it landed with a lumbering thud. In death, the Bright-Eyed returned to its monstrous state, and now lay sprawled on its side, wings stretched in broken angles, fractured in the fall, its face forever frozen in a murderous snarl.

Greer's insides thrummed; her heart was pattering so fast she felt it might burst from her chest. She'd killed another Bright-Eyed, this time without the power of her scream.

That made two.

She glanced down into the mine's tunnels, watching, listening. Somewhere in that darkness were more. They did not know what had happened to Elowen. They did not know Greer was here at all.

That left just the wolf and one other outside.

But Elowen . . .

Elowen could be anywhere. With no tracks in the snow, Greer had to assume she'd managed to fly away.

But which way had she gone? Into the trees or down the tunnel?

Greer tried to focus on the sounds coming from the mine, but there were too many tunnels full of too many echoes. Noises bounced off rocky walls, repeating their cadence until they were a jumble of sound, falling over themselves in a mess of confusion. She couldn't pinpoint their source, couldn't make sense of the rustled whispers.

Turning to the forest, she wondered why Finn had yet to return. She pictured the way Ellis had fought against him. Had he somehow wounded Finn, causing both of them to fall from the sky? Before she could stop herself, she imagined them broken and bloody, impaled upon the rocky outcrops below the mine. What if they were both dead, and it was now only her against the Gathered?

Greer's fingers jangled against her thighs.

Two in the forest.

Elowen missing.

She sighed. The tunnels were her best choice, the one she'd have taken in Elowen's place. Giving the tree line a final sweep, Greer picked up the cloak and slipped into the mine.

Even with Finn's blood coursing through her, it was difficult to see far ahead in such shrouding darkness. The tunnel was roughly hewn.

Greer could make out individual marks made by the miners' shovels and pickaxes as they'd bored into the mountain. Wooden beams and layers of bricks helped support the arched shaft. Farther down, the tunnel split into two corridors. Greer hurried down the length and stopped at a small niche just before the junction.

Before she went any farther, there was something she needed to do.

Greer shook out her mother's cloak. It was so dark she could barely see its inky form, but she felt its energies all the same. Before putting it on, she paused, listening to the overlapping echoes of sound washing over her.

From the tunnel's entrance came the padding of footsteps, slow and cautious. Then a sharp sniff, a predator testing the air. Greer peeked around the corner and caught sight of two wolves poised at the mouth of the tunnel, their ears pricked with curious agitation.

She ducked back, holding her breath and trying to not make a single sound.

The wolves were enormous, far larger than any Greer had ever seen in the wilds. If they'd stood face-to-face with her, their gaping maws would be right at her eyes. She did not doubt that their teeth were just as oversized.

Greer listened as they crept into the mine, taking one step, then another, drawing ever closer to where she hid. Their scent filled the closed space, a sharp musk, feral and biting. In seconds, they'd be alongside her.

Now, now, do it now.

The voice in her head—her conscious, her other, inner self—sounded just like Finn. Was it his blood or just solid reasoning that now turned her thoughts, spurring her to action?

A chilled sweat broke over her as she fought back a sudden rush of nerves.

It didn't matter who said it—she herself or Finn—the words held truth.

It was time.

Wincing, she pulled Ailie's cloak over her head, feeling like a frightened child gripping the magical belief that if she couldn't see the monsters, they wouldn't see her. The velvet fell over her hunched form, covering her completely, and all at once, Greer realized she'd made a mistake.

The energy she'd felt all day sank into her, seeping across her skin like drops of ink on paper, staining everything it touched.

She scrunched her eyes, biting into the flesh of her palm to keep from crying out.

The magic burned, as potent as a forest fire sweeping through dried brush. Her blood tingled, and her teeth felt too large in her mouth. She wanted to toss back her head and howl out her anguish, but the wolves were too close, and she was in no position to fight.

The magic's heat settled deep into the marrow of her bones, warming her with such ferocity she wanted to cast the cloak from her, rip off her clothing, and peel away her undergarments. She wanted to race into the frigid night and dive into an icy stream, certain it was the only thing that would bring relief.

Her ears pounded, stretched and overwhelmed by the new rush of sounds she caught. She could hear the wolves' heartbeats, the blood pumping through their veins. As she listened to the soft whooshes, her mouth watered; she was suddenly parched, suddenly aching to brandish her new teeth. They were longer, sharper; she imagined how good it would feel to sink them deep into flesh, bursting apart skin like overripe berries.

Greer's eyes flashed open, and the muscles in her legs trembled, readying to act.

The wolves were in striking distance, but a small part of Greer rebelled against these new, wicked desires. It grabbed hold of her racing mind, tried to stifle the hunger seizing her middle, and harnessed the surge of impulses flooding her system.

The wolves passed the niche and wandered deeper into the tunnel; Greer let out a silent sigh of relief. With her hidden beneath the cloak, they'd been completely unaware of both her presence and just how close they'd come to death.

She swiped her arm out, ready to fling away the cloak and all its dizzying powers, but it was no longer there. Greer searched the floor of the niche, horribly aware of how clearly she could now see in the dark, but it was gone, as if it had never existed. As if it . . .

Greer raised her hands, studying the shaking fingers.

She recalled the fiery feeling of the velvet against her skin, the sensation sinking inside her.

She'd absorbed the cloak's magic. It was a part of her now, integral and inextricable.

Holding the wall for balance, she rose, as wobbly as a newborn foal, standing on legs new and too long. All her senses were heightened. The tunnel seemed impossibly bright, as though she were outside, basking in the glow of a midday sun. Details she hadn't noted before were now emblazoned onto her retinas, in sharp clarity. She could see the residual grime along the ceiling from smoke cast by lanterns that had not burned in decades. She saw water trickling down the walls, each drop as brilliant and sparkling as a tiny jewel.

The air was cool and scented with minerals, and when she took in a breath, she could smell the Bright-Eyeds, could sense their heat. She knew exactly which tunnels they'd gone down.

The odor of the wolves was obvious, but there was a difference to the batlike creatures, a meatier funk, like warmed body oils and hair that hadn't been washed in weeks, and above even that, a scent Greer recognized instantly from the night she'd been attacked by the river. An earthy, loamy blend of bog water and peat moss, crushed violets and prickly thistles.

Elowen.

She had gone into the mine, and now Greer knew exactly where to find her.

43

GREER SLIPPED ALONG the empty tunnel like water over river rocks. She felt as if she'd become a shadow, noiseless and nearly invisible, joining the very darkness itself. Her limbs moved with easy grace, swinging loose in their joints. Her gait was long, her cares were few.

Ailie's powers had gone straight to her head, intoxicating her with a confidence she'd never experienced before. She was giddy with it, delighting in her ability to stretch and move, to skulk and scheme.

Everything felt so different.

Everything felt so *good*.

She ran her tongue over the ridges of her teeth, certain there were more of them crammed into her mouth now. They felt sharper, stronger. They felt ready to bite and rip, and she regretted that she was so far into the mine now, so far away from the reflective surface of a quiet pond. She wanted to see herself, admire the changes, revel in her mother's sovereignty.

Her sovereignty.

She wanted to see what she looked like with this dark magic running through her, molding and making her into something new and dangerous, something strange and threatening.

And yet . . .

There was still one piece of her that had not quite changed. Vulnerable and human, full of worries and softness, compassion and anxieties. That part—that small, tiny part—was screaming.

Ellis, what about Ellis? the little voice cried, causing her to stop.

What *would* Ellis think of this new Greer? What would he think of all her new teeth?

The thought took her breath away.

She tried filling her lungs, but there was something wrong, something pressing against her throat, heavy as an anvil, sharp as the spike of a naturalist's pin.

Not pressing, she realized as dark stars began to dance over her vision, leaving her light-headed and ready to sink to her knees. *Encircling*.

She was choking, her airway closed off as if caught in a hangman's noose.

Greer ripped open the buttons at her collar and felt for the beaded necklace from Hessel's study. This was what choked her, even though it hung low and loose. Tension did not cause the pain; it came from the stones themselves.

With a gurgle of disgust, she tore off the necklace and flung it from her. It skidded a few feet down the tunnel, and instantly Greer felt better. She drew in deep, gasping breaths, staring at the innocuous little bauble.

It looked so harmless, flickering against the darkness. The flashes of red again reminded her of the Warding Stones, and suddenly Greer understood.

Those *were* the Warding Stones, or little pieces of them. Just like the monoliths, they, too, had been enchanted by Resolution Beaufort, as a means of protection. Protection for the townspeople. Protection against the Bright-Eyes.

Those beads had allowed Greer to roam away from Mistaken without being pulled back. But putting on Ailie's cloak, taking its magic into her, must have tipped the scales so that whatever words Resolution had used now worked against her. Just as it did the Bright-Eyes.

But I'm not one of them! she wanted to shout, feeling helpless.

It didn't matter what magic she'd taken on, what powers she'd gained. She could not undo this. The cloak, the magic, had become part of her, and she did not know how to wrest herself free of it.

I can never go home, she realized, and though she'd spent most of her life yearning to leave Mistaken and travel far from its shores, the knowledge that she couldn't ever return filled her with overwhelming dread.

She was more Bright-Eyed than human.

It was a truth too terrible to bear.

What was she doing here, in this mine, ready to kill monsters who were now more a part of her than the humans she wished to save?

"What *are* you doing?" she whispered aloud, feeling small and broken, damaged beyond repair.

You're spiraling, Greer. Your mind is running wild. An echo of Ailie's voice rushed over her. *Ground yourself in truths.*

"I don't want any of this to be true," she admitted, running her tongue along the sharp edges of her new teeth. Ailie's powers tugged at her limbs, trying to seize hold of her hands, turn her fingers to claws, ball them to fists. She could feel her mother's power pulling at her, eager to make her move to its accord, as if she were a marionette on a string.

"You're in the mines, north of Laird," Greer mouthed to herself, fighting for control.

One truth.

"You put on Mama's cloak."

Another, even though she wished it weren't.

"You're doing this to save Ellis." She paused, acknowledging the veracity of her words, but they weren't enough. She needed something more, a truth bigger than just her and the man she loved. "You're doing this to save Mistaken, to save the world, even if you've never seen it. Even if you don't make it out of this alive, the world needs to."

Greer breathed deeply, centering herself in the utter rightness of those words, of that love. She'd wrested herself away from the dark currents writhing beneath her skin, from the doubts, from the fears, from the horrors of what she'd become. She'd found the last true piece of herself and was going to hold on to it with all her might, for however long she lived.

She opened her eyes and ventured deeper into the mine.

44

THE SMELL WAS so much worse than Greer could have ever imagined.

The Gathered apparently dragged their kills into their roost to feast upon, letting the bloodless corpses remain wherever they fell. The shaft was littered with bones and body parts in a wild range of decomposition. The air did not stir here, not even with the smallest draft, and every smell was left to sit and fester.

Greer covered her nose with the back of her hand, breathing through her mouth, but that only left a dank film across her tongue that no amount of saliva could fix.

How could they live this way?

She tried picturing Finn here, tucked in a dark niche, teeth deep in the neck of a nearly lifeless buck, but couldn't do it. He seemed part of the forest, belonging to the tree line and the airstreams. She wasn't forgetting the creature beneath his human shell, but he didn't seem like *this* kind of monster.

"What do you mean, you lost her?"

Elowen's voice ripped from the darkness, echoing off the walls and sounding closer than Greer had guessed. It was raspy and strained. Though Ellis's attack hadn't killed her, she was still gravely hurt. Her note of pain gave Greer hope.

Farther down the tunnel, she had to skirt around a hulking lump that looked too much like Hessel. His wrists were ragged with puncture marks and Greer looked away before she could catch sight of anything else. There would be time to mourn him later.

If she had a later.

The corridor was so steeply sloped that Greer had to run one hand along the chiseled wall for balance. The stone had been softened by dripping rainwater and snowmelt, and she wondered uneasily at the thousands of tons of it above her.

At the next junction, she stopped, smelling at the air to determine which split to take. Though carcasses littered both sides of the tunnels, the ones on the right seemed older, more bone than body. The left, then.

But before she could venture down it, Greer startled, pulling her hand back as if something had bitten her. She clutched the wounded palm to her chest, tears stinging at her eyes. She expected to feel blood, certain she'd torn open skin, but when she flexed her hand, there was nothing.

Studying the wall, she could find no obvious barb to have nicked her, no sharp jut of granite or toothy shale. But when she ran an experimental fingertip lightly over the stone, she jerked away, hissing as her skin burned.

Greer narrowed her eyes. A thin vein cut through the stone, running up the wall. It was a rich umber, far darker than the rest of the tunnel. Curiously, she pressed her finger directly onto the vein, then instantly withdrew it, bewildered at what could cause such pain.

When the answer came to her, Greer wanted to laugh.

It was a line of iron.

Sandry had been a mine for iron ore. Most of it must have been cleared out long before Ailie arrived and—exhausted from her travels and ill-prepared for the harsh winters of the new world—she'd settled her small court there, never realizing they were roosting on a spot so dangerous to them.

Greer wondered that they hadn't sensed it, but she hadn't, either, not until her skin brushed directly over the deposit. She followed the vein, watching it trail up and across the tunnel, wondering how much ore might still be left in the mountain. In the back of her mind, a plan began to form.

She took off, exploring the tunnel with a discerning eye, her focus fixed on spotting more of the iron veins. Greer was so intent on finding a larger cache that she didn't hear the skittering of claws on stone until it was too late.

"Starling," Elowen said, coming out of the darkness like a demon. Torn strips of cotton were tied around her neck, the bandages stained with drying blood. Though the cut had already begun to heal, Greer noted that the surrounding skin was a violent shade of red, irritated from the knife. "You've finally come home."

It was the first time she'd stood this close to Elowen. She was so much bigger than Greer would have guessed, even with her wings tucked away. She filled the narrow space, her head nearly brushing along the ceiling. The muscles in Greer's legs flexed; she wanted to turn and run, unable to imagine a world in which this confrontation went in her favor. But she swallowed and stayed put.

"This isn't my home."

"Of course not," Elowen said, taking a step forward. "You think I'd allow Ailie's daughter to join the Gathered, to become one of us?" Her laughter felt forced in its gaiety.

"No one wants that, least of all me."

"So you say."

Greer peered around Elowen's shoulder, squinting to see if she'd brought others with her. For the moment, it seemed they were alone. "So—we what? Fight to the death now? All because you think I want to take your place?"

"Don't you?"

"Of course not. I came for Ellis. You can have . . . whatever this is." She gestured at the tunnels. "It's all yours."

A shiver of anticipation ran through the Bright-Eyed's limbs; she was hungering for battle. "It wouldn't be much of a fight anyway."

Elowen shifted, almost carelessly, into a smaller, human form. She looked so much like Greer they could have passed for sisters. Same height, same slight frame. She'd even taken on her shade of hair, letting the dark waves hang long and loose down her back. But her eyes . . .

Greer squinted, unable to tell exactly what was wrong with them. The irises were two-toned and misshapen, pinched into strange whorls.

Her left eye didn't seem to have a pupil at all. She noticed that Elowen also wore a replica of the plaid dress Greer had donned only nights ago, for the Andersans' barn warming.

She really has been watching me, she realized with an uncomfortable start.

"Since it's just the two of us, why don't we speak candidly?" Elowen began, tucking a strand of hair behind her ear with such studious care that the gesture looked wrong. She'd once been human, but was only playing at the role now. "I don't want you anywhere near my court, and you don't relish the thought of wasting your life between those tiresome stones."

Greer only blinked, waiting for her to continue.

Elowen sighed, as if the coming offer pained her. "I will let you and your intended leave these lands. Alive," she added, smiling too brightly. "But, in return, I want the mantle. Give it to me and you and the boy can go."

"Do you think me so foolish?"

"If you truly have no desire to rule, then what use is it to you?"

Greer shrugged nonchalantly. "I always thought it terribly pretty. Perhaps I'll wear it on my wedding day. To Ellis. After we stop you."

Elowen dared a step toward Greer, now within striking distance. "Give me the cloak and you and your human can forget you were ever here, ever a part of this."

Greer pressed her lips together, unable to stop the curve of a small smile. "No."

Elowen lashed out, smashing her fist into the side of the tunnel, releasing a shower of shale and rock. "Tell me where you hid it!"

"Isn't it obvious?" Greer asked, then smiled widely, showing off every one of her too many teeth.

Elowen sucked in a quick breath, unable to hide her surprise. "You . . . you claimed it for yourself?"

"I took what my mother left for me."

Without warning, Elowen burst into a flock of starlings, hundreds of birds strong. They zipped throughout the small space in fantastically sculpted murmurations, appearing as a lynx, a serpent, a fox. Each shape flew at Greer to peck and claw, screeching out cries of rage.

Greer fumbled for the knife, but there were too many of them, their bodies too small and agile to hit. They twisted and turned, evading her strikes with impressive aerial feats. They went after her hands and face, seeking blood. They swarmed at her neck, swiping and screaming so shrilly that her head rang with the echoes. She couldn't see around them, couldn't hear above their calls. They were everywhere, thousands strong, and she felt as if she'd go mad, unable to escape their slashes, their insistent screeches, their relentless and persistent—

A sudden mass charged through the murmuration and struck Greer squarely on her chest. It hit like a battering ram, crushing the air from her lungs and squeezing out any chance to scream. She crashed backward, cracking her head against the stony ground with a meaty thud that made her stomach heave. Reflexively, she curled up, trying to protect her soft middle, and felt a searing spike of pain along her back as the beast bit into her. Its wide jaws clamped down hard and tore away a chunk of skin as it thrashed its head, snorting with fury.

It was a bear, massive and white, with monstrous paws. It pounced upon her, mauling and mashing, and Greer didn't know what to do. It was so much larger than she was, filling the width of the tunnel, a vast and immovable force.

Over the grunts and growls of the monster, Greer heard laughter and caught sight of Elowen farther down the tunnel. The starlings were gone, and she'd returned to her batlike form, all tendons and wings and malice. She watched the battle with rapt interest, her eyes shining in the darkness.

One of the bear's front paws slammed into Greer's face and began to press down, scraping her cheek roughly into chiseled stone. A terrible burst of crackling white noise filled her head, and her vision began to dim.

It's going to crush my skull, she thought, panicked.

She squirmed and flexed, using every bit of her strength to wriggle from the bear's hold. But it was too big. It weighed too much. This wasn't an even fight.

It isn't a fight at all.

Ailie's voice filled her mind, and Greer wanted to sob. Even now, knowing what she'd been and the things she'd done, Greer longed to fall into her arms. She wanted to disappear into the protective power of her mother's embrace, losing herself in Ailie's comfort and strength.

Let me do this, her mother insisted. *Stop fighting against the mantle, and let me help.*

"I'm scared," she whimpered, and she must have said it aloud, because, somewhere down the tunnel, Elowen cackled.

Greer, Ailie pressed, and it was the only encouragement she needed.

Greer let go. She felt the moment Ailie's blood took hold. Her limbs thrummed with muscles she did not possess, lengthening and shifting, and hefting the bear from her. Her back arched as her spine grew longer, suddenly crowded with too many vertebrae. Inside her chest, she felt her sternum expand, growing into a wide, protective shield. Joints popped as her fingers extended, and wickedly curved talons pushed from her flesh.

She waited for the pain, waited to be struck dumb and dizzy as her body shifted into new shapes and angles.

It did not come.

Greer knew she'd changed, knew she no longer resembled herself, knew she was now one of them. But it did not feel wrong, only different.

She pushed herself up, feeling all the ways gravity tugged at her new frame, changing her sense of balance and equilibrium. Her back hulked, bowed against the weight of longer sinews and muscles and wings.

The white bear let out a deafening roar but did not attack.

Greer waited for it to change, matching her form with one of its own, but it remained low, its ears flattened, snorting and smacking at the ground. Its claws raked across one of the veins of iron ore, but it did not flinch. It didn't even register it.

It's not a Bright-Eyed, she realized. *It's just a bear.*

It growled again, bellowing its anger first at Greer, then at Elowen.

She brought it here, Ailie whispered in her daughter's mind. *She controlled it. Our blood is wilder than even the most barbarous of creatures. They submit to us, not the other way around.*

Greer remembered the night of Reaping. The moths. The bats. They hadn't been a swarm, concentrating together to migrate or hunt.

They'd not been an omen from the Benevolence. They'd been possessed, their blood seized by Elowen. They'd been a diversion, a way for her to leave a note stabbed on Hessel's door. The note that started this whole bloody affair.

How? she asked, and felt something in her mind shift, reaching out for the white bear.

Before she could seize hold, a terrible commotion came from above. With a shuddering rumble, the tunnel's ceiling broke apart, falling away in a shattering of slate and granite. Rocks rained down, striking at all three of them. The bear thundered in terror and charged down the shaft, knocking Greer over as it fled, running as fast as its lumbering gait would allow.

Greer tried to call it back but stopped short as a Bright-Eyed, far larger than any of the others and camouflaged as the very mountain itself, slammed to the ground behind her. He towered over both her and Elowen, a veritable gargoyle come to life, with murderous intent shining in his eyes. He swiped at Greer, catching her arms and wrenching them back with such force that her spine cracked.

Elowen pounced, covering Greer's mouth to stop her rising scream. Greer bit into the fleshy palm as hard as she could, tearing flesh and drawing blood, but the Bright-Eyed didn't so much as flinch. She rammed the heel of her hand upward instead, and Greer's vision exploded in dark stars. Still Elowen wouldn't release her, and Greer gagged, sputtering and choking on the Bright-Eyed's blood.

She flailed, lashing out with her feet, but could not find purchase. The stony Bright-Eyed tightened his grip, digging bruises into her skin. She felt a rib crack. Then another. Greer's sight fell in and out of focus, and she heaved, unable to draw breath.

"Since you won't give me the cloak, I'll take it myself," Elowen snarled, and in a flash, her mouth was pressed to the crook of Greer's neck. Rows of serrated teeth sank deep.

Greer choked on her own scream as her captor sank his teeth into the curve of her shoulder blade, feasting from behind. Their mouths roved across her skin, licking at the punctures, massaging the wounds with their lips to draw out more blood, to draw out all of Ailie's magic.

Greer wanted to shut her eyes and roll into the dark, welcoming void of oblivion, but the sounds would not let her escape. Lips smacked, tongues laved. More mouths joined in, snapping at her wrists, grabbing hold of a thigh. The Bright-Eyeds made grotesque noises of pleasure, murmuring and groaning as they fed. She could hear their heartbeats—three, four, five of them now, maybe more, maybe an entire court—quicken with bloodlust. She could hear her own heart, slowing to a sluggish pulse.

I'm dying, she thought, and was distressed to realize it didn't bother her as it should. She idly wondered if there was something in the Bright-Eyeds' saliva that sank victims into a state of hazy apathy, allowing the predators to feed at their leisure.

"Greer."

Her eyes flashed open at the sound of Ellis's voice.

She heard it distinctly, as if he was there in the tunnel with her now, but she couldn't see him. She couldn't see much of anything past the tufts of black hair at Elowen's ears.

"Come find me," he beckoned, and, despite everything that was happening to her, Greer smiled.

Their old whispering game.

"I need you to come find me," he instructed.

Greer thought she nodded.

"Now, Greer. Find me now."

His insistence pulled her from the drowsy fog, wrenching her back into the pain, but it was good. There was pain because she was present. There was pain because she was alive.

And if she was alive, she could fight.

Carefully, as if falling into a swoon, Greer arched back against the stony Bright-Eyed. She shifted, bringing up her legs till her feet were on Elowen's chest. The queen, so intent on feeding, didn't seem to notice. The sound of her blood being gulped down in great swallows made Greer's stomach twist.

She tensed the muscles in her calves, preparing for the inevitable pain to come, then kicked as hard as she could, ripping Elowen from her. Elowen stumbled backward, and Greer fell. Using the swing of momentum, she pulled her captor toward the spot the white bear had scratched. She swiped claws across his rocky face, pressing the lacerations to the iron.

His roar of pain scattered the other Bright-Eyeds who had gathered round. Greer recognized the tusked guard, the pair of wolves, and counted three new others. How many Bright-Eyeds did this mountain hold?

Without warning, a dark shape whizzed by, racing along the side of the tunnel wall and slashing at two of the Bright-Eyeds. The largest wolf and the tusked guard hissed, falling to their knees as they clutched their throats, trying in vain to hold back the curtains of blood pouring from the deep and ragged wounds.

The figure skittered to a stop, stomping on the stony Bright-Eyed and snapping his neck. The monster fell slack, a mountainous mass of unmoving flesh.

Greer looked up in wonder, unable to contain her smile.

Noah Finn had returned.

45

"WHERE'S ELLIS?" Greer demanded as Finn pulled her to her feet.

The tunnel was a mess of shrieks and death rattles. There were too many bodies sprawled in too many severe angles for Greer to truly understand what was happening. The bites on her body pulsed, screaming with hot, fiery agony. She could feel where every fang had sunk in, each puncture ragged and inflamed.

"He's safe."

Finn tugged her through the mess of wounded Bright-Eyeds, moving the two of them deeper into the mine with a skittering speed that made Greer want to throw up.

Elowen's rage echoed after them. "Bring her back!"

There were murmurs of protest, cries of outrage and death rattles as the Bright-Eyeds Finn had wounded took their last, heaving gasps.

"Stay with me," he ordered.

Greer wondered who he was talking to. She was right beside him, keeping up as best as she could, though now that she thought of it, she wasn't entirely sure her feet were moving. Perhaps Finn was moving so fast that she flew along, trailing after him like a pennant in the wind. She could feel pounding jolts ricocheting through her body, but wasn't certain if they were her footfalls clattering down the stone corridor or the painful clunk of her blood pulsing through her veins. She was woozy with blood loss; her thoughts were as lethargic as her heartbeat.

"Greer!" he shouted as the tunnel faded in and out of focus. "You have to stay with me!"

He means me, she realized, the thought imploding through her like a dying star. *Why wouldn't I stay with him?*

Greer didn't know how much of her mother's magic had been drunk from her. She could still feel a residual dark energy lingering in her limbs, wanting to strike and bite, but it no longer consumed her every thought and impulse.

I'm here. She wanted to say it, but pain spiked across her shoulder as Finn jerked her arm, hard. Electric fury radiated into her fingers. She reached out, disoriented, but couldn't find him anywhere. Greer blinked, trying to push away the haze filtering her vision. She gasped.

Elowen had caught up to them, emerging from a split farther down the corridor. She'd snatched Finn away from Greer and now struggled to hold him back. She swung her legs forward, scratching at him with curved talons. Her wings snapped forward, striking punishing blows at his head, smothering him in an enveloping embrace.

Their brawl left lingering phantom trails across Greer's retinas. As she watched Finn's shape blur, stretched and elongated into impossible forms, a terrifying realization struck her.

I've been poisoned.

Something in the Bright-Eyeds' bite obscured her reason and made clear thoughts impossible. She knew some predators used venom to stun their prey, subduing them to an apathetic death. She tested her reflexes—opening and closing her hands—and felt certain the Bright-Eyeds were behind her indifference.

Greer slapped at her cheeks, trying to rip herself from the fog. She needed to help Finn, but she struggled to understand the fight. A thrown punch, the tear of talons across webbed membranes. Bared fangs and the smash of skulls knocked together. She caught only slivers, and could not stir herself to action.

But then Elowen was down, screaming and clutching at her face as her form sank into the shadows, and Finn was back, his grip an insistent pressure, digging into her shoulder.

"We need to go," he gasped, fighting for breath. His voice sounded garbled and choked with blood; Greer didn't know if it was his or Elowen's.

"Go?" she echoed.

"You can't face her in this state."

She lost track of where they were. Tunnels bled together into a labyrinthine nightmare. There were too many turns to follow, too many corridors that looked just like the ones that had come before.

"Where are we going?"

"There's another way out. A back entrance, from when the cave was first explored. It's hard to get to. It was never mined."

"Are we going to see Ellis?"

As the words fell from her, she knew they were not the right ones, knew there was other things that should be asked. They needed to form a new plan, strategize and plot. But the only thing her muddled mind could focus upon with any clarity was Ellis.

Finn didn't respond.

"Where is he? Does he know . . ."

She stopped, unsure of what to ask. Did he know what she was? She'd seen the look of understanding cross over his face before he'd thrown the knife at Elowen. Did he know about Ailie, about what her mother's plan had been? Had Finn explained it? She doubted any version of the story Elowen might have told would have been accurate. Greer barely comprehended it all herself.

Did he know—despite everything that had happened, despite the thing she'd become—that she loved him still?

Greer would never be able to voice that question aloud. Not to Finn. Everything he'd done had been to help her achieve what Ailie had dreamed of. Greer didn't know if it was his devotion to her mother or an affection for her, but to ask now would be too cruel.

Ahead of them, the tunnel opened up, revealing a large cavern. With what remained of Ailie's heightened senses, Greer could just make out the larger space; she estimated it was at least a few hundred feet long. A questionable-looking bridge of ancient ropes and wooden planks spanned it.

They stopped at the end of the tunnel, where the ground fell away, plummeting to depths that even Greer could not see.

"What is this place?" she asked, reaching for Finn. Her head spun from confusion and vertigo. She worried that if she toppled over the edge she'd never stop falling.

"The way out," Finn said, shifting so he could steady her with human hands. "We'll find somewhere you can clear your head." He peered down with such concern, she wondered how wild she must look. "You can't fight them like this, and I can't hold off so many on my own."

Even through her bewildered haze, she noted the deep gash blooming across his chest, reddening his shirt. She opened the collar and caught sight of four deep gouges carved into his chest. "You're wounded."

He nodded. "We need blood. There's nothing in these tunnels."

"It feels bad here," she whispered, her lungs tight in her chest. The air around them seemed off, too thick and bristling with unseen barbs.

Finn nodded across the bridge. "The miners had only just begun clearing out this section of the caves when Laird was attacked. There's still so much iron . . ." His eyes flickered over the dark rocks on the other side with trepidation.

"Is that why they aren't following us?" Greer glanced back down the tunnel they'd come from and coughed. "It hurts too much."

Finn nodded. "And they're taking stock of their dead, I'd guess. I saw the remains out in the yard." He offered her a faint smile of praise. "You did well. I think . . . when the time comes, the court will respect you."

Greer looked up at him. "I don't want to lead them," she admitted. "I don't want to have anything to do with them, with this place, with any of it."

Finn considered the cavern, taking in the ancient bridge, the thick, rocky walls, the entire weight of the mountain pressing down upon them. "It doesn't have to be like this. If we lead them north, out of the mines and into the wilds, we could—"

Greer shook her head, silencing him. "They'd still be cruel. They'd still be calculating and crave human blood. They don't listen to Elowen; what makes you think that would change with me?"

"But with Ailie's—"

"It's nearly gone!" Her head throbbed with the force of the outburst. "They drank almost all of it."

Finn looked horrified. His jaw clenched, and she could practically hear his grinding thoughts. "Then we finish them," he finally said, his words surprising in their simplicity, ringing as hollow as a bird's bones. "All of them."

Greer stared up at him, wishing her head was clear so that she could say everything she wanted to. But it wasn't, so she only nodded, her throat tight.

"But first . . ."

"Blood," she agreed.

"You take the lead," he said, gesturing to the bridge.

It was too narrow for them to walk across together, but as Finn nudged her forward, Greer's hand slipped into his. It was an act of solidarity, a promise of commitment. They would do this terrible thing together, as a team. And after . . .

Greer didn't know.

Though she couldn't guess at what her future now looked like, she felt certain Finn would have a place within it. Not as consort, not as husband or lover, but as a partner all the same. What they'd done, what they would do, would forever bond them. They were sealing their fates in blood.

Every step forward hurt.

Greer felt the iron like a wall of fire. Its sharpness singed at her, sizzling little dots of red blisters along any exposed skin. Her throat and nasal passages were raw and stinging. Her fingers swelled and hurt to move.

"Why do they live here?" she gasped, struggling to put one foot in front of the other. "Why would Mama have ever chosen this place?"

"The other tunnels aren't bad," he began, his words strained and tight. "They're warm and offer protection against the worst of the winter storms."

"Isn't there any other way out?"

"Not without doubling back to Elowen."

Greer groaned and pressed forward. To distract herself from the pain, she darted her eyes around the massive cavern. The rocky crevices had been smoothed to a polished luster by millennia's worth of rainwater and snowmelt. Spiky stalactites dripped overhead, looking like a colony of roosting bats.

They hung across the ceiling, each one unique, a sculpture made not by the chiseling of man, but from the steady drip of water. Some were simple fangs, blunted points of minerals, but others had formed into fantastical masterpieces. Greer's overwrought imagination turned them into undulating curtains, upside-down castle turrets, creatures with gills and fins, tails and feathers, folded wings . . .

"Finn?" she asked slowly as her gaze landed on the shape directly above him. It was large and dark and shifting with the smallest of movements, the slightest of tremors. It was *breathing*.

The attack began before she could finish her warning.

The cavern erupted, a messy swirl of noise and chaos as all around them, stalactites unfurled, revealing themselves as hidden Bright-Eyes.

This was not the five monsters Greer had thought remained, nor even the twelve Finn had guessed at. This court was dozens strong, a hundred, maybe more. It was an army, a horde, a legion.

Greer took in the magnitude of the flying bodies with grim realization.

They would not survive this.

She would not survive.

But Ellis would.

Ellis would, and Mistaken, too, and all of the other outposts and villages, the land's first people, and all the others who came after, the mountains to the west, the plains to the south, the whole world over.

With one bold action, she could save them all.

And so she ran. Gripping Finn's hand tightly, she raced across the rest of the bridge, pulling them into the inferno of iron. The bridge swayed, boards creaking and ancient ropes hissing as their fibers stretched and snapped. Greer worried the entire thing would pull apart, spilling them into the endless depths of the chasm below.

The only thing she could do was clutch Finn tighter, grabbing at his forearm as he tried to fend off an attacking Bright-Eyed. She pulled them through the confusions of bodies, the slicing talons, the poisoned fangs.

The end was so close, only a few planks away.

Greer dared a quick glance back and noted that the Bright-Eyeds were not as close as she'd feared. They hung back, hurling threats and occasionally diving in threatening feints, but never getting more than a few feet from the cliff, unwilling to face the iron ore, even for their queen.

A smile grew on Greer's lips as she began to hope that favor had found them. The court was too fearful of the iron to blindly follow Elowen's screeched orders. Brazenly, Greer began to plan her next steps, daring to believe that there would be a life beyond the bridge. They'd have to endure the last of the tunnel, fighting through the waves of pain and heat, but then they'd—

In an instant, Finn was gone, pulled from her so fast that the silk ribbon he wore looped around his wrist, the silk ribbon Greer had unwittingly given to him so many years ago, ripped.

Greer found herself holding on to only the tattered bracelet and turned in confused horror.

Elowen had swooped out of the swarm, daring to go where her court would not, and had seized hold of Finn.

He struggled in her grasp, thrashing and flipping his body as he fought to shift back into his Bright-Eyed form. But before he could, Elowen's teeth sank into the crook of his neck, snapping at tendons, tearing apart flesh. She drank deeply, guzzling down blood in great, gluttonous mouthfuls, letting it run down her chin as her eyes rolled back into her head. She let out a groan of pleasure, then bit again.

There was nothing Greer could do.

Elowen was too high, well beyond Greer's reach, and too ruthless by far.

Finn's gaze landed on Greer—first panicked, and slowly glazing over with resignation. His hand twitched, reaching for her, telling her to run. Then . . . he stopped and moved no more.

Before Greer could cry out, the Bright-Eyed tossed his small, broken body down into the cavern without even a hint of remorse.

Greer heard him strike a rocky outcrop, landing at his final resting place with a dull thud. She wanted to call out to him, wanted to believe that he was still alive and could somehow answer her, but she was too horrified to move, too broken to make a sound. Sorrow and rage swirled within her frozen body, racing through her veins like a storm. Without an outlet for release, their energies built, growing concentrated and deadly, until, using up every bit of breath left within her, Greer opened her mouth and screamed.

46

It was a scream strong enough to shake apart a mountain.

A scream loud enough to bury a mine, bury a court, bury its queen.

As Greer's voice ripped across the cavern, great crumbling rocks fell upon the Gathered, covering them with iron ore. The air turned foul with it, scorching and blistering everything it touched. She could hear other screams blend with hers: Elowen and her swarming court, and the horde of unseen Bright-Eyeds hidden throughout the caves. Their screams filled the mine, filled the tunnels, filled the entire mountain, until there was nothing but a storm of sound, a great crashing wave of noise and chaos, an old world shattering apart as a new one rose.

Greer had intended for the scream to bury her as well. She had accepted the certainty of her death, knowing her sacrifice would ensure that the Bright-Eyeds never left the Severing Mountains, never made it into the wider world.

But, impossibly, she had not died.

When her scream finally came to an end, Greer found herself in a painful heap at the edge of the forest, small and human once more, and staring down a wall of stones and debris. She remembered being thrown through the tumult, pushed by the force of her voice. It had torn apart the tunnels, felling walls and timbers with ease, but the waves of sound had pushed the destruction away from her, leaving her safe and out of the mine.

Another thundering blast roared from the remains of the tunnel, spewing out a shower of shale and dust, as more rocks shifted, tumbling down to seal the entrance forever. Greer scrambled to avoid the falling chips of stone, and then collapsed in the forest's undergrowth. She lay on her back, letting the snow numb the worst of her pains as whatever remained of Ailie's blood began to heal her, knitting together broken bones, mending gashes, healing bruises.

She stared up at the gray sky, watching it lighten by degrees. Sunrise wasn't far off. Impossibly, she'd lived through the night.

But Finn . . .

Her hands balled into fists, clutching at his frayed ribbon.

They'd been so close to leaving together, to surviving it all.

She didn't know what would have come next, how they would have carried on, but to have had the chance ripped away like that, right at the end . . .

Finn had remained faithful to her mother for so many years, had watched after Greer, had gotten her here, and helped her succeed. And for what? What had been the point of his journey? What consolation could she take hold of?

Greer relaxed her fists, studying the intricate designs embroidered across the ribbon she held. These stitches were here even though her mother was not. They remained when all the other pieces of Ailie—her schemes, her cloak, Finn's devotion—were gone.

Almost gone, Greer mentally amended, the power of her scream still echoing in her ears.

"I'm the last of the Bright-Eyeds," she said aloud, and her voice was so small against the vast wilds surrounding her. She thought of what the hunters in Laird had said, how the Bright-Eyeds had disrupted the rhythm of the land, devouring everything they came across, hunting life to near extinction. Now she was all that remained of that insatiable appetite. "That blood will die with me," she whispered; she tied the ribbon around her wrist as she made this promise to the land.

Only the wind responded, howling out a keening pitch that made her insides ache with an icy loneliness. She rubbed her hands over her goose-bumped arms, cold for the first time since the night she'd drunk Finn's blood. She needed to stand, needed to warm herself with movement and purpose, but couldn't seem to stir to action.

Greer kept her gaze fixed on the sky instead, watching and waiting for the approaching sun.

After a time, footsteps stirred her from the haze. Though the worst of her injuries had passed, her head still reeled from the force of the scream, and it was difficult to focus on the figure making his way through the trees.

He cupped his hands over his mouth and called out her name.

"I'm here," Greer gasped, unable to raise her voice above a whisper. "Ellis, I'm here."

He was beside her in a flash, his kisses falling on her as soft as snowflakes, as tender as the first shoots of spring. He held her close, her pounding head heavy on his chest, vowing he'd never walk away from her again. They spoke in low, quiet tones, telling the stories of how they'd gotten here, of leaving Mistaken and venturing into the unknown, of Ailie's secrets and all of Greer's changes. It wasn't until the sun was well over the tree line, spreading its cold winter beams, that Ellis noticed the bracelet now tied around her wrist.

"I remember this," he said, bringing it up for closer inspection. "I haven't seen it in years."

"Finn had it." Her eyes darted toward the impenetrable wall of rocks now piled up at the start of the mine.

Ellis's gaze followed hers, understanding. He hesitated before speaking. "He took me down the mountain, down into a little clearing with old carts and broken tracks, and said I'd be safe." He let out a sigh Greer couldn't read. "He said he was going to get you. He said he'd bring you back. But he didn't . . . and then I heard that horrible rumbling . . . it sounded like the mountain was splitting in two, and I couldn't stay put. I needed to find you."

"He's gone," she whispered, pushing aside the heartache, grounding herself in the truths of the here and now. She'd done what she set out to do. She'd found Ellis. She'd saved him and the whole world beyond. "They all are."

"Except you," he noted, and Greer's heart clunked heavily, missing a beat.

"Yes."

A long moment of silence passed between them. Greer longed to fill it with explanations and sworn oaths she wasn't sure she could keep, declarations of love and good intentions, promises that she still was herself, no matter how much of her mother now raced through her veins.

Ellis trailed his thumb over the bracelet thoughtfully before taking her hand in his, silencing the flood of words that were ready to pour from her. His simple gesture said all that was needed.

"What do we do now?" Ellis asked, lacing their fingers together into an unbreakable knot. "Where do we go?"

Greer squeezed his hand as her blood quickened with the familiar stir of wanderlust. Her lips parted into a faint smile, revealing a row of small and even teeth. "Anywhere we want."

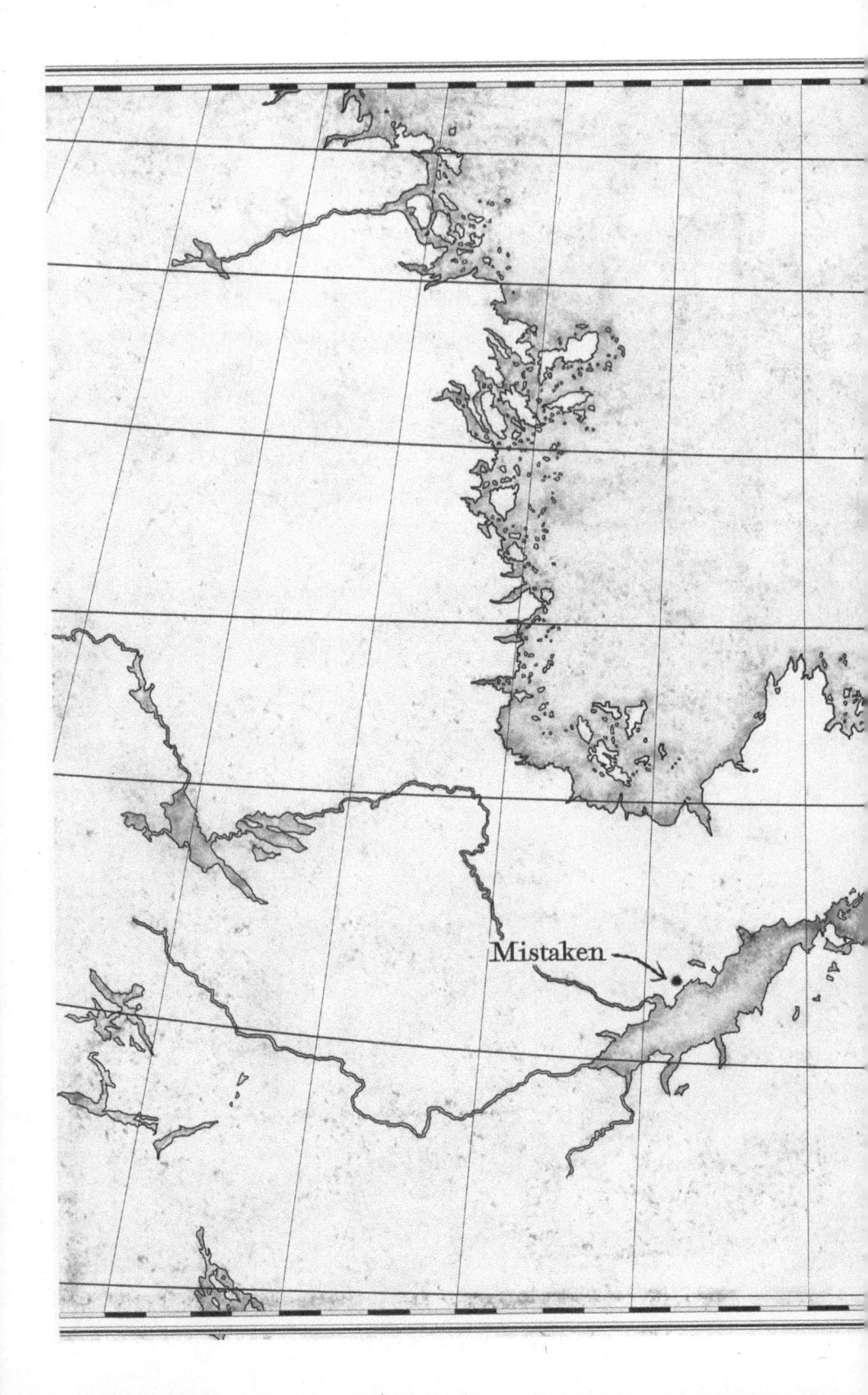

Mistaken

Beyond this there is no certainty...

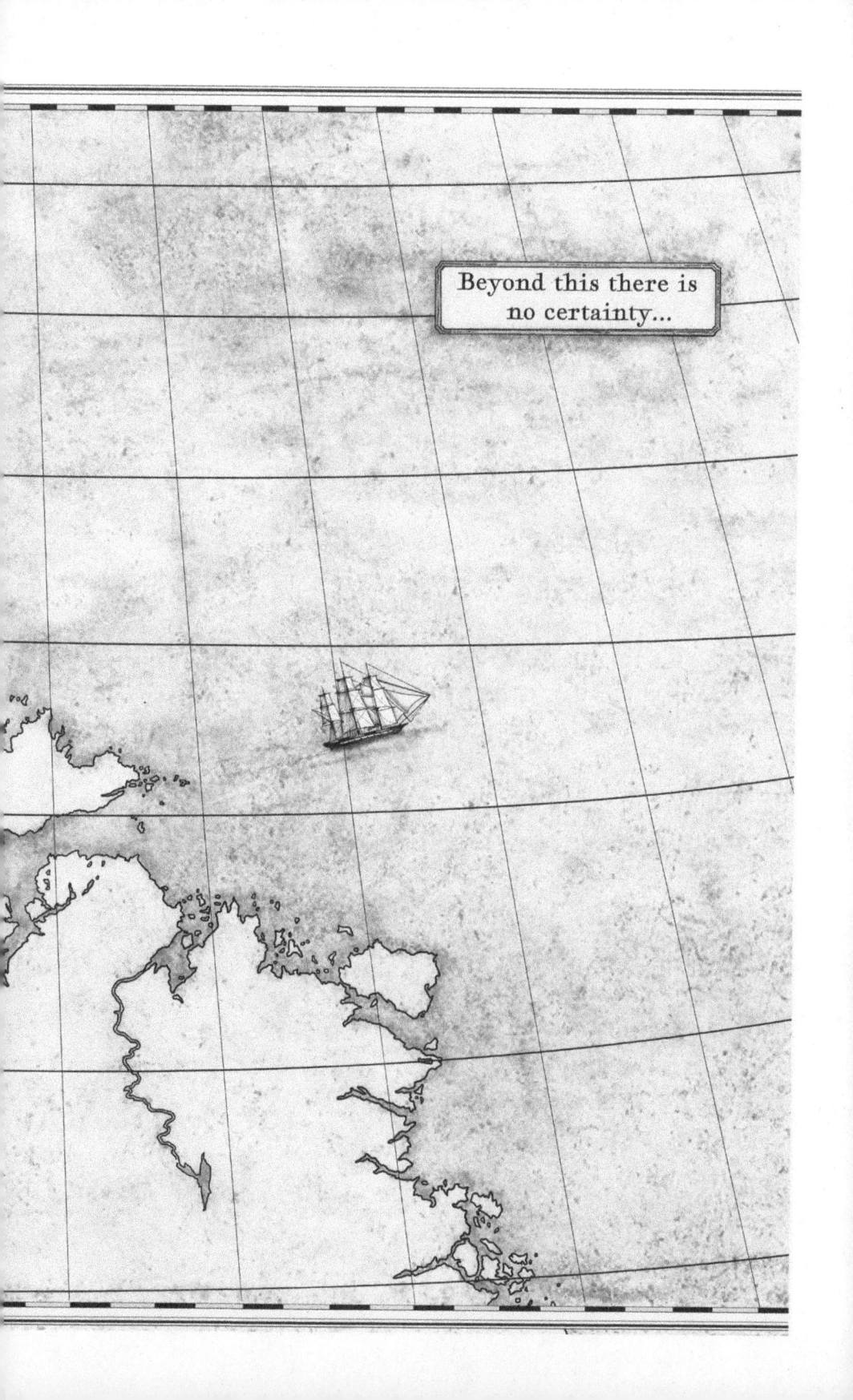

1768

THE JOURNEY OUT of Mistaken began with one final scream. The Warding Stones were no more, blasted into nothing but impotent rubble.

For the first time in their lives, the townspeople did not fear the setting of the sun.

For the first time in their lives, they wandered past the boundary line, going farther than they'd ever dared, seeing new sights, pulled by new desires, dreaming of things bigger than their little cove.

They traveled to the coast and boarded a great ship, bound for a far-off world. They watched the silhouettes of Redcaps fade into the distance before turning to face the wonder of the open sea. They didn't know what to expect when they arrived in the old world—the land of their blood and family names, the birthplace of their stories and mother tongue—but they were eager to find out.

At the bow of the ship, not far from their family and friends, stood a pair of travelers. Their arms were wrapped around each other to form a lovers' knot, and they watched the horizon with hopeful hearts. So focused upon the waves, they did not notice the dark shape skittering across the sky, riding the wind high above them, strong and wild. Two talons flexed, as if seizing hold of the blowing westerlies, before the Bright-Eyed shifted, soaring off into the approaching night, drawn toward the vast promise of uncertainties strange and new.

ACKNOWLEDGMENTS

Just as there is no one right way to write a book, there's also no one right way a book gets made. While *A Land So Wide* is my fifth novel to be published, it was my first foray into the world of adult fiction and I'm so very grateful to the absolute dream team who has helped me, Greer, and the Bright-Eyeds find their way through woods both dark and deep.

I was lucky enough to have two editors on this project and I am forever grateful to both Caitlin Landuyt for first believing in my Scottish vampires and to Anna Kaufman for helping me polish and refine their story. You are wonders! So many thanks and heart-hands to all the fantastic people working at Pantheon Books, especially Natalia Berry (you are so wonderful!), Kathleen Fridella and Terry Zaroff-Evans (I owe you both a zillion gold sticky stars for catching all of my many mistakes!), Katie Anderson for the incredibly haunting cover, Cassandra Pappas for making the inside of the book look just as magical as its outside, Rhys Davies for taking my terrible doodles of Mistaken and turning them into the most gorgeous maps, Lisa Frenette for your thoughtful insights and early reading, and Rose Cronin-Jackman and Julianne Clancy for shouting about and loving on this book so hard!

Evergreen (see what I did there?!) thanks to Sarah Landis for putting up with my dreadful puns, as well as being a top-tier agent and friend!

So thankful to the entire team at Sterling Lord Literistic for helping spread my eerie little stories into the world.

Endlessly thankful for the many friends who have been cheering on and supporting this book. I'm so grateful to have Hannah Whitten, Lindsey Landgraf Hess, Shea Ernshaw, Ava Reid, Marisha Pessl, Kiersten White, Charlene Honeycutt, and Aftyn Shaw in my corner. Y'all are the best ride or dies!

I wouldn't be here, doing any of this, without the deep support and love of my family. Thank you. Thank you. Thank you. I love you so.

Thank you, Paul, epic fort-holder-downer and maker of the world's most perfect fried egg sandwiches. You're better than any love interest I could ever dream up.

And Grace . . . I love your imagination and quick wit, your smiles and your sunshine. You truly are the best writing partner and I'm so grateful.